BEC MCMASTER

THE BURNED LAND SERIES

The Last True Hero: A Burning Lands Novel
Copyright (c) Bec McMaster

Edited by: Hot Tree Editing
Print formatting by: Cover Me Darling and Athena Interior Book
Design
Cover Art (c) Damonza.com

ALSO AVAILABLE BY BEC MCMASTER

LONDON STEAMPUNK SERIES
Kiss Of Steel
Heart Of Iron
My Lady Quicksilver
Forged By Desire
Of Silk And Steam
Novellas in same series:
Tarnished Knight
The Curious Case Of The Clockwork Menace

DARK ARTS SERIES
Shadowbound
Hexbound

BURNED LANDS SERIES
Nobody's Hero
The Last True Hero

OTHER
The Many Lives Of Hadley Monroe

prologue

THE FIRST TIME Adam McClain put the gun in his mouth, he couldn't pull the trigger.

He'd found a nice, lonely spot out in the Wastelands, far enough away from his sister that she wouldn't find his body, and one with a beautiful view over the Great Divide, which split the continent in half.

Thou shalt not suffer a warg to live.

That was the first law he'd ever learned at the knee of his stern bounty hunter father. Adam had followed in his footsteps, hunting the wargs and shadow-cats that lurked in the gloom of the wastelands. He'd seen the massacres firsthand, blood sprayed across timber floors as he walked slowly through a homestead, and broken bodies scattered and torn as he searched room after room, looking for the perpetrator.

One particular memory sprang to mind.

"I didn't mean it," the man whispered, his hands covered in blood and his eyes filled with utter horror at what he'd found when the sun finally rose and he returned to himself. "*I didn't want to hurt them."*

But the warg inside him made him do it, and Adam lifted the gun and shot him. He'd always considered it mercy.

It was only now that he recognized the irony.

He *knew* what he was facing. The barely knitted wounds across his abdomen still ached, but he could feel the maliciousness that worked its way within him. Two nights ago a warg buried its claws in his gut and tore his future away from him, and now it was he who had to deliver mercy to himself.

And he couldn't do it.

Adam took the coward's way out. He pulled the gun out of his mouth and dropped it to the ground, gasping hard. Night was slowly falling and with it came the heat in his blood, the moon's curse. He could feel it whispering through his veins as the monster within fought to free itself. The partner he'd once ridden with, Luc Wade, would be staring at the same sky, feeling the same rush of blood through his veins that Adam felt as the moon became a glint on the horizon.

And it was because of Adam that Luc shared the same fate.

As muscle ripped and bones tore themselves in half and re-formed, he screamed his rage and shame into the empty night. It was the first time he'd shifted and the agony of it was blinding. Soon there was nothing more than a monster remaining, and the man that Adam was lay buried deep inside the brutish beast's heart.

When the sun rose in the morning, he found himself a man again, naked and panting on the blistering sands of the desert floor with blood on his hands and the taste of it in his mouth. The sight of the deer—or what remained of it—made him vomit. It was a long walk back to where he'd been, his feet healing even as the harsh rocky floor tore them apart.

Adam put the gun in his mouth again. This time he knew the bone-deep truth of what he'd become. His hands shook. His sister, Eden, flashed into his mind. Eden, who would be wondering where he was...

"Promise me, you'll watch over her, boy," his father's voice whispered in his mind, from a long time ago when his father had ridden out that last time.

Adam always kept his promises, even if he'd had to stab his best friend in the back to do so. His hands were shaking so hard when he pulled the gun out of his mouth the second time that he actually crushed the hand piece. Without him there to protect her, Eden would be forced to find her feet in this harsh world.

He didn't know what to do.

A wink of pewter caught his eye from the bag he'd brought with him. Adam stared at it for a long time, knowing he didn't deserve it. The medallion was a promise. A dream of another life. He'd taken it from Bartholomew Cane, the warg who'd changed him into... this. Cane wore one himself, as did his partner, Johnny Colton. Though Adam wanted both their heads, he wanted what the medallion represented more.

A way to keep the beast at bay. A way to hide what he was in a crowd of humans. A means to pretend that nothing had changed, that he was still the man he'd always been. He'd worn it last night and managed to escape the change.

Until now.

Luc Wade had promised them all vengeance. That was the only thing that kept his once-partner sane after what had happened between them. But Adam had something else to live for.

Atonement.

So he dressed himself in the spare clothes he'd brought with him—perhaps he'd known he couldn't really do it—and then he started back toward the beaten-up old motorcycle that had brought him here.

Eden would be wondering where he was, and Adam had promises to keep.

one

Nine years later....

"ANOTHER," ADAM MCCLAIN slurred, shoving the empty tumbler across the counter.

The woman behind the bar arched a brow and stayed where she was, polishing a glass. Then she pointed to the white line that had been painted across the timber floors.

Adam stared at her. Mia stared back. This was one argument he had no hope in hell of winning, despite the fact she barely reached his shoulder.

If there was one thing that drove him utterly crazy, it was hardheaded women.

Scraping the chair back, he stood and crossed to the start of the line. Holding his arms out, he walked swiftly along the line and then turned with his hands held wide in a somewhat mocking salute.

Mia's dark eyes narrowed, but she poured him another whiskey. That was her rule. Walk the line and you got another drink. But she had to be wondering how he'd downed nearly two bottles of the stuff and wasn't even staggering.

Casual slipups like that might get him caught. He was just drunk enough not to care.

"Any particular reason you're trying to drown yourself in my good whiskey?" She slid the full glass toward him then held it there, her gaze a challenge.

"Nothing I'd like to share."

"You missing that kid that was riding with you? Where'd he go, anyway?"

Adam sighed. Cole had insisted on following him over the past year, ever since Luc Wade clawed the boy up and turned him into a warg. But he'd grown tired of Adam's lack of motivation, and finally decided he was going home to see his family.

There'd be no home for him there. Adam could have told him that. Nobody in the Wastelands welcomed a warg back into their familial embrace.

But some things you had to learn for yourself.

"Kid's gone home. And he's welcome to it." Adam threw the glass back, and the fiery liquid burned all the way down. Within half an hour his body would have burned through it, so he had to drink fast to stay drunk these days. Not that getting drunk made the world any rosier.

"If you wanted to talk about it, McClain," Mia picked her words carefully, "I'm a good listener."

"Why? You want to make it all better?" He leaned closer. "We don't need to talk for that."

Those dark eyes narrowed again, the thick lashes doing nothing to obscure the heat in them. It seemed to be her favorite expression. "Now I know you're drunk." She screwed the cap back on the whiskey bottle. "No more."

Frustration lanced through him but he tipped his head to her. Mia Gray reminded him of another woman he'd once known. Sometimes he wondered if that was why he'd lingered here in this tiny shitforsaken town for over a month. Oh, she looked nothing like Riley, and she had far more tact than Riley had ever had, but Mia's favorite word was also no.

Tracing a puddle of amber liquid on the timber counter, he wondered what Riley would be doing right now. He'd lost his chance with her over a year ago—or maybe he'd stepped aside when it became clear that she was the only person who could find Luc Wade's heart, let alone cause it to beat—but Adam still thought of her now and then.

Of what could have been.

He felt so lost now. At least after he'd first become a warg, he'd had a plan. He'd been driven then, searching for his own redemption, building a town, gathering people together where he could protect them and striving to create a life for himself. He'd thought he'd found redemption, but it was all gone the second his people discovered they had a warg in their midst. Who was he now? A clapped-out bounty hunter who spent more time in bars than hunting?

A brutal lesson to learn. No matter what he tried to make of himself, to everyone else's eyes he was still just a monster.

"That looks like woman trouble in your eyes," Mia noted.

She swiped a rag through the sticky puddle he'd been fingering, then lifted his wrist and cleaned his finger too. Her touch was cool; her bronze-colored skin wasn't as warm as his. The fever burn in his veins promised that the full moon was only three days away.

He could always feel it now.

The full moon was the hardest to ignore, despite the burning cold of the amulet against his chest that kept the monster at bay. And the feel of Mia's skin on his awoke all manner of longing. Before he knew what he was doing, he'd turned his wrist, capturing her own in his strong fingers, his thumb rasping over the sweet kick of her veins. Just a faint caress, but from the sudden shocked flash of her eyes, she felt the burn too.

They stayed like that as the clock ticked out long seconds.

"No women," he said, "but plenty of trouble."

Adam's gaze lowered to her mouth; that dangerous mouth that liked telling him no. He wanted it to say yes. He wanted to capture the word on her lips and steal it deep inside. Mia's mouth parted... but the word never came.

Heat simmered in her cheeks and Mia turned away quickly, rubbing at her wrist. "I'm not the answer to your problems."

"I know." He crossed his arms over his chest and leaned back a little in his chair. "I'm not looking for an answer, but maybe I'm looking for a distraction. Maybe we both want the same thing."

"What's that?" Her eyes met his in the mirror.

"Something uncomplicated."

Those broad shoulders straightened and she tilted her head to the side, as if thinking. Her entire outfit was no-nonsense: tight denim jeans that showcased a fine ass, a white cotton tank, and only a pair of pretty jade earrings to hint at femininity, though she had that in spades. The tank clung to her rounded curves, and though he'd rarely seen her without her black hair knotted back or in a tight braid, little tendrils of it constantly escaped. The effect was immediate. And effortless. He'd be surprised if she even knew how often men's gazes lingered on her, though they rarely pushed for more than that. The sharp tongue had its own ball-tightening effect, but it scared off most of the locals, he'd noticed.

More fool them.

"Turn around," he said. "As much as I enjoy looking at your ass, I much prefer your pretty face."

Mia leveled a force-one glare upon him. "Sometimes, McClain, you just shouldn't open your mouth."

"My mouth does wonderful things, or so I've heard. Maybe you should teach me to put it to better use."

"I run my own bar. I'm a respected woman who can earn her own way, and I do *not* need a man for anything. Even something *uncomplicated*. So don't go looking at me as a means to scratch that itch you've got. Why don't you visit Jade?"

"Jade's never going to scratch this itch," he replied. "This itch has got a mean mouth, the prettiest pair of eyes north of the borderlands, and skin that just begs to be licked. Why else do you think I drink here? The service with a smile?"

"I thought it had something to do with the best whiskey this side of the Divide." Mia crossed her arms over her chest. "Christ, McClain. Is that what the women fall for up in the Wastelands?"

"How'd you know I come from the north?"

"I've got a gift for dialect. We get all sorts wander through here; bounty hunters, Nomads, sometimes even Confederate militia."

"Hmm." He considered her. "One night. That's all I want." Then he could burn the yearning for her out of his system and move on.

"Why me?"

A tricky question. "You remind me of someone...."

"Oh, hell no." Mia bristled. "You want to switch off the lights, and pretend I'm—"

"No, I didn't mean it like that." With a scowl, he raked his hands through his hair. It was getting long, the ends of it faintly curling. He needed to razor it again. "You're the type of woman that catches my eye."

Mia leaned back against the bar, slightly mollified. "And what type of woman is that?"

"The strong-willed, determined, take-no-prisoners type," he growled. "The type that I can't have. Usually."

Mia considered it, chewing on her lower lip. Then she shook her head. "You're the type of man I stay far, far away from, McClain. I don't need to know your story to see the shadows in your eyes. You're trouble. You don't know what you want, nor do you know how to get there. You're a man without a map or a compass. A hero without a cause to fight for. And," she said, with the faintest smile, "you're far too pretty for your own good."

"I'm not a hero."

I'm the monster every Wastelander fears.

"Interesting." Mia poured them both another shot of whiskey. She nudged one toward him with a curious glint in her eyes. "You protest that, but you don't protest the part about you looking pretty."

This time, Adam was the one trying not to flush. She had a way about her that struck him straight to the gut. He lifted his glass of whiskey. "Here's to what could have been."

"Cheers," she said, lifting her own glass and bumping it against his. Her voice grew a little husky. "It's not just you, McClain. You're not the only one who's a little lost. I'd be bad for you and I know enough to know you'd be bad for me." She took a deep breath. "Here's to finding our way." She threw the whiskey back, her long, smooth throat working. He watched her for another long moment, fighting the urge to touch her, then threw his own back.

Both glasses hit the counter.

"You moving on soon?"

Adam nodded. There was his answer, right there. "No other reason to stay."

Mia looked troubled again. "You know, sometimes you say things that make me want to smack you upside the head. And sometimes... sometimes you know just the right thing to say."

"I—" Adam shut his mouth, hearing bootheels ringing on the front porch. Company by the sounds of it.

Mia followed his gaze toward the door. "What?"

Three seconds later a pair of hands hit the doors, sending them swinging inward. A man appeared, wearing a long trench and a black Stetson he dragged from his head. There were small weathered lines at the sides of his eyes, a Kevlar vest shielding his chest and a pair of guns at his hips. Adam's gut clenched hard. A bounty hunter by the look of it, just like him. If anyone could recognize the signs of a warg in human clothing, this stranger would be it.

Mia sucked in a sharp little breath as if hit.

That made Adam's gaze jerk back to her, but she was hastily polishing the clean counter again.

The bounty hunter pulled up a chair at the bar and tossed his hat on the counter. He eyed Adam with hard eyes, but didn't seem particularly curious. "Mia, long time. How 'bout a drink?"

"Sinclair." She tipped her head politely, pouring him a whiskey and sliding it his way.

The man sipped it, arching a brow. "You know you can call me Jake," he said. "Now that I'm married to Sage."

"I keep forgetting," Mia said, with a tight little smile. "Since you've been gone so long."

That earned her a wry twist of the mouth. Adam sat very still. He still wasn't certain if he was reading things correctly, but there was tension here, and he didn't like leaving a woman behind to deal with a strange man who may or may not be dangerous.

"Just as long as your sister doesn't forget," Sinclair replied firmly.

"Oh, she doesn't. Sage always did think that men'd keep the promises they made." Mia looked dangerous. "I'm the one who knew better. That's why it was so easy for you to break her heart."

"Well, I haven't missed that mouth," Sinclair said. "That's enough, Mia. I'm tired, I'm hungry, and I don't enjoy walking into this war zone every time I ride in. Can't we just form a truce, for once in our lives?"

"That depends," she said, "on how soon it will be until you ride out again?"

"Not soon enough." Sinclair glanced again at Adam, clearly eager to talk to someone else. "You hunt?"

"Yes."

That earned him an appreciative look and a deeper perusal. "That bike out front yours?"

Adam sat back. "Yeah."

"Gas is hard to find out here."

It wasn't quite a question. "An old friend of mine rigged it up for solar. Sunshine's the one thing we've got no problem finding here in the Badlands. That, and scavengers."

"Man or beast." Sinclair grunted. "That's the truth. Catch anythin' lately?"

"Just trouble." Certainly no sign of Johnny Colton, the warg he'd been hunting until the bastard vanished clean off the map. He spared Mia a faint smile, which only seemed to set her back up more. "You?"

"Been north." The man raked a hand through his dark hair with a sigh. "Chasing rumors of some warg who'd been living in the heart of a town up there for well on eight years. Nobody even knew what was hiding in their midst. Hell of a strange story. Wouldn't tell me his name, wouldn't tell me where he went, or how he did it. Just clammed up real tight whenever I mentioned it. Let's just say I was *encouraged* to leave quietly."

Hell. Adam froze. Those were his people. After they'd asked him to leave, he'd have expected them to sell his secrets for the price of a glass of whiskey. Eden. It had to be Eden, pleading for the town to spare her brother and keep his secrets. They might shun him, but they sure as hell wouldn't risk incurring the wrath of the only healer in that part of the Wastelands. Eden was worth her weight in gold for her doctoring.

Mia's eyebrows shot up. "How in the seven hells did a warg hide in plain sight for so long?"

"Don't know." The man looked troubled. "Makes me nervous. They're isolated hicks, but they're not stupid. Everyone knows the signs out here, and how the fuck did he hide his nightly rampages? That's the true question I want to know. 'Cause if one of them can do it, then how many of them are sitting here, right beneath our noses?"

If only you knew.... Adam smiled grimly. The "hicks" comment put his back up. Wastelanders grew up hard and they were wary, but they weren't stupid. Down here in the Badlands, where it rained more and towns were closer together with more supplies running up from the borderlands down south, they grew too soft. Soft and arrogant. "Sounds like a tall tale to me."

"That's what I thought when I first heard it." Sinclair leaned on the counter. "Found a reiver gang out there.

Once I were done cutting them down, I got some time to ask the last survivor a few questions."

"You trust a reiver?" Reivers were lawless, barely human scum who rode in gangs, stealing whatever they could lay their hands on, burning down settlements, and either raping, killing, or taking the people there for slaves.

"I had good reason to believe what he was telling me," the man replied, and Adam knew exactly how he'd asked the questions. "He said he ran with a pack of wargs who wore some sort of medallion to keep their monster under wraps. A couple of others came looking for them, and killed his warg friends. That leaves two of them out there, wearing amulets, maybe three, if this warg at Absolution wasn't the one who came down on them reivers. What do you think of that?"

The medallion burned as a cold reminder against his chest. Adam forced himself to relax, grateful that it was the kind of thing he kept hidden, beneath his shirt. *I think there's four of us with medallions*, a part of him whispered, *and that you might just be a dangerous man to keep alive*. But he wasn't a killer, no matter what others thought of him, and there were better ways to deal with this. "A single warg killed that many people? I think stories grow. That's what I think. Besides, if they're content to kill each other then let them."

"Maybe. It's still troubling."

"Damn right," Mia said, pouring them all a shot and throwing hers back before they could argue.

"Hell, Mia," Sinclair said, leaning on the counter. He didn't take her hand, though a part of him clearly wanted to. "I didn't mean to remind you of the past."

What past? Adam glanced at her from beneath his lashes, but she shook her head.

"Just shut up, Jake."

She was the wrong kind of woman. Or maybe he was the wrong kind of man. And he was just drawing this out. There was no point staying, especially now there was a bounty hunter in town, out to claim his scalp, and a woman who'd shoot him if she ever knew what he really was.

And wasn't that the kicker, for he realized that a part of him would actually hurt to see that look of horror in her eyes. *Idiot.* He needed to get moving. He'd stayed here too long, started to feel something for the town. Or perhaps, for one stubborn woman.

He couldn't do that again.

"Well, thanks for the company—and the story." Adam slid his chair back, tossing a few coins on the bar to clear his account, and grabbed hold of his black Stetson. "Time for me to move on, I think."

Mia looked startled, just for a second. Then she shuttered her emotions and nodded. "Good luck, McClain. I hope you find what you're looking for."

"You too," he said, taking the time to look at her one last time, as if to imprint her image in his memory. Just one more lost dream. Adam swallowed hard, then turned for the door, giving Sinclair one last nod, bounty hunter to bounty hunter.

Time to remember what he was.

You don't belong here and you never did.
You don't belong... anywhere.

two

"DIDN'T THINK HE was your type," Jake said, tapping his fingers on the bar and watching as the doors swung shut behind McClain.

"He's not." Mia pulled her mind out of wistful nothings, and gathered up the coins McClain left behind. They were stamped with New Merida symbols, no doubt paid out in blood money. She didn't particularly like that they came from the slave towns down south, but money was money, and it was far more than what he'd owed. Most of the time she was paid in Wasteland coppers—the square bits that were stamped with whatever the maker decided to put on them and worth only the metal that they were made out of. A good bar owner could tell when someone mixed too much metal with the copper. A good bar owner also knew when she was holding on to solid gold. She looked toward the fluttering doors and had a moment of doubt.

That itch she couldn't scratch.

Maybe she shouldn't have been so hardheaded, but McClain made her nervous, and she'd burned her fingers before. Indeed, she wouldn't be in this situation if she'd listened to that quieter, warier part of herself.

"Yeah?" Heat darkened Jake's eyes, a mix of jealousy and something else—something he had no right in feeling. "I know what you look like when you want a man."

"You would know." She turned away, sliding the sticky glasses toward her. Once he'd been her best friend, her only ally. Now? "That doesn't mean that this is any of your business. And you heard him. He's leaving."

Too late for her to do anything about her choices. Maybe it was for the best?

"Hey." Jake caught her wrist, leaning forward. "It's not my place to say it, I know that, but he's not the type of man—"

"You touch me again, and I *will* cut off that hand," she told him, staring him down.

With a grimace, he let her go. "I'm trying to—"

"You're married. To my sister." That hadn't stopped him once upon a time, when they'd been barely adults, though she'd been completely unaware of the promises he'd made to Sage just four fucking hours earlier. Four hours. Mia shut her eyes. All of it had been a mistake— telling Jake that she wanted something more than him, wanted to see the world, and him taking all that fury and rejection and asking her sister for something he shouldn't have.... And then later that night, for not telling her the truth of what he'd promised Sage when Mia changed her mind and went looking for him.

Yes, she'd kissed him. She'd done a hell of a lot more than that. But he'd had his chances to tell her he'd proposed to Sage, and he hadn't. Now Mia had to feel that crawl of guilt every time she looked at her oblivious sister.

Sage had been so happy to marry the man they'd both loved, that she'd never even known what was in her sister's heart. Maybe it was Mia's fault, for not telling her how she felt about Jake? Love wasn't something to hide, but she'd been wary, even then.

She didn't know how to fix this. Sage's heart broke every time Jake rode out of town, but he couldn't stay here with everything that lay between them. They just kept cutting at each other, and Sage didn't know why.

"I've been thinking," Jake said. "About... this."

Mia buried her hands in the sink. She just wanted him to go. It had been seven years since that disastrous night and she felt sick every time she saw him.

"Mia, are you listening?"

"Only occasionally." She sounded weary. "You should go home," she said. "To your wife. She misses you."

"I know." Jake's hesitation lingered. "I'm thinking of taking her north."

"*What?*" Mia smacked her head on the shelf above the sink. Her heart plummeted into her feet. "You can't take her away. This is our home."

"But it's not mine," he said firmly. "I can't keep doing this. I care for your sister, and you're the one who keeps throwing it in my face about the promises I made her. How do I fix this? You want me to make her happy, but you don't want me around." He let out a sigh. "I know you

23

don't want to see her go, but she and I could make a life together, away from all of... *this*."

Her was what he meant. "And what about me? You're going to take away the one piece of family I have left? Haven't you done enough damage?"

"I care for your sister, Mia. Really care. Sometimes I think there could be more between her and I, if we gave it a chance. I don't want to see her hurt any more than you do. Maybe she'd be happy? I could divorce her and leave forever, but you know what she was like after she lost the baby." His voice dropped. "I'm a fool who's made a lot of bad decisions, but I'm not a bad man, Mia. I hate being the villain in all of this. I fucked up. I fucked up badly. But I don't want to drive my wife back into that walking-zombie state by leaving her, and I can't see any other way out of it."

That hurt. Mia didn't love him, not anymore, and he didn't love her. There was too much bitterness between them for that to have lasted. But why did she have to be the one who kept missing out?

"I owe her better than what I've given her," Jake said. "I owe *you* better, but I can't change the past. The only thing I have left is to change the future."

Tears sprang to Mia's eyes. She knew what he was saying was the truth, but that didn't make her feel any better. Sage was her only... anything. "You bastard."

"I'll wear that," he said in a roughened voice. "Let me pay my dues, Mia. Please."

Swallowing hard, she brushed her wet cheek against her shoulder. Enough of that nonsense. "Where will you take her?"

"Thank you," he whispered, as if she'd given him her blessing. "I don't know. It's a hard land up north, but there'd be plenty of work for me and Sage would fit into the communities up there. They don't take to strangers easily, but when they do it's forever, and Sage's talent in salvaging electronics makes her valuable."

"When?"

"I don't know. I'll have to ask her first." He hesitated. "It would help if she knew she had your blessing."

Mia smiled bitterly. "More lies I have to tell my sister. Don't you ever get sick of it? I do."

"I—"

A commotion sounded outside, engines roaring and tires squealing. She'd probably have noticed it earlier, if not for her absorption in their argument.

Jake found his feet, his body tense. Salvation Creek was a quiet town, and no commotion was ever a good omen. "Stay there," he said, with a sharp cutting motion of his hand, then turned toward the door, one hand on the pistol holstered at his hip.

"Like hell I will," Mia grumbled, grabbing her shotgun from under the bar and then leaping over the counter.

Outside, dust hung in the air as four vehicles jerked to a halt in the street. Three of them were salvaged from scrap with different-colored doors, but one of them was whole, a dull red that had once been shiny.

Her heart dropped through her boots again as she saw it. "Thwaites," she whispered, pausing at Jake's side. The rancher owned a good portion of the land near Salvation Creek.

His farmhands spilled out of the vehicles, two of them carrying another. Then Thwaites himself appeared. There was blood smeared up his face, and his shirt was soaked with it.

Mia's heart twisted as she searched through the faces. No. *No.* She darted forward, shoving through the men, searching for the one face she didn't see. "Sage? *Sage!*"

Ethan Thwaites turned toward her, his arm hanging bloody at his side and his face smeared with dirt and sweat. Normally a big man with a hearty laugh and a booming voice, he'd never looked so beaten down, so small. "Mia," he breathed. "I'm so sorry."

"What happened? Where is everyone? Where's my sister?" Sage worked on retainer for Thwaites, and the last Mia had seen of her sister, she'd taken the old jeep out toward his place last night to see to some problem with Thwaites's water pump. Sage had planned to stay the night there.

She barely felt Jake's presence at her back. All she could do was cling to Ethan Thwaites's coat.

"Reivers," he said. "A good forty of them. They hit us this morning, just before dawn. Came in quiet-like with no cars or bikes. One minute I was eating breakfast, the next they were there shooting at us. Jesus." He scraped his good hand over his face. "They dropped Maggie in the kitchen whilst I still had a fucking spoon of porridge in my hand. If I hadn't reacted as quickly as I did, then this"—he gestured to his limp arm—"wouldn't be my worst problem."

"What about the outposts?" Jake asked, his voice hard. "How'd they come in so quietly? The men on duty should have seen something."

"Don't know," Thwaites replied dully. His eyes were glassy with pain. "No word from them."

"Those men had radios." Jake searched Thwaites's eyes.

"Then maybe they didn't see the reivers coming either? I gathered those I could and came here. The rest of them I left at the ranch, to bury the dead."

Dead. "What happened to Sage?" Mia demanded.

Thwaites wouldn't meet her eyes. "They took all of the women they could, Mia. Those that didn't die in the first attack. We were holed up in the barn trying to keep them at bay, but most of the household staff were trapped inside the main house. I don't know where Sage is— maybe she got free, maybe she ran—but I didn't see her body anywhere."

Her breath caught in a half sob. "You left them in the main house, defenseless?"

Thwaites flinched as if she'd struck him. "*All* of the women, Mia. You don't see my wife here, do you?" he demanded. "Or my daughters. I was trying to gather the men to fight them off. We were trapped like fucking rats."

"Mia," Jake warned, grabbing her arm.

"I'm sorry." This couldn't be happening. She clapped a hand over her mouth. She'd lost both parents to a shadow-cat attack when she was only fifteen. Her aunt Jenny had taken her and Sage in, but Mia had always known that it was just the pair of them now against the world. Maybe it was the fact they'd both been adopted and had no one else, but Sage was her entire world.

She'd sat in the dirt at her parents' grave and promised them she'd look out for her little sister. No matter what happened.

"What are we going to do?" Jake asked, low and soft.

"I'm riding after them," Thwaites said. "I need men though. And guns. Are you with me?"

"Never any doubt." Jake's lips thinned. "That's my wife out there. I know what reivers do to women, Ethan. If we don't get them back and soon, there might not be much left to get back."

Tears shone bright in the old rancher's eyes. "I know."

"And I'll be riding with you," Mia declared, daring either of them to say no.

three

ADAM SLID HIS shotgun into the holster on his modified motorbike. The word Yamaha had once stretched across the tank, but now it was bleached clean. He didn't even know what the word meant. A lot had been lost in the years of the Darkening, when the skies blackened with dust and ash, and the temperatures dropped a few degrees. The only ones who survived were those who had access to underground bunkers or storage sheds, where they'd stayed for nearly five years before the ash cloud settled. Wasn't much left alive then, but food was running scarce, and so the survivors had to adapt.

They said that people showed their true selves then. Some banded together and struck out west across the Great Divide, where there was still land to settle; others stayed in the east under the harsh thumb of the Confederacy—there were still cities there in the east, some said, though his mind couldn't even conjure what that meant; and others became scavengers.

The Yamaha was his sole relic of the past, and most of it was patched and recrafted. The tires came from the factories down south where rubber trees were found, and there were men here in the wastelands who could craft steel and aluminum, others who'd managed to rig up solar panels, which were worth their weight in gold here out in the Wastelands. People made do. They had to. Any man could own a dozen trades.

Noise and raised voices spilled out into the courtyard behind the public house where he'd taken rooms, but it wasn't his business. Time to move on. He'd shaved his face and cropped his hair, then packed up his stuff.

The only thing he had left in his life was one last quest: to find Johnny Colton, the warg who'd helped turn him into a monster, and bury him so deep nobody ever found the body.

Adam slung a leg over the bike, flipped the choke out, and then stiffened.

Blood. He could smell blood.

That caught his attention. The warg shifted inside him, as if pushing against his skin.

Following the scent, Adam found himself back in front of the bar. He couldn't see Mia, but several jeeps idled in the street, and people were streaming from every other business in town to discover what was going on.

A huge man with a barrel for a chest and blood soaking his sleeve stepped up onto the porch of Mia's saloon, where he could see the crowd. "As you all know by now, a band of about forty reivers hit my ranch this morning and took half my womenfolk and some of the kids. They'll be headed south, where they can sell them at the border towns, and we all know what happens then.

"I've been a part of this town for near on fifty years. I've sacrificed my own blood and sweat to build Salvation Creek, and now I'm standing here asking you folk to lend me your blood and sweat back. They've got a four-hour start on me, but I'm plannin' on gathering some men and going after them. I can't pay you. I don't know if you'll come back. But I need to know... are there any here that will ride with me?"

Several hands shot into the air, but it was clear from the look on the man's face that he'd expected more. Silence became almost thick, and then one hand started to lower, then another.

"Jenny," the man said, looking at someone in the crowd. "Please. They've got Helen, and all the rest of the girls, including my two."

A hard-looking woman in front pursed her lips together. She was short and slim, with gray in her dark hair and dark skin the color of tea-stained paper, but she didn't look scared. More thoughtful. "I can shoot, Ethan, but hell... what are we meant to do against forty reivers? And by the look of that arm, you ain't gonna be much help. Nor half your men."

"I'll go," a female voice called out, and then Mia stepped up beside the man. "That's my sister they've got. That's your niece too, Jen." She looked out over the crowd. "I see a lot of faces here that know those girls, or share some blood with them. What are you all going to do next time, when it's your girls you're crying over? Thwaites is right. We need to stick together."

Mia. That made him stand up straight. He looked around. People lowered their eyes, muttering under their breath. He couldn't stand to see her there alone.

"And what if they come back when everyone's gone?" another woman called. "What about those of us left behind? I'm sorry, Mia, but we've got children here. We need to protect the town."

More voices rose up, a sudden chorus of arguments.

"They won't come back," someone called. "We've got the General on our side."

"The General don't give a shit about us out past the Divide," someone else yelled. "He only rides through when he's got reason to."

"What if they come back—"

"And what if they don't?" someone else called. "How do you look your daughter in the eye, Crane, when you let her best friend get taken off into slavery?"

It was chaos. Adam could almost taste the anger and fear in the air, and the vein in his temple throbbed as his heart started beating a little faster. He could feel the icy cold burn of the amulet against his chest as his inner predator sat up and took notice of all the weakness in the air.

In that moment he was stepping back years into the past, where he'd been forced to step forward and gather together the small tribe of settlers who were being hit hard by wargs in the Wastelands. Those people helped him form the fortified town of Absolution, but they'd need a push to get there. And while he'd never wanted to put himself forward as a leader—not with his secret—he couldn't leave them there alone. Just as he couldn't keep quiet now.

He stepped up on the porch next to Mia and Thwaites. "That's enough," he said, and though he didn't raise his voice much, it carried, and people began to settle down, turning curious eyes on the newcomer.

They might not know him, but people understood an air of authority. They recognized strength when they saw it, and Adam had long grown used to commanding respect from people.

"A lot of you don't know me, and I don't know a lot of you, but you can't allow this to stand. You can't afford to look weak. The reivers have never hit you this far east, but I grew up in the north. I've spent most of my life hunting these bastards and fighting them off. In the north, we have walls and guns and we look at you down here and call you the 'soft-landers.' Maybe we're not the only ones who think that? Most reivers prefer to raid the Wastelands for the scarcity of the militia, but it's getting harder to take the settlements up there. Their slave routes are drying up. If they start getting a taste for how easy it is to come a little further out of their way, then do you think this will be the only attack you bear?"

Silence lingered, but he saw several people shifting, not liking what a stranger had to say.

"I want you to look at your daughters gathered here today, or maybe your sons too, for the slavers like some big strapping boys to work their fields and their factories. I want you to think about what happens if the reivers come back, or heaven forbid, get a taste of the softer times here." He looked around, daring any man to meet his eyes.

"Easy for you to say. Who are you to tell us what to do?"

"I'm the man who's going to ride with your rancher here and get those women back. I'm the man who's going to tell you what you need to do to keep the reivers off your back." He let a faint smile show. "I'm the man who hunts these scum for a living, and I enjoy it. I'm good at it. Same as your own boy here, Sinclair, is good at it." He turned and met the other bounty hunter's eyes. "Is there anything I've said here that you don't agree with?"

Sinclair tipped his chin back. "No," he called. "I've been north. I've seen their walls at the settlements up there. I've seen how the reivers are getting more desperate by the day, and I've killed 'em too." He had the kind of cocky grin that the crowd ate up, but Adam could smell his sweat. "Reivers are scavengers, they're not even really predators. Why'd they sneak in at dawn? I'll tell you why. They've got rusted out guns, and piecemeal body armor sewn together out of scrap wheel hubs. They needed surprise on their side. Hell, maybe they got the numbers, but we've got something they don't have." His voice grew louder, and he thumped his chest. "We've got men, good men. We've got women"—he tilted his head toward the one they'd called Jenny—"who can shoot the eye out of a squirrel a hundred yards away. Our guns are good, our bullets are hard, and most of all, we've got a righteous kind of wrath to spare." His voice lowered, but it was no less powerful. "Reivers are cowards. We hit 'em with everything we've got and they'll run. They won't stand together. It's every man for himself out there, but if we ride as one, then we'll scare the ever-living daylights out of them."

It might take a little more than that, but Adam kept his opinion to himself.

With a flourish, Sinclair handed the floor back to Adam.

"Do you know what the strength of the northern settlements is?" he called. "We live together, we work together. One settlement gets hit and the others send relief troops their way. You want to protect your town? Then you need to get the other settlers hereabouts to work with you. You find a common building." He gestured toward the town hall behind them. "Something strong and easy to fortify. Gather enough food and water to last you a few weeks, until we return. Work together. Watch each other's backs. Have men on guard at every hour of the day with guns. Work out a roster. Radio in to the nearby towns and get them on alert, watching for reivers."

"But what about our houses?" an older woman called, nursing a kid on her hip.

He stared her straight in the eye. "I've seen a house rebuilt. I ain't ever seen someone put a person back together though, once they're full of holes. Take care of yourselves, then worry about your... replaceables." He gave the word the respect it deserved.

He had them.

Turning to Thwaites, he nodded. "All yours."

"We can't pay you much," the man said. "Or we can't promise you'll get anything if we return. There may not be much left."

"I don't do this for the money," Adam replied. He met Mia's eyes then. She looked shocked, but also curious. "I do this because it's my map and compass, as someone once said to me."

Thwaites stared at him for a long moment. "It'll get harder before it gets easier, son."

Adam just smiled. He couldn't remember the last time someone had called him son. "I've been to 'hard' before. It's not a place I enjoy, but it's a place I know well."

four

"WANNA HAND?"

Mia crouched in front of the small fire she was trying to light with her flint. She knew who it was. She just wasn't entirely certain she wanted company. "No. I'm fine."

McClain dumped an armful of small sticks and twigs at her feet. Mia kept striking the flint, waiting for a spark to feed. One latched on to her tinder and she scrambled to her hands and knees and blew on it, until she had a nice flame glowing there. The task was simple, and it kept her mind busy.

McClain had spent most of the day scouting ahead, whilst she rode in Thwaites's jeep. It was hard travel over barren plains and rocky gravel, and sometimes she had to wonder if McClain was just seeing things when he said there were tracks. Even Jake looked hard at the ground and chewed on his lip, though he didn't disagree.

"How far ahead do you think they are?" Mia asked, staring into the flames. Night meant that they had to stop, but night also meant the reivers would be making camp, and that meant they'd want to celebrate what they'd captured.

Don't think about that. Mia snapped a twig in half and fed it into the flames. Ever since she lost the baby, Sage had been prone to bouts of moodiness and depression. The simple fact of the matter was that Mia feared for her baby sister's state of mind, and she'd give anything to trade places with her right now.

"About four hours still," he replied. "We lost a lot of time getting supplies and making sure Thwaites and his men were ready to ride out, but we're moving faster than they are. Here." He broke a piece of hardtack and handed it to her.

Mia shook her head. "I'm not hungry."

"You need to keep your strength up," he replied.

"I feel sick," she shot back, sinking both her hands into her hair. "I couldn't possibly eat. What about my sister? Do you think she's eating right now? Or do you think...." She couldn't say the words.

Putting the hardtack away, McClain hauled a stump closer to her and sat beside her. "Mia, if you start thinking about the what-ifs and the could-bes, then you might as well turn back now. Stick to the facts. Face them as they come at you. Focus on the plan."

"She's my baby sister," she whispered. "She's strong, but she's always had that softer side I could never manage. What if they break her?"

"You might be surprised." The fire crackled as he fed it. "People sometimes find a kind of strength in hard situations that you'd never believe they owned. Maybe she's never had to be fearless, because you were there beside her? Or maybe she knows that her sister would shift hell and high water to get her back? Maybe that's her strength, right now, knowing that you're coming for her."

That gave her some hope. If there was one thing that Sage would believe in, it was that her sister would come for her. And her husband, Mia had to reluctantly admit. "I'm scared."

"I know you are. I would be too, if that was my sister out there."

Mia glanced toward him. "You have a sister?"

"Baby sister," he said, "though she'd take affront at that. So I can guess at how you're feeling. There's five years between me and Eden. She's always been mine to protect, but it's as though she grew up when I blinked, and it took me far too long to realize that." His smile faded. "It's not easy to let them be grown-ups, but I kind of figure she's twenty-nine now, with her own life and her own destiny. Hell, she's a doctor who's patched me up more times than I can tell, so maybe she's been the one looking after me? It's not easy to admit that though, especially when you're the type of man who likes to protect. I've been told I'm... overbearing."

"And who told you that? Your sister?" There was something in his voice though, that hinted at the answer.

"No." He met her gaze. "There was a woman. Once."

Mia looked back into the flames. He'd spent a month drowning himself in her bar. In that time he'd flirted with her, butted heads with her, and outright driven her crazy. There'd never been a promise of more though, even if his words sent an odd twinge through her. "What happened? To the woman?"

McClain sighed. "She fell in love with the man who was once my best friend."

"He took her from you?"

"No. It's complicated. Luc and I weren't friends toward the end, though that had little to do with Riley." McClain moved slowly, taking over her fire and setting out a small pan and some tins of beans. He set them to broiling, then poured water from his canteen into a pot. "I never had her, Mia. She was never mine, and I didn't even know what really made her tick. I wanted the promise of her. I liked her hard head even though it drove me crazy, but I never really understood her. I asked her once, why him? And do you know what she said?"

"What?"

"She said that he let her stand at his side, while I tried to hide her behind me. He trusted her to guard his back, while I tried to force her to stay out of danger. He let her be who she was, and even though I was attracted to her attitude and personality, a part of me tried to change her." McClain stirred his beans. "Maybe I learned a little bit from her. I'm not going to lie and say that I like the idea of you riding along with us, or the other women—I've always been a bit old-fashioned like that—but I'm not going to stop you. You deserve to be here, and I hope we can stand side by side when this shit with the reivers goes down."

It explained a lot. Mia drew her knees up, watching him over the top of them. "Sometimes you drive me crazy too."

He laughed, though it was never the type of laugh that overtook his face. More like a faint sign of humor that he couldn't stop from escaping.

"And if you tried to stop me," she told him, "you'd end up wearing that fork you're stirring the beans with, in your thigh."

The faintest hint of a smile curled his mouth up. "The strangest thing is that hearing words like that gets me all hot and bothered." Glancing up at her from underneath the brim of his hat, he kept stirring the beans but his focus was 100 percent locked on her.

Mia's breath caught. He had dangerous green eyes, the kind of eyes that always made her want to linger there, staring at him.

"I'm not into that kind of thing," she said primly.

"Me either. I'm starting to think I have a serious weakness for strong-willed women though."

"Even though you want to change them?" she asked.

Another smile. "Poor choice of words. Darlin', I wouldn't change a damned thing about you, but if push came to shove I couldn't just stand by and let you walk into danger. I have this idiot complex about taking bullets in the chest for pretty ladies."

Wouldn't change a damned thing about you.... Mia swallowed. He had a way with words sometimes. A blunt kind of honesty that took her breath. "I guess we'll have to cross that bridge when it comes to it," she replied. "I bet I can shoot more reivers than you can."

"So you know how to work that thing?" He gestured toward the shotgun at her feet.

"My Aunt Jenny can put out a squirrel's eye at a hundred paces. I can shoot the cigarette out from between someone's lips. She taught me how to defend myself, but her eyesight's struggling these days. You wouldn't have wanted to cross Aunt Jenny ten years ago. She rode with the Nomads for a time."

"I don't want to cross your Aunt Jenny now," he replied. "She's still sitting there with your friend, Sinclair, watching my every move. Has been ever since I walked over here."

Mia looked up and squinted in the darkness. He was right. Jake glanced away as if he hadn't been caught looking, but Jenny arched a brow as if to ask her if she knew what she was doing.

Mia shrugged, then looked back down at McClain. He was pouring some of the beans into the pot lid for her. Firelight washed over his tanned face, highlighting the stark line of his cheekbones. He was one hell of a handsome bastard, but she thought his slow manner of moving, almost a kind of careful *gentleness*, and his brutal sense of honesty were more appealing than his looks.

And, she had to admit, as he handed her a share of the beans, he'd very neatly manipulated her into thinking about something other than her sister.

Mia ate her beans, watching him and brooding. Nobody had ever quite tied her up in knots like this, not even Jake.

And McClain did it without even thinking.

"I'd better take the first watch," he said, putting his makeshift bowl down.

"You're not tired?" Mia asked.

"I can go a few days without sleep, if need be. And not that I doubt your friends but I know what to look out for in the dark. We don't need an ambush."

"You think that would happen?"

"I think that reivers are unpredictable," he replied bluntly. "They're not overly educated, but some of them are cunning. Whoever's leading this band took us straight out over these plains, which leave barely any tracks, instead of making straight for Fort Phoenix. They're heading southeast, which is unusual as there's not much out there. Maybe they'll swing back but I can't guarantee that, so we're forced to follow them and play their game for the meanwhile."

Mia stared into the flickering flames. "Do you think we'll get them back?"

McClain knelt in front of her, capturing her hands. "Look at me, Mia." She obeyed, and then couldn't look away from those intense green eyes. "I promise you I'll do my best to get your sister and your townsfolk back, but you have to promise not to give up. I'm very, very good at what I do. I promise you I'll find her, eventually."

He didn't promise he'd find Sage alive, but Mia appreciated that. "Thank you," she whispered.

"For what?"

"For not lying to me." Lowering her gaze, she licked her lips, unable to take the scrutiny of his stare any longer.

"It's the one thing I can't stand—being lied to." Letting go of her breath, she released his hands and stood, brushing them against her jeans. "We'll get them back." Determination washed through her. "And you're right... I need to take care of myself in the meantime. If I don't eat or get enough rest, then I won't be at my strongest when we catch those bastards. Good night, McClain."

He was watching her, still kneeling on one knee. "Good night, Mia."

The darkness swallowed him whole. Adam climbed up onto the bluff overlooking the camp and stared out into the night, feeling the pull of it through his veins.

It was harder to contain that inner edge at the moment. He was a mess of want, of need, of hunger; though he knew most people wouldn't think it from his appearance. Adam had had a hell of a lot of time to learn to hide what he was underneath. His men in Absolution once called him the epitome of control, but now he started to wonder if all those years had merely been a conceit of his own. Ever since they'd discovered what he was, the bars of this particular cage seemed a little ragged. He could remember the looks on their faces with blinding clarity. He'd spent six years ruling them with a fair but firm hand, he'd lost blood for them, given them food off his own table and risked his own life to fetch back their women and children from reiver raids, but none of that mattered in the end.

For a few years, he'd forgotten what he was. He'd lived as a man, begun to even think he was one.

Now the warg within was making it clear that it had never gone away. Just hidden within him, waiting for its chance to dig its claws deep and remind him of what he was.

It didn't take Sinclair long to find him. The other man tipped his head in greeting, staring out into the darkness. "Do you think we've gained any time? The reivers would have had to stop for the night too, no?"

There were tiny, twinkling lights out there on the horizon. Adam pointed them out. "They're there. I can see their campfires. They might have pushed on past evening, but it's too dangerous to drive around out here in the dark. Not as many wargs hunt the nights here as they do in the north, but there will be enough. And if they blow a tire out in the dark, then they're screwed and they know it. Best to set up camp and have a guard on the perimeter. I'd say we're only four hours behind at this stage, so we've gained a little during the day, but lost too much earlier, when we were setting out."

Sinclair grunted. "Can't see a bloody thing. Just stars."

Adam stilled, aware of how close he'd come to slipping up. Of everyone here, Sinclair was the most dangerous, for he alone knew what to look for in a warg. "I've been out here longer. Maybe your eyes are still adjusting from the firelight."

"Probably."

Adam stared at the twinkling lights in the distance, a faint frown wrinkling his brow. They were further to the south now, almost back on the original road.

45

"What's wrong?" Sinclair asked.

"Nothing." But that irritating itch tickled at the back of his senses. No point in keeping it to himself. "I feel like I'm missing something. The reivers swung southeast earlier in the day, and I couldn't work out why. There's nothing out here and the slave towns are directly south. They should have taken the Southern Road toward Eagle Canyon, but they cut out across the desert here, like they were going to go straight over the Serendipity Mountains, toward the Rim."

"And?" Sinclair watched him carefully, his eyes intent. "I've had hunches like this before, out on the trail. It's saved my life several times over. I'm not doubting you, McClain."

"Now they're almost back on the road." Adam couldn't explain it. He met the other man's eyes. "Why? Why did they swing out of their way? What brought them here? There's nothing here, and they obviously intended to go south all along. All it's done is cost them time."

"Maybe they wanted to throw us off the scent?" Sinclair rested his hands on his hips, staring out into the velvety night. "That was hard tracking today. Maybe they were hoping we'd miss their trail, and head...." He paused.

"Head straight south along the road? If we had, then they'd be sitting right on top of us right now, which is not where they want to be. They wanted us to follow them. There were just enough traces left to track, even through that rocky gulch that threw us off a few times."

"Threw me off," Sinclair admitted dryly. "I couldn't see shit. You were the one tracking wind over rocks."

"Yeah, well—" He caught the scent of something faint on the breeze, but it was enough to turn his stomach.

Sinclair noticed his distraction, his body tensing and his hand falling to the gun at his belt. "What is it?"

Adam pushed past Sinclair, his hand held in the air to shut him up, as he tried to get a better fix on what exactly he was smelling. It was sickly sweet, just a gust of it on the air.

Rot. His mind finally put a name to the scent. He could smell rot.

Adam's blood froze. Everything coagulated in his mind. *This.* This was why the reivers brought them here.

"We've got incoming," he yelled, grabbing Sinclair by the arm as he wrenched them back toward camp. "Deadheads! Wake up! We've got deadheads incoming!"

"Fuck," Sinclair cursed, scrambling along at his heels. "Revenants? Out *here*? There's nothing out here."

The plains surrounding them were as barren as some parts of the wastelands up north. The only sign of life in the area was this tor, jutting out of the plains like some fucking mecca.

"It was a trap," Adam shouted over his shoulder, leaping over boulders, and slipping and sliding down the shale. It rained beneath his boots, like a miniature stone avalanche that he surfed. "I bet the whole tor's riddled with caves for them to hide out in during the day." That's why the reivers swung this way. It might be an hour or two out of their way, but if they'd timed it well—and they had—their pursuers would see the tor as the perfect place to make camp. "The reivers wanted us to stop here."

Adrenaline pumped hot blood through his veins, the darker side of him surging forth in glee. It could scent death on the wind, and knew it would be called to deal it in return. The sudden fierce urge to kill almost overrode him.

Not now. Sweat gleamed at his temples as he held himself tightly reined. The medallion burned cold against his chest. Its magic held the warg within him and helped keep it chained up tight, but even the medallion fought to contain the fierce hunger that roared through him. If the warg broke free, tearing its way out of his skin until he was nothing but rage, need and desire, then he wouldn't differentiate between friend and foe.

"Wake up!" Sinclair bellowed. "Wake up, and hands to rifles!"

"Incoming! Revenants!" Adam screamed. Christ, would they be in time? All those people rolled up in blankets, with only two guards posted... they'd be like fucking human tacos.

The camp came alive, fire flickering to life. People called out, shadows shifting in the night as Adam thundered toward camp. He saw the odd shambling gait of a revenant appear out of nowhere behind Jenny, and didn't think, simply threw himself toward her. Jenny screamed, then they were rolling straight over the fire. Sparks flew up around him, and he felt his shirt catch alight. It died a short death in the dirt, but there was no time to worry about being burnt.

"Fire," he yelled, snatching at one of the burning brands he'd just rolled over. "Use fire!"

The revenant lumbered toward them, its hair hanging in matted hanks that had slowly bleached of color until it was a sandy, dirty nothing. Its white eyes were filmed over with death, but its nose was twitching, trying to track him by scent. Adam hurled the branch at it, and the faded rags it wore went up like dry tinder. The flames spread, engulfing its hair, and burning a sickly green. The whole fucking thing stunk like an open grave.

Not long dead then, perhaps only a matter of months.

"Thanks," Jenny gasped, rolling to her feet. People were screaming around them and fleeing out into the night, which was the worst mistake they could make. God only knew how many revenants were out there, waiting in the dark for easy prey.

He had to do something.

"To me!" Adam bellowed. "Grab a branch of fire, and form a ring around me!"

"Over here!" Sinclair yelled, lifting the shotgun he'd appropriated and spraying buckshot into the nearest revenant's knees. Someone who knew what he was doing then. Sinclair stepped forward, blowing off the revenant's head as an afterthought. They'd keep crawling after you, if you let them.

"To us!" Jenny screamed.

Panic began to slow down. Out in the bushes people screamed. One particular cry hit notes he'd associated with dying animals before, and Adam knew what had happened. Revenants didn't wait until you were dead to begin eating.

Thwaites hobbled closer, using a shotgun for balance. He looked like he'd twisted his ankle in the rush out of his blankets. "Over here," he bellowed. "To McClain!"

Someone tossed Adam a spare shotgun. More people found their way into the circle.

But he couldn't see Mia.

"Wait here," he told Jenny. "Burn anything that comes at you."

"Where are you going?" she demanded, grabbing his arm.

"To find your niece."

five

THE FIRST SHOUT barely woke Mia. She drifted in the realms of exhaustion, trying to run after her sister, but never quite catching her. A boot in the side did the trick, however, as someone tripped over her.

The next thing she knew, she was surrounded by chaos. It took far longer than it should have for her to snap out of it. Screams filled the air, and people tackled each other to the ground, and then a lurching shadow straight out of her nightmares staggered toward her, and Mia finally realized what was happening.

"Sweet Jesus," she cursed, scrambling out of her blankets. It had been cold, and she was knotted up good and tight.

Her gun... where was her gun? She found it, kicked out of the way by someone—perhaps even her—and scrambled toward it. A revenant staggered over it, blocking her path, and Mia found she was all alone with not a single weapon to her name, and only her blanket still snagged on the toe of her boot.

Blood pumped through her veins, bringing with it a surge of adrenaline. Mia grabbed her blanket and didn't think, just attacked. She threw it over the revenant's head, snagging its ragged hands in tight, and then tackling it. Teeth gnashed beneath the blanket, far too close to her cheek as they rolled. There was a strength in its wiry body that she hadn't expected, and she found herself beneath it, trying to fight it off.

"Help!" she screamed, but there was no one to help her. Everyone else was either fleeing or under similar assault.

Out of the corner of her eye, she saw another filthy shape lurch toward her. Desperation forced her legs up between her and the figure pinning her down, and then she kicked it back, toward the fire.

Its arms flung free of the blanket as it fell, its face with its drawn-back lips and stained teeth turning toward her. Then the smoldering blanket finally caught fire. The creature jerked, throwing its head back in a silent scream as green flames engulfed its entire body.

Mia dove and snatched at her shotgun. She rolled onto her back, staring up at her new assailant, and pumped two rounds straight through its chest. *Jesus.* Nothing happened. The revenant lurched and black ichor splashed from the holes there, but it kept coming at her.

How...? No time, no time....

Swinging the shotgun's barrel into her hands, she flinched at the heat of it, then swung the butt round and took the revenant's legs out from beneath it. Ground... on the ground was dangerous. Had to get up.

Shadows darkened her vision. They were everywhere. Circling her, their eerie sightless eyes seeming to track her. Mia had a moment where she simply froze, her blood seemingly sluggish in her veins. Time slowed down. There was no way out. No. There had to be a way—

"Head or legs," someone bellowed.

And then *he* was there, leaping over the burning revenant behind her and sailing through the night. McClain landed in front of her, spinning with a sharp axe in his hands and decapitating one of the revenants. He stepped back, crouching low long enough to haul her to her feet. "You're not bitten?" His eyes were a little wild, sweat tracking runnels down his dirty face.

"N-no," Mia managed to croak. Was she? She knew what happened if someone was bitten, but patting herself down showed she was whole. She felt so disembodied that she wasn't certain she'd have felt it.

"Good." McClain stepped forward, swinging the axe again and burying it with a meaty thunk in the back of the nearest revenant's knee. It went down, but he spun, and then another head was soaring through the darkness. "Head or legs, Mia! Take them down, and then finish the job." Lifting his head, he caught sight of someone beyond the revenant. "Here! To me!"

It was a nightmare. Mia found her feet, smashing the butt of her shotgun into a lifeless face, then whirling and sending another sprawling. McClain barely paused to decapitate them both, before grabbing her arm and hauling her through the sudden gap in front of them.

"To me!" he yelled.

"Here!" Mia screamed. "To us!"

She grabbed a flaming branch out of a nearby fire, and set a revenant aflame. It lit up like a Christmas bonfire and kept shambling forward, staggering into a pile of dry sagebrush. The flames surged, lighting up the night.

"That's the way," McClain said. "Over here!"

A younger boy suddenly found them, shaking with fear. There was blood splashed up his arms, and his eyes showed so much white that she thought it was a miracle he'd made it to them.

Mia let go of McClain and grabbed his wrist. "I've got you, Joe. Keep an eye out, and let's keep moving."

"Where did they come from?" the boy bleated. "They've got my dad."

She caught a glimpse of Wayne Erris on his back, his body twitching, and his abdomen spilling viscera across his jeans. Too late. "This way," she said, turning Joe away from the sight and hauling him after McClain.

McClain made it feel all right. He cut through revenants as if they were cows to be slaughtered, drawing survivors toward them and leaving her to sort them out. There was no fear in him, nothing but brutal focus, and everyone felt it. Suddenly the nightmare was less compelling, less real, against the sheer magnetism of the man leading them. If McClain didn't fear them, then why should they?

And then it was over.

Mia started trembling as their small group was absorbed by the larger one surrounding her Aunt Jenny and Thwaites. Jenny hauled her in for a hug, her chest shaking against Mia's.

"My God," her aunt whispered. "I didn't think I'd see you again, my girl."

"You almost didn't." They shared a bleak smile, and then Mia looked around for McClain.

"He saved you," Jenny said, her hand sliding into Mia's. "Told me he'd go bring you back and he did."

They watched as he barked out orders, snapping the small band into a well-organized unit. Mia and Jenny set up a makeshift infirmary, checking everyone over from top to bottom for any signs of bite marks. They were almost home free when Mia dragged up Joe's left sleeve and saw the bloodied gash there, the teeth marks painted clearly in the boy's flesh and the mottled blackness beneath the skin as the pathogen took hold.

Her gut dropped. Joe was still out of it, his face pale and his eyes wide as he looked around. "W-where's my d-dad?" he kept asking. "Mia, did you see him? We have to get him. W-we have to—"

Her ears were ringing. She couldn't hear him anymore. All she could see were the teeth marks in his skin.

Joe Erris. Her Joe, the boy who made her deliveries every Wednesday when she'd finished with her latest batch at the still. Joe, with his stutter that he'd worked so hard on diminishing, and the secret crush he'd had on Sally Evans at the store.

Boots stepped into her vision and someone grabbed her arm. She had the feeling the newcomer asked her something too. Mia looked up and sound suddenly broke back into her world.

"Mia," McClain repeated. "What's wrong?"

"It's Joe," she said, suddenly feeling like she could move again. Life surged back into focus, and with it came determination. "Jenny!" she yelled. "Get me the tourniquet out of the kit, and the cauterization knife!"

"Shit." McClain saw what she'd seen, and wrenched the kid's arm out.

Joe looked down. "No," he whispered. "N-no!" He started screaming, tearing at his arm.

McClain grabbed him and held him down. "Stop moving. The more you move, the faster the pathogen travels through your bloodstream."

"Jenny, the kit!" Mia bellowed.

McClain's hard eyes met hers, and he gave a little shake of his head. "Mia—"

"Shut up," she said fiercely, undoing her belt and ripping it free from her belt loops with a meaty slap. She knew what his eyes were telling her, and she didn't want to hear the truth of it in his words. Joe wasn't dead, not yet. Mia wound the belt around Joe's arm, up under his shoulder, and wrenched it so tight that his circulation stopped.

"You don't have time for the kit," McClain said.

She just stared at Joe's arm. "I don't have—"

"Here. Swap places with me." McClain dragged a clean machete from his belt. It was a simple tool a lot of Badlanders carried.

Joe saw the machete and lost it. Grabbing the end of her belt, Mia shoved the hard leather between his teeth, forcing him to clench them around the leather. "That's it," she murmured. "Bite down hard."

He shook his head.

"I'm sorry, Joe. This is the only way."

Joe's nostrils flared, his breath coming in harsh pants and a scream building in his lungs.

"I've got you," Mia told him, grabbing hold of his other hand. "Hold my hand, Joe. Look in my eyes. I've got you."

The trust there... it almost flayed her. For she didn't know if she had the answers. A revenant's bite was often fatal, with almost 90 percent of the bitten beginning the transformation. You had to burn the bodies then, make sure there was no chance of them coming back. It was a fate worse than death, and nearly every Badlander had lost someone to the damned plague.

The meteor that caused the Darkening brought with it the revenant pathogen, or so her mom told her when she was a little girl. When a research team went into the pit to examine the meteor, they didn't come out again. By the time the rescuers dug the researchers out, every single one of them had been dead, though strangely unmarked. Half an hour after they hauled the first body out, it got up and tore out a doctor's throat. Unprepared, almost all of the medical staff were slaughtered before they could escape and fetch help. Too late, though. Three of the revenants escaped, carrying with them the hunger for flesh, which had spread through the heart of the country.

The scientists of the time managed to locate a virulent pathogen in the tissues of three of the bodies that could bring the dead back to life. There'd been a concentrated effort to wipe out the revenant scourge, but then the riots started breaking out, a couple of nuclear plants poisoned the earth, and there'd been no time to finish the job.

The machete flashed up in the corner of her vision. Mia didn't dare take her eyes off Joe's. Blood splashed against her sleeve and Joe's eyes widened in shock and pain. The scream pouring from his ravaged throat was the worst thing she'd ever heard. He kept screaming, even as McClain worked swiftly to staunch the blood flow, and then slowly, slowly, his eyes rolled back in his head and he was out of it.

Mia almost threw up. "Jesus," she whispered. The fingers clamped around hers slackened, and she pried them loose.

Jenny appeared with the med kit, panting swiftly. "Shit," she whispered, taking in the scene.

"Heat the knife," McClain instructed, using gauze to staunch the blood.

"Did we get it?" Mia demanded. Joe's severed arm lay at her feet, the veins in his elbow a roadmap of black beneath his pale skin, but the decay didn't seem to have travelled further. "Did we get it in time?"

"Won't know." McClain wouldn't look at her. "Just heat the knife, Mia."

six

LIGHT GLINTED off metal, somewhere on the valley floor below them.

"There she is, boys," Ethan Thwaites murmured the next day, idling the jeep on the top of the cliff. "Vegas."

Mia slid to the edge of her seat, peering down. Afternoon sunshine gleamed back off metal and glass. "Is that where the reivers are?"

"They'll likely make camp there," Jenny muttered. "Used to be flat plains here, but the Darkening tore the earth apart pretty good down here. Some kind of dam broke and cleared out half the population, but a lot of the buildings still remain. It's the only city from pre-Darkening days that survived out here, beyond the Wall."

The Wall cut the Confederacy of the Eastern States off from the West. Nobody from this side of the Wall had ever crossed it, as the Confederacy soldiers manned it and were ruthless in employing their weapons. Rumor abounded that there were still cities out East full of people and technology the likes of which the Badlanders had never seen.

The cough of a motorbike ripped through the air, and then McClain pulled up beside them, dust pouring through the windows. "They're down there," he said, leaning forward to peer in.

"You sure?"

McClain pointed toward the far side of the city ruins. "Smoke. It's nearly two hours until sunset, but they look like they've made camp."

"What's wrong?" Mia asked.

McClain frowned. "It's unusual, that's all. Even the reivers usually avoid the ruins. I haven't been down this way for nearly ten years, but the local mole people tribes all say that you don't stay the night in Vegas."

He'd stayed with the mole men that haunted this valley? The mole men were notoriously private thanks to their conspiracy theories on how the Darkening began, and strangers were rarely admitted into their underground silos and bunkers. They'd been underground since before the Darkening began, and now had entire tribes down there, somewhere. Mia was almost impressed. "Deadheads?"

"Not deadheads." He shook his head. "Not sure what it is. There's a ton of predators around Vegas, so it could be anything. The mole men say that *ac'tun ahili* haunts the city, though hell if I know what that is. Every settlement they've tried to start in the ruins has disappeared, so now they don't bother. It's a long valley and the mole men *really* don't like reivers, so maybe they decided to stay somewhere the mole men won't enter."

Thwaites stroked his moustache as he peered at the ruins. "In two hours, we might be able to find the reivers."

"Maybe, but we'd be walking into an ambush if we did," McClain countered. "If they're smart, they'll have set up defenses, and last night's ambush at the tor suggests there's at least one reiver in control with above-average intelligence. For a reiver. I suggest sending in a scouting party of two or three people, some of your best, and work out what we're dealing with before we make any rash decisions. The others can stay at the edge of the ruins, fuel up, and prepare a quick camp where the reivers won't notice."

Thwaites looked toward Mia. "What do you think?"

"Sounds good. I'll put my hand up for the scouting party." If only so she could get closer to see if her sister was still alive. She also needed to move her body, get out of her head. All morning, all she'd been able to think about was Joe. The boy survived the night, but this morning a raging infection had bloomed and his cousin decided to take him back to Salvation Creek. She just hoped he was okay.

"Anyone else?" McClain asked.

"Jake," she said, without a moment's hesitation. Jake had skills she could only dream of, despite her resentment. "Maybe Jenny?"

McClain nodded, and kicked the bike out of gear. "Alright then. Hopefully we don't find out what this *ac'tun ahili* is."

"What is this place?" Mia whispered, turning in slow circles, examining the debris. She'd known the city would be in ruins, but she'd never expected the buildings to look the way they did.

McClain remained focused. Intent. Hunting. He barely gave the empty fountains a glance. They were getting closer to where the smoke came from. "Vegas used to be a city for pleasure-seekers."

Pleasure-seekers? Was that something like the slave towns down south? Mia stared up at the iron scraps of some sort of tower. It looked kind of like something she'd seen once, in a picture. "Paris," she whispered. This place was like nothing she'd ever seen. She was *fairly* certain she'd seen some sort of ship earlier, after all, and none of the maps about the pre-Darkening world indicated any sort of body of water nearby, beyond the huge dam that flooded the nearby river system and towns. "What kind of people lived here?"

"Don't know. Before my time."

"Before anyone's time, smart-ass." Mia snorted. A good ninety years at least.

McClain held out a hand to quiet her. He cocked his head on an angle and listened, and Mia froze. Could be Jake and Jenny he was listening to. McClain had partnered them up to cover more ground. But she wasn't sure.

Jenny learned to hunt squirrel and deer as a young girl, and despite her limp she moved like a ghost. And Jake had experience, like McClain. He wouldn't be making a lot of noise.

No, he was listening to something else. Her heart ticked a little faster.

Water bubbled up out of a crack in the ground, despite the desert surrounding the place. It seemed to spring from where a huge building had crashed down into the sodden mire. Maybe a quake during the Darkening unearthed the water table? Not that it looked drinkable. Green slime covered the pond, and lush vegetation surrounded it.

A critter chirped in the slowly descending night. Frog, maybe?

"What is it?" Mia whispered.

"I thought...."

She was going to have a heart attack from the suspense.

"Thought I heard something following us, but it's either really quiet or we scared it off." McClain knelt down, pressing his fingers into a faint impression in the dirt. "There's some kind of animal living here. "

"Shadow-cats?" A chill ran through her and she spun, her gun quivering as her hands shook. A pack of mutated shadow-cats had taken her parents when she was younger. She could still remember finding their abandoned jeep covered in claw marks where the shadow-cats peeled it open like a tin of rotten beans. Jenny had tried to shield her from it, but that bloody image was burned straight into her brain.

"I don't think so. This is smaller."

"Maybe kits?" She looked around nervously. The problem with shadow-cats was that you never saw them coming. They'd been cloned back before the Darkening, with intense camouflage patterns that made them almost invisible in the dark, which just happened to be their favorite time to hunt.

"Not sure." McClain straightened. "But the reivers are definitely here. I can see bootprints."

And they were the focus. Mia let out a slow breath. Sage. Sage could be here with the reivers. *If* they could find them. This place was enormous with its hulking buildings, ruins, and strange oddments peeking through the vines....

"And whatever left these tracks is long gone. These are hours old."

Hours. "Ha. Yeah. Long gone. That's really comforting."

"You wanted to come."

She gripped her shotgun tighter. "And I still do. I just hate knowing there's something out there that probably wants to eat us."

"Good thing I brought you then," he said. "I can probably run faster than you."

She stared at his muscled back. Was that a joke? "I'm leaner than you are, and shorter. I probably look stringy. You, however, are Grade-A rump. If I were looking for plenty of meat, I know who I'd pick."

McClain glanced over his shoulder at her. He paused. "Did you just...."

Mia smiled, and looked him up and down. "Jade used to say that you could bounce a pre-Darkening penny off that ass."

Jade wasn't the only one who'd commented on it. Mia scrambled past him, climbing up what looked like a fallen pile of bricks.

McClain moved a little slower, as though he were chewing over what she'd just said. "I thought you'd prefer to sink your teeth in my ass? Wasn't that what *you* told her?"

Mia jerked to a halt. She'd definitely said that. "How did you...?"

"You're not as quiet as you think you are." He held out his hand, as though to help her step over a fallen beam.

Mia's eyes narrowed. She remembered that night. She'd had one too many sips of her own homebrew. But she knew McClain had been across the room from her.

There was no physical way he could have heard her.

"Do you read lips now?"

His smile was hot and slow. It burned her all the way through. "Maybe. Or maybe I was just focusing real hard on yours. I couldn't stop thinking about them that whole month."

"You were dreaming if you thought I was going to kiss you," she said, with a snort. Anything to defuse the sudden situation she'd found herself in.

"If I were dreaming," he countered, "then I wouldn't have been imagining your mouth on mine. Those lips would have been elsewhere."

She had a sudden intense flash of what his naked body might look like. All tanned skin, like the darkened gold of his arms, and cut with muscle.

Shit. Every nerve in her body lit on fire. She was pretty sure her nipples just flagged his attention. McClain had spent the entire month in her bar uttering sweet nothings at her. It hadn't ever gone further than that, and he'd remained politely distant, as though testing out her intentions but not quite pushing hard for them.

Probably a good thing. For if those words were a hint of the heat smoldering beneath his still surfaces, then she wouldn't have stood a chance if he decided to pursue her.

The drought in Salvation Creek hadn't just affected the local farms.

"Fine," she said, trying to ignore the heat in her cheeks. She accepted his hand and eased her way over the iron beam. *Keep things cool....* "It's a fine ass. And pickings are slim in Salvation Creek. Once upon a time I might have made you an offer."

"Pretty sure you knocked mine back." His hand squeezed hers. Their eyes locked for one tempting second.

Mia swallowed, then hopped down the other side and away from him.

"I thought about it," she admitted. Thought hard. And often. Alone in bed, with her hand down her panties.

She brushed sweaty strands of hair off her face. Between the buildings, where there was no wind, it was hot as hell. Sweat slicked between her breasts and down the center of her back. She fanned herself. "Take a break?"

McClain smiled at her as if he could see straight through her, and suddenly the sweat on her skin wasn't the only thing that was wet. "Sure."

Mia leaned back against a wall. Neither of them had been alone since they rode out. She was suddenly shockingly aware that there was not a single soul within a one-mile radius.

Think of all the things you could do to him in that time....

McClain paused and tugged his water canteen out of his pack. Every movement was careful and precise, as though he'd always been big and had learned to control every inch of his body, for fear of breaking things as a boy. She could imagine him as a raw-boned young man. He had that look. Heavy muscle now, as though he'd finally caught up to the sheer height of himself. He had the kind of hands that looked like they could soothe a startled colt, or leave a woman in exquisite pleasure.

He unscrewed the flask, offering her a mouthful. Always polite, damn him. "Why'd you say no?"

"You're not the first stranger to wander through town." She lifted the flask and took a mouthful. "Maybe we could have made sweet memories, but there's also the risk that I could have ended up alone and pregnant."

He scowled. "I wouldn't do that to you."

"I know that now. I don't think you're the type of man to just leave a child behind." No, he was all about protecting those he considered his. She eyed him out of the corner of her eye. Made her wonder just who made that list. He'd mentioned a sister. An old flame. Even a little girl he'd considered a niece. "But that only works if you knew I was pregnant," she pointed out. "You were moving on eventually and sometimes these things don't show up until it's too late."

His eyelids hooded, leaving his eyes impenetrable. "I think that if something had happened between us, I would have made a point of returning. You're not the sort of woman one forgets."

There went her heart again, making another one of those mad leaps in her chest. "I bet you say that to all the ladies," she replied, keeping it light.

A part of her didn't know what she was doing.

"No." McClain didn't take a single step toward her, but suddenly he filled the space between them. All of that focused intensity locked on her with absolute absorption. "Ever since the day I met you, it's only been you. Standing there in that bar, asking me if I wanted a damned drink, or whether I intended to stand there staring all day." His smile was slow as he lifted a hand and brushed a strand of hair behind her ear. "You smelled like whiskey and sage, and your skin glowed like polished bronze. It looked so smooth, I wanted to lick it. All over."

Not only was he the hottest man she'd ever laid eyes upon, but there was something about him that made her want to throw all of her rules out the window.

Mia put the flask to her lips, but she couldn't take her eyes off him. He was destroying her, inch by inch. And she wasn't sure she could handle that. Not right now.

"If you keep looking at me like that, Mia, then whatever's out there might not be the only thing looking to eat you all up."

She swallowed a mouthful of water down the wrong pipe, and sprayed it all over him. A wet hack tore through her throat and she coughed desperately while McClain thumped her on the back.

Jesus. "Are you trying to kill me?" she croaked.

His shirt clung to his chest. She'd spat water all over him. McClain raked a hand through his sweaty hair.

Real suave, Mia. No wonder she was single.

68

Apart from the whole fingers-burned situation. Which took her thoughts to Jake, and from there, right back to Sage.

Who was somewhere in these forsaken ruins while she was flirting with McClain.

She felt sick all of a sudden. What was she doing? Tears blurred her vision, taking her by surprise. A whole wave of anger and grief suddenly erupted within her, like it had been lurking within, waiting for a moment to take her down.

"Hey," McClain murmured, his warm fingers closing over her arm. "Are you okay?"

She was *not* going to fall apart right now. Sage needed her.

Mia's throat felt dry and achy, as though there were a silent scream threatening to tear itself free. "No. No, I'm not," she admitted. "I want her back and here I am flirting with you, and... what type of person does that make me?"

Those green eyes looked almost silver now, in the night. "A human one," he said gently. "You're not made of stone, Mia. And you've been pushing yourself hard."

And he'd been playing along, taking his cues off her. She'd flirted first, before he got involved, almost as if he hadn't wanted to push her too far.

"I'm an emotional mess," she whispered. "I don't even know what I'm doing right now."

"I know." There was that inexplicable gentleness again. McClain stroked her arm. "I'm not going to take advantage of that."

"It might be nice if you did," she blurted, thinking about what it would feel like to be in his arms while he held her. She couldn't fall apart when his arms sheltered her from all the darkness around her.

Which was probably the stupidest thing she'd ever thought. Especially when McClain froze. Right. That just confirmed it. He'd definitely been playing along. And now he was being nice because he didn't want her to break down on him and cry.

Mia offered him the water canteen. "We'd better get moving."

"Mia, are you—"

"I'm fine," she muttered. Apart from being an idiot for a few minutes. "And we're not getting anywhere standing here talking. Time to go find some reivers."

Lights twinkled in the distance. She smelled cooking smoke, and could almost make out the figures below them as the reivers moved around their makeshift camp.

McClain peered through a set of binoculars. He lay on his belly in the dirt beside her, resting on his elbows. Mia snuggled next to him, little shivers of nervousness shooting up her spine.

"Can you see the captives?" she whispered, practically itching with the urge to get closer.

Sage was down there. She could feel it in her bones.

"No, but there's a pit or something at the back of the camp," he murmured, lowering the binoculars. A small line etched itself between his brows. "You want a look?"

Of course she did. Mia snatched them and peered through, searching the camp hungrily. Her vision shot forward until she could make out individuals. A tall reiver stood on guard, wearing a rough leather jerkin that bared his belly and a scruff of beard on his jaw. Another reiver behind him joked with another man. The pair of them pushed each other, settling into a shoving match, but they were of little interest. She found what she wanted and zoomed a little closer.

"That's definitely a pit," she whispered. "They've got five men on guard there. They look like they're arguing."

"Three of them are bleeding," he said, "and there's two bodies at least, laid out beneath old sheets of tin thirty feet from the camp. I can make out their boots."

She tilted the binoculars to where he was pointing. "Why would they…?"

"Did you count the reivers?"

Mia shook her head.

"I did. There's only sixteen of them down there."

What does that mean? "Where are the rest of them?"

"I don't know, but we were following at least fourteen vehicles today; three motorbikes and the rest cars of some description. There are only seven vehicles down there."

She looked again. McClain was right. "Over half the camp is missing." Mia slowly lowered the binoculars. "Do you think…?" She couldn't say it.

"Don't know." McClain stood and dusted off his pants. He reached out a hand to haul her to her feet. "Could be a trap, but I can't see the other vehicles anywhere. At least we know where they are now, and what the circumstances look like. Time to get the others."

seven

NEITHER JAKE NOR Jenny waited at the rendezvous point, but someone had tied a torn piece of shirt to the dented grill of an old rusted car. It hadn't been there before.

"Jenny's," Mia said, examining the piece of linen. She couldn't imagine Jake wearing pale pink, even if it were so faded that it was more like a blush-white.

"Where'd they go?"

"Don't know." She looked up. There was a thin silvery gray arrow in the concrete wall straight ahead of her. It looked like someone scratched something metal along the wall. "That way. Camp."

McClain drained his flask, giving a satisfied nod. "Good. Hopefully they'll bring the rest of the group with them and meet us half—"

Mia looked up from where she was retying her bootlace. "Half—?"

McClain stood frozen, his head cocked to the side. He stared back in the direction they'd come from, and Mia swallowed. That stare told her a thousand words.

"What is it?" she whispered.

McClain grabbed her by the arm and set her to moving. "Don't look now, but there's something following us again."

Damn it. She caught herself before she looked. "Is it that thing you sensed before?"

"Maybe." He kept moving, just a little faster than they'd been going. "This must be its hunting ground. It's near where it stopped tailing us before. "

Thick vines draped from broken balconies. All of a sudden she realized how quiet it was here. The two of them felt all alone in the world. And they were right out in the open.

Anything could be hiding in the rubble around them.

A horde of revenants.... Some kind of critter like a shadow-cat or warg. Even the rest of the reivers.

"Tell me about your bar," McClain said suddenly. "Why whiskey? I mean, your beer's not bad, but you obviously care more about the whiskey."

"What?"

He helped her around a pile of rubble. "Try and act normal. It already knows where we are, and it's stalking us. If it attacks we might be able to take it by surprise."

"Whiskey, right." Mia eyed the enormous hunting knife at his side. "It was my dad's favorite drink. Rare though, because of the price. You couldn't get it up here in the Badlands, you had to import it from down south where they grow heaps of corn. After he died, I wanted something to remember him by. This traveller came through once who knew how to make whiskey. He showed me how to make it, and I rigged up an old still behind the bar. Then I talked to Thwaites and he started growing corn. I'm the only one north of the border forts who makes it, I think."

"Which makes you worth your weight in gold," McClain muttered, but most of his attention was behind them.

A piece of stone tumbled down from a ledge, ricocheting off the concrete below. Mia nearly leapt out of her skin. Only that warm hand on her wrist kept her from breaking into a run.

"It's above us," McClain said. "Up on that balcony there."

Nervous sweat trickled down her spine. She wanted to look so badly that she could barely breathe. "What do we do?"

"We can't risk using a gun," he murmured. "The reivers might hear it."

"I'm not so worried about that," she shot back. "If we shoot it, it won't eat us. We can hunt the reivers down later. You're the world's best tracker, aren't you?"

He made a noncommittal sound. "It won't eat us."

"I'm pretty sure it's not just following us because it wants to be friends. If we don't shoot it, then maybe we won't get a chance to rescue Sage from the reivers."

"I'm a bounty hunter, Mia. This is what I do. It won't hurt you, because I won't let it," he told her firmly. "I can kill it with my knife, if it gets close enough."

His confidence was a suit of armor. And it worked, because her nerves died down just a fraction. She wasn't used to this. Sure, she knew how to work a shotgun, ride a motorbike, and skin a deer. She was handy with a knife and knew how to throw a punch, thanks to growing up with Jake.

But she was also just a desperate bar owner who wanted to get her sister back.

A shard of glass still clinging in the gaping window of a jeep reflected back a monstrous white creature behind her. She gasped. "What the hell *is that*?"

"Keep moving," McClain told her. "I can smell it now. Smells like a cat. A large cat."

Shadow-cat. The very name of it obliterated all her senses. Mia began to panic. Nobody had ever seen one and lived to tell the tale.

Her feet were still moving. Her body felt distant though, and she realized her hand was on the butt of the shotgun she had strapped over her shoulder.

"We might have to run," McClain told her. "If we do, you go on ahead." He glanced back as they turned the corner. "Can't see it anymore, but it's still there. I'll cover your back."

I don't know if I can. The words dried on her tongue. All she could see were her parents lying dead in that truck. Her mother's dark arm hung out the smashed window, those fingers lifeless.

"...got this," McClain was saying. "Mia? Mia, are you listening?"

She looked at him blankly. "Shadow-cat."

His thumb rubbed the inside of her wrist carefully. "I don't think so. It's got stripes, but it's white. That doesn't sound like a camouflaged creature of prey. And shadow-cats are larger than this. They were created by gene-splicing in a lab. This... this looks like something natural caught a few rays of radioactive chemical somewhere along the way. It's all warped, from what I've seen on it."

Mia focused on breathing. Okay. Not a shadow-cat. She could cope with that.

"Mia, I won't abandon you," he told her. "I just need you to focus. Can you do that?"

She nodded. The feel of his hand grounded her. Somehow McClain was so solid that he made her feel safe, despite the state of the world.

"Good. Let's move. It vanished, but I can still smell it out there. Somewhere. I think it's circling around ahead of us."

They paused at the next intersection. Mia unabashedly held his hand. Broken cars cluttered the streets like a metal graveyard. Some were parked right in the middle of the pitted asphalt. Others looked like their owners had just stepped out of them, except for the rust and body damage. One door hung awry, swinging in the wind. She had the sudden thought that people had fled from their cars here. Maybe it happened right after the meteor hit the earth 140 miles east of this place. The cars were packed in along the road, as though people had been trying to escape something.

There were dozens of places the creature trailing them could hide. Rubble was strewn into the streets from an enormous building. The walls looked like they'd been pink or red once, but now they were bleached a faded peach. Wind stirred a few dry leaves. Nothing else moved. No matter where she looked.

McClain's nostrils flared. "It's between us and the camp."

"Deliberately?"

He hesitated. "I don't know. It knows this terrain better than we do. Maybe it just thinks a better place to ambush us lies ahead. It knows we saw it." He looked to the left, down the street that cut across the one they stood on. "We could circle around."

"We don't know what's around any of the corners," she pointed out.

McClain looked uncertain again. "I'll hear if there's something coming."

"You and your super freaking senses," she grumbled, slinging the shotgun off her shoulder. "And don't look at me like that. I'm not going to use the shotgun unless absolutely necessary."

A tail lashed ahead of them. Mia froze as an enormous cat appeared in the street.

A growling huff of warning came from its throat. She could see it now. Face twisted with mutation, those golden eyes locked on the pair of them.

And then something that sounded like a strangled baby cried out.

"Aw, hell," McClain suddenly swore. "It's not hunting us. It's protecting its kits. We walked right into its home territory."

"Is that... a tiger?" She'd seen an old world animal book once. Sage adored the book as a kid. Mia vaguely remembered something golden with black stripes and a regal expression.

This was neither golden, nor regal. It *did* have stripes, however, and a massive tumor growing up the side of its face.

The creature picked up its kitten by the back of the neck, watching them with dangerous eyes. It suddenly leapt from the street onto the balcony of a faded pink hotel, a distance of almost eight feet that it cleared in a single bound.

McClain let out a breath. "I didn't think they were white."

"We don't exactly know everything about the old world," she pointed out. "Only what survived in books, or was passed down by word of mouth once our ancestors came out of the underground bunkers."

"I do know that those were big teeth," he replied, his hand settling in the small of her back. "Come on. Let's go around so we don't disturb her, or whoever fathered that cub. I'd rather not kill them."

"Strange attitude for a bounty hunter."

"I kill predators, Mia. Not defenseless animals."

"Do you think we just saw *ac'tun ahili*?" Now that the danger had passed, she felt a little breathless. Most of the animals that survived the Darkening were predators, but there'd been something about the way the tiger moved that spoke of grace and power.

She'd never seen anything like it.

"Maybe," McClain muttered. "These ruins are immense. There could be anything hiding here."

As if to concede his point, a strange roar lit up the night. It sounded almost like it came from some sort of horn. Birds screamed, and took off from a stand of trees several hundred meters away.

"What was that?" Mia whispered. It hadn't sounded like the tiger. Which might be a good thing. Or might not.

McClain stared in that direction, his nostrils flaring. "Hell if I know," he finally said. "But I'm not inclined to stay around and find out. Let's get back to the others."

Which was the most sensible thing anyone had said today.

eight

THE JOURNEY BACK through the ruins with the rest of their people was far simpler. Nothing bothered them, most likely because of the numbers. McClain took the lead, with Thwaites and his fellows following as quietly as they could. A long walk, but then nobody wanted to risk the reivers hearing them coming. The reivers had every advantage already; the position they'd been camped in was tucked up against the walls of a ruined hotel, and the camp was fortified with old jeeps hauled into a circle around it. McClain's little group would have to clear the jeeps to attack, and that meant leaving themselves open to gunfire for a crucial second. Plus the reivers could escape into the bowels of the building if they needed to.

Mia couldn't help feeling like they were walking into a trap. Where were the other reivers? She'd expected them to leap out at any moment as the group made their long journey, but they were almost upon the camp and there were still no signs of them.

She hurried ahead to catch up to McClain who was working point. "Got anything?"

Flies buzzed. McClain scented the air, the moonlight catching on his irises for a second as his nose screwed up.

He held up two fingers, and then dragged his index finger across his throat.

Two dead reivers. Right.

"How?" Mia mouthed.

McClain shrugged. "Lots of blood," he whispered.

Something had gotten to the reivers—or maybe they'd fought amongst themselves. She hoped for the latter. After all, they still didn't know what this *ac'tun ahili* was. Maybe it was the tiger creature they'd seen, but maybe there was something else out there. She'd be quite happy to ride out of this hellhole still not knowing.

They crept past the dead bodies. Smears of blood on the asphalt revealed the reivers had been dragged here and then discarded. She tried not to look at them. Something stunk to high hell—their bowels opening after death probably. And they weren't even covered over. Just left out here to rot.

McClain paused beside them, kneeling down to press his fingers to the blood. He looked around.

"What is it?" she whispered.

He slowly withdrew his fingers, frowning. "They dragged four more of them out here. But the bodies are missing."

The second he said it, she could see the signs. Scuff marks in the dirt showed where something had hauled the other four bodies away. They led directly to a hole in the ground. A sewer grate?

Mia looked sharply at McClain. *Ac'tun ahili?*

He understood her. "Let's get moving," he said quietly. "We're not alone out here."

In the distance, shadows rippled behind a shattered statue. Jake and Jenny, she guessed. They blended into the statue, whose head had been half-dismembered by the fall. It had been pale green once, and the blank eyes stared sightlessly at her, its head crowned by a diadem of spikes. Mia eyed it uneasily. Now that she knew something preyed on the dead bodies, she couldn't stop feeling like they were being watched.

Best to get this over and done with, then get the hell out of here.

McClain made some kind of gestures, and Jake nodded, flicking his fingers back in some sort of unspoken language. McClain urged her forward, his warm hand firm on the small of her back.

They took shelter behind a car.

Pressing close to her, he breathed in her ear. "There are sixteen reivers here," he whispered. "Fourteen in camp, and two on guard. Your people are definitely in the hole in the ground."

"Good," she murmured, gesturing to Thwaites and his group to creep after them. She couldn't help wondering where the rest of the reivers had gone.

As soon as she thought it, her gaze shot to the two bodies. Some kind of fight *had* broken out—she just knew it. Or maybe whatever was snatching the bodies had taken live ones too.

"How many of our people are in there?" Mia whispered, a breathless feeling almost choking her.

McClain shook his head. He didn't know.

What if Sage was not here? She'd been so certain she would be, but… maybe the reivers fought, and some of them separated from the group?

Worry about that later. She gripped her shotgun in clammy hands. She and Jenny were the best shooters, which meant they were to get around back and pick off as many reivers as they could.

I've never killed someone before.

"Stop it," she whispered to herself. Adrenaline punched through her veins. It made every little noise echo in her ears.

"Okay," McClain murmured. "I'm heading in with Jake. Are you ready?"

Ready to get my sister back. She nodded firmly, pushing aside all her doubts. There'd be time to think over everything later. Right now, she needed to focus.

"Then go."

Mia crept across the pitted asphalt, and slipped in next to Jenny. They both squatted behind a rusted out car.

"You know what you're doing, girl?" Jenny pumped a pair of shotgun pellets into the chamber.

"Yes." *No.* Her hands were wet with sweat.

"Just remember: they ain't men or women. They're scum. Scavengers. This is just like picking off the coyotes near Salvation Creek."

Mia nodded. "I know."

It didn't make this any easier. She wasn't shooting to warn someone off, the way she had in the past. This was killing, plain and simple.

Jenny had it easier. Once upon a time, she'd ridden on the back of a Nomads bike, one of the bikie gangs that owned the coastlands. Susan—Mia's mother—told stories of her when Mia was a little girl. It wasn't until Susan and Greg were killed that Jenny returned home, and when she came she said little about her life out West. Mia knew she'd left her man, but she never spoke of him. Instead, she'd settled into their home and finished raising both Mia and Sage.

Jenny wasn't mother material. Nothing like Susan. She'd been hard and fair, but she wasn't the sort you went to when you wanted a hug. She usually preferred her own company, and when Sage moved out with Jake, and Mia moved into the bar, she had the run of the house.

But when it came to protecting her own, Jenny had your back.

"There they go," Jenny whispered, watching Jake and McClain slip through the shadows of the evening.

Two guards on rotation meant two targets. McClain had laid out the entire plan with military precision back at their camp. Where she'd spent time trying to see her sister through the binoculars, he'd been making ruthless calculations.

Mia stilled, almost holding her breath.

A scrape sounded to her left. Then a hushed noise, as if someone lowered a body to the asphalt.

Another sound—louder this time. A startled "*mmph*" that was swiftly cut off with a quick hand over the mouth, she imagined. A boot lashed out, scraping along the ground. She caught a glimpse of it through the dusty windowpane of the car they sheltered behind.

Jake.

Shadows rippled behind her and Jenny. Thwaites and his men running low across the ground to take cover behind the cars near them.

Jenny made a quick slashing movement with her hand, and Thwaites nodded, pressing his back to a jeep.

Silence. Stillness.

A faint bird cry whistled. A mountain bluebird. That was the sign.

Go, go, go. Mia followed Jenny, bending low as they scuttled around the cars and the crumpled statue.

A scream suddenly echoed. It cut off abruptly, but it was clear they'd lost the element of surprise.

And it also meant Jake and McClain were in the reiver camp with no backup.

"Move out!" Jenny bellowed.

She went left. Mia went right. The plan was for the pair of them to circle the camp and hit the reivers from the sides. It also meant that the women and men trapped in the pit were protected, in case the reivers realized they were losing the fight and decided to go down bloody.

Bullets ricocheted as Thwaites and his group hit the camp. Mia caught flashes of the fight as she ran. Reivers swarmed out of their blankets, laying hand to sawn-off shotguns, knives, and on one occasion, a chain.

Flames flared as someone threw something on the campfire. Suddenly the whole world flared bright, and she lost her night vision even as the fire died down just as suddenly.

Shit. She was blind. Mia caught a shadow out of the corner of her vision and ducked. The chain rippled through the air an inch above her head. She spun around and fired the shotgun.

The shot almost blew her back off her feet. She wasn't prepared, and staggered into the side of the building.

Stupid. Stupid... She knew better than that. She'd spent years filling old cans with holes. Funny how different it seemed in the heart of the action. Cans didn't shoot back, for one. Mia jacked the shotgun rounds out. Her hands fumbled as she hastily reloaded.

Don't look down. She still caught a glimpse of the female reiver she'd just shot. Mia stepped forward, ignoring the body, the fight taking shape in front of her again as her vision slowly returned.

Too late. A baseball bat swung toward her. Mia flinched backward. Pain exploded through her shoulder, and she lost the shotgun as she went down.

"Mia!" McClain's voice.

She scrambled to her feet. Move or die. Those were the options. The reiver came out of nowhere, swinging the baseball bat again. His head exploded right in front of her. The body jerked, knees caving out from under it.

Okay. Okay. Mia panted as she stared at him. Her shoulder ached, but she wasn't dead. Yet. A shadow moved in front of her. Another reiver. Mia didn't think this time. She slammed a palm up under the bastard's chin, snapping his head back. Her good hand. The second he went down, she turned and snatched at the shotgun, swinging around and jamming the butt of it into another reivers face. Something in her shoulder felt like a knife going in, and she knew she hadn't hit hard enough.

Swinging the butt back into her hands, she pumped the shotgun, her left hand moving weakly, and fit the butt of the shotgun to her shoulder this time, welding her cheek to the stock. Her lower arm felt numb, but she managed it. Then she pulled the trigger.

More blood. More... stuff.

Mia nearly threw up, her throat constricting on her. *Move!* She screamed at herself.

But the fight was dying down. Jenny put another round into the second reiver near Mia's feet, her face blank as though this were just another day. Thwaites stood behind the fire, directing men. And McClain stared at Mia across the camp, blood spattered up his arms and firelight reflecting back off his eyes. He met her gaze, then nodded.

Good work.

It was done. She and Jenny had taken the brunt of it as the reivers tried to flee from the onslaught. Cowards, one and all.

"Get the girls out," Jenny told her, limping around the camp. She pumped another round into a groaning reiver and he fell still.

"Are you hurt?" Mia demanded.

"Just a scratch," Jenny shot back. "Get moving."

She didn't quite believe her aunt, but there were other concerns right now. Sage.

Scrambling to her hands and knees, Mia peered over the edge of the hole. Dirty faces looked up and flinched away from her. Some of them were crying. One girl rocked, blood on her skirts and wrists. Genevieve Adams, she thought.

Then one of them gasped. "Mia!"

And a wave of hope spread from soft lips. Hands reached toward her. Desperate faces. Maura Adams... Jin Cho... Ellie Thwaites... Tara Macklemore... on and on, until a small cold fist formed in her chest. No Sage. There was no sign of her sister and it was hard to look at the women they'd rescued—those hopeful, relieved faces— and not feel some small scrap of despair, when she knew she should be relieved too.

"Is Sage here?" she demanded.

Ellie Thwaites shook her head. "No. Mia, I'm so sorry. They took her."

"Who?"

"Rykker. The one in charge." Ellie visibly swallowed. "There was a fight, and he and his men took a handful of the girls. They were planning on taking us all, but then Yanno and his crew rallied and they fled."

Every one of her worst fears came true. Disappointment lodged like a fist in her throat, and rage screamed inside her chest.

"Mia?" Ellie asked softly.

Sage wasn't the only one she'd vowed to rescue. Mia stuffed all her emotions into a little box deep inside. It was the same way she'd gotten through her parents' funeral, and the long aftermath.

"We're here," Mia said, tossing the rope ladder the reivers had used into the pit. She couldn't think about Sage right now or she'd break. There were things to be done in the meantime. "Let's get you all out of here."

nine

"ELLIE! OH, ELLIE! You're back!" Thwaites wrapped his eldest daughter in his arms, dragging her against his chest so tightly that the girl cried out.

"Dad!" she said, pushing him away just enough to look at him. "What happened to your arm?"

Thwaites shook his head as if it didn't matter. "Where's Alice? Where's your mother?" He brushed past Ellie, looking around until he caught sight of Alice. The young sixteen-year-old hurtled into his arms and he closed his eyes, relief shining across his stark features. Just for a moment though. "Helen?"

"Dad." This time Ellie caught his arm, her eyes shining suspiciously. Reaching out, she drew her little sister, Alice, into a one-armed hug.

He looked at them. And he knew. Mia saw it in his face as he looked between both girls' faces. "No," Thwaites whispered, sinking to his knees. "No!"

Something in Mia's chest shriveled up and died. She wasn't the only one missing a piece of her heart right now. And if she told herself that often enough, then she wouldn't feel bitter.

At least she still had a chance to find her sister. Helen Thwaites was never coming home. Ellie and Alice would never hold their mother again.

"Mom wouldn't listen," Ellie told him, cradling his shaking head against her waist. She looked up and met Mia's eyes, as if aware they had an audience. "She went down fighting," she said fiercely, as if that mattered.

All around the camp the same scenes echoed. Men sobbing as they hugged their wives and daughters to them. Marisol, the young woman who'd insisted upon coming even though she'd never held a shotgun in her life, yanked her bruised brother into her arms as if she'd never let him go again. And others like Mia looked around, as if the very absence of their loved ones had been a punch in the face.

Six. There were six people missing who should have been there.

And Sage was one of them.

Mia could only stand it for another minute before she had to get out of there. Nobody noticed her leave. Pushing through the door into the hotel foyer, she found herself in the courtyard beyond, a half dozen frogs and crickets chirping in the night and the breeze sloughing away the grief that stained her. The floor was filthy. Leaves and rubbish piled up in the corners, as if blown there. The courtyard looked like it had been covered in a glass roof once, but now the plants had taken over. Moonlight streamed through the open hole, but the garden was mostly shadows.

McClain followed her, snagging her wrist. "Hey."

"Please," she whispered, letting her hair fall across her face to hide her gleaming eyes. "I need a moment alone."

He hesitated. "I don't know if that's a good idea, right now."

Those missing reiver bodies.... A chill ran through her, but it felt like she was walled off somehow. She should care. She should have thought about that.

But she didn't.

"Here." Warm hands cupped her cheeks, tilting her head up. Those green eyes swam into view, his brow notched down in a frown. "Do you want a hug? No judgment, no reading into things. If you need someone to lean on right now, I'm offering it."

Tears sprang into her eyes. It sounded like everything she'd ever wanted—and perhaps he was right. She didn't need to be alone right now, even if it was her usual modus operandi.

"My sister's not there," she said hoarsely as he opened his arms. She could remember the first time she'd ever seen Sage, a girl of around three, with ragged red curls and tear-stained eyes. Her mom had brought her home after Sage's mom's funeral, and told Mia that Sage was hers to look after now.

"I know."

There was a weight of meaning in those two words, and she didn't want to deal with it at this moment. Mia slid into his arms, burying her face into the crook of his shoulder. Strong arms curled around her, holding her against a body that was warm and strong and comforting.

She let a shudder rack through her, swallowing hard. All of those emotions were fighting to get out of that box. If she let them, she'd drown. "Thank you."

"It's all right, Mia." A callused palm snagged in her hair as McClain stroked her skull. "You're not alone and this isn't done. If she's not here then we'll find her."

We. The word struck her straight through the heart. It meant everything right now.

"Why are you doing this?" she whispered hoarsely.

McClain owed them nothing. He'd just been a stranger riding through town, one trying to find himself in the bottom of a bottle of her finest whiskey.

"Every hero needs a cause," he replied jokingly. "Isn't that what you said to me once?"

She realized she was crying, and tried to wipe her eyes. She was wetting his shirt. God. Mia struggled but he shushed her, rocking her gently. She settled for dragging the back of her hand across her eyes.

"Where were you when I was eighteen?" A man like McClain would have bowled her straight off her feet, and then the entire mess with Jake would never have happened.

He laughed under his breath, his entire chest expanding against hers. "Probably trying to rope an entire town into order."

That was the first she'd heard of that. Mia brushed the backs of her fingers against his nape. His tawny brown hair was cut short, and it prickled her skin.

It had been a long time since she'd touched a man like this.

A long time since she'd wanted to.

And that was when she realized her breasts were pressed flush against him, all soft lushness against the hard planes of his body. Sweat dampened his collar. Suddenly the heat against her skin wasn't simply his body heat. Mia shifted, and he must have felt it for he looked down, just as she looked up.

Those strong arms—as reassuring as they were—weren't what she wanted, right now.

No. She wanted oblivion. Sweet oblivion. To feel and not think a thing at all. Something to fight off all those emotions swarming her. She could barely see in the dark, but she could just make out his lips. Firm lips they were, not the kind of mouth that curved in a smile very often, but still dangerously tempting. And she was so close to breaking that she desperately needed to drive the image of her sister out of her mind before she lost it.

Tilting her mouth to his, Mia slid a hand behind his nape and dragged his face down. Their lips met, hers hungry and ravening; his hesitant.

McClain froze. "Mia."

"Shut up and kiss me," she breathed against his skin.

There was no more resistance. McClain melted against her, capturing her mouth in a gentle caress. She'd expected more, but the simple affection in the touch rocked her, just as much as the sensation of passion did. His hands slid from her arms, down to her waist and back up again. His hesitation vanished as Mia thrust her tongue against his, earning a growl from his throat and a faint, teasing thrust of his hips, as if he couldn't help himself.

Yes. Mia planted both hands in the center of his chest and pushed him against the wall.

Kissing him grounded her, in more ways than one. Not alone. Not right now. She threw herself into it, hands greedy as McClain made a growling protest sound in his throat.

The hard press of his erection dug into her belly and Mia slid her hands between them, wrenching his shirt out of his jeans—

"Christ," he cursed. "Mia... Mia." Capturing her face in his hands, he drew back. Inches separated them, McClain's eyes flashing green in the faint moonlight. Tension knotted his body into a faint rebuke, and Mia hesitated.

"You don't want it?" she whispered. When had that changed? He'd made it clear two days ago that if she wanted a fuck all she had to do was ask.

McClain shuddered, closing his eyes. "Of course I want you. You don't know how damned much." Taking her hand, he dragged it toward him and for a moment she thought he was going to place it over his cock, but he lifted it instead, eyes opening to lock on hers as he pressed a gentle kiss to her palm.

The scrape of his stubble made her palm tingle, but more than that was the look in his eyes... both scorching and tender, the green blaze of his irises softening into regret.

Mia's heart shifted in her chest. She felt utterly breathless. This was more emotion she couldn't deal with right now.

"Not now," he said softly, as if reading her thoughts. "When we come together it's going to be amazing, Mia. But this isn't amazing—this is just using each other for a moment's respite."

"It would still feel good."

Heat flared in his gaze, but he didn't move toward her. "Your sister's missing, and you're upset—"

"I wouldn't regret it," she told him, placing her hand flat against his chest. The steady throb of his heartbeat pulsed against her palm. Mia licked her lips. "You wouldn't be taking advantage of me, McClain. I'm a grown woman with a mind of my own and I'm not afraid to take what I want, when I want it. You and me—"

"You're presuming I want to be some anonymous fuck."

That shocked her.

They regarded each other in silence, the hot rush of blood drowning out every other sound—but for the racing pant of her breath. And his. Mia dragged her hand away from his chest, curling it in a fist in front of her.

"McClain...." She didn't know where to start.

A slightly bitter smile kicked up the corner of his lips. "Exactly."

"You wouldn't have minded two days ago," she told him. "In fact, the shoe was on the other foot then."

Faint shadows swept through his eyes. "Two days ago I was heading north and we were never going to see each other again."

"In two days we might have Sage back and you'll be heading north again," she countered.

"It's not the same."

Mia pushed away from him, crossing her arms over her chest. Bloody men—running hot and cold. "Oh? What changed?"

McClain's face twisted in that stubborn scowl she was beginning to recognize. "It doesn't matter, Mia. This is not happening, not now. Maybe in a few days.... Come and talk to me then. Maybe you wouldn't regret it, but that doesn't mean that I wouldn't. I hate the idea of taking advantage of your grief, regardless of whether you think I would be or not. I like you," he said bluntly. "A lot. And you're going through a bad time right now.

"If you want a shoulder to cry on, then I'm here. If you want a hug, all you have to do is ask. But I'm not taking things any damned further until I know you're in the right frame of mind."

Mia stared at him wordlessly.

He held out his hand to her. "Let's get back to the others. I want to check that shoulder out. You took a nasty hit."

She barely felt it. Maybe only peripherally, though she knew tomorrow would be a bitch. "I'm okay."

"Just let me fuss," he told her. "It makes me feel better."

Fine. Mia settled with a huff. Exhaustion was starting to ride her shoulders. "I didn't realize you were such an old woman."

"It drove my sister crazy."

"I can empathize."

McClain smiled. It faded suddenly, as though he'd thought of something else. "You also need sleep. Tomorrow we're going after your sister and we need all the advantages we can get, because I don't think Thwaites and his men will be coming with us."

The words were like a shock of icy water to the face. "What?"

"Some of the men are wounded, Mia. Others... well they've got loved ones to look after now."

And they'd want to take their girls and the young boys home. She completely understood, even as her heart ached. How were they going to get Sage and the other girls back now?

"Jake and I got our hands on a live reiver. We need to ask him a few more questions, but he told us enough. Whoever was leading this company rode out five hours ago. We can't catch up, not at night, and several of the others who still have missing girls are injured, including Jenny."

"Jenny's injured?" Her head began to clear.

"Not that she's admitting it," he replied, "but she's limping. Badly. That was why I came to get you. I wanted to see if you were hurting too."

"It's nothing I can't handle." Everything faded. Lust. Pain. Heartache. Mia started thinking again. "Where are they taking the girls?"

McClain must have seen her shutter away her emotions. "We don't know." His voice darkened. "Yet."

Yet.

But someone did.

ten

"I'M NOT SAYIN' nuthin'." The reiver spat on Adam's boot, his eyes wild and crazy—but holding hints of fear. "And you won't torture it out of me." He tilted the side of his jaw to the light, showing all the burn scars there. "Ain't nuthin' you could do to me that ain't been done before."

It was enough to make the monster within Adam shiver with delight. It could smell the fear.

And it sickened the part of him that was still a man.

Adam swallowed the lump in his throat, forcing the warg back down. It had spent years hiding quietly within him, watching through his eyes for a chance to escape, and for nearly ten years he'd thought he'd won the battle—that he'd beaten the warg within him.

He'd been wrong.

The second Eden pulled the medallion off him last year in order to save his life, the monster tore its way from his body, leaving him howling in pain on the floor. He might have been able to push it back down the next day, when Eden gave him back the medallion, but this time the warg remained, shaking the bars of its cage as if testing them. This time he could never quite escape the feeling that it was just watching for another chance.

The lie had been revealed. He didn't control it; the warg would always be waiting for another chance to break free.

And as much as he pretended that he wasn't a monster, sometimes it felt like every day was a step down a dark path. Mia needed answers—she needed to know where her sister was—and he was going to get those answers for her.

No matter what it took.

No matter how hard it was to hold on to his humanity.

"I don't have to torture you," Adam said, tugging off his leather gloves slowly. "You'll tell me what I want to know."

Maybe it was the tone of his voice. Maybe it was the look on his face. The reiver swallowed, and tried to press his back through the wall. "What are you going to do?"

Adam began unbuttoning his shirt. A part of him hated that he knew the suspense would do more than showing rage or fury ever would, but he forced that part of him back down deep. Where the warg lurked. It was interested now. He could practically feel it prick its ears. "There are worse things than torture."

He lifted the medallion off his chest and instantly felt the warg hold its breath. *Yes*. It whispered. *Feed me*.

The reiver's lips trembled. "What are you doing?" He scrambled back as heat lit through Adam's veins. "What the fuck are you doing?"

"Showing you what happens if you don't tell me what you know," Adam replied, through lips that were no longer quite human.

The reiver screamed as he saw Adam's face.

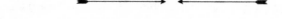

Mia paced impatiently.

She'd heard the screams. She knew what was happening. Maybe she should have felt sick about it, but the only thing she could think was *Sage, Sage, Sage*, like a drumbeat in her ear. And the second she thought of her sister, the reiver became the monster. Who knew what her sister had gone through? He deserved to suffer.

Jake lit a cigarette, rubbing at his temples, his eyes a million miles away. For whatever reason, McClain had insisted that he question the reiver alone and Jake had been quiet ever since.

"Are you okay?" she asked, watching the tremble in his fingers.

Jake flicked ash from the glowing tip of the cigarette, his gaze skating around. "No. No, I'm not."

She swallowed.

"I thought she was going to be here," he said, finally meeting her eyes. "I really thought I'd be holding her in my arms right now—" His voice broke and he tossed the cigarette, grinding it out with his heel and watching the movement as if to hide his glittering eyes from her. "It's the only thing that's kept me going these last couple of days. That I would get her back. Before...." He couldn't say it.

Mia wrapped her arms around her waist. All along she'd been lost in her own agony, not even thinking of how Jake would feel. Despite their arguments, she couldn't deny that he loved her sister. Maybe not in the way that Sage loved him, but if Mia were honest with herself, he did care for her.

"We'll get her back," she told him, taking those few steps between them and grabbing hold of his hand. "Hey, look at me." He did, his face a mask of anguish that tore through her own heart. Mia's voice hardened. "I don't care what I have to do. I will get my sister back and so will you."

He nodded. "When we do, I'm going to tell her the truth, Mia."

The ground dropped out from beneath her.

"She deserves the truth and I should never have kept it from her." Jake dashed moisture from his eyes. "It was never your fault. It was all on me and my stupid, pigheaded self. I fucked up and she needs to know it was my fault and—"

"Maybe we should wait until we see—" She hesitated. "—what kind of condition Sage is in. Emotionally," she clarified, when his face went white.

"Yeah," he rasped.

"But right now, if you want to help her you need to pull yourself together," she continued. "I know how you feel. That same fear is gnawing me up inside, and if I let it, it could swallow me whole. I can't breathe without feeling my chest tighten. But that's not going to get my sister back." Mia reached up and hesitantly hugged him. "You're not alone, Jake. We'll deal with this together, because we're family. We're Sage's family." Tears suddenly wet her own eyes as Jake squeezed her back hard, as if he hadn't expected her to comfort him. "We'll get her back. You, me... and McClain."

Jake held her for a long time and despite everything that had come between them in the past, she realized that she needed this too.

He'd been her best friend once, and a part of her missed that crazy young boy who led her and Sage into every bit of mischief he could conjure as a kid.

Turning sixteen had screwed up the dynamics of their relationship. Mia knew that his feelings for her had changed, even if she hadn't been entirely certain of her own. She'd cared for him, but at sixteen Salvation Creek began to feel too small for her. With Sage two years behind her, she'd been tied to the town, but as time passed and Sage began her own apprenticeship in electronics salvaging, Mia began to feel that restless itch again.

The second she got an offer to join a hydroponics cohort out east, Jake changed. No longer content to hint at his feelings, he'd begun to pursue her, as if he could feel her slipping away.

And Mia hadn't known what she truly wanted.

Freedom? A career in hydroponics? The ability to see more of her small part of the world? Or Jake? Jake, who was safe and familiar and meant security for the rest of her life?

She drew back slowly, looking up. This was a night of revelations, the pair of them dealing with fallout from years ago. And she needed to do her share.

"I used you," she admitted suddenly. "I didn't know what I wanted but I knew I didn't love you. Not... not enough. And when I chickened out on heading east I turned back to you because I knew you would be there, even though I'd told you there was no chance of anything growing between us. Saying that scared the shit out of me. I kept telling myself that I loved you as a friend, maybe a little bit more, and that true love could grow between us if I gave it a chance. But... I was also using you and that wasn't fair."

Jake's brows narrowed. "Why are you telling me this?"

She moved away, wiping the tiredness from her face with a hand. "You know why."

Jake cleared his throat. "It's him, isn't it?"

"Partly. I don't know," she admitted. "There's something there and I don't know what it is, but I've never... never felt like this before. And it scares me more than anything else ever has."

"Mia...." He hesitated. "Do you ever get the feeling that McClain's not telling us something?"

"Yeah." She definitely got that feeling, all right. "I'm not committing to anything. He's holding back from me and I know it. But... he also makes me feel safe." Mia shook it off. "Let's not talk about that. Let's focus on Sage. I owed you an apology."

"You don't owe me anything, Mia. Like I said, this was all my fault." He took a slow breath. "Well. That was unexpected. You and I working shit out, acting like allies rather than enemies."

"I can't help thinking that if I hadn't been such a bitch to you, then you might have stayed and my sister wouldn't have been working at the ranch that morning," she admitted, her voice dropping to a whisper.

That was the thought that kept her awake at night.

"You don't know that. And you *can't* know that," he pointed out. "Do you think Sage would have been content sitting at home, waiting for me to get back from a hard day's work? She liked what she did, Mia, and she could have been there all the same. This isn't your fault. Any of it."

"I know." She pressed her thumbs up under her aching eye sockets. "I know. I'm just thinking too much." Mia frowned. "What's taking so long, what's—"

"It's quiet," Jake replied, cocking his head.

And so it was. The screams had stopped.

"Do you think it's done?" she whispered.

"I'll go—"

"No." She shoved past him. "I'll go and see."

Hammering down the flight of stairs, she stepped into the cell where McClain had gone about his business. The stench hit her first: the reiver had voided his bowels at some point, but as she glanced at his crumpled body she couldn't see any blood. Not even a mark on him.

Mia stopped in her tracks. Even before she saw McClain's face she knew something was wrong.

McClain washed his hands in a bucket methodically, his shoulders stiff. Every movement was careful-like, as though this was some sort of routine he needed.

"Adam?" she whispered.

"They've taken her south, to one of the border towns," he replied quietly, still scrubbing each finger, as though to remove nonexistent blood. "We were right. This wasn't just the usual sort of raid. The man leading the reivers is named Rykker. He brought the group together for some sort of raiding party, but he's not one of them. There were two groups of reivers working under him, and his handpicked sortie of men. When they got here one of the groups wanted to"—his face screwed up in distaste—"enjoy the spoils of war. Rykker and his men preferred the girls were kept clean. They're worth more on the slavers' blocks down south if they haven't been touched. That's one good thing, at least. A fight broke out and Rykker's men killed half the reivers, but he was shot so he and his men pulled out, taking the best of the women and one or two of the young lads."

She took a moment to accept that. "Then Sage hasn't been—"

"Most likely not. Yet." McClain looked up, his eyes glittering with rage. "But when they arrive at Rust City there's a chance she'll be put on the auction block. I'm not sure, as the reiver muttered something about Rykker offering some of the women to a man named Cypher as tribute."

"Rust City?" Jake broke in, and she realized he was standing in the doorway, listening. "I've heard of that. It's not one of the border forts."

"Another day's ride south," McClain replied. "It's a trader town formed out of scrap and run by this Cypher.

Filled with scavengers, reivers, slavers, and anything not good enough to get credit in the border forts."

Jake's eyebrows shot up. "The border forts have standards?"

"Apparently."

"And the reiver?" Mia asked, glancing at the slumped body.

"Dead." McClain grabbed his shirt and dried his hands on it, then paused, his voice a little hollow. "I broke his neck."

She'd never felt more like he needed her in his life. "Hey." Mia stepped forward, sliding her arms around his waist. "Are you okay?"

"Yeah." He drew away a little, trying to turn, but she wasn't going anywhere.

"Did I ever tell you how much I hate it when people lie to me?" she asked lightly, her hands resting on his hips.

That was when he met her eyes. Mia's heart broke a little in her chest. McClain looked like he'd been at a funeral. And worse, he looked like he'd been the one to put the body in the dirt.

"That man lived a life of rape and murder," she told him, rubbing her thumbs against his hips. "You shouldn't have done that alone."

McClain sighed and rubbed his face, but something about the set of his shoulders looked like he'd lost a little of the weight he'd been carrying. "I know that. Killing's never bothered me, not when it comes to reivers."

"Oh?"

"It's the... up close and personal of it," he muttered. "I can do hard things. That's always been my role."

"It doesn't mean they're any easier to do," she pointed out. "Or that you should do them alone."

This time he let her curl her arms around his waist. There was still some hesitancy in his eyes when he looked down at her. "Mia—"

This shouldn't happen, said his unspoken words. "Shush. Just let me hold you for a bit." Burying her face against his chest, she squeezed him tight. A part of her knew keeping him at arm's length would be the smarter, safer option. But he'd been there for her when she needed it. The least she could do was to return the favor. "This is the part where you wrap your arms around me too."

McClain hesitantly dragged her closer. He gave hugs that made everything feel better, even if it were just for a moment. Those muscular arms held a strength that could keep off the weight of the world.

Movement shuffled behind them. Mia caught Jake's eye. "*Give us a moment*," she mouthed, as he hesitated in the doorway.

He shot McClain a hard look, then nodded and disappeared.

Mia shut her eyes and sank into the embrace. Only an hour ago, he'd been the one offering her comfort. This time it was her turn.

"Thank you," she whispered, in the still, dark warmth of the room. "For riding with me, protecting the people that I know, and doing what it takes to get my sister back." Her nose wrinkled up. "But now I think we need to get some fresh air. It stinks in here. Come on," she said, drawing back and slipping her hand into his. "I've been doing a little bit of exploring, and I found something I think you should see."

Tugging on his hand, she drew him up the dirty stairwell. Dozens of years of dust and debris caked the upper stairs, and she even saw a faded pink toy of some description in the corner. Three flights up, a fracture line appeared in the walls.

"Is this safe?" McClain asked.

"I've been poking around up here." She found the hole in the wall where she'd slipped through before, and ducked through it. "It feels secure."

McClain ducked under the arch, his eyes widening in surprise as he stared around. Miles of desert and ruined buildings stretched around them, as Mia turned in a circle, her arms spread. "Must have been some sort of balcony once. Isn't it amazing?"

Lush green vines grew over the railing. They'd enveloped the entire building once, though half of them had died and their dried husks shivered in the wind. Still, this part remained green and vibrant. Her favorite book as a child had been an ancient copy of The Jungle Book that survived the Darkening, and she couldn't help but think of that now as she breathed in the scent of flowers.

"It's beautiful," McClain admitted, leaning on the rail.

Strange how she could find beauty and peace in this moment. Her sister was in hell. This entire chase had ended in disappointment. But she still felt it, just for a second.

"It makes me wonder what sort of people lived here," she mused. From this vantage point she could see almost everything. Huge buildings with crazy statues and adornments lined the street. Everything was faded, half-broken and washed out, but she could still see traces of what this place must have been like. "What do you think it was like before the Darkening?"

Her mother told her once that the pre-Darkening people knew the meteor was going to hit almost a year before it did. There'd been a lot of panic. Talk of missiles to blow it up, only there wasn't time enough to build one with the capabilities required to destroy the meteor before it hit.

Some cults and Doomsday preppers owned underground bunkers, so there'd been fights in the shops over food and water. People killed each other in riots, and stole what they could. Panic was widespread and people headed for cabins in the wild, or bunkers they knew of. All over the world, people prepared, though Mia had no idea whether anyone still survived in those countries. They were simply colors on an ancient map to her, and the impact cloud killed off most of what the radiation and revenant plague didn't.

Sometimes, Susan admitted, she wondered whether they called it the Darkening because the skies turned black from the dust cloud, or because that's what happened in people's hearts.

"It was a place for pleasure," McClain murmured. "They have some kind of machine in the big rooms downstairs. Thousands of them. I don't know what they did, but there's carpet in there and what looks like a bar." McClain examined the vista. "We know they had technology we can only dream of. The only place that wields that sort of power now is the Confederacy."

"Cameras, cloning, and cannons," she muttered, for everyone knew the Eastern Confederacy was hiding technology and secrets behind their walls. Rumors came back from the odd traders who managed to get within their city-states. She couldn't imagine it, but apparently the people there called each other citizen, and they were all supposed to have equal rights. Even the leaders.

They wore numbered tattoos and old Jefferson, the trader, said that they waved some kind of machine over the tattoos that could automatically tell them who a person really was and if they had a criminal record or not. Confederacy leaders strictly controlled information, and citizens were actively encouraged to report upon dissenters within their families and friends. It was the only way for the Confederacy to survive according to their leaders, Jefferson said.

Scary, in a way.

"Do you ever think about how easy it would have been back then?" he asked. "They created wargs and shadow-cats in their labs, but they weren't a widespread affliction. There were no revenants—they came with the virus the meteor brought with it. So they had no predators, not really. Just cars, and huge buildings...."

"And planes," she said, getting into the swing of things. "My mom's grandfather once flew a plane. Said it could take him anywhere in the world. That would be amazing."

"My sister used to complain that she'd kill to get her hands on some of the medicines they used," McClain said, with a faint smile. "She's a doctor. She's really smart, and she's saved a lot of lives. But she always wishes she could save more."

"You love her," Mia said. "I see it on your face every time you mention her."

He nodded.

"When was the last time you saw her? Does she know where you are?" It struck her then, just how little she knew about him. "Why did you leave her behind?"

Suddenly reluctance filled him. She could see it in every line of his body. "Mia, it's kind of complicated. I didn't want to leave. I promised my father that I'd protect Eden with my dying breath. But... I did something bad and the people in my town—the people I trusted—they didn't want me around anymore. I left because I didn't want to drag Eden down with me."

She couldn't imagine this man doing anything bad. But it was clear he didn't want to talk about it. And that rankled a little, for she'd thought that he trusted her. She trusted him.

"Then they're fools," she said, and bumped shoulders with him. "You're actually quite handy. You're practically a superhero."

"Thanks," he muttered.

"For?"

"The distraction," he replied.

She was wise enough not to comment on that. Maybe he saw right through her, but they both needed this right now.

In the distance something gave a coughing roar.

Both of them turned.

"What the hell is that thing?" she asked, with a frown. The moon shone bright enough to make out a few things in the streets below. "Do you think it's the white tiger?"

"It's out there somewhere." McClain peered into the distance, moonlight gilding his jaw. "But it's not my main concern. There's something moving down there in the street." He frowned. "Two somethings. They've come for the bodies."

Mia lifted onto her tiptoes, but all she could see were shadows and glimmers of moonlight reflecting back off broken glass and metal. She shuddered. "*Ac'tun ahil?*"

"They look like people," McClain finally said. "Deformed people. They're all hunched over, and I'm pretty certain I can see tumors on one of them."

The earth wasn't the only thing that the meteor had torn apart. Nuclear reactors went haywire, and radiation was still the number-one threat to people in this land.

One of the reasons most of the people stayed in such an inhospitable place as the Badlands was precisely because there were no Dead Zones nearby.

The wind slid straight through her, and she shivered. "Why do they want the reiver bodies?"

"Let's not go there," McClain replied, his lips firming. Good decision.

Footsteps echoed in the stairwell. Jake stepped through, rapping his knuckles on the wall all polite-like, as if to interrupt the pair of them.

"Jake," she said. "What's wrong?"

He had his funeral face on, and he fanned himself lightly with his hat. "Mia, you mind if I have a minute with McClain?"

"Sure." She stared at him for a long moment. The two men looked at each other like a pair of wolves sizing each other up. Something was wrong. But she could find out later. So she shot McClain a faint, tired smile. "Thanks for the company. I'll go let Thwaites know what's out there, and get the guys to set up a watch. Then I think I desperately need some sleep."

"I know what you are," Jake told him, the second Mia was out of hearing distance.

The words took him by surprise. Adam looked up sharply, still hearing Mia's footsteps fading down the stairwell.

"What?" he asked, but ice was sliding down his spine. Surely he hadn't heard that right. Surely Jake was speaking about something else? But one glance at Jake's face, and the floor dropped out from under him.

"Open your shirt," Jake said, striding toward him.

Adam stilled. Of all the things to happen to him, this, right now, was the worst. "No."

A hand caught his collar and Jake was in his face. "Open it," Jake insisted, reaching for the buttons. "You show me what you fucking are. I know you're wearing one of them—"

Adam didn't think. Just reacted. He shoved a hand into Jake's chest and the man slammed back into the concrete wall, the breath rushing out of him. Jake stayed pinned there, as if sensing the sudden violence in the air, his face showing echoes of it.

Adam slowly withdrew his hand. He knew now. Jake didn't just suspect him, he was certain of the truth. It gleamed all over him. Wariness. And something else Adam could remember seeing, back at Absolution.

Fear.

He held up his hands, backing away. Jesus fucking Christ. It was too late. The game was up. Jake wouldn't back down from this, and from the amount of white in his eyes, Adam would be lucky if Jake didn't shoot him.

"You son of a bitch," Jake hissed. "Why are you here? Did you think it would be fun to ride along? Or were you just waiting until we were someplace out in the open. Or...." Thought raced in his eyes. "Were you luring us somewhere? Who's out there? Who's out there *waiting for us*?"

"I'm not going to hurt you," he said, like soothing a man down off a ledge. "If I were really a monster, do you think you'd still be walking around without your throat torn out? I could have done it several nights now. And I'm alone. Use your head. You're a bounty hunter. You think this is a trap?"

"I think you were awfully insistent upon riding along with us." The anger was back.

And suddenly he was angry too. He was sick and tired of people looking at him like he was a monster.

"Christ, the reivers stole fucking women and kids! What type of man lets that slide? I could help. I knew I could help," he yelled back. Then his mind caught up with him. He couldn't afford to let anyone else hear this conversation. The warg was already aroused; it didn't need the anger either. His voice dropped. "Do you think that this curse changes who a man was before? Do you think—for one fucking second—that there's no part of me that merely wants to be just a fucking man? Because I still am. That's the worst of it. I'm still a man, even with that *thing* lurking inside me. I still care. I still... hope. And I still give a damn about the innocents of the world. All this means"—he tapped his chest—"is that I have to fight even harder to keep the warg inside me. Where it can't do any harm to anyone."

Jake's eyes narrowed, but the anger melted out of him. He too was thinking now.

Adam turned, crossing toward the edge of the balcony. Dry leaves crumpled beneath his touch. Adam stared blindly out at the city, his chest heaving. Jake might have a gun and he might be behind him, but just as he could have ripped Jake's throat out several times over by now, Jake had had just as many chances to put a bullet in his heart.

A silver one.

After all, he'd been watching Adam for days now. Clearly putting together the pieces. At first he'd thought Jake had been keeping an eye on Mia and him, but now.... There'd been something else in the man's eyes. Suspicion.

"I'm not a monster," he said, wondering who he was trying to convince. All of the calm that being with Mia brought him evaporated. "I just wanted to help."

"Okay. I believe you."

Didn't sound like Jake liked it though.

All of the weariness came crashing down upon Adam. He'd been going for days, forcing his body to the edge, running high on adrenaline. This moment wiped him.

"How?" he asked gruffly.

Jake audibly swallowed. Fabric rustled as he pushed away from the wall. "You hear things I can't hear, McClain. And see things I can't see. That first night when the revenants attacked you could see the lights from the reivers' camp, out there in the blackness. I couldn't make out shit and I'm good at what I do." Jake cleared his throat. "You didn't torture that reiver down there. I checked the body out. So how'd you make him talk, huh?"

With a sigh, Adam glanced down at his quivering hands. In his mind's eye, they looked like claws for a second. "You know how. Reivers aren't normal men. I've seen bands of them who've cut off their own fingers or hands even, to prove their loyalty to their crews. Torture wasn't going to break him. I needed him to be afraid of me."

"You threatened him." Jake's voice strengthened. "You threatened to make him one of the monsters."

McClain flinched. "Yeah. What's the one thing every man fears, whether he's a Wastelander or a reiver?"

"I've been putting the pieces together. And you heard me in that bar, back in Salvation Creek, talking about wargs who didn't change, wargs who hid in the towns. Looking back now, you couldn't have gotten out of there any quicker." Jake tipped his chin up. "Who are you?"

"I'm the warg from Absolution," he said, meeting the other man's eyes. "The one you were asking about."

"Then it's true." Jake looked stunned. "You've got some sort of medallion that keeps it at bay."

No point hiding it now. Adam grunted, and opened his shirt just wide enough for Jake to see the pewter.

"How's it work?"

"Don't know," he replied. "Just know it keeps the warg contained. If I lose this...."

"Yeah." Jake didn't quite shift his hand to the gun at his hip, but it was in his eyes. "I'll take care of it."

They stared at each other.

"What are you going to do now you know?"

Jake crossed his arms over his chest, leaning his back against the wall. The first hints of dawn began to lighten the sky. "Fuck. I don't know. I can't—I don't.... All I've ever known is that your kind are monsters. But then I remember how you saved all my friends at that tor, how you decided to ride along with us to save women and children you've never even met. How do I reconcile that?" He pinched the bridge of his nose. "And then there's the fact that we need you."

"To get your wife back."

"Thwaites is taking the rest of the men and women home. They're not cut out for this shit. And Jenny's injured, else she'd be at my back too."

"We're not a large enough group to attack a slave town," Adam replied in a weary voice. "Better off without them. Maybe a couple of us can blend in, pretend we're something we're not."

"And that's exactly why we need you. You think like I do. Fuck."

It set off another round of curses. Adam merely watched. Jake was no friend of his, that much was clear, but maybe, just maybe, he'd keep this secret.

For there was one person who wouldn't accept this.

"What are you going to tell her?" Adam asked.

He might as well have lit a match near a powder keg. Jake stabbed a finger in the air toward him. "You stay as far away from her as you can. Mia's not for you."

"Do you think I don't know that?" he growled, even though he couldn't help remembering the way she'd wrapped her arms around him. For a moment he could pretend that he was just a normal man with a chance at a normal life.

For a moment when she kissed him, he'd forgotten that he was anything else.

Now the truth reared its ugly head. He'd been wasting Mia's time. There was no future between them. Adam didn't have a future.

"Not from the way you're looking at her." This time, Jake's eyes narrowed. "You look at her like a man in the desert finding his first oasis in three days. And while I might be willing to... overlook certain things for the moment, you so much as breathe in her direction and I will—"

"What? Shoot me?"

Jake didn't have an answer to that, but his eyes remained narrow.

Adam scrubbed both hands through his hair, lacing them at the back of his skull. He stared at the faint rays of sunlight creeping over the horizon, watching the light begin to paint the desert a glorious pink. All this beauty in his life—the desert, Mia, the way Ethan Thwaites wrapped his arms around his daughter as if he'd just seen a glimpse of heaven—and he could only ever be a bystander. Of course he wanted to reach out and touch it, touch her. Even as he knew that he couldn't. "She's an amazing woman," he said, his voice raw and harsh. "And I know I can't have her. Do you think that stops me from wanting to? And hell, I'll stay away from her—because I'm not *that* much of a monster—but I won't pretend that there's not a single part of me that doesn't want to know her, just once."

"She'll never forgive you," Jake warned. "And if she knows you lied to her...."

"Yeah, I picked up on that. Woman doesn't like secrets." Just once he wanted to push back. "After all, she hasn't forgiven you yet."

That earned him a dirty look. "Probably never will either."

"Bad lie?"

"The worst." Jake's voice came out hollow. He didn't bother asking how Adam guessed. It was written all over the two of them whenever they were in the same room together. That kind of hate didn't just happen. It was caused by bitter betrayal, or something else.

Like a broken heart.

"So you're not going to tell her?"

Again the man's lips thinned. "Not my secret to tell. And maybe that's another mistake, I don't know. I'm only human." He sighed. "I can't get Sage back without Mia. Or you. And right now, Mia's feelings don't matter half as much as my wife's safety." His voice broke on that last word.

Adam scrubbed at his stubbled jaw. "They haven't raped her yet."

Jake's head shot up.

119

"The reiver... he said they're not allowed to ruin the women. Not the ones they want to sell anyway. Cypher won't pay for damaged goods."

"Who the fuck is Cypher?"

"I don't know." Adam shrugged. "I guess we'll find out when we hit Rust City. But the reiver was scared shitless of the bastard. He was actually begging me to kill him at that point, so this Cypher wouldn't know he'd ratted him out."

A shudder ran through the other man. "Okay," Jake said, and his voice sounded rusty, like he'd been trying to hold himself together, but Adam's words about his wife only confronted his worst fears. "Okay." He took a slow, steady breath, then let it out. "I'm going to get a few hours' sleep. If I can. You'd best get some too. As soon as the sun fully hits the skies we'll head south for Rust City and get my wife back."

Adam nodded gruffly.

"I'm not going to tell Mia and I won't shoot you in the back. Not until this is done. But I can't promise anything else," Jake said, still looking like a man caught between two demons as he turned for the stairs. But at least he wasn't looking like he might reach for that shotgun. "We're not friends, McClain—hell, I don't even know if I can trust you completely—but I need you. So I'll set all this aside until we get out of this mess."

He backed away with a sharp nod, man-to-man, and turned for the stairwell.

Leaving Adam alone. Again.

Forever, whispered that little dark voice in his head. Adam curled his hand into a fist. He'd beaten that voice a couple of times now, when it sought to take him to a dark place where it seemed like there was no light. The last time it had taken a couple of months to crawl out of there. To keep putting one foot in front of the other. And he wasn't going to listen to it this time, even as he knew that it could sink its hooks in him at any time.

You serve a purpose, he told himself. A mantra he'd used to protect himself far too often. The list of purposes ran through his head, only this time he'd added a couple of items: Find Mia's sister and the other girls. Kill the reivers. Find Johnny Colton, the warg who'd helped do this to him. Kill Colton. Make sure Eden was safe and loved, even if it had to be from a distance.

The warming desert wind stirred through his clothes. There was a nice bottle of hard liquor in his bags, but that was another demon he was starting to lean on just a little too much.

With a tired sigh, Adam raked his hand through his hair and started toward the stairwell.

That had gone better than he'd expected.

At least Jake wasn't going to kill him.

He might be saving that honor for Mia, if she found out.

eleven

THE HEAT STARTED to make people sweat as the sun gleamed far overhead. More than time to get going, but McClain wanted to talk to them first. Mia bustled about camp, seeing to the people they'd rescued and making sure the injured were drinking enough water. Jenny insisted upon following her around, despite her leg. Jenny's "just a scratch" turned out to be a nasty-looking cut from a machete. Mia didn't like the look of it. The heat and the lack of proper medical attention meant that Jenny was dead certain to be facing a fever, despite the fact she'd cauterized the wound herself.

In fact, taking stock of those in the camp revealed a newer problem. The fight with the reivers had been short, bloody, and brutal, and most of the rescuers weren't trained fighters like McClain, Jenny, and Jake. Mia couldn't stop seeing memories of her own brief experiences. She was damned lucky. That was the truth.

Others were not so lucky.

Mia paused by McClain's side. "There are only five people here who are still in good condition. Three are women who've barely lifted a shotgun in their life, one's a kid, and the other's a ranch hand from Thwaites's. Most of those without serious injuries are the girls we rescued."

He stared down into the pot of water he'd set on the fire to boil. "Will any of them come with us?"

There was no time to be optimistic. "No," Mia said bluntly. "That fight took a lot out of everyone. The fact that as many of them rode along with us as they did is surprise enough. I doubt they'll come any further." She swallowed a little. "What about you?"

McClain looked up sharply, then his face softened. "I'll ride with you until we get those girls back."

"This is not your fight."

"If I don't go you'll only get yourself killed," he replied, slowly though, as if he were editing his words carefully. "You *and* Jake. I can't live with that."

"If the reivers make it to Rust City, then we're walking into a trap," she replied. "The odds of us getting in and out of there alive aren't great."

McClain's lashes lowered. He always looked like he was the calm at the center of any storm. And it settled her nerves even now, as it always did. "One problem at a time, Mia. Besides," he glanced around. "We can't take Rust City with force. The reiver I questioned said there're over two hundred reivers there, and we don't have the manpower, not even if everyone here was fighting fit and experienced in a gunfight. In a way, this might work out better for us. A smaller group can slip into a crowd and blend."

"Blend?" she blurted.

"None of us look like reivers," he pointed out, "but there are enough bounty hunters out there who get tired of riding long hours for minimal coin. Sometimes they take up a darker trade. That's our way in."

Mia chewed it over. Her stomach twisted at the thought of what she was about to do. If this failed, she'd be the one wearing a slave collar. But he was right. It was their only chance to save Sage and the others. "Okay."

"We have to make a move and soon," McClain said, reaching out and using his sleeve to lift the pot off the hot stone it rested on as soon as it started boiling. "The reivers who took your sister might be at least fifteen hours ahead of us."

Fifteen. Her stomach sank.

"Maybe less," he continued, "depending on whether they stopped to rest."

"We should have gone last night," Mia whispered.

"In the dark? Mia, we're tired, we're injured, and we're distinctly lacking in resources. I don't work off knee-jerk impulses. At best we might have gotten ourselves killed in the dark. We don't know what's out there. I've only ever been south once, and that was years ago. If we do this, then we need to plan and we need to think." His voice softened when he noticed the look on her face. McClain rested his hand on her knee, squeezing gently. "We'll get her back."

"You shouldn't make promises you can't keep."

His thumb rubbed the inside of her thigh. "I don't make promises I can't keep. If I say we can do this, then it's because I know we can. I wouldn't let you go in there if

I didn't think there was a chance I could keep you safe. No matter how much your sister means to you."

"If you think you could stop me...."

He smiled a little. "Yeah. Then there's that."

Mia curled her hand over his. She didn't know what she'd do without him right now. McClain was a rock. And she couldn't help believing in him. "Okay. We do this."

"Who've we got?"

"Jake," she replied promptly.

"Jenny?"

Mia glanced at her aunt. Jenny rested in a chair now, her eyes glazed with pain and exhaustion. "She's hurt and she needs medical attention, even if she won't admit it."

McClain examined Jenny too. "She'd be handy, but you're right. We'd only end up nursing her, and we don't need that complication."

Footsteps echoed behind her. McClain jerked his hand off her knee and moved to pour them both a cup of coffee.

"Someone say my name?" Jake asked, squatting down beside the pair of them. His bloodshot eyes revealed just how much sleep he'd gotten last night.

Mia managed to snatch a few hours, but it only felt like it exacerbated how tired she truly was. A constant ache drove into the back of her left eye. "We need to head after Rykker and the girls they took. McClain thinks we should go in small and infiltrate the place. Pretend to be bounty hunters turned wannabe slavers."

Jake scratched his jaw. "It's dangerous."

"It's the only way you're going to get your wife back," McClain countered.

Jake sighed. "Yeah. I know. Who else we got?"

Pointed silence.

"Fuck me," Jake said.

"Sideways," Mia added.

McClain slowly pulled a slave collar from his bag, and handed Mia her coffee. He turned the collar over. "Got this off that reiver. If we do this, we need a slave."

Mia's stomach jerked sideways. The entire thing was repulsive, and her blood ran cold.

"I'll do it," a voice from behind said.

All three of them spun around.

Ellie Thwaites stood there, her fingers curled in fists and her face pale but determined. Her frizzy blonde hair knotted behind her, making her mass of freckles and red-rimmed eyes stand out. "I can't fight," she said, "but they took my friends. I can pretend to be your slave to help you guys get in."

Hell, no. That idea was going to go down like a sinking ship. Mia found Ethan Thwaites in the crowd. He moved slowly, looking a million years old right now. "Ellie, we might not be coming back."

"I know." Ellie knelt on McClain's sleeping blankets. "I know that," she said fiercely. "But I grew up with Thea, Sonya, and the others. How do I slot back into life at Salvation Creek knowing what might be happening to them? How do I look at myself in the mirror every day when they're wearing collars out there somewhere and I didn't do a damned thing to stop it? Do I just let my mom die for nothing?"

"She didn't die for nothing," Mia countered. "She died to keep you and your sister safe."

"If we have a fourth person along with us," McClain interrupted, "then that leaves three of us to act as bounty hunters. I know you can shoot, Mia. It gives us a few more options, otherwise Jake and I will have to do all of the legwork."

Mia shot him a look. She didn't want Ellie along. It was hard enough taking McClain with her, when this wasn't his fight and there was a chance that he might not come back. Sending one more soul straight to hell.

Jake obviously felt the same. "What about your dad?"

Ellie quieted. "He's injured and he just lost mom. He won't be any use to you. And Alice.... She's not coping very well."

"Precisely why she needs her sister there with her," Mia said.

"Maybe that's true." Ellie tipped her chin up. She wasn't going to back down. "But Thea Haynes is my best friend in the world. And she doesn't have a sister. Or a dad. Right now, all she's got is me. Alice's safe now. But Thea's not."

There were no arguments to that.

"I get why you don't want to bring me along, Mia. I know I'm only nineteen. You think I'm throwing away everything, especially after the trick hand of luck I was just dealt. But you were nineteen once too. How would you feel?"

As if she'd move heaven and hell to get her friends back. Mia sighed. Ethan Thwaites was going to be a problem. "There's no way your dad will allow this."

"I can handle Dad," Ellie said. "Those bastards killed my mother and they took my friends. I want to make them pay. Dad will respect that."

Personally, Mia thought that was one argument that wasn't going to go headstrong Ellie's way. But as she looked around, she could see that even Jake was nodding now.

They needed all the help they could get, and even though Ellie knew next to nothing about fighting, she was one more set of eyes.

"Good luck with that," she told Ellie as the young blonde got up to go tell her father her plans.

⟶   ⟵

Mia was wrong.

Apparently Ellie Thwaites knew exactly how to get her way, because the argument with Ethan only lasted ten minutes before his shoulders slumped and he started to cry. Ellie hugged him for another five minutes, before wiping her eyes and making her way over to where Mia checked over the supplies they'd need.

"What did you tell him?" Mia muttered, as she stripped the vest and weapons off a female reiver someone had killed last night. She paused with her hand on a set of goggles. Might be useful to protect her eyes from the stinging desert winds, but she was definitely going to drop them in a pot of boiling water first. Same with the neck scarf. Mia brushed a fleck of dried blood off it.

Ellie's face paled, making her freckles stand out even more as she stared at the body. "The truth. That Thea's not just my friend."

Mia looked up in surprise. She'd never noticed. Ellie knelt down to undo the dead reiver's belt. Neither of them had much in common, except for the fact they both had sisters. Clearly she'd never bothered to pay much attention to Ellie's goings-on.

"Then we'll do our best to get her back," she said, squeezing the other girl's hand.

"Thanks," Ellie muttered, and removed the reiver's belt. "This feels so wrong."

"She doesn't need them anymore." Mia collected the belongings she planned to take. Two days ago she'd probably have blanched at the thought as much as Ellie did. Amazing how much could change in such a short period of time.

She felt vaguely numb to it all. Shock, perhaps.

All she could do was focus on putting one foot in front of the other.

Sage, Thea, and the other girls. Poor Sara, Sonya, Bethany, and little Tommy Hannaway, who was probably not so little anymore.

They were the only things that mattered.

"Let's go," Mia said, and headed off to sterilize the goggles.

A subdued air hung over the camp as the four of them prepared to leave. Guilt, perhaps. These people had their families and friends back, and they wouldn't risk anymore. Maybe it was unfair to blame them for that.

Mia made her way from person to person, accepting hugs and good wishes.

"I promise I'll look after her," she told Ethan when she finally stopped in front of him.

The big man nodded gruffly. He'd never been a man short of words, but apparently Ellie's decision cost him.

"You're a good girl, Mia." Thwaites hugged her awkwardly, his other arm knotted in some sort of sleeve sling. "Good luck with your sister. I wish I could do more than I am."

"You've done enough," she whispered, then hugged him back.

Jenny waited patiently beside him. Mia clasped her hands. "You look after that leg."

Jenny snorted. "Are you telling me what to do, girl?"

"Mom always said I might as well try and hold back the tide."

Jenny caught her at the back of her neck, an almost affectionate pat, then turned to the matter at hand. She started unbuckling her belt. "You'll need this. It's all the ammo I've got, plus I'm giving you my Remington. The bolt action's a little stiff these days, but it's the best I've got." She flipped a heavy hunting knife from its sheath. The handle bore a gorgeous hunting hawk pattern etched into the polished wood. "This too."

Mia's chest felt several sizes too small. "Jen, I can't take this. This is Hawk's." The last thing Jenny's man ever gave to her before they parted.

"It's a knife, Mia, which is exactly what you need." Another snort. "I've got another back at home."

But this one was special. Nobody had ever been allowed to touch it, and sometimes Mia caught her aunt rubbing oil into the steel lovingly, long after it needed it. "Thank you."

It meant so much to know that Jenny—who'd never been the sort to give hugs or take much interest in the day-to-day things—was surrendering her most precious object into Mia's keeping.

"You watch your back, and you get those girls home," Jenny said. Her gaze slid sideways, and Mia's followed it.

McClain strapped his bedroll onto his bike, next to where Jake was helping Ellie into the jeep he'd commandeered. Those strong hands jerked hard at the strap, McClain's shirt clinging to the muscle in his broad back. Last night sprang sharply into her mind. A desperate kiss that she could remember every detail of. Mia jerked her eyes off him before she betrayed her thoughts. Jenny always could see straight through her.

"One thing else you ought to consider," Jenny said. "This is a hard world, Mia. And I don't regret a single second of my life. I know you think I gave up too much when I left Hawk to come home and look after you girls. Maybe I did. But he understood. He knew that the years we rode together were the best moments of our lives, and that they were never going to last forever. *Love hard, ride fast, and don't know regret.* He taught me that. You've got to cherish every moment, Mia. I know you locked your heart up nice and tight after Jake screwed you over..."

Mia opened her mouth to protest—she'd never told anyone that.

But Jenny rolled right over her. "And no point denying it. I got eyes. But you're riding straight into hell. And you're riding there with a man who's got you knotted all up in a way I've never seen you before. Maybe you ought to take some of those moments and enjoy them a little. Let yourself love him, even if it's only for a few days. Or nights." Jenny squeezed her shoulder. "Because you don't know if you're coming back."

The words echoed within her, like a truth burned into her skin. Mia clapped Jenny on the shoulder one more time, then turned to go. "I'll think about it. Thanks, Jen. For everything."

"Ready?" McClain called.

"Ready," she replied, slinging her leg over the back of the bike and nestling her thighs around his.

McClain revved the throttle to warm the bike up. It buzzed beneath them, as if it were as full of nervous energy as she was.

Time to go rescue her sister.

twelve

THERE WAS SOMETHING wrong.

Mia nibbled on the quick of her thumb as she watched McClain and Ellie refill the water canteens from a stream he'd managed to locate in the middle of a winding canyon. She couldn't stop thinking about Jenny's words. The last thing she needed was to deal with the temptation McClain presented for her. *Don't pin your hope on a man.* She'd put those rules in place for a reason. But Jenny spoke truth. What happened if she got shot? Would she be satisfied with her life if she looked back on it? That answer was a definite no.

Love fast, ride hard, and don't know regret.

Damn Jenny for planting that seed in her head. At least it kept her mind off darker matters, like her sister.

However, she might be the only one dwelling on that kiss and what it represented.

All morning McClain had been distant and focused, and there was definitely something going on between the two men. Jake looked like a dog watching another dog enter its territory. He tolerated McClain's presence, but he sure as shit wasn't welcoming him here, and he looked like he was just waiting for that other dog to attack.

What the hell happened last night?

The last time she'd seen him, McClain had given her that honey-slow smile of his that warmed his entire face. Now he was purely professional.

And the Jake that had been glued to McClain's side ever since they left Salvation Creek was long gone.

"What did you say to him?" she hissed in Jake's ear, the second she thought McClain and Ellie were far enough away not to hear. "What's going on?"

Jake shot her a look from beneath heavy lids. "I'm just watching out for you, Mia."

"You've got no right. Whatever's going on between McClain and me is none of your damned business."

"I know it isn't," he shot back. "But that doesn't mean I'm just going to leave you out here for the vultures."

Mia drew back with a frown. McClain wasn't a vulture. But something had gone down between the two of them, and from the way they were both acting, it seemed an agreement had been reached.

"Focus on Sage," Jake told her, still looking grim. "He'll ride away after all this is done and not look back. I don't want to see you get your heart broken. I know you need something to hold on to right now, but he's not the one to do that for you. And I wish he were, Mia. I really do."

"And who else have I got?"

"You've got people who love you," he replied firmly. "Your sister, Jenny... me." Jake's lips pursed. "I wish... I wish I could say more, but keep in mind that I'm only looking out for your best interests. This has nothing to do with what happened between you and me. I promise you that. Can you trust me on this one?"

Swallowing down that little knot of anger in her chest, she patted him on the back. "Just stay out of my love life, Jake."

And then she headed toward McClain.

"Let's talk," McClain said. "About how to get into Rust City safely."

Mia looked up from the sleeping kit she was rolling. She, Ellie, and Jake had snatched a couple of hours sleep that afternoon. It had been a long day of travel, with barely any of them speaking to each other. She ached to get going again, now that they were so close to Rust City, but McClain insisted. Tired minds made mistakes, and Rust City twinkled in the desert below like a junkyard out in the sun. They all needed to be at their best. "What's the plan? We're three bounty hunters looking for a way to get rich quick...."

"With one slave," Ellie said, looking like she faced down a firing squad.

"You're not going to like it, Ellie." McClain knelt down at Mia's side on the small ledge overlooking the plains below. Tired lines fanned around his eyes, and his cheeks bore evidence of several hard days' ride. Funny how the scruff along his jaw was several shades darker than that on his head. In the sun she could almost see strands of gold in his short-cropped hair.

Ellie bit her lip, zipping her duffel shut. "I don't have to like it, McClain. If it gets me closer to Thea...."

There wasn't a great deal that any of them wouldn't do.

McClain sighed, then reached inside his coat and dragged out a leather circlet. When he shook it out, Mia realized it was the slave collar with silver links fastened into the leather so that a chain could be clipped there.

Women were commodities in the slave towns, unless they'd managed to earn their reputations, and some of those particular women were just as dangerous as the men.

Reaching out, Mia brushed her quivering fingertips against the leather. It made her feel sick just to touch it.

McClain wouldn't look either of them in the eyes. "Think you can do this, Mia? You're going to have to play the part. Look them in the eye, spit on their boots and keep your hand on your gun at all times. The women in these towns don't take shit. They can't afford to."

She'd killed one of them back in Vegas. It all happened so quickly, but afterward she'd gone back and examined the body. The woman had shaved both sides of her head, and her hair was ruthlessly braided down the center of her skull. Tattoos scrawled up her gaunt cheeks, and she'd been missing several teeth, but the thing that made her stand out in Mia's memories was the absolute lack of humanity in the woman's eyes, that she'd glimpsed before she pulled the trigger.

"I'm not much of a fighter." Vegas made that clear. Mia considered it for a moment. "If someone tries to take me on, then I don't know if I can stand my ground. I made it through Vegas, but most of that was taking the reivers by surprise."

"I'll protect you," McClain said, earnest and raw, as if he sensed how much it scared her. "You're my woman. That's the cover story. And I protect what's mine."

"Why not mine?" Jake interrupted.

He and McClain stared at each other for a long moment.

"Because you and I get along like two cats in a burlap bag," Mia pointed out. "Plus you're in the market for a new slave. Preferably Sage."

"And you're the lucky owner of this one," Ellie said, buckling the collar around her throat. Despite her unwavering voice, her hands shook. "No offence, McClain, but you're a bit too old for me."

The look on his face was priceless. "I'm thirty-four."

"And I'm married," Jake squeaked, as if Ellie had just propositioned him.

"And I'm gay." Ellie rolled her eyes. "Relax, guys. We're playing pretend, remember?"

Jake's eyes near bugged out of his face. Mia couldn't resist a smile.

"How are you going to cope down there?" McClain asked Ellie seriously. "We're going to stop most of the touchy-feely, but we can't play too nice."

"I can bear being touched, McClain." Ellie replied. "

To a point. They'll want to see the merchandise too, I expect." Her jaw tightened as she glanced at the three of them. "And I know you won't let it go too far, but you guys need to promise me that you won't break our cover. If you're a slaver trying to sell me in Rust City, then you can't be too protective. There's a lot I can handle. You need to promise that you can keep your mouths shut and let some of it happen. Just enough to get us in."

"It's not going to come to that," Jake growled. "I'll think of something. But if you think I can just stand there whilst someone feels you up... Christ, you're like my kid sister."

"We might not have a choice."

"Like hell. There are always choices. Apparently you're *my* slave, and I don't like sharing either. If someone puts their hands on you, then I can rip their heads off without retaliation."

Ellie let out the breath she'd been holding. "Thank you."

"Just one problem," Mia said, realizing something they'd all overlooked. "If this Rykker and his reivers see Ellie, they might recognize her."

That slammed their plans to a halt.

"Shit," Jake said.

"Maybe," Ellie said, with a frown. "They kept me in the trunk of a jeep while we were travelling and it wasn't always good light."

"That blonde hair's kind of distinctive," Mia pointed out.

Ellie ran a hand through her curls, then her expression firmed. "Anyone got a knife?"

"What?" Jake blurted.

"I'll shave it," Ellie said, with pure determination. "We can work some charcoal into my brows and my across my face to make me look dirtier. And I'll keep my head down if I see one of the reivers that hit the ranch."

"Might work," McClain muttered.

"We don't have much of a choice at this point," Mia murmured. They couldn't just leave Ellie here.

McClain drew his knife. "I'll do it. You're not used to shaving with a knife. Better leave you with both ears."

Ellie flashed him a grim smile. "Preferably."

"What about us?" Jake asked, his boots crunching on dry gravel as he turned on McClain.

"You and I are cousins," McClain said, peering toward Rust City. "We're both bounty hunters—it's easier to keep it simple, then we don't have to worry too much about slipping up. Except the pair of us realized there could be some of the finer things to be had in life. We want gold." He curled his lip. "Mia, you're not really a fighter, but you're training to ride along at my side. Sorry to be old-fashioned, but you're basically my woman."

"Do you want me to flutter my eyelashes at you a few times?" she drawled.

"No, but if I slap you on the ass once or twice, try not to jump out of your skin."

"You slap me on the ass, and I will personally grab a handful of your balls."

McClain smiled. "That's the reiver spirit."

"Are we buying or selling?" Jake asked. "Because I don't think we should bluff when it comes to Ellie."

"Buying," McClain said firmly. "Ellie doesn't leave our sight. We work in pairs at all times, and don't go anywhere by ourselves. Ellie's a girl who did you wrong, so you took your revenge on her. But we also heard that we can fetch good coin buying up here, and selling to the south. So we're looking for slaves, preferably women. Maybe a boy or two. If need be, then we buy your wife back."

"And the other girls," Mia hastened to point out. "Sara, Sonya, Bethany, and Thea. Plus the Hannaway kid. He's about fourteen."

"Do we have enough coin?" Jake asked bluntly.

There was a lump in her throat the size of the Wastelands. What would she do if the choice came down to Sage and Thea, or the others? "I don't care if we have enough," she told him firmly. "We're not leaving any of our people there."

A jingle sounded as McClain dumped a small pouch of coin on the rock in front of her. He opened it up, coins dripping through his fingers. "I've been hunting an old friend of mine, but along the way I took the time to do a few jobs. One of them paid big."

Jake tossed another leather purse next to it. "Twenty gold. It's all I've got on me. Thwaites gave it to me when we were saying good-bye."

"And I've got this," Ellie said, untying the gold locket around her neck. "It was my mother's."

Mia hadn't even thought about bringing extra money. All she'd grabbed was her duffle, a few spare clothes, her medical kit, and her gun.

"What happens if they don't want to sell?" Mia asked, staring at the haze in the desert and the glittering scrap city in the distance.

"Plan B," McClain said, pocketing the money. "Shoot everyone, burn the joint, and get the hell out of there with our friends."

Mia couldn't stop a faint smile from forming. "I like that idea." Slavers needed to know that their kind couldn't be tolerated.

"Let's hope it doesn't come to that," Jake added grimly, dropping the cigarette he'd been smoking, and grinding it under his heel. "I don't think I've got enough ammo."

"And I'm a terrible shot," Ellie added.
"We'll deal with that when we get there and sound the place out," McClain replied. "Let's go shave that head, then roll. The sun's starting to set. I'd like to be in there before the gates close for the night."

"To keep the wargs out," Jake said, and the two men looked at each other for a humorless moment.

"To keep the wargs out," McClain gently echoed, then hauled his ammo belt over his shoulder and headed for his motorbike to fetch his shaving kit.

"Yeah," Jake muttered, rising and dusting off his jeans.

"Anything you want to tell me?" she asked, regarding the sudden hostility between the two men.

He hesitated, glancing behind him at Ellie and McClain, as they started for the river. "Just be careful. I've got your back."

Their rescue party had dwindled down to four, and she had to hope that was enough.

Especially when two of them were barely speaking to each other.

Adam's first glimpse of Rust City soured his stomach.

Riding directly for the gates in the barbed wire fencing, he examined the place. There were gun turrets on top of the towers on either side of the main gates, with several guns mounted at odd spots along the walls. The walls looked like they were hewn out of solid rock and the city nestled in a small canyon, with sheer cliff faces rising above it.

This wasn't just some reiver town, cobbled together out of scrap.

"You okay?" Mia called in his ear, giving his waist a squeeze.

He tried to ignore the way her thighs straddled his own, her breasts pressing into his shirt. "I don't like the look of this place," he called back. "It looks more organized than I'd have expected, and they have some serious hardware mounted on those walls."

He should know. It was similar to the setup at Absolution when he'd been running the town. Enormous chain-wire gates loomed ahead of them. Rolls of barbed wire crowned the perimeter fences. Anything clearing that fence would then have to contend with the stark walls beyond it—where they'd be sitting ducks for the turret guns.

"One way in," Mia noted.

"There's always a back door," he said. "We just need to find it. You ready?"

Men stared at them, dressed in reiver brown with padded vests over their chests and rifles in their hands. One wore a leather face mask. Adam eased off the throttle, dust spewing out from beneath the bike as he began to slow. Six guards. Two more in the gatehouse by the look of it.

Whoever was running this place, they had military experience, he'd bet on it. Which suggested someone from the Eastern Confederacy who'd escaped the heavy-surveillance state, or maybe one of the road warriors from the Nomad bands who drove up and down the coast, hiring out as small mercenary armies.

Adam pulled in as a guard stepped forward, his hand on his shotgun. There were nails sticking out of the reiver's helmet, and he had an old gas mask hanging around his throat. Typical reiver, in a faded pair of much-patched pants, a vest, and a grotty shirt underneath that might have been white once upon a time. A bandolier slung across his broad chest, with little shiny caps on the ends of each shell. Freshly made by the look of them.

That was interesting. A lot of people knew how to make ammo, but getting your hands on critical components like gunpowder wasn't so easy.

"New to Rust City?" the reiver demanded, spitting on the ground beside Adam's boot.

Adam glanced around. The other guards looked curious, but not suspicious. "Heard you could get a good time here. Thought we'd check it out." He let a slow smile bloom. "Just finished a job and I've got coin to spend." He jerked his head behind him as Jake pulled up beside him in the jeep. "So does he."

"Bill of sale?" the reiver asked, strolling in a slow circle around the jeep and eyeing Ellie.

"Who said I bought her?" Jake replied, meeting the reiver's eyes.

A nod. The reiver stepped closer to Mia, whose hands trembled faintly on Adam's waist. He reached out but Adam caught his wrist, and not gently.

"Don't touch the merchandise?" the reiver asked.

The click of the safety on a pistol being removed echoed in Adam's ear. Mia pointed the barrel directly in the reiver's face. "I'm not merchandise, you piece of shit."

"She's with me," Adam drawled, sweat licking his spine. "And I wouldn't piss her off if I were you. She bites."

"I only bite you," Mia pointed out. "Everybody else gets a bullet. I don't know where they've been."

"Aren't I special?" He clapped a hand on her thigh, and Mia laughed.

The reiver stepped back, hands in the air. "You should play nicer."

"You should wash, and I might consider it."

"Oh, Cypher's going to like you." The reiver's sly leer at Mia made Adam's hand itch.

He wanted to punch those dirty teeth out and see if the bastard would pick them up. "Like I said, she's with me," Adam reminded him.

"We'll see." The reiver shrugged.

Adam couldn't quite tell what the reiver meant by that—had he just brought Mia within the realm of a man who took all that he claimed? But at least the reiver nodded and waved at the guards to open the gates.

"First rule of Rust City: everything here belongs to Cypher," the reiver said, patting the hood of the jeep. "So you three need to pay your respects first. We don't take too kindly to strangers here. But if Cypher says you can stay, then you can stay." The reiver grinned. "But if Cypher says that the girl ain't yours, then that's the way it falls. As for your slave... well... Cypher insists on taking a cut of all profits."

"We're not interested in selling," Jake cut in. "Heard you could buy good product here. My man—and the lovely lady at his side—are looking for something similar to share."

The gates began to slide open with a grinding noise. The reiver walked backward through them, gesturing them in. "Market's open in the morning," he called. "You can look then. Tonight's the start of the War Games. Three nights of action. We've got reiver packs coming from everywhere to spend their coin. You don't want to miss it."

"*War Games*?" Mia whispered.

Adam gunned the bike and zipped through, a squirt of red dirt pinwheeling through the air behind him. Shit. Just what they needed. More reivers to contend with.

"Moko!" the reiver bellowed, gesturing to a one-armed man with scars slashed up his cheeks as if by a razor. "Come and show our guests where to park, then take them to Cypher."

Moko ambled over, moving oddly, as if his foot had been smashed at one point. His head gleamed bald, and his gaze kept lifting to Adam's then shying away, somewhat like a kicked dog. "Yessir. This way! This way! Hurry."

The electric gate kicked into gear behind them, and all the hairs on the back of Adam's neck rose, but he rolled the bike after Moko. They passed between the two gun turret towers and under a makeshift arch decorated with an old cow's skull and a pair of rusted wheels.

"That was easy," Jake breathed.

Adam couldn't stop himself from checking everything out. Ten, twelve reivers in the marshaling yard behind the gate towers... more strolling through the dusty streets beyond. Looked like a market back there, scraps of faded tents strung here and there, with street kids holding trays of food running through the crowd, trying to hawk their wares. Could be a couple of hundred reivers in the shanty city. Jesus.

"Getting in's the easy part," he muttered, idling the engine as he pulled up where the reiver gestured. A dozen bikes of various conditions waited there. "Getting out...."

"We'll deal with that when we get there," Mia whispered. "We're in. That's the first step."

"Hey you! Moko!" Jake called, resting his arm on the edge of the jeep's shattered window and peering directly at the bald man. "Will these be safe here?"

"Nobody will touch 'em," Moko replied.

"Yeah, well, I'm holding you personally responsible if my jeep goes missing. You understand?" Jake slammed his door shut, dragged his duffel and rolled sleeping kit out of the back of the jeep, and slung it over his shoulder. He jerked Ellie's hand, and she slid passively across the seat, slipping out of the car.

The scent of nervousness and determination rolled off her, but she kept her eyes lowered. Talk was cheap. Now she stood here in the heart of the reivers' shantytown, Adam hoped her nerve held.

"Nobody steals in Rust City," Moko replied. "If they do, Cypher feeds them to the arena."

What the hell was the arena? Mia slid off the bike behind him, and Adam eased the engine off. The bike sighed into silence as he rested it on its kickstand.

"Got to hurry," Moko called, limping toward a small arch that led into a wire fence tunnel. "Cypher's got to start the War Games, so we don't have long. Doesn't like to be late."

Adam exchanged a long look with Jake.

"Nothing for it, I guess," Jake replied, eyeing the mesh tunnel with distaste too. Once inside they'd be sitting ducks.

Jake took the leash from his pocket and hesitated before he clipped it to the collar around Ellie's throat. "Sorry."

"Just do it," Ellie muttered. "The sooner we pay our respects, the sooner we can start looking for Thea and the others. I can be practical."

Mia's hand stroked the small of Adam's back. "Stop looking like you want to kill everyone here. We've got this. But if you greet Cypher with that look on your face, I'd expect fireworks. To rule this place he's got to think he's got the biggest dick around. You need to prepare to back down a little."

Adam let out a slow sigh. It was good advice. "Sorry. Just on edge."

"We all are," Mia murmured, and again she caressed his hip. "Think about how good it's going to be to set this place on fire."

Adam smiled. Yeah. That would be nice.

Mia slapped his ass, then shot him a wink. "That's better," she said loudly, in her reiver voice. "You look prettier when you smile, McClain. Maybe if you're nice I'll give you a rubdown later?"

Hell, if she wasn't the one thing that could make this ordeal better.

She'd intrigued him from the start with her no-nonsense attitude and stubbornness, but there was a gentler side to her too, a nurturing side that he hadn't expected. As if she were just as concerned with his feelings about this whole situation as her own.

And he had little defense against that.

He wanted to kiss her right now, to tell her with his mouth just how much she amazed him. To silently vow that he would get her out of this safely—no matter what he had to do—but there was no time. And he couldn't get her hopes up. Nothing could happen between them. Jake's discovery of his secret yesterday only reminded him of that.

It wasn't fair to her to start something he had no intention of finishing.

"Let's do this then," he murmured.

He didn't like it—hated it in fact—but he followed Mia into the tunnel, focusing on her ass. She'd put a strut into her stride that drew all eyes, and he figured it was safer to think of how much he wanted her, rather than give rise to the feral feelings inside him. Adam rubbed his chest, the cool pewter of the amulet beneath his shirt. Every day felt like the warg grew a little bigger inside his skin.

The tunnel led to a huge adobe building with steel doors. Moko waited for them nervously. Inside the doors, the building opened into a huge courtyard with dirty walls, yet there were lush plants everywhere and water trickled from somewhere. On a balcony overlooking the courtyard stood a man in flowing white robes, a neatly trimmed beard, and a pair of loose pants around his waist. His bare chest was oiled, and his blond hair was pale.

Cypher?

The man didn't look dangerous. Adam watched him as they strode up the stairs, but... he wasn't getting the right vibe.

"Newcomers," Moko said, pausing at the top of the steps and not daring to venture any further. He reeked of nervousness all of a sudden. "Here to pay their respects to Cypher."

The man's blue eyes looked glassily uncurious. "I'll take them."

He gestured the four of them toward the canvas curtains blowing in the arch. Behind them, Adam could smell faint traces of motor oil, gunpowder, and blood.

Time to meet the master of Rust City.

thirteen

CYPHER WAS NOT what he expected.

To begin with, he was a *she*.

The second the pale man shoved open the canvas flaps on a tent in the middle of the camp, Adam found himself in a room lit with harsh electricity. An enormous chair hovered on some sort of dais, covered in sheepskins and wolf hides, and there was a woman leaning over a table in the middle, marking items off a piece of parchment.

"Got a guest for you, Vex," the pale man announced, letting the flap fall shut behind them.

The woman looked up, her skin polished bronze and her head shaved at the sides. A shock of dyed red hair swept in a ridge along the top of her skull, and her blue eyes were lined in kohl. Silver bands circled her upper arms, and another one circled her throat. Leather straps hooked onto it, and were attached to the bustier of her custom leather corset. A glint of steel flashed at her waist as she turned, but he couldn't see what she was carrying.

Hard. That was the word he would have used. That, and "dangerous."

"Mmm," she breathed, her eyes lighting up like she'd just spotted cake the second she saw him. "Is this gift all for me?"

Adam froze.

"Well, aren't you as pretty as a picture," she announced, and eyed him from head to toe, virtually stripping him naked in her mind's eye. She wasn't young, though he suspected she was older than she looked.

"Vex Cypher," she announced, circling him slowly and examining every inch of him with hungry eyes. He had a sudden sickening feeling that he knew exactly how the slaves in Rust City felt.

Like meat.

"What's your name, handsome?"

Alright then. "Adam McClain. And this is my cousin, Jake, my woman, Mia, and—"

A hand cupped him firmly between the legs and Adam caught Vex's wrist, his eyes nearly bulging out of his face.

"Jesus," he breathed, as Jake made a strangled sound in his throat behind him.

For a second he didn't know what to do. He couldn't shove her away, or punch her in the face as he would have done to a man.

"It's impressive, isn't it?" Mia drawled. "You ever feel like you want to take that cock for a ride, you let me know and maybe we'll invite you to share our blankets."

Somehow he had to salvage this moment. Hard to do when a woman's hand was on his dick. "I told you, we don't share," he shot toward Mia. "Nobody else gets to touch you."

Mia crossed her arms over her chest and gave a somewhat predatory smile that she shared with Vex. "Sorry. I'm open to it, but he's not." With a sigh, she fixed those gorgeous dark eyes on him. "Are you still pissed about that guy at Fort Phoenix?"

"That's okay, princess," Vex said with a smile, caressing his cock as she stepped back. "Didn't realize you were so shy." She raked a nail up over his belt. "A shame though."

His cheeks flamed. He didn't know what to say. Thank Christ Mia had got them out of that predicament.

"Uh, we were told we had to present tribute or something?" Jake cut in.

Vex collapsed back onto her throne, hooking one long leg over the other. "And just what are you going to offer me?"

The arch of her brow suggested she'd be far happier unwrapping him, and Jake cleared his throat and took a faint step backward. "Uh...."

Vex snorted. "What a pair of disappointments." She tapped her painted lips. "Still... you both look cute when you blush."

There was silence. Of all the possibilities they'd prepared for, this hadn't even been considered.

"They look pretty, but they can be dumb as oxen sometimes." A pouch of coin flew through the air, and then Mia stepped forward. "Ten gold pieces do for a tribute? Maybe if we drink on it, they might lose their shyness?"

Vex snatched it out of the air, as fast as a viper, and hefted the bag. "It's a start."

When Vex glanced at Jake, Adam saw the edge of cunning in her. This whole thing was a game to her, a way to put them off-balance. It had succeeded. She'd picked him as the leader, and she'd gone after him, just to cut him down to size. Then Jake.

The woman was dangerous.

Especially when she turned those considering eyes on Mia.

"You aren't reivers," said a low, feminine voice from the shadows in the corner.

A faint blade rasped on stone, and Adam realized there was another woman kneeling in the corner, sharpening her knife. Vex's appearance threw him so far off balance that he'd not even noticed her.

Her brown braids were bound tightly across her head, and she had the same kohl-rimmed eyes as Vex, the same features in a younger face. She watched the four of them with a flat expression that reminded him of a predator like a coyote. Not quite strong enough to match up, one-on-one, but there the second your back was turned.

"No, you aren't," Vex agreed, watching the young woman with an inexplicable expression. She leaned forward, resting her elbows on her knees. "This is my daughter, Zarina. And as she has pointed out, you clearly aren't the type of men who walk through my doors every day. What brings you to Rust City?"

Time to pull himself out of the nosedive. Adam gestured toward Ellie. "As you can see, we've had some luck out East. We're all growing tired of bounty hunting. It's long hours, alone, with little reward to show for it. We were paid to protect a small settlement out there along the Rim. They were having some problems with wargs, so we took care of the problem for an agreed-upon price. Only thing was, when we came back for the other half of our money, they told us they didn't have it." He crossed his arms over his chest. "Mia suggested other compensation. They disagreed, so we shot the place up and took what we wanted."

Vex lit a cigarette, watching them unemotionally. "You get any others?"

Jake ruffled his hair, almost apologetically. "Yeah. Sold a couple three days ago, just to the south of here."

"How far south?"

"Fort Phoenix," Adam interrupted, sweating a little. It was the only place where he knew the name of the man who ran the slave town.

"And how much did De la Vega give you for the product?" Vex asked.

Proving that she was no fool. "De la Vega?" Adam shot Jake and Mia a look, as if confused. "We dealt with a man named Thurston. He gave us thirty gold coins for the other girls. I thought that was kind of low, but we don't have a lot of experience in these matters. Wanted to sound out a new buyer. There are a lot of settlements out east that we know of, and nobody's touching them."

"There's a reason for that," Vex said dryly. "You'd take on the Confederacy militia that roam outside their territories?"

"It's better than ending up as some shadow-cat's last meal working for minimum pay as a bounty hunter. And let's be honest," Mia added, running with the story they'd worked out. "Competition is fierce down south among the reiver packs. That's why they're all heading north, looking for fresh pickings. But the north is sparse. Whoever doesn't get eaten alive by the revenants or the wargs up there is wizened by drought and protected by stone walls. Hardly prime product. Along the coast the Nomads rule, and I'm not suicidal enough to take on a bikie gang. That leaves the no-man's-lands along the edges of the Great Divide and the Rim as the last option. Settlements are few and far between, but nobody's trying for them and the three of us have experience in dealing with the critters out there. The militia makes a lot of noise, but we know the lay of the land, and we know their regular routes." She shrugged. "It makes sense."

"How do I come in?"

"You have a market," Adam pointed out. "We have a resource route. And we didn't think much of Thurston's offer."

"Nero, fetch me something to drink," Cypher told her slave, then gestured with her fingers. "Sit. You have my interest. Make sure you keep it."

Adam sank into the chair opposite her, with Mia at his side. "The Confederacy is tied up in building their wall to shut us all out," he pointed out. "They have militia riding the edges of the Great Divide, true, but if you know the territory then you know how to hide. And we don't like working in a large band. That's the sort of thing that gets you attention. Jake, Mia, and I are real good at slipping in and out before we've been noticed."

Vex accepted a glass from Nero. The blond man seated himself at her feet, and suddenly the implications of what he was began to take shape in Adam's mind. The shaved and oiled chest. The blank eyes. This was Vex's personal slave, and he could only imagine how the man served her. Vex tapped her long, painted fingernails on the sides of her chair. "The three of you can't haul much stock. Not much profit to be made from one or two sales."

"It's enough for us to start with," he replied, with a shrug. "And we pick the best."

For the first time, Vex took a good, long look at Ellie. "Gorgeous skin," she noted. "In her prime childbearing years too."

"Oh, I'm not selling this one," Jake cut in. "I have a personal stake in keeping her."

"She do you wrong?"

"Turned me down a few years back." Jake looked uneasy but he forced a smile. "Let's just say, I'm sure she regrets it now."

Vex drained her cup, watching with those witchy eyes that told Adam nothing. "So why are you three here if you've got nothing to sell?"

"We're interested in viewing your market," Adam replied. "We have a supply route, but we want to know where we can get the best price for prime quality. And my cousin here is in the mood to buy another woman of his own. This one's a cold fish. Thought we'd kill two birds with one stone, and maybe Mia and I might have a look and see if there's someone at the market that catches our eye."

"Some*thing*," Vex corrected. She eyed Jake. "I could help him out with that."

"I don't think you'd like what I like," Jake replied.

"Oh?" She turned all of that hawklike attention upon him, along with a sleazy smile. "You might be surprised."

"You look like you want to be in control." Jake smiled his own insincere smile, though the look in his eyes was faintly murderous. "So do I."

Vex sighed. "Pity. But you're right. We'd either end up killing each other, or I'd break you."

Jake flinched a little.

The smile on Vex's face vanished, almost as if it had never been there. "Rust City is mine. Which means I make 50 percent off each sale here."

"Twenty," Adam countered quickly, playing his part. He knew what she would be expecting.

"Forty," she bit out. "We're the closest slave market to the Great Divide. You're looking at an extra day's ride to find another, and you've already found Fort Phoenix is not as generous as I am."

"Hell if I'm paying forty," Mia said, nudging his foot. "Sixty split between the three of us is piss weak."

Adam frowned. "Thirty. There are at least five slave towns within a day's drive of here. And they're selling direct to New Merida."

"Not for prime stock, they're not," Vex pointed out. "They want field laborers to tend the plantations and farms down south." She tapped her nose. "I have a direct route for *prime* stock. It leads to someone who'll pay a lot of money. Forty percent."

"Who out here can pay that kind of money?" Mia blurted.

"I never said it was someone 'out here.'"

The implications shocked him. No wonder Vex Cypher was in control here, if she had some Confederacy general or higher-up in her pocket. Jesus. That was a dangerous supply line, and he had to wonder what she was getting out of it. The Eastern Confederacy had access to technology and medicines that were worth more than gold in this new world.

"It's better than nothing," Jake muttered. "Take the deal."

Adam rubbed Mia's thigh while she considered it. She finally gave a curt nod.

"Done," he said. "Forty percent."

"You try and cheat me, and I'll cut your throat. You bring me less than the best, and our deal goes south." Vex leaned closer, catching his gaze. "And if you steal from me, I'll take your balls and sell you myself. Understood?" That viper gaze extended to Mia. "Her I keep. I like her."

"I don't shit on my business contracts. If I give my word, then I mean it." Adam fanned himself abstractedly. Man, it was hot. "But I'm also not the type of man you should cross."

"Ooh, you are an interesting pair." Vex sized him up again.

"And I don't mix business with pleasure," he pointed out.

Vex drained her cup. She hadn't offered any of them anything to drink, which made it clear who ran this business discussion. But to roll over and show her his belly would be the end of them. "That doesn't sound like much fun, but I respect your thinking. Do we have a deal?"

He stood, and offered her his hand. "We have a deal."

Vex's hand was callused and firm. "Good. Then I want young women and men who look pretty and can handle the transition. Fit, healthy livestock. My buyer wants girls who can breed, primarily. The boys are for pleasure."

"We'll do our best." Fuck. He'd heard rumors that the Confederacy struggled with fertility. Something about radiation poisoning passing from generation to generation.

But kidnapping young women just to bear children for them?

That had to be stopped.

All of a sudden, this wasn't just about Mia's sister and the rest of the people who'd been stolen from Salvation Creek.

"Zarina, show these three to some quarters." Vex stood, dragging one of the wolf furs off the back of her chair. She draped it over her shoulders. "Then bring them to the arena. My box. We should celebrate our new partnership."

Snapping her fingers at Nero, she headed for the door. "Zarina will see you fed and watered. And then I expect you to attend me. I have some War Games to open."

fourteen

ADAM CUPPED HIS palm in the basin of water, then poured what he'd captured over the back of his bare neck. He'd scrubbed himself clean and it felt good, but hell, he was tired. Three days of hard riding, a fight or two, and no sleep would do that to a man. It didn't help that Jake knew his secrets, and Mia kept pushing... pushing against those walls he kept trying to put up between them.

You're not invincible.

You're also not a saint, he thought, as he smelled her coming.

And now they were sharing a narrow bed in a small room, and everyone watching thought Mia belonged to him—or the other way around. There was no escaping her, or the thoughts she aroused.

Just when he needed to put as much distance between them as he could.

"You parade around like that in front of Vex, and Jake and I might be able to steal the others back right out from under her nose," Mia said.

Adam let the washcloth fall into the basin. The small bedroom Zarina had led them to was in a different compound to Vex's stronghold. Nobody stayed under the warlord's roof, but some reivers rented rooms to newcomers—for a hefty price. There went five more gold coins, but at least the rooms were clean, and separate from the main building. Jake and Ellie shared the other one.

Adam made sure his towel was tucked in, and turned to find Mia in the doorway to the small washroom, looking fresh and clean. He'd let her wash first and the smell of his soap on her skin made something possessive sit up and take notice inside him. "Real funny."

Amusement lit her whiskey-brown eyes. "I'm not going to lie. You and Jake nearly tripped over your shoes in there. I could have sworn the pair of you were rugged bounty hunters with a bit of experience under your belts...."

"Yeah, well, she didn't have her hand on your cock," he growled, and snatched up a small towel to blot his face dry. His cheeks felt ridiculously sensitive after that shave. "And while I don't usually complain, there was a possibility she'd have used her knife to remove it. I wasn't quite sure which way she was going to go. Makes a man nervous."

Mia leaned her hip against the door, crossing her arms over her black tank. Her gaze slid down his bare chest and hooked on the towel. "You don't look nervous right now."

No. His cock was partially erect. The side effect of having her here in the room with him when they were talking about cocks. "I think you almost like playing a female reiver."

Mia arched a brow. "Is that an insult?"

"No. I just meant that you're a little more open like this." Adam tossed the small towel aside.

Mia frowned. "The take-what-you-want attitude... it's wrong when it affects other people and their freedom," she admitted. "But maybe there's something to be said for admitting what you want in life, and going after it."

"And if you could take what you wanted?" Instantly he wanted to take the words back. This was not helping the situation.

Mia looked up slowly, those dark eyelashes shading her eyes. "I don't know. I think I'm still figuring that out, but I've been thinking... about what I'd regret if I died tomorrow."

"You're not going to die tomorrow," he growled. Not if he had anything to do with it.

Mia rolled her eyes. "Way to bypass the subject, McClain."

"Adam."

"What?"

"My name is Adam." For some reason, he desperately wanted to hear that name from her lips.

"Adam," she said, and there was the Mia he knew. Gentle, wary, and full of shy warmth. "And what about you? No regrets?"

A lifetime of them. He groaned. "Mia, we're not starting this."

"You're about a month too late with your warning."

"Reivers," he pointed out. "A psychotic warlord. Your sister."

"We're one step closer to Sage." Mia looked away though. "And you're right. I shouldn't even be thinking of this. Not right now. But...."

"But?"

"Nothing." She shook her head. "Just something Jenny said to me. I can't stop thinking about it." She stepped closer, making every muscle in his body tense. Mia tugged playfully at the towel around his waist. "And you never answered the question."

Adam clapped a hand over hers, keeping the towel in place.

If you could take what you wanted....

What did he want?

Her. That much was simple. The second he'd walked into her bar he'd known that Mia was different. Gorgeous, brusque, and clearly warning everyone off, she'd barely warmed up to him in the first week. But there'd been moments when she'd looked at him as if intrigued. Moments where her eyes tracked him and hinted that she didn't mind looking at him, even if she wouldn't let herself pursue anything else. Maybe that was what caught his attention: the loneliness that he saw echoed in her eyes.

He'd told himself a thousand times he couldn't have her. But every day only twisted that tension tighter. Every day he realized the attraction between them was growing.

Everything about this was wrong. Wrong timing, wrong situation. Right woman.

Wrong man.

She'll never forgive you, Jake's voice whispered.

Adam pushed away from her. "There's a reason for that. I don't have an answer. I can't afford to live in the abstract. We all have dreams and wants, Mia, but sometimes we have to accept that those dreams don't always come true."

"Adam." That hand drifted across his lower back, splaying over the base of his spine.

And he wanted so much to turn to her—

A knock sounded sharply at the main door.

The breath exploded out of him. Saved by an intruder. This was going to be hell: trapped in here with her at night, trying to do the right thing, when both of them wanted to explore the wrong so badly. He was only a man. That kind of willpower was for a monk.

"Who is it?" he called. The smell of Mia's soap covered all others, and he was reining himself in so tightly that he didn't have access to his better senses.

"Zarina's here," Jake called. "Are we ready to do this?"

Adam dragged a fresh shirt over his head, then reached for his jeans. He paused and glanced at Mia.

She rolled her eyes and headed for the bedroom. "I'm not likely to tackle you right here, with Jake behind the door. Not the time. Not the place. Besides, I want to go look around a bit. I'm just opening up the discussion of what happens when we blow the candle out tonight. I'll give you a minute to get dressed."

"Nothing happens."

"We'll see." She paused with her hand on the door handle. "McClain?"

"Yeah?"

"Consider this discussion postponed," she said. "It's not over yet."

That was precisely what he was afraid of.

fifteen

MEN AND WOMEN howled their fury, shaking fists and calling offers as Adam stalked down the aisle with Mia at his side. The canyon at the back of the town was round, hollowed out by what looked like millennia of water running through it, and it formed the perfect arena.

The War Games. He had a feeling he knew exactly what was going to go down. The air had that feel of violence to it, like a thunderstorm about to shatter the peace of the evening.

Yes, whispered the warg within him, scenting the fury in the air around it.

It had been restless ever since they entered this godforsaken place.

There were benches carved into the sandstone, and they were covered with maybe two hundred reivers. A huge wire fence circled the arena, with a couple of strands of wire at the top. As a moth flew into one of those strands, it sparked and the moth's ash carcass dropped to the floor. Huge generators stood at either end of the arena, no doubt providing the electricity, and a couple of flare lights lit the sands. Thousands of insects buzzed in the path of the light.

At the center of it all stood Vex Cypher in her wolf fur, despite the heat from the lights. She held her arms up in the air, and the reivers packed into the arena screamed their love of her. He barely knew the woman, but her face seemed lit from within at the sounds of their adulation.

And that told him enough.

He'd considered Vex dangerous: anyone with this much power over a slave town was. But now he wondered just what drove her. She didn't do this for the profit, she did it for the awe of having others kiss her boots, and that made her temperament unpredictable.

Women in gauzy white danced in the arena. Mia stumbled against his side when she saw them, for they all wore collars. He caught her and they shared a look, but he couldn't afford to look too compassionate.

There were more people held as slaves here than he'd anticipated.

"Watch your feet," he told her, in a harsh voice that belied the look in his eyes.

Ahead of them stalked Zarina Cypher, who looked dangerous in leather. She hadn't said much as she showed them their rooms. Just: "I'll be back in half an hour. Don't be late."

For all of her mother's showmanship, Zarina was the opposite. She ignored the crowd as she led them directly toward Vex's stand of chairs. Somehow she seemed insulated, locked away from it all. Vex was easy to make out. Dangerous, unpredictable, damn near psychotic. But Zarina was a mystery, just like her surname.

"Here," Zarina said, gesturing them to the row of chairs set behind Vex's throne. "Nero, bring beer."

The blond slave nodded and slid to his feet with an elegant grace.

"Boys and girls!" Vex called, stepping up onto the thick rail that ran along the front of her box. The wolf fur slid from her shoulders, pooling on the floor around her boots. "Are you ready for the War Games!"

The crowd screamed back at her, but Adam couldn't take his eyes off the fur on the floor.

The fur wasn't from a wolf. He could just make out hints of a monstrous face tangled in the bottom of it.

Vex Cypher wore the skin of a warg in beast form.

He didn't know why that made him cold. Wargs were monsters through and through, but they'd been human once. Every time he put a silver bullet through one of their skulls he made it quick, because that could be him one day. Taken over by the beast inside him and forced to crave flesh and blood. There was no worse fate known to man than to lose himself so completely, and to be utterly powerless about it.

He looked up, sensing eyes on him. Zarina didn't disguise the fact she'd been watching his face. Her dark almond-shaped eyes glittered with something he couldn't name.

Vex continued, hurling out encouragement and ratcheting the tension in the arena higher. Every now and then something roared in the distance, like a throttle or an engine being gunned. It seemed to vibrate in the rock beneath his feet.

Vex waited a moment to take it all in before she lifted her hand, palm held flat. "Last man standing! Begin!"

She chopped her hand down sharply.

There was a coughing grumble of engines and then a huge truck came screaming out of one of the caves beneath the stands, its front grill transformed by iron spikes, and its flatbed empty. Another car exploded out of the darkness hot on its heels, and this one looked like someone had fused together an iron porcupine with a turtle.

Car after car exited the tunnels. The dancers fled, vanishing into a smaller tunnel, and sand and smoke sprayed as the cars and trucks circled the floor at breakneck speed.

They'd all been heavily modified, with spears welded to their hoods and enormous crush bars on the front. One of them limped along behind the others, but someone had removed the wheels and undercarriage and mounted the top of the car on the bottom of a tank.

Steel screamed as the truck slammed one of the cars into the stone walls at the back of the arena. The tank-car inexorably pushed another into the walls, and slowly rode up over the hood, crushing the other car beneath it.

There was a man inside it, screaming.

No, not a man. A reiver. Adam blinked slowly. It didn't make any difference. No one deserved to die like that.

"My money's on RoJo," Vex said, watching the spectacle with glittering eyes.

Two cars drove into each other, and one flipped up over the other, landing on its back like a turtle. The crowd screamed, fists waving, and men moving through the aisles offering odds on some battle that was coming up next. Adam took the seat Nero directed him to.

It was over blessedly soon, with the reiver from the truck staggering out of his crushed metal carcass and holding his arms in the air as the announcer pronounced his victory. Vex thrilled at the spectacle, and turned back to her party as the cars and bodies were dragged from the ring.

"Just a starter," she promised. "Next up is the Creature Feature, and that's the one we don't want to miss. Ten wargs, only the winner survives."

Adam accepted the mug of beer that Nero offered him, nearly spilling it in surprise. "You fight wargs?"

"What the hell else are you supposed to do with them? They're a plague on the countryside, and when all it takes is one scratch from their claws or teeth to start the transformation, they'd overrun us fairly quickly if they wanted to," Vex said. "My reivers hunt down as many wargs as they can. Cleans them out of my territory, gives my reivers something to do, and this"—she gestured to the arena—"pays for their upkeep."

"Until they die on the sands," Adam said softly.

Jake shot him a sidelong glance from where he sat, with Ellie at his feet.

"Where do you keep them?" Adam asked. He couldn't let it go. The warg within him seemed to have curled up tight and small, which was unusual. He'd never felt fear from it before. "Aren't you scared they'll escape?"

171

Vex snorted. "Not from my cages they won't. I keep them below the arena, and the only way for them to get out is if someone lets them out. My warg cages are Confederacy-made. Nothing's getting out of them once they're in it."

Another link to the Eastern Confederacy. Was this how Vex was paid?

A female reiver begged her captors as they dragged her toward two enormous posts at the edge of the arena. Ignoring her, the guards chained her between the posts, and stepped back out of the way as the crowd began to chant.

"Slash! Slash! Slash!" cried a section of the crowd nearby.

"What are they doing with her?" Mia whispered in his ear. She'd curled against his shoulder, as if a little intimidated.

She was just sheltered enough that the answer didn't spring immediately to mind. Adam, however, had seen far too much of human nature. Maybe it wasn't the wargs that people should fear. "She's their prize."

"Correct," Vex said, sipping her drink and proving just how much attention she was paying to their little group. "Bitch tried to steal from me. I might make her sweat a bit before I rescue her and send her to the slave markets. Or I might just let the match decide her fate."

He flinched as the iron gates at the opposite side of the arena rattled open, and a warg spilled into the midst of the sands in full shift. A monster of disjointed proportions, its black fur shaggy and thick, it ran on all four feet, revealing lean flanks and enough ribs to show how hungry it was.

Vex clearly didn't pay too much for their upkeep after all.

Adam's nostrils flared. He sat up and clasped his hands behind his head, trying to feign nonchalance, but seeing the beast below him confronted all of his worst fears. He felt like he couldn't breathe.

Hurtling forward, its silver eyes gleamed feral as it launched itself at the woman. She screamed, and the warg hit the end of the chain that was leashed to the collar at its throat. Its legs whipped out in front of it as it hit the ground.

The crowd roared.

"They give their women to the monsters?" Mia breathed.

Monsters.... She might as well have cut out his heart.

"Mia." He rested a hand on her knee, aware that she saw herself down in that ring just as much as he did. Only, both of them took a different perception of events. "Keep your voice down." A quick glance showed that no one was paying attention. A second warg had been brought into the pit, and this one moved slowly, still mostly a man, unlike the other one that scuttled about on all fours and snapped and snarled on its leash.

"And the match you've all been waiting for...." The announcer laughed. "His opponent, Reaper!"

The huge warg in his leather pants pumped both fists toward the sky. Matted fur clung to his monstrous head, his wolf teeth snapping. Another section of the crowd cheered.

Now that Reaper stood in the ring, the warg on all fours eyed him, his lip curling back slowly.

Without the medallion around his throat, that could be him down there. Half-human, half-animal, all monster. There was nothing as terrifying in his life as that thought.

I'd rather kill myself.

Could he truly blame the people of Absolution for turning their backs on him? For wanting him out of their lives? Out of their town? Sweat trickled down his spine, and he held on to Mia's thigh tightly.

"Who do you think will win this bout?" Vex asked, tossing a couple of coins at Nero. "Reaper, or Slash?"

"What?"

"Reaper or Slash?" she repeated, reminding him that the wargs in the arena were the least of his problems.

Adam considered them both. Reaper was a giant of a man, with a close-cropped beard and tattoos that crawled up his arms and throat, peering through the straggly fur. As he lifted an enormous iron hammer, the crowd screamed again. But there was something about the way Slash paced to and fro, watching his opponent's every move, that made him hesitate. This one was more wolf than man.

"How many bouts has Slash won?" he asked, trying to avoid offering his opinion.

Vex cast shrewd eyes his way. "All of them, so far, though he hasn't yet faced my champion. I'm saving that match for the third night, if he wins here. Reaper's been brought up from Fort Henry, where he's the champion. Do you think he can kill the beast?"

Everything he saw decreed this match should go to Reaper: the scrawny Slash looked lean, scarred, and underfed. "Slash will win," he said softly.

Vex's smile turned oily. "Put my money on Slash," she told Nero. "I like the way you think, McClain. Slash is mine. Let's hope you don't cost me my coin."

"He's not here for the cheers of the crowd, or whatever else they're promised. He just wants to kill."

"That's because I don't treat them as anything other than what they are. Raiden from Fort Henry nurtures his wargs. Promises them things. Thinks they're human. I don't. They win, or they die. Then they feed my other wargs."

As he looked away, he caught Zarina's eyes. The younger Cypher watched him, and suddenly the sweat down his spine chilled him. She faded into the background so easily that he needed to remind himself that Vex wasn't the only danger.

The bout began. Reaper launched forward, swinging his hammer as Nero hurried off to place Vex's bet.

"Ah. Here comes my favorite." Vex's attention caught on something else.

A tall man strode up the stairs, black hair streaming over his shoulders and an eye patch covering one eye. His short black beard was neatly trimmed, and he wore expensive black leather that seemed not to fit in with the rest of the crowd. They wore scraps of clothing and armor that were clearly salvaged; the very look of this man screamed that he had coin to buy his own. Behind him was a tall redhead on a leash, her eyes downcast and one side of her face bruised. Her pale skin gleamed beneath the floodlights, like polished pearl, and a taupe robe barely covered her.

Reivers reached out to touch her, but the man shot them a fierce look and they cringed backward, away from him.

Jake cursed under his breath and straightened in his chair. "Son of a—" He jerked to a halt, as if remembering himself.

Adam knew, even before he heard Mia suck in a sharp breath, that the woman before him was one of hers.

Blood spattered the sands.

Mia flinched, despising the way it only drove the crowd to a higher frenzy. The poor woman in the chains squirmed and sobbed, trying to free herself, but her fate lay in the hands of the warg who won her.

Or Vex, if she felt merciful.

Swallowing bile, Mia looked up—just in time to see her sister jerked to her knees beside a man wielding a leash in his fist.

Every molecule in her body went still. *Sage.* She started to move, but a hand yanked her back into her seat. McClain. Mia froze. Now wasn't the time to let control slip through her fingers for even a second. Jake eased out a breath at her side, and Mia's hand found his.

Mia willed her sister to look up. Sage wore a couple of bruises on her pale skin, but her lips were pressed firmly together, still hinting at defiance. Whatever she'd been through in the past few days, it hadn't broken her.

That had been Mia's biggest fear, after Sage lost the baby. It had taken months for her sister to recover, and she feared losing Sage to that blackness again, more than anything.

Come on, damn you. A breathless moment as she waited—needed—her sister to look up.

Slowly, as if sensing eyes upon her, Sage lifted her gaze. Their eyes met, and Sage's mouth fell open.

"Nice-looking slave you've got there," McClain said sharply, his hand still resting on her thigh.

Sage's head jerked to him, then she looked down again.

Mia forced herself to control her racing heartbeat. Her baby sister was alive. That was all that mattered. And it didn't look as though she'd broken. There'd been mutiny there, in Sage's green eyes, when she first looked up.

"Rykker," Vex practically purred, extending her hand.

The black-haired man knelt on one knee, kissing the backs of her fingers. "Warlord." The pair of them shared a fond look.

"Good hunting, it seems," Vex said, raking Sage with a mercenary look. "She's glorious."

"Hit upon a small mother lode," Rykker replied. "Got myself a new route."

Son of a bitch. Those were her *people* that he spoke so callously about.

"Relax," McClain murmured, his breath stirring the tight curls that brushed her ear. His steady hand stroked soothing circles on her thigh.

"It seems tonight's the night for people offering me fresh slave routes," Vex said.

Rykker's gaze cut to Mia and the two men with her, but he lingered longest on her, and there was something dark and canny in his gaze that unnerved her. Better if he was looking at her, rather than Ellie, who he *might* recognize, even if the girl kept her face lowered as she knelt at Jake's feet. He dismissed Mia eventually, his flat gaze locking on McClain as if he knew who his adversary was. "I don't think we've met."

"Most likely not," McClain said, not bothering to offer his hand. "I'm McClain. Bounty hunter by trade, someone with his eye on the cash by necessity. This here's my cousin, Jake McClain, and my woman, Mia. We came to pay our respects to the Warlord of Rust City."

"Where you from?" Rykker demanded.

"The Rim."

"Rykker," Vex called, leaning back in her chair and lighting a cigarette. Clearly she didn't like the attention shifting from herself for the moment. "I like this talk of a mother lode. Enlighten me. Just what have you brought back for me?"

"A gift for you, Warlord," Rykker said, yanking Sage forward.

For once, Mia was glad that she and Sage were adopted from different parents. Physically, there was nothing to link them. Nothing to make anyone suspicious.

Cypher examined Sage with a satisfied smile. Mia's hands curled into fists, but she didn't dare open her mouth. Any misstep and she'd condemn them all. Even if the mere thought of shooting Rykker in his sneering face made her heart beat a little quicker.

"She's beautiful. All of that red hair will look wonderful in my menagerie. Well done, Rykker." Vex gestured her daughter forward. "Give Rykker his reward."

Zarina withdrew a small pouch from her belt, and tossed it to Rykker, whose eyes lit up. He slid the pouch in his pocket with a faint smile. "You're generous, Vex."

"I can be. Sit. Enjoy my new friends. We're just getting acquainted."

Rykker settled in the chair directly next to Vex. Clearly the other woman was playing games—she'd deliberately left the chair empty as if she expected him.

"So how many others did you bring me?" Vex murmured, stroking his arm.

"Five," Rykker replied. "One or two of the girls might suit the General's causes."

"Five?" Those stroking fingers stopped. "I thought you said you hit the mother lode."

"A slight difference of opinion developed in Vegas," he replied, gesturing to the shoulder wound he carried. "Yanno and his men double-crossed me. The bastard shot me in the shoulder, and I was forced to retreat with what I had."

Vex blew smoke in his face. She'd withdrawn her hand. "And yet you ride in here like a champion."

"Yanno's a dead man walking," Rykker replied. "I just needed to get this shoulder stitched up, and then I'm going to find that prick, cut his throat, and take back what's mine."

"They'll be ruined by then. Good for little more than fieldwork, or maybe the brothels." Vex ground her cigarette out.

Mia's rage brewed.

"Something wrong?" Rykker asked, noting it.

"I've barely met you," Mia said swiftly, "and already you seem like the kind of man who likes to make excuses."

Rykker paused. "You let her speak for you?" he asked McClain.

That hand squeezed her thigh in warning. "I think you underestimate our relationship. Mia and I are partners. In all matters. The words that come from her lips might as well come from mine."

"What kind of man lets a bitch do his talking for him?" Rykker asked.

"I don't know, Rykker," Zarina suddenly interrupted. "What kind of man does?"

He slowly became aware of whose side he was sitting at.

Vex tapped those long elegant nails on the side of her chair. "Yes... do tell."

Rykker flashed his teeth at Zarina, his lip curling before he turned to placate Vex. "You and your daughter are warriors, Vex. Not bitches. You know what I meant."

"I like the girl," Vex said. "She seems like a warrior to me."

Mia curled back against McClain, resting her head on his shoulder. Point to her.

"You come in here," Vex said, looking fierce now, "calling my guest a bitch. You know I don't like that word."

"My apologies." Rykker started to sweat.

"You bring me one slave as a tribute, and barely have a handful of others to show for your efforts." Vex's eyebrow lifted. "And you let Yanno steal your mother lode."

"That's where you're wrong," Rykker argued.

"Wrong?" The word was laced with caution.

"The mother lode wasn't the first batch of slaves we took. No. I was referring to the area we took them from. Got a real good look. Lots of women and children. Not a great deal of security. Ranchers, townsfolk... there are whole settlements there, virtually mine for the taking. I just need the manpower."

The glacial look in Vex's eye became distant. "Talk is cheap. I want to see action. You owe me another tribute for the offense you've caused tonight. Bring me another and maybe I'll forget the bad taste in my mouth."

Rykker pushed to his feet. "I will."

"Oh, and Rykker?"

"Yeah?"

"You might be my favorite, but there are many others at your heels. It's a long way to fall. Now get out of my sight."

As he strode past them, he shot Mia a dark look, one she had no trouble reading.

She'd just made an enemy.

A dangerous one.

sixteen

———➤

"I SHOULDN'T HAVE said anything."

Adam undid the collar from Ellie's throat and curled the leather around his fist as Mia paced.

"Thanks," Ellie said, with a sigh. She rubbed at the red mark where it had rested.

"We can't afford to be seen as weak," Adam countered, tossing the collar on the bed. "Besides, I think Vex likes you."

"Vex liked Rykker," Mia pointed out.

True.

The four of them reconvened in Adam's room following the massacre at the War Games. Mia couldn't stop pacing, but Adam suspected that had more to do with the shock of seeing her sister and not being able to do anything about Sage's imprisonment. The jitters extended to Jake, who seemed far too quiet. Trouble brewed within the other man's hard body.

Only he and Ellie seemed unaffected.

"Do you think he'll come after us?" Ellie asked.

"He doesn't seem the sort to let bygones be bygones," Adam replied. He'd met men like that in the past. Rykker didn't seem the sort to kiss Vex's heel and enjoy it, so he'd probably take this upset out on the four of them. "Watch your backs, okay. What's the rule?"

"Nobody goes anywhere alone," Ellie parroted. She looked tired. "We know Vex has Sage now. Where do you think they took the others?"

Mia squeezed her shoulder. "Rykker said he had five others, so that means they're all still alive. We can work out where he'd keep them in the morning."

"This is fucking bullshit," Jake declared, tension radiating through his body. "How can you all just sit here? That bitch has my wife. Who knows what she plans to do with her?"

"For now? Not much, I think," Adam replied.

Mia stepped closer to Adam's side, as if she subconsciously looked to him for protection now. "Jake—"

"No!" Jake jerked to his feet and headed for the door. "I'll be damned if I'm letting my wife stay one more night in this hellhole."

"McClain!" Mia warned.

"On it." Adam moved fast. He grabbed Jake by the arm, but Jake moved with furious grace, swinging a punch toward his face.

The blow glanced off the forearm he hastily flung up, and then he used his greater weight to shove Jake against the door. They wrestled furiously for a second. Anger gave the other man a strength he could barely match.

Adam pinned Jake against the hard timber, his forearm pressed across Jake's throat and his other hand twisted in the man's collar.

"You get your hands off me, you filthy fucking—"

"Jake! Stop it." Mia touched his arm.

Jake sagged against the door, his breath coming in ragged gasps, and his eyes showing far too much white as he glanced at her.

Adam sucked in a lungful of air. That had been close.

"I'll let you go the second you start acting rationally," Adam replied, cutting him off fast. If Jake blurted out his secret right now, who knew how Mia would react? He needed them both to listen.

Or they'd get themselves collared for real.

Jake glared at him, the pulse in his throat throbbing.

"You walk out that door," Adam growled, "and you not only sacrifice any chance of getting your wife out of here safely, but you condemn Mia to the same fate. And I won't let you do that. You understand me?"

"Who the fuck are you to order me around?"

"Jake!" Mia snapped.

"I'm the only one thinking clearly right now." Adam held him there for a long second, but he felt the tension melt out of the other man, and finally eased up. Thank God. "I know this is hard for you. The both of you. You need to trust me."

"We do," Mia replied promptly.

Even if she shouldn't. Damn it, she'd hate him when she realized what he was keeping from her.

Jake looked away, his nostrils flaring. "How do I do this?" he asked hoarsely.

Ellie slipped her hand into his and rubbed his shoulder. "The same way we all do. One foot in front of the other."

"You listen to me," Adam replied. He included Mia in his glare. "The pair of you are emotionally tied to this. I get that." He let go of Jake's collar. "You brought me along for a reason. So let me do my job here. I'm in charge. I call the shots right now. And the pair of you need to be patient. Vex doesn't trust us. Not yet. She made that perfectly clear in her private quarters, and with that display tonight."

"Yeah. She's scary." Mia shivered.

"And she's probably not the dangerous one," Adam pointed out. "Vex is unpredictable, but I think I've got a handle on her. Zarina's the one I don't know much about. And she was watching everything that went on tonight, especially the way the pair of you reacted when you saw Sage."

Mia's face paled. "You think she'll tell her mother?"

"Who knows?" He rubbed his mouth. "Like I said, I can't read much of her intentions yet, but we all need to be very careful of the way we act around her. I don't think she likes Rykker much, if that helps."

Mia looked thoughtful. "Well, Vex isn't going to touch Sage. Not tonight." She wrapped her arms around herself, her voice hardening. "Can't touch the merchandise, right?"

"I don't like this any more than you do," Adam pointed out. "But Sage and the others aren't being mishandled right now." He took a step back, allowing Jake some space, but staying close enough that he could grab him again if he tried to do anything stupid. "So we need to assess the situation. We need more information, and to get a good look around. We have time. What we don't have is ammunition, allies, or an escape plan."

Jake sank onto the bed, his hands clasped firmly between his legs, the very picture of stillness. "Vex won't sell her," he said, looking up slowly, his eyes revealing the horrors of a man who'd seen the end of his world. "When I saw her there I was so relieved because I thought that at least she wouldn't be touched, but now.... How can we get her back from the fucking warlord who runs this place? She's clearly got buyers lined up, so she'll take one look at our money and laugh in our faces."

"It they're Confederate buyers, then she can't afford to cross them," Adam mused. "And they can pay more than we could even dream of. So that's out of the question now. We're going to have to steal her and the others back. Plan A is down the drain."

"So what?" Mia drawled. "We go to Plan B? Burn the place down?"

"Don't forget Vex's nice little promise to castrate the pair of us and sell us into slavery if she catches us stealing from her," Jake shot back.

"You did turn an interesting shade of green," Ellie noted.

Adam dragged a chair out from the table and gestured the three of them to sit. "Sage is now Vex's pet. We don't really know what that means, but it buys us a little time. I'll head out tonight to have a decent look around."

"We need to know when Vex's supply route to the Confederacy leaves," Mia added. "Do they come here? Or does she send the people to them? You say we have time, but how many days do we have?"

"That's what we need to find out," he replied.

"I'll come," Mia said, taking the seat next to him.

Adam folded his arms on the table. "I can move faster—"

"You're not winning this argument," she replied, a fiery glow in her dark eyes. "So save your breath. There are only three of us, and we *need* you. You've probably got mad skills that I can't even imagine, but even you can't watch your own back. So it's either Jake or me, and he looks fit to fall over. Plus—nobody goes anywhere alone. Your rule."

"I'm alright," Jake protested.

Mia arched a brow in his direction. "You've been going for days with barely any rest. I know you're not sleeping. I barely am either, but I've had more than you. And let's be honest, Jake, right now I could take you one-on-one and you know it. You need sleep, or the next time someone looks sideways at Sage you'll blow up, exactly like you just did before."

Jake clearly didn't like it, but he shut up and then dragged out the third chair for Ellie. "So... reconnaissance tonight?"

"Mia and I will check out Vex's stronghold, see where they're keeping Sage and what the security is like," Adam continued. "The streets are full of reivers partying after the War Games, which gives us some cover."

"And a lot of potential eyes."

"We'll deal with that," he replied confidently. "Reivers aren't known for their sanitary habits, which means we'll probably smell them coming, if we don't hear them."

Jake's eyes flashed to his in wary understanding, but Mia merely nodded.

"I was speaking to Zarina after the games," he continued. "She mentioned that the slave markets reopen tomorrow. Rykker's got a fresh haul he wants to sell, which no doubt includes your other friends. Jake, you get some sleep tonight. You and Ellie are on the markets tomorrow. Buy the others back if you can." He dragged out the money pouch he carried and counted out just enough coins to keep them here for a few days, if everything didn't go to plan. He tossed the rest to Jake. "If we can't buy them, then track who does. We'll reassess after breakfast. Any questions?"

Mia chewed on her lip. "We need to work out how we're going to get out of here once we free our people. We need transport."

"And probably a distraction," Jake added.

Adam merely smiled. This fucking place made the skin on the back of his neck rise. "When the time comes, I can provide the distraction."

Plan B it was.

It would make him feel a hell of a lot better to know Rust City was in ashes.

The night echoed with howling as drunken reivers chased each other through the streets and fought in bloody brawls that seemed to be for pure enjoyment.

Mia shivered as she watched a pack of them cheering two bloody comrades on as they grappled each other in the center of their circle. McClain halted at a corner, drawing her against his side. So far they hadn't been challenged as they slipped quietly through the streets, ignoring the mayhem. Just two more reivers in the crowd. Mia had braided her black hair back fiercely, and dirtied her face a little to look like some of the other female reivers she'd seen. She had both knives at her hips, plus her pistol, and she kept reminding herself to strut as if she owned the place.

"There it is," McClain murmured, his hand on the small of her back as he guided her into the shadows of a doorway.

She peered around the corner. Vex's stronghold loomed in the night, its stark white walls bleached in the moonlight like a skull. The wire fence around it wasn't patrolled. Mia pointed to where the fence met the wall of the building. "We can't come at it from the front without being seen from a mile away. But maybe there's somewhere to climb that wall around the back?"

"Mmm." McClain's breath warmed her ear. "I'd be happier if it wasn't so frigging bright. We'd stand out against those walls like—"

A shot suddenly echoed, and they both jumped.

A gun? No, a flare gun.

The flare sailed into the sky with a hiss and the world erupted in violent light. Cheers went up, and a couple across the street stopped kissing long enough to look at the flare.

Rust City lit up like frigging Christmas, painting the pair of them vividly in the doorway.

McClain swore, and Mia tugged him around the corner into a run. They darted past tin shanties and dirt alleyways as she listened for an outcry. None came. Mia slowed to a trot at McClain's side. Running here would only look suspicious, especially considering they were right outside Vex's stronghold.

Still, it took everything she had not to leap out of her skin when a cat suddenly hissed and darted between their feet.

"Hell," she whispered. She wasn't made for subterfuge like this. It was rapidly becoming clear that she wasn't cut out for any of this; shooting people, fighting hand-to-hand, and trying not to show how much she bled inside when she saw what these reivers did to innocent people. But she would just keep doing what needed to be done. Find a way to survive this hellish experience.

It helped having McClain there, a steady, calm influence at her side.

"This way," McClain said. He eyed the stronghold across the street. "Focus on what we're here for."

Sage. Her heart rabbited in her ears, but she nodded. *Right.*

Somewhere in that building her sister lay awake, no doubt listening to the same rabid howls.

They took refuge tucked against another tin shanty. McClain knelt in the shadows, examining the place. Bars lined the windows, but the wire fence was lower here, and outbuildings inside the yard provided some cover.

"That's Vex's chambers right there," McClain pointed to the top of the building. "And those five rooms there at the back have bars on the windows. It stands to reason that she'd want to keep the slaves she's shipping to the Confederacy close. She wants them untouched, and despite her hold on them, I wouldn't trust the reivers either.

"I can climb that wall," McClain said. "I'll see if I can find your sister, to let her know what we're up to. She's just as dangerous to us right now as Jake is, but if I can talk to her...."

"What about me?"

He began unbuckling his hip holster. "You're watching my back. You see something unusual, then give a yell, so I can get the hell out of there."

She ached to see her sister. But he spoke sense. The adobe walls were sheer, and she was tired. Her body still ached from the blow she'd taken to the shoulder in Vegas. There was no way she could climb that wall. *Patience. Just a little patience.* Then she could get her sister out of here.

"Tell her I love her and that we'll get her out," Mia whispered.

"I will." McClain handed her the holster. "The gun's loaded. You have any hassles here, then don't be afraid to use it."

"I won't." Mia caught his hand as he turned to go. Breaking into Vex's complex took dangerous to a new level. And he'd done more than enough for all of them. "Watch your back."

McClain's face softened, as if he saw something in her expression that she couldn't quite hide. "I'll be back for you, Mia. I promise." His voice was rough sand, and he stroked the back of her hand with his thumb.

A thousand thoughts sprang to mind. A thousand words she didn't think she could say right now. Instead, Mia lifted onto her toes and pressed her lips to his cheek. "I'll hold you to that promise," she told him. "You and I.... It's the worst time in the world to start anything, but I think we've already passed that point. I want you back, and I want you unharmed. Got it?"

His warm palm caressed her jaw, and his breath whispered over her lips as he turned and pressed a gentle kiss to her forehead. "Got it."

Then he was gone, vanishing into the night as if he owned it.

Mia settled in to wait.

The climb gave new meaning to the word "brutal."

Adam's shoulders ached as he finally cleared the ledge just below the first barred window. The past few days were starting to catch up to him, and he'd need to get some rest tonight. Even a warg had limits.

Pressing his back against the wall, he scanned the streets below. Nothing moved. He couldn't see Mia, but he knew where she was. And if he couldn't see her, then neither could anyone else.

Scenting the air, he eased his way along the narrow ledge. The rough walls scraped his skin through his shirt, but there was nothing to hold on to here. Two more steps until he reached the first window.... Adam reached for the bars, his shirt flapping in the warm desert night breeze.

Made it. His fingers curled around the bars and he hauled himself closer, taking a good look down. The distance to the ground blurred. He looked up sharply. Heights were one of the few things that made his balls tighten.

He'd caught just enough of Sage's natural odor at the arena that he thought he'd be able to track her. Hunting like this played up his other senses, ones he'd denied for far too long. For the past nine years he'd fought too hard to smother all of his otherworldly instincts. Now he needed them, and it was strange to admit that.

The warg inside stretched, intrigued, as he loosened the reins of control he strapped it down with.

Come on, he snarled at it. *Find me the girl.*

The warg lived for pure instinct alone. Blood, flesh, hunger, need. He'd never tried to steer that instinct before, and it felt like wrestling with himself. Sweat dripped down his forehead as heat filled his eyes. Every shadow around him suddenly grew clearer, and he could feel his vision growing stronger. Scents exploded to life around him as his body made minute changes. His muscles quivered as he stood on the edge of total transformation. His body wanted to push further, to complete its monstrous act, but he needed his brain to be in control. Not the warg.

It was harder than he'd expected to hold himself there. If he could just bloody operate like this, it might almost be worth it.

With the partial change he could experience the world better, his senses coming to life like a barren desert after the rains, but with that came the rest of it. The heat in his mouth. His teeth threatening to burst through his gums. He'd seen others lost to the monster within, hunting beneath the moon. It terrified him so much that he couldn't force it now. It was either lock it down tight, or let it take over, and he couldn't do that.

Adam slumped back against the wall. The warg receded. His vision faded again. Still better than human, but nowhere near what it could be.

Fine. He'd do this with his own instincts. The ones that made him the man he was.

Scent filtered through the open window behind the bars. He didn't think it was the right cell. Someone slept on the narrow bed in there, but the musky fragrance of a man made him withdraw. The last thing he needed was someone crying out in surprise.

He moved on, placing foot over foot on the narrow ledge. Nothing to hold on to up here, not until he reached the next window. Wind whispered through his clothes, reminding him of just how open this position left him.

Cold sweat poured off him. He snatched for one of the bars at the next window.

"Hello?" someone whispered fearfully. "Who's there?"

Scent shifted past him. Pure and clean. "Sage?" he breathed.

A pale face swam into view. Sage peered at him hesitantly, then glanced over her shoulder. "Who are you?" she whispered, crossing swiftly to the window. Recognition dawned. "You're the man who was with Mia, Ellie, and Jake." Her eyes narrowed. "I've seen you before. In Mia's bar. You're her McClain."

Her McClain?

He'd heard Mia mention a sister, but he'd spent most of his time in Salvation Creek sleeping off a hangover. He'd never noticed a redhead there, and probably wouldn't have presumed the pair of them were related. Mia had kept him well away from her private life. "She talked about me?"

"A regular pain in her ass was how she put it," Sage whispered.

That sounded more like it.

Sage's wariness vanished however, and she gave him a disconcertingly thorough stare, as if there'd been more to it than that.

"I'm a bounty hunter working for your sister." The room behind her was bare; a metal bed with a lumpy mattress and a single blanket. Water basin on the floor and a refuse bucket in the corner. Nothing much else. Clearly Vex valued those she took as slaves more than the rest of the reivers did, but there were limits. "Can you talk?"

"Quietly." She gripped the bars. "Is Jake there?"

"No. Just me. Mia's keeping watch."

Sage released an unsteady breath, her knuckles paling around the bars. Those big green eyes suddenly glistened. "You have to get them out of here. It's not safe. If Vex realizes who they are, and why they're here—"

"Hey." He curled his hand around hers. "Look at me."

Sage did. The blind faith in her expression nearly undid him.

"I won't let anything happen to them. But if you think that I can convince the pair of them to turn around, then you don't know them very well."

Sage laughed under her breath, a fierce, sucked-in little sound that told him how close to breaking she was. It died swiftly. "You don't know what Vex is like. If she finds them here...."

"She's not going to. I promise. You just need to keep quiet, and try not to look at the others too often. We told Vex we're here to buy slaves. We just need a little time to work out how to get you out. Can you hold on until then?"

It was clear she didn't entirely believe him, but some of the life was starting to come back into her eyes, now that she knew she wasn't alone. "Yeah. I'll be alright."

"Are you okay? Nobody's hurt you, have they?"

Sage shook her head. "Just bruises." She hesitated. "Some of the reivers got a little touchy and they talked about doing things... but it's... it's okay. I'm okay. Rykker didn't want them touching us."

"What about the other girls? And the Hannaway kid?"

"Thea's in the cell next door. They brought her in after me, but I could hear her voice. I don't know what happened to the others," Sage admitted.

Which made his job just that little bit more difficult. Two parties to rescue, instead of just one larger one. Jake could look for the others in the morning when he made his rounds of the slave markets. At least there was one more confirmed safe in Vex's stronghold.

"We're going to get you out," he promised. "All of you."

"You can't. This place is locked up tighter than a prison. There's got to be at least two hundred reivers in the town. Possibly more."

"We'll deal with that," he replied. "Can you describe the interior of Vex's stronghold to me? We saw her courtyard and her throne room, but I need to know a little about the layout inside. And what her security detail is like."

Sage paused.

"There's no detail too small," he prompted. "I just need to know what the situation is like inside."

That got her talking and once she started, it seemed to calm her. The place was exactly as he'd suspected. Vex's private quarters; Zarina's chambers below; and cells for the private slaves Vex had plans for. Sage had seen at least five guards slinking around—dangerous-looking men who resembled Rykker more than they did the other reivers—but she didn't think Vex was overly concerned with security.

"I don't think she believes anyone would attack her," Sage murmured. "She laughs sometimes, and calls the reivers wild dogs. Makes them cower and kiss her boots, and they do."

A serious mistake to underestimate them like that. Unless Vex knew she had some other sort of hold on them?

"Tell me about Zarina."

"Zarina?" Sage squinted through the bars at him. "I don't know much about her. She hasn't said a word to any of us girls."

It still bothered him. "Is she friendly with her mother? Any of the other reivers?"

Thought raced in Sage's eyes, but she ultimately shrugged. "I don't really know. She seems quiet and... just there, I suppose. Watching everything."

Which was the same impression he'd had.

"I'd better go before someone sees me." His voice softened. "Both Mia and Jake wanted me to let you know how much they love you."

A shaky breath escaped her. "I love them too. Make sure they know that. And that they're fools to even attempt this."

"You don't know how lucky you are to have people like that who are there for you."

Sage smiled sadly. "I do know. It doesn't mean I'm not going to kick their asses for doing something so stupid."

In that moment she sounded so much like Mia that he saw the resemblance. "Be prepared for anything. It might take us a day or two, but we might need you ready to move at a second's warning."

"Got it. I'll get word to Thea somehow. Thank you... for looking after Mia. She needs someone like you."

His heart fell in his chest, but he managed a smile. "It's not like that."

"Isn't it?" Sage arched a brow. "I saw the pair of you at the arena. I've never seen my sister look so... trusting... with a man. She's never let anyone in. Guarded like a bank, that's my Mia, but I know there's a heart of gold under there." Sage paused. "Just as long as you know that too?"

"I know it."

Sage patted his knuckles. "You'd better go. They do rounds every hour or so."

Adam looked around. Light beams soared into the velvety sky nearby, as though someone was having fun with the flare lights. "Look out for yourself. We'll spring you both as soon as we get a chance."

McClain materialized out of the shadows. Instantly Mia straightened.

"How is she?" she demanded. "Is she okay? Is she hurt?"

"Bruises," he replied, his gaze still raking the streets. "Not much else. She's scared, but she was more concerned with you being here. She's afraid Vex will get her hands on you. Promises to kick your ass once she gets out of there. Both you and Jake."

That alone gave her reassurance where nothing else would have. A choked cry caught in her throat and she launched herself at McClain, burying her face in his shirt. Strong arms caught her tight, until she could feel the thump of his heart against her chest and smell his soap. Closing her eyes, she breathed in the scent of him. Sage was safe. She hadn't let herself think too much about what exactly might be happening to her baby sister in the past few days. "Thank you for everything."

"We're not finished yet." McClain cleared his throat. His hand soothed her braided hair, the calluses catching. "You all good?"

It was becoming far too easy to find refuge in these arms. "Yeah. You give the world's best hugs, do you know that?"

Their fingers laced as they stepped apart. Just a simple thing really, but her chest tightened. McClain looked down, as though he didn't know what to do about the gesture. "Yeah. Eden gave me plenty of practice."

His sister. Mia squeezed his fingers at the way his voice softened. There were wounds there, and she could empathize. "We'd better—"

Footsteps suddenly echoed on the concrete outside the stronghold. Mia's eyes widened, and McClain tilted his head to listen, his entire body going still.

"Move," he rasped, shoving at her. "It's a couple of reivers."

Mia raked the area, but there was nowhere to go. Any move they made would only draw attention. She grabbed his wrist, and dragged him back into the shadows.

"Mia! We need—"

Grabbing a handful of his hair, she dragged his face down to hers and met his mouth with hers.

McClain stiffened against her, and Mia kissed him for all she was worth. Adrenaline slammed through her veins and her hearing pricked up as she listened to those footsteps come closer. *Come on, damn you.* She could feel the moment McClain realized what she was doing. All of the reluctance slid out of him, and he opened his mouth, capturing hers with a renewed intensity. One step toward her, then he hauled her against the wall of his chest.

Suddenly it wasn't just pretense. Mia's tongue darted against his own, teasing, coaxing him in. And where she led, McClain followed.

She could feel all of that delicious tension lock the muscles in his arms, as she rubbed them.

Her back hit the wall, the ridged tin digging into her butt and shoulders. She tore her mouth free, enough to whisper in his ear, "Haul me up."

Those large hands caught her behind the thighs, and McClain obliged. Mia's hips nestled around his as he used his body to grind her against the wall. She gasped. Vex wasn't wrong. That was one hell of a weapon in his jeans.

Her fingertips grazed the short buzz of his hair, and she bit his lip as she kissed him back. She didn't want to stop. Ever. Maybe this was pretend, maybe it was just an act to fool the reivers, but it felt real.

And worse, it ignited the need in her blood.

She didn't think she could keep her hands off him after this.

"Give her one for me!" one of the reivers shouted.

Mia broke the kiss long enough to shoot the guards a fierce glare and the finger. "Fuck off, you bastards. Can't you see we're getting busy here?"

One of them chuckled and grabbed his crotch at her, but the other two barely shot her a look as they continued on their path. She'd seen how the female reivers behaved at the War Games.

Her heartbeat still kicked like a mule in her chest as the reiver guards vanished. She could feel McClain silently watching her, his own breath coming short and excited. Mia looked up, one hand on his chest. For a second she forgot everything: the danger they were in, the reivers around them.... Suddenly, all she could see was him.

And she could feel him still.

That hard erection pressing exactly where she wanted it. The wetness of her panties. They stood frozen, staring at each other. Mia made a little sound, her hips rolling faintly. The seam of his jeans rode over her clit.

McClain's fingers brushed against the sensitive skin above her hips. He shuddered. "Mia. Stop. I can't think while you're doing that."

Precisely the point.

McClain stepped away, her legs sliding down his as he helped her to stand. If she could. She felt shaky all over. Nipples hard. Exhausted, but riding the edge of something she didn't think she could let go of so easily. Every inch of her body felt alive.

"You nearly gave me a damned heart attack," he murmured.

"I don't think that's all I gave you." Jesus. Was that her voice?

Their gazes clashed. Something smoky and hot danced through his green eyes, turning them almost gray. Feral intensity lit his features as he honed in on the press of her hard nipples through her shirt. The fingers on his left hand curled into a fist.

"This isn't done yet."

"It's done," he growled.

Arguments chased through her mind, but suddenly she could hear reiver voices echoing in the streets. Curse them.

"Time to get back to the rooms." McClain's voice held the faint note of regret.

"Great idea," she replied, but she didn't add anything more.

She'd made her decision.

She was tired of running.

seventeen

THEY SPOKE NOT a word on the swift return to their rooms. Jake's snores echoed in the narrow hallway, and Mia slipped through the door, into the heat of the room.

Outside it was growing cold, the desert night laced with chill. In here, the shutters contained the heat, and thin bands of light were all that crept through. They slashed across the bed, drawing her attention to it.

As if she wasn't still alight from that moment in the alley.

Behind her, McClain closed the door quietly. She felt like that moment stole all of the oxygen in the room. Every movement he made was small and concise. Thoughtful. Careful. He couldn't have dragged out the moment any longer if he'd tried.

Well. There was more than one way to skin a cat. Mia dragged the bandolier from her shoulder, discarding it on the floor.

McClain's shoulders stiffened. Warily, he turned, his gaze lighting on the discarded leather. Then he looked up.

And suddenly the room was far too small.

"We're not doing that again," he told her.

"Doing what?" she taunted, tugging at the snap on her belt. It rustled as she dragged it through the belt loops on her jeans. McClain's hungry eyes watched every movement. "I wasn't planning anything." Mia tossed the belt aside. "I was just intending to get into bed."

Reaching up, she pulled the tie free from her hair. Silky black curls tumbled over her shoulders, and she brushed her hands beneath them, trying to cool the back of her neck.

"Yeah, right. You've got that look in your eye."

"What look is that?" She took a step back toward the bed and eased onto it. Her fingers went to her boots, but she watched him the entire time.

McClain bared his teeth at her. He paced. "The look that says 'trouble.' I know what you're thinking is going to happen. It's not."

Who was he trying to fool? Mia tossed one boot aside, then the next. Groaning at the feel of freedom from her narrow boots, she lay back on the bed with her arms spread behind her. "For a man who protests so much, you didn't seem to be averse to kissing me."

Mia rolled her head to watch him.

"We didn't have a choice. And that was your idea, not mine." Fanning himself, he headed for the corner and the small electric fan there—more for something to do, she thought, than for any desire for a breeze. It buzzed to life with a groan, streamers of paper fluttering off it.

The sluggish breeze cooled her damp skin, but not by much.

"I can still taste you, did you know?"

"Mia." A warning growl.

"What changed?" she asked.

He started unbuttoning his shirt, then clearly thought better of it. "What do you mean?"

"You made me a lot of dirty promises when you were drinking in my bar."

"I was drunk, Mia." McClain tossed his belt aside. The single bars of light through the shutters highlighted the erection straining his jeans. "I said a lot of things I didn't mean."

She rolled onto her hip. "I call bullshit." Draping a hand down over her breasts, she caressed herself through her tank. And he watched every movement. "Every word you've uttered since you walked through that door is a lie.

"Something changed," she said, reading his reaction. "You wanted it then. And you want it now. Every time you touch me, or look at me like that, I can see how much you want it. But then you get this constipated look on your face, like you're trying to tell yourself you don't." Mia slid her hand up under her tank, tracing circles across her hip. "Something happened that night that Jake wanted a quiet word with you. What did he say?"

Those hungry eyes narrowed. "The truth. That you and I have no future together. I like you a lot, Mia. I genuinely like you. And I don't want to break your heart when I leave. Please stop doing that. I'm just a man, one trying to do the right thing. And you're destroying me right now."

Mia's hand stilled. Guilt descended. Guilt and frustration, and a bittersweet loneliness that ached in her chest. She'd wanted more but instead she was pushing him, shredding his willpower. And that wasn't fair.

Even if her body—her heart and soul—ached with denial.

Something haunted him.

Slowly Mia sat up, trying to cool the furious ache beneath her skin. She'd come here to get laid. That wasn't going to happen, and it physically hurt. Or maybe she was so fucking tired that she couldn't tell if it was her body or her heart that burned. The fan buzzed. "All I want is for you to stop pretending. To stop lying to me. I know barely anything about you, McClain. Every time I look around you're there for me, but you won't let me near. And. It. Is. Killing. Me."

Exhaustion painted dark rings beneath his eyes. "I know."

She wanted to growl with frustration. One step forward. Two steps back. "That's it? *'I know.'* That's all you're going to give me?"

"It's easier this way," he said.

"Easier for who?"

"Easier for you."

"That would presume that you were finding any part of this difficult." She couldn't keep the bite out of her voice.

"Mia." He pinched the bridge of his nose. "I'm trying not to hurt you. Really trying. If I didn't give a damn about you, we'd have been in bed weeks ago. But there are things about me that you don't know. I'm not a good man."

At least he was honest about keeping something from her. "I hate secrets."

"I know."

"Fine," she said in a low growl as she collapsed back on the bed. "Let's pretend that kiss never happened." Even as she said it, she could feel the ghost of its caress on her sensitive lips. "No kissing. No touching. No sex. You can sit down. It's not like I'm going to push where I'm not welcome."

McClain hesitantly sat on the end of the bed. "If I could be the man you needed, Mia, then I wouldn't be saying no. But... it's complicated. If you knew my secret then you wouldn't look at me the same way. And I don't think I could bear that. Not from you."

Mia stared at the ceiling. "You don't know that. Maybe you're underestimating me?"

"I do know that."

Fine. "I just can't imagine you doing something bad. It's not your style." She laughed bitterly. "Hell, if you were really the kind of man you paint yourself as, you wouldn't be warning me off. You'd have taken what you wanted and kept your mouth shut."

Silence fell. McClain rolled slowly onto his back at her side. Inches separated them. It might as well have been miles. "Can we talk about something else?"

"Like what?"

"Sage is adopted," he murmured.

Mia glared at him. Oh no. She wasn't going to go spilling everything about her life when he barely gave her anything. "What gave it away?"

McClain flinched.

And suddenly she felt like a bitch. A tired, frustrated, grumpy bitch. She dragged the heels of her palms to her eyes. "Sorry. I need sleep. Badly."

"We both do."

Mia sighed and reached for his hand. She couldn't lose him. "Still friends?"

McClain eyed her, his head twisted to the side. "Friends?"

They'd never been that. She didn't quite know how to classify their relationship. "If you want."

"I would like that," he whispered.

Mia rolled onto her hip, tucking the pillow under her head and still holding his hand. "We were both adopted. Susan and Greg Gray couldn't have kids of their own, so they raised children for those who couldn't. They were almost sixty when we came along, so I kind of have other brothers and sisters, technically, but Sage and I were raised together. The others had their own lives by that point, and we don't see them much anymore. They moved on.

"I don't know who my mother was, but she left me on their doorstep when I was a baby. I used to get upset over that but as Susan pointed out, this is not the sort of world that makes it easy for young girls who fall pregnant. Whoever my mother was, she knew that Susan and Greg were renowned for raising other people's kids, so she must have loved me. Enough to find me wonderful parents."

"Do you miss her?"

"I miss them all," Mia corrected. "Sometimes I regret the fact that I never got to know her, or what her story was. And I miss Mom and Dad terribly. They were great people. Wonderful parents. And they gave me Sage too, which is the biggest blessing in my life. I don't know what I'd do without her."

"Kid sisters," he said dryly. McClain lay flat on his back on the bed, scrubbing a hand over his face. "Can't live with them sometimes, can't live without them."

"Yeah." She looked at him. "Sometimes people don't get it. What family means to me."

"I know. The rest is just a technicality." His voice trailed off and he stared at the ceiling, going someplace distant.

She recognized that distance. It had been in his eyes when he spent all of that time in her bar, staring into his glass of whiskey as if it held the secrets of the world within it. McClain had demons. She'd known that the moment she met him.

"That sounded like it had hidden meaning to it," she said softly, sounding him out.

McClain's head rolled toward her. He'd shaved that afternoon, but she kind of missed the scruff of dark beard that had taken over his jawline in the last day or so. In all the time she'd known him, she'd never seen him looking anything other than clean-shaven. It put a dint in the myth of him. Made him seem more human to her. More touchable. He was so in control of himself that sometimes it seemed like she'd never breach that gap between them. Maybe shaving was just another means to take ownership of his life?

"There was a little girl that I was raising," he finally admitted. Exhaustion created dark hollows beneath his eyes. "I was always 'Uncle Adam' to her, but it felt like she was mine. I would have moved mountains for that kid."

"What happened?"

Please not something bad.... But maybe that was the secret he carried, the one that weighed heavily on his shoulders, and wouldn't let him reach out to her.

"Her name was Lily," he said, voice soft and confessional in the darkened room. "And she belonged to a friend of mine, Luc Wade. He couldn't raise her for a long time, so I stepped in. At first it was a duty: I owed him that. But Lily... she was the most loving little kid. She used to have these nightmares, and she'd come up to my room as though she wanted to sit out front of my door. As though that made her feel safe. So I'd call her in and... I remember the first night she fell asleep in my arms. The way she curled herself in against my neck, as though nothing bad could ever touch her again when I was there. That was when I knew she was mine." His voice trailed off. "Or she was. Wade came back, and you know, of all the losses I've had in my life that one was the worst."

"So he just rides back in and picks up where he left off?"

McClain tilted his head toward her. "It's not like that."

The moment stretched out and it became clear that he wasn't going to say anything more.

Right. Half a confession then. Mia sighed and rolled flat on her back, staring at the ceiling. Every time she thought she was getting somewhere with him, he backed away.

And she didn't know why that bothered her so much. This wasn't going anywhere. She knew that. She'd been telling herself those words ever since he strolled in through the doors of her bar, his boots caked with dust and his black cowboy hat hiding his eyes. That moment had nearly knocked her off her feet, and she realized that she still hadn't fully recovered from it.

A single moment and she knew that Adam McClain was going to leave scars on her life that she might never recover from.

The question was: would it be worth it? A touch of paradise, maybe just one night in his arms, branding that memory on her skin for all the long years ahead.

Would it be enough for her?

Every bone in her body felt like lead. Mia closed her eyes. She couldn't answer that. Everything in her past told her not to take that risk. All she knew was loss. The woman who'd given birth to her; the parents who'd lovingly raised her as their own; the boy who'd broken her heart.

But she also knew what years of guarding herself felt like.

No one to sit beside at night and whisper all of her daily musings in his ear. No warm arms around her in bed. She was tough enough to survive by herself. She had Sage, after all, and a job that kept her busy.

But was it enough for her to merely survive? Longing filled her chest, an aching chasm that threatened to swallow her whole. *Just once, just once, just once*, that longing whispered. Just once to pretend, and then she could cherish that memory for the rest of her life.

If he would let her in....

"There are so many things I can't tell you," McClain said, as if trying to explain.

"You're not married, are you? No other woman tucked away somewhere?"

"No."

"You're not a murderer, or diseased, or——?"

"No." McClain shook his head in frustration. "Mia, I can't——"

She pressed her finger to his soft lips. Fine then. "I'm not dreaming of happily ever after, McClain. All I want is one night. And I get it. You can't tell me something. Or maybe you don't want to break my heart when you're gone...?"

His lashes fluttered shut, blond at the tips. "Mia." There was a wealth of need in that one word. Every inch of his body said one thing, while his lips said another.

Maybe McClain doesn't want to break his own heart?

"We live in a dangerous world," she whispered, "I want to take my chances where I can."

McClain simply looked at her.

"I know." This was the worst time to be trying to think her way through this. Exhaustion slid through her veins, a heavy drug.

"Mia." He rolled toward her. She felt the bed shift and then his warmth seemed to envelop her, as if their auras connected. A hand brushed her arm, and she felt the longing in that touch too.

Knew that she wasn't the only one who felt that chasm. Maybe that was why she'd connected with him so instantly?

"I owed Luc a debt," McClain murmured, so quietly she almost didn't hear him at first, "and I repaid part of that by looking after his child. It was my fault he had to leave, and when he came back I couldn't say no when he wanted to take her. Lily was his, and the only reason she'd been forced to grow up without her father was because of me. I betrayed him. I cost him everything he ever had. It tore my heart out of my chest, but she was his before she was mine."

McClain's shoulders blotted out the light of the moon through the window, leaving his body a dark mass in the night. But she could still feel the heat contained beneath his skin.

"Thank you," she whispered, reaching out and hooking her index fingers through his. "I'm sorry that you lost her."

He released a huff of breath. "So am I. This last year... riding alone... I don't think I let myself look too closely at all that I'd lost. But the truth is, I miss her. The way she'd look at me as if I could solve every problem in the world. I miss my sister, Eden, and I miss having a home. Having friends."

"You could find a new home." She rubbed her thumb against his. "Maybe you could see your sister again?"

No. The answer was no. She felt it in him.

And it hurt her heart.

She at least had something.

McClain shifted. "Mia...."

Here it came.

"I should sleep in the chair," he said, withdrawing his hand from hers. Swinging those long legs over the bed, he made to sit up, but she scrambled after him and caught his wrist.

"Don't be ridiculous."

"Nothing can happen between us. You know that, right?" Shadow sliced across his high cheekbones as he glanced back at her.

"Yeah, I got it." *Thanks.* She nursed her injured feelings. "I wasn't going to do anything."

"Every time you touch me you make this harder."

Mia withdrew her hand and knelt on the bed. "Then I won't touch you. The bed's just big enough for two of us. And even if I *were* tempted, I'm fairly certain I don't have the energy anymore. I'm wrecked. And I won't pretend you don't do all kinds of bad things to my willpower, but I need sleep." She lowered her butt onto her heels. "You're exhausted too. And we're both adults. We can share a bed for one night without it going any further. Besides, that chair looks uncomfortable."

McClain sighed. "It is uncomfortable."

And that was about as much capitulation as she was going to get tonight.

"Stay," she told him. "I promise I won't ravish you in your sleep."

McClain lay back down, clasping his hands under his head. Despite her words, she couldn't resist looking at the powerful muscles in those upper arms. "Good night, Mia."

Later. Maybe. She wasn't going to give up on that hope. Tonight he'd reached out to her. That was something. Mia squeezed her eyes shut. "Good night."

Slipping her jeans off, she slid under the blanket and gave him her back again, ignoring the pointed silence from the other side of the bed. He would just have to deal with the fact her legs were bare. She was too tired, too ratty, to give a shit anymore. Especially after that latest rejection.

Or was it?

Her eyes shot open in the dark as she thought about his words. Nothing *can* happen between us... Not *I don't want anything to happen.*

Every time you touch me you make this harder....

Mia caught her breath in the dark. The problem wasn't the fact he didn't want her. No. He clearly did.

Just what was he hiding?

It made her uncomfortable and she snuggled in under the blanket, pondering this latest revelation.

She was going to find out McClain's secrets. This constant to-and-fro threatened to drive her crazy. And the one person who knew McClain's secret was Jake.

Mia's eyelashes fluttered closed. Tomorrow. Definitely tomorrow....

Game on, McClain.

eighteen

SOMETHING HAD CHANGED.

Adam realized that two seconds after he woke the next morning. He'd half expected Mia to be wrapped around him—last night she'd come perilously close to tempting him to break his promise. But there was no sign of her in his sheets beyond the scent of her and the imprint where she'd lain. Mia smelt like a woman. The soft musk of her natural body odor, the soap she used in her hair—chamomile—and that hint of warm linen....

Fuck. Adam scrubbed his face with his hand as his cock woke up. It had been half-hard when he woke, but now it was alert and ready for action.

Only one thing missing....

"Behave," he muttered, rearranging himself in his underwear. He'd stripped his jeans off sometime during the night, thanks to the heat.

Inside the washroom the shower turned on. Adam couldn't stop himself from turning his head that way. Mia. Wet. Naked. His mind supplied a generous image, and he groaned. Now he was losing the battle within his own head.

Would that be so bad?

She'd made it clear last night that she didn't expect anything more from him than sex. No broken hearts. Just a memory.

He hadn't realized how much the thought of that tempted him.

She knew he was keeping a secret. She'd been okay with that.

In the light of day it was easier to work his way through this mess. Adam rolled out of bed, still not entirely certain what he was planning. All he knew was that he wanted to see her, and that not having her was starting to hurt more than he'd expected.

The door to the washroom cracked open half an inch. Adam rapped on it with his knuckles. "Mia?"

"Come in."

If she was naked, he was not going to be able to stop himself. But when he nudged the door open, she was still wearing a shirt. His shirt, he realized. The black cotton hung down the back of her thighs, caressing the rounded curves of her ass, and highlighting her dark skin. Her panties lay discarded on the floor.

It looked good on her. It was also a little confronting to realize that a part of him wanted to see her in his shirt every morning for the rest of his life.

That thought was not *just friends*. Even with benefits.

"We need to talk," he said.

"I thought we did enough of that last night."

Mia's face remained carefully neutral as she waved her hand under the water spray, testing the warmth. Her black hair was a riot of gorgeous curls. Most of the time she tried to tame them, either by knotting it all back or braiding it. He liked it like this. Fresh out of bed in the morning. He could almost imagine wrapping his fist around a handful of it and pinning her beneath him.

"I'm just having a shower," she murmured, grabbing the soap off the bench. "I'll be out shortly."

And suddenly he couldn't keep this up anymore.

"Here are the rules," he grated out. "One fuck. No holds barred. And we don't talk about it afterward. No messy emotions. No future. No expectations. Just a memory to warm ourselves with forever."

Mia dropped the soap. "What?"

Those dark eyes blinked in surprise.

"I know what I said last night. I changed my mind." Adam took a step forward. "Jake left for the market an hour ago. I heard him and Ellie shifting around in there. We're shut in here until they return, and we have maybe an hour to kill."

Mia swallowed, her eyes darting here and there. "Well, yeah, I'm not saying no, but... why the change of heart?"

"I'm tired of fighting this," he said, instead of admitting that he knew walking away from her without being able to hold her, just once, would make him regret this moment for the rest of his life. "And I keep thinking that maybe we could handle the fallout from this."

"Okay." Suddenly she looked nervous. "I would really like it if you could just make up your mind though. You pull out on me now and I *will* kill you."

"It's made." He reached over his shoulder and dragged his black tank over his head. "You were right last night when you said we could both be adults about this. The truth is, we want each other. It doesn't have to go any further than that. We can share a bed like last night, so we can share our bodies. Like adults." Rational adults. And if he walked away after they got her sister back, and Jake kept his mouth shut, then she'd never know his secret.

He couldn't hurt her. Nor could he give her the curse, not unless he was in his warg form. Just one more time keeping up the pretense that he was just a man.

It all sounded so simple in his head now he'd made this decision. Why then was his gut filled with butterflies?

Because this matters more than I'm pretending it does.

Mia's eyes rounded as he dropped his tank on the floor. Suddenly he was wearing only his briefs, and there was no disguising how much she affected him. Mia slowly smiled. "No future. No expectations. Do you have protection?"

He reached for his shaving kit and plucked out a condom he'd paid ridiculous money for. Next to gunpowder, there were certain necessities that men—and women—paid a small fortune for. "It's Confederacy standard." Adam paused with his thumbs hooked in his underwear. "No regrets, Mia?"

"No regrets." She took a step toward him, plucking the condom packet from his hand and tossing it on the vanity. "Shut the door."

Relief filled him. This was happening.

Adam did. Steam curled out of the shower. A rare luxury in this part of the world. Maybe Vex kept her honored guests here? Mia reached out to turn the shower off.

"Leave the shower on." He wanted her under that water, where he could lick it from her skin. His gaze dropped to the shirt she wore. Time to stop talking in full sentences, like his brain was in control at the moment. "Then take the shirt off."

Mia's fingers curled in the hem of his shirt, but that fire lit her eyes again. The one that drove him crazy. "Or?"

He smiled, all of the nerves finally leaving him. "Or maybe I'll just have to strip it off you, nice and slowly." Adam took a step toward her. "You always have to challenge me, don't you, Mia?"

This time it was her turn to smile that slow smile that turned his knees to water. Seeing it felt like she'd punched him in the chest.

"Maybe just this once I could be obedient." Mia dragged his shirt up over her shoulders.

"I'd like to see that—" His breath caught.

The dark triangle of hair between her thighs drew his attention, then her full breasts. More than enough for a handful. She was a wet dream put together; wide hips, strong athletic thighs, a narrow waist, and broad shoulders. Everything he'd ever imagined and more. His fingers shook as he reached for her. The second the shirt cleared her head, he dragged her into his embrace, capturing the mouth that had taunted him for so long.

It was as though giving himself permission made everything about this moment blisteringly better. He didn't have to hide the fierce need inside him in this moment. It felt like he was able to let himself truly *be* for the first time in nine years. No hiding. No denying. No lying. He told her all of his truths with this kiss, and from the way she rubbed her breasts against his broad chest, she knew what he was telling her. Adam's hands slid down her back and cupped her ass, even as he chased her tongue. She was his in this moment. That's all that really mattered.

The desperation in her touch made him haul her closer. He wasn't the only one feeling this way. Adam groaned, and Mia swallowed up the sound, her spine bending as he tried to take more, to take all of her....

"McClain," she breathed, drawing back with a gasp for air, one hand clasping his neck to hold herself upright. Those gorgeous whiskey-brown eyes looked glazed again. This time, for all the right reasons. "Give me more."

More. He wanted *everything.*

Adam nudged her back against the glass shower screen. He dragged his mouth lower, unable to resist anymore, and captured her nipple between his lips, swirling his tongue around it. Mia gasped.

She captured a fistful of his hair. "I'm not very experienced," she breathed, as if he couldn't tell from her unabashed responses. Every lick of his tongue seemed to surprise her, especially the way her body reacted to it.

"That's okay." He curled his arms around her waist, kissing her mouth again. Slowly. Teasingly. Mia melted. "I'll take it slowly, Mia. I promise I'll make it good for you."

A good reminder for him too. His cock ached. He wanted her. Now. But if she wasn't used to this, then he'd need to work her body slowly, get her ready for him. Worship her. There was no time for selfishness, and Adam had never been interested in conquering women. He liked bringing pleasure first.

He pushed her under the water gently, then shucked his underwear. Mia's gaze dropped, and she smiled as his cock bobbed in response to the sudden attention. "I think he likes me."

"He definitely likes you." Adam stepped inside the shower himself. "And maybe later, you two can get a little better acquainted."

Water drove onto his skin, shattering off it. Mia slid her hands up his chest. "I remember what you said: about how you wanted my lips around your cock."

His turn to shudder. "Do you know what I want even more?"

"What?"

"To be inside you. Here." He slid a teasing finger between her legs.

Another kiss. More skin beneath his hands. Mia was slick with need. His cock threatened to erupt. It'd been a long time for him too, and this was like having all his dreams come at once.

Time to slow them both down. He turned her around, drawing her body back into the warm embrace of his own. Water sprayed off his shoulder and he kissed the back of her neck. "You're so beautiful, Mia. I've been dreaming of this." He ran his hand down over her breast, cupping the full weight in his palm. They both gasped. "But reality is so much better than wishful thinking."

"Did you ever think of me when you made yourself come?" she whispered.

"Every. Damned. Day."

That was a faint smile on her mouth as she turned her face toward him shyly. Adam cupped her hips from behind, the head of his cock brushing against her ass. All of that smooth brown skin. All his. Adam curled a hand in her hair and drew it over her shoulder, revealing the slope of her neck.

"Did you think of me?" he whispered, his heart ticking a little faster. "Did you touch yourself, Mia, and think of me?"

"*Yes.*"

His cock jerked. "Give me the soap."

Mia shuddered, handing it to him.

Denial was a bitch. He wanted this so fucking badly that every part of him ached. But there was no way in hell he was rushing a single moment.

Adam brushed his mouth there, where the slope of her neck met her shoulder. Mia shuddered, arching her back a little, and he bit her, then suckled the skin gently.

He cupped her hip. "Hold on to the screen."

She did so.

Adam rubbed his fingers against the soap to slick them up, then brushed his hand closer to the black curls between her legs. Mia's breath hitched. "McClain."

"Adam," he breathed, and slid his index finger into the lush folds around her clit.

A shiver ran through her. Soap gleamed on her skin, and he used it to lubricate his touch, tracing small circles there, where it ached the most. Mia jerked, biting her own arm as she tried to hold herself up. "Oh, God," she breathed.

One arm beneath her breasts, he held her there against him, his cock sliding between the valley of her thighs and gliding through the slickness of her folds. The soap vanished in the water, leaving only her own slickness. Water sprayed off his broad shoulder as he teased both of them.

"Spread your thighs," he told her, driving a knee between her legs.

She widened her feet, leaning back against him fully. The trust in the action made something in his chest twist. *Mine. Just once.* Adam slid a hand down her ass, then entered her pussy from behind with a finger. God, she was tight. He rested his forehead against the back of her shoulder, working her a little. "Do you like that?"

From the way she was thrusting her hips back against him, the answer was a firm yes.

Mia shuddered. "Please."

"Can you take more?"

"*Yes*," she promised, and he worked a second finger inside her as she gasped.

Hot. Wet. Intense. Cum wept from the head of his cock as he rubbed it against her ass cheek. Any more of this, and he'd be over before he began.

"Turn around."

Mia obeyed.

He couldn't resist tasting her breasts again, dragging his mouth across her aching nipples. Mia moaned. "I want to touch you too."

"Later," he said, capturing her hand when she tried to curl her fingers around his cock.

Adam kissed his way south. His golden skin stood in stark contrast to the bronze of hers. Beautiful. Just beautiful. Desire pulsed through him, the warg slithering through his veins. He didn't want to be gentle right now, he just wanted to take.

But Mia was special. He wanted to make this a memory she'd never forget.

"Hold on," he breathed, and cupped her ass in both his hands.

She curled her hands backwards over the screen for balance, her thighs splaying wide. She was darker here, slick and wet. Adam nuzzled into the juncture of her thighs, breathing in her scent. The second his tongue touched her, she moaned.

"Oh, God," she breathed. "Yes!"

She's so close.... He sucked her clit into his mouth, teasing that hard little knot with the tip of his tongue.

Mia came with a faint stifled gasp, as if, even now, she held a part of herself back.

And that wouldn't do.

One last gentle kiss against her mons, and Adam turned the shower off. Instantly they were surrounded by a curtain of heated mist. Water beaded on her skin. He licked it off, slowly rising to his feet.

"God, you make me wet."

"The next time you come," he told her, whispering the words in her ear, "I want to hear my name on your lips."

Glazed eyes slowly focused on him.

Adam caught her in his arms, capturing her mouth. He'd lost any trace of control now. Mia bit his mouth as he hooked her legs around his hips and carried her toward the vanity. Lush breasts caressed his chest. Every inch of her stripped bare, and his for the taking. Setting her on the vanity, he kissed her once more, his ruthless fingers finding her again.

Sharp nails raked into his hair, and she gasped. "Oh, oh... *oh*."

Capturing her wrist, he dragged his mouth to her ear. "Turn around. Face the mirror."

A devilish light gleamed in her eyes. Mia panted openly. "Aren't you bossy?"

Always. If he was going to do this, then he wanted full control.

"Mia," he warned.

She turned, looking thoughtful again. Her broad shoulders curved down to narrow hips, and then that ass. He'd always been a breast man, but he'd make an exception for her ass. Adam dragged his fingernails over the soft flesh there. Mia bit her lip, bracing herself against the vanity.

"Are you wet?" he demanded, even though he knew the answer. She'd been dripping before.

Mia nodded, and he slapped her ass, cupping her there. She jerked in surprise.

"That's not an answer."

"Yes," she whispered.

He scraped a hand across the fogged mirror, revealing her startled face in the glass. Water droplets beaded together, and their images began to haze over again. But he could still see her. Adam bit her shoulder, tracing soothing circles on her ass where he'd slapped her with his hand. He reached for the condom and tore it open with his teeth. Its lubricated rubber slid down over the head of his cock, and then he rolled it on with one hand.

"Ever since I met you, I've barely been able to get you out of my mind," he snarled, the hot crown of his cock breaching her. "I wanted you. God, I wanted you. And maybe this is wrong. I promised I'd protect you— even from myself. But I can't be that man anymore, Mia. I'm not a saint." Just a man. One who wanted to touch heaven, just once. He flexed his hips and earned himself another inch inside her. Jesus. He couldn't stop himself, couldn't deny either of them any longer. "I want you too damned much."

Mia moaned as he slid all the way inside her, until his thighs slammed against her ass. Every molten inch of her locked around his cock like a vise. Adam lost himself in that moment, his eyelids fluttering open to find her watching him in the mirror. She'd wiped it again. All the better to watch him with.

"Are you okay?" he whispered, shaking with the need to claim more of her.

Mia shuddered. "More than okay."

He cupped her breast with one hand, damp fingers slipping over her nipple. The other slid between her thighs again, teasing her exactly where she wanted it. Mia's inner muscles locked on him like a clamp.

"Hold on," he murmured, thrusting hard within her.

Every thrust took him closer to the edge. He wound his fingers through her hair, dragging her head back to reveal her throat. Teeth skated over the smooth skin there. Mia jerked against his fingers.

"Harder," she breathed, that inner spasm locking tight around him as her body teetered on the edge. "More."

He'd leave marks on her skin with his fingers. But there was no stopping himself. Not anymore.

Mia cried out as she came, her hips jerking. She clapped a hand over his, squeezing his fingers where they lay over her hip. "Adam!"

His name on her lips. It was that which undid him.

Adam came, his cock pumping hot seed within her. Every muscle in her pussy locked around him, milking him like a glove. The world spun, white light obliterating his vision as pleasure took over.

He rested his forehead on her shoulder, shudders tripping through him as though she dragged her fingers over his ticklish spots. Mia collapsed forward on the bench, and he slid his hand up her back, fingertips grazing the roughened indentations of her spine.

Truth dawned. He'd been lying to himself when he told her he only wanted this one memory.

The truth was: he wanted all of them.

Afterwards they lay on the bed, both naked. He'd taken her a second time, sweeter this time, a little slower, staring down into her eyes as he rocked atop her, those powerful thighs locked around his hips. She'd come with his name on her lips once more, and he got to watch every moment of pleasure bloom in those glorious eyes.

Adam curled around her now, listening to the rise and fall of her breath and hating himself even as he knew he couldn't have resisted.

He'd broken his promise—not the one to Jake, but to himself.

Don't touch her. Don't take that step. He'd known even then that there was something different brewing between them. A storm of such epic proportions that he'd never felt anything like it before.

Because there couldn't be anything else.

He was going to walk away from her after this, and, despite the fact that she'd burned the memory of herself into his mind, let alone his body, he knew he'd both revere and regret this moment. It would ache inside him whenever he stared up at the stars on another long, lonely hunt. A reminder of everything he'd lost and everything that could never be.

There was a new loss festering in his heart, and it had a name. Mia.

His blunt-tipped finger traced the delicate shell of her ear. Mia shivered, sharing a look with him that said more than words ever could.

One moment in her bed.... Why had he ever thought it could end there? Mia was in his blood now, under his skin. Even the warg within him gloated at his possession of her, purring beneath his skin as if he'd somehow released the pressure.

"Thank you," she whispered, and pressed the gentlest kiss to his cheek. Slowly she sat up, swinging her legs over the bed. "Guess we'd better get moving."

"Yeah." Adam rocked onto his elbows. "Guess we'd better."

nineteen

THE GOOD VIBES just kept coming.

Mia took a second shower, even though she couldn't stop feeling McClain's hands and mouth on her skin. She felt both relaxed and utterly destroyed. Her heart skittered in her chest like a newborn foal, but she didn't dare dwell too much on the rush of feeling through her veins. That way lay dragons. The rules had been simple. Once, and once only.

Even if she couldn't quite keep her eyes off him, despite the fact Jake and Ellie returned from the slave markets, bringing with them two familiar faces.

"Look who we found." Ellie grinned, dragging Sara into the room by the fingertips.

Bethany slipped through the door, looking around warily. When the girls saw Mia, both their faces lit up.

"Mia!"

She stepped forward, hugging both girls to her. Bethany sobbed on her shoulder as if she'd been trying to withhold her tears since this entire ordeal began. Mia clung to her, letting this hug act as surrogate for the one she intended to give her sister when they got Sage out of there.

Mia stroked the damp curls off Bethany's forehead. The girl was barely seventeen, a shy, sweet thing who always had her nose buried in a book. "It's okay, sweetie. You're safe now."

"I can't believe you guys came for us," Bethany whispered, wiping her eyes. "We thought we were never going to get free."

Shadows stained her eyes. No doubt those fears included others. Sara caught Bethany's hand, squeezing it gently, as though she'd been looking out for the younger girl.

Jake removed his felt hat, and wiped the sweat ring around his forehead. "Ellie filled them both in on our plans. We didn't have enough money to rescue Tom or Sonya, but nobody else was buying. They locked the pair of them back in the pens. Sonya said she'd prefer if we got these two out first."

"I overheard the overseer saying that there's a buyer coming tomorrow," Ellie broke in. "I couldn't get too close, but he seemed to think Tom and the girls would be going out with the buyer, so he's obviously someone with a generous amount of coin floating around."

"Confederacy," Mia murmured, that sick feeling twisting her insides. They had a timeline now.

"What else did you see?" McClain asked.

Mia sat the pair of girls down at the table as Jake explained the security details of the slave yards. She broke out some of the bread they had leftover from breakfast. Both girls fell on it, hurrying to fill in the gaps with what they knew.

McClain scratched his jaw, listening intently to the security details, and Mia knew that mind of his was quietly sorting information into plans.

She ached to touch his hand. But it was time to put her feelings aside and start concentrating. They were one step closer to their goal, but nowhere near success yet. "What's the plan for today?" she asked, the second the girls fell silent, both their eyelids fluttering with exhaustion.

"The girls can get some rest," McClain said, eyeing the pair of them. "Ellie, you and Mia right to keep an eye on them here?"

Mia looked at him sharply. She'd expected the pair of them to work together today.

"We need to know more," he continued, meeting Jake's eyes. "Today's all about information. If tomorrow's our deadline, then we need to get moving."

"On it," Jake said, snatching up his belt.

"You want me to stay?" Mia repeated, not quite understanding.

McClain's gaze caught hers, then skated away as if he were trying not to give the game away. She could see a faint mark on his neck where she'd bitten him. "Thought the girls might want to see some familiar faces."

Female faces. She nodded slowly. "Okay." She and Ellie could fuss over the pair of them, make them feel safe. "What time will you be back?"

McClain grabbed his gun. "Not sure, Mia. Just make sure you keep your gun on you. It should be safe in here, but you never know." He looked at her then, and the room and all the others fell away.

Until Jake cleared his throat.

"Do what you need to do," Mia said quickly. "Just watch your backs."

"Will do," McClain murmured, and headed for the door.

Ellie arched a brow in her direction. One person wasn't fooled. Heat rose in Mia's cheeks, and she pasted a smile on her face, then headed for the bed, shaking out the blanket there.

Jake tossed the empty money pouch on the table. "Two down," he said.

Mia picked up one of the thin pillows. "Four to go."

Jake nodded, looking harried. "And we're out of coin."

Sweat dripped down Adam's spine as he and Jake worked the town. Ostensibly they were interested in the coin to be had, and the beers to be drunk. They idled in one little shit-hole tavern that was little more than a tin shack, listening to reivers boast about fighting, coin, and women for over an hour, before moving on. Buying a couple of small items like bread and cheese in the markets. Working out the layout of the town, even as they tried not to arouse suspicion.

"Town works as a funnel," Jake noted, as they headed back through the slave markets so Adam got a look. "The canyon at the back protects it, and everything leads back to the main gates."

"One way in," he confirmed, "one way out."

"That's not a good sign."

Agreed. Adam caught a hint of unwashed bodies, and his blood boiled as they passed the slave markets. The reivers kept people in cages in there, Jake had told him.

"Who are we rescuing first?" Jake asked. "Thea and Sage, or Tom and Sonya?"

The muscle near his left eye ticked. "All of them," he said quietly.

"What?"

"I'm not leaving a single person in those cages," he replied, striding straight through a pair of reivers. They scattered around him and Jake, spitting over their shoulders at him, but when he shot them a look they fled. He knew he had murder all over his face. Right now, he just wanted to get Mia and her folk as far away from this shit hole as he could. "We take them all."

"Right." Jake chewed it over. "Could work in our favor. More hands to take up a gun."

"Got to get the guns first."

"Well, that guy with no teeth did say there was an armory near Vex's stronghold."

Adam forced his clenched hands to relax. He'd been quietly brewing ever since he hit this place, but the feeling twisting his chest was new. He couldn't quite work it out, but it had something to do with Mia, and he had a horrible suspicion the warg within him was involved.

He wanted to kill. No, he wanted to destroy this entire town. And get her out. *Protect her*, whispered the warg, which was new.

Adam stopped dead in the middle of the street.

What had that been?

He'd always been at odds with the monster inside him. It seemed for once they were on the same path. *Protect Mia.* That was the only common ground they shared, and it bothered him a little, because he didn't want that part of himself having anything to do with her. What had changed?

Smooth skin, her moans filling his ears as he worked his way inside her tight, wet pussy— Shit. He felt his face heat. Making love to Mia meant something to him, but had it also meant something to his darker half?

"You alright?" Jake frowned at him.

"Yeah," he said slowly, and started walking again. Later. He could think it all over later.

Coming into the main square—an enormous patch of dirt with an old fountain in the middle—they both hesitated. A man sat on the fountain, with four of his reivers standing in nonchalant poses around the square. As they entered, a pair of old men took off running, as if they didn't want to get involved.

Rykker came into focus, licking his cigarette paper, then carefully rolling it. A man knelt at his feet, a spiked iron collar around his throat and his hair matted in dreads. "Ah, my new friend. McClain, was it?" Rykker said.

Adam paused, his fingers itching toward the gun at his belt. "I wouldn't have called us friends."

Something about the man at Rykker's feet bothered him, and it wasn't just the collar. His nostrils flared, and the warg inside him growled.

Fuck. That wasn't a man. That was a warg, his knuckles broken and torn, and his own nostrils flaring as he drank in their scents. Adam knew the beast within him wasn't very close to the surface right now, but who knew if the other warg would smell it on him?

Rykker smiled as he lit the blunt. "Vex asked me to show you around. Said you was interested in opening up a new slave route. She thought I'd be the best person to help you out, since I know everything there is to know about Rust City... and slaves." He slowly stood up, one hand curled around the warg's chain. "Only, it seems as though you're already having a good look round."

Adam's senses screamed at him. It had to be a trap. He hadn't felt anyone following them, but with secrets available for the right price here, it stood to reason that others would have mentioned them passing. "We were trying to find a decent beer in this place, but that seems like chasing a myth after tasting all of this rat-piss."

"Decent beer *is* a myth," one of the reivers at Rykker's side laughed.

Rykker shot him a look, and the big fellow shut his mouth abruptly.

"And it looks like we've got a couple of hours to kill before tonight kicks off," Rykker said, pasting that oily smile on his mouth, "so I thought why not?"

"What's happening tonight?" Jake asked.

"Don't you know?" Rykker's smile held smug touches. He sucked back a lungful of smoke. "Thought you were Vex's favorite new pets."

"Sorry." Adam refused to back away as the other man stepped closer. "But I ain't nobody's pet."

Rage smoldered in Rykker's eyes. There was a second where Adam thought it was going to spill into violence. The other man barely held himself back. "Vex wants me to show you the warg cages."

An instant chill ran down his spine. "Why?"

"She said you had a good eye last night. Picked every winner for her, so she wants you to have a look at tonight's crop of dogs. The war games run for three nights, so this is night two." Rykker clapped a hand on his shoulder. "And the general might arrive tonight, he might not. But if he does, then Vex wants to impress him."

The general. That had to be the buyer that the auctioneers thought would be arriving soon. "Thought he wasn't due until tomorrow?"

"He radioed through. He wants his bedchambers set up, and one of the new girls sent over. He likes the war games. They're not allowed to do that shit in the Confederacy."

"Guess I can take a look," Adam said slowly. "Though my cousin here is due back at our rooms." He glanced at Jake, trying to get the message through. "Make sure Mia gets something to eat. She'll be pissed if I'm late. I promised her a warm shower, and a back rub."

"Sounds like she's got her hand on *your* chain," Rykker said nastily.

Adam ignored him. He was far too aware of the other warg watching every movement he made. It growled at him as he shifted, and Rykker looked down in surprise, then aimed a boot at the warg. "Shut up, War Dog."

"Why you got a warg on a leash?" Adam asked.

Rykker crushed his cigarette in the dirt. "Hunts for me. That way I can't get ambushed out on the trail, and nobody escapes when we hit a village."

"Dangerous act," Jake muttered.

Rykker rubbed the warg's head. "Bastard knows not to screw me over. Don't you, War Dog?"

The warg sat very still. Adam thought he could see burn marks down its back, and that made the bottled rage within him rise up until it nearly choked him. This was wrong too. Wargs were monsters, but you didn't torture them. A clean bullet through the skull to put one out of its misery was the kind of mercy he preferred to deliver.

"Let's do this." He couldn't exactly avoid it, unless he wanted Vex breathing down his neck, demanding to know why. Maybe it was one of her little games? She could be punishing Rykker, or trying to fuck with him, who knew?

The thought crossed his mind that maybe Vex hadn't requested this at all. The warg cages and the arena were the only place he hadn't really explored, but he knew not many people lingered there.

The perfect place for an ambush.

"Get the girls," Adam said out of the corner of his mouth, as Rykker walked away, presuming he'd follow. "I'll go see what he wants, but we might have to make some quick plans."

"We don't split up," Jake hissed back. "That's the rule."

Adam looked him in the eye. Urgency rode through his veins. "Just get Mia and the others. This is happening now. Because if this general arrives, then he might be entertaining your wife tonight."

Not to mention the militia that would no doubt be at his side.

Adam strode along the narrow hallway between the warg cages, the creatures snapping and snarling at the bars as they passed. Some of them were ragged men, others already changed into the beast form, as if they'd given up any semblance of staying human. Those were the kind who'd never change back. The moon might provoke a shift, but once a warg gave up, they'd stay there.

Two of Rykker's reivers followed Adam, with Rykker, War Dog, and the other man, who'd answered to Gnat, in front of him. He was deadly aware of the men behind him, every sense on high alert.

But so far, no sudden movements.

Only War Dog kept looking at him and curling his lip, but that might be more about the scent of him. Nothing more.

"Which ones are fighting tonight?" Adam asked.

"Through here," Rykker said, unbolting the next door and swinging it open to reveal a new row of cells. "Some are fresh, unblooded. Then there's our reluctant champion."

Adam stilled. He wasn't going through first.

Rykker bared his teeth in a smile. "What's wrong?"

"I trust you about as far as I can throw you." Rykker seemed just the sort to stab him in the back—or send him into a tunnel full of open warg cages and hungry wargs.

"Guess I'll just have to prove who's got the bigger balls," Rykker shot back, and entered ahead of him, dragging War Dog.

Adam gestured to Gnat. "Ugly first."

Gnat shook his head. "You sure know how to make friends."

"Like I said earlier: I wouldn't have called us friends."

Gnat strode ahead of him. The next section was crowded, and darker.

"Thought you might want to check out our champion first," Rykker called, kicking the bars on a cell. "Get up, you piece of shit."

"Make me, you cockstain."

That voice. Adam's head turned swiftly, his nostrils flaring.

Movement shifted in the cell. A man stepped forward out of the darkness, his face bisected by the shadows of the bars.

Adam had a feeling, even before he saw the man— his stomach free-falling, the bottom of it dropping through his toes—that fate had something horribly wrong in store for him.

And that was before Johnny Colton gripped the bars, melting out of the shadows. "McClain," he said in some surprise. "Long time, no see."

twenty

"YOU TWO KNOW each other?" Rykker demanded.

"We've met," Adam replied roughly, tension radiating through him. "A long time ago."

Eden screamed as Johnny Colton dragged her toward the small hut. "Adam! Adam, help—"

"You leave her alone!" he'd roared, straining at the shackles tied to his ankle. The ring he was tied to moved a fraction of an inch, but it was driven deep into stone. Adam grabbed a fistful of the chain and yanked, but there was no shifting it. Thwarted, he looked helplessly at his sister. "If you fucking touch her, I'll—"

Laughter echoed, rough-edged with pure sadism. Bartholomew Cane—the bastard who'd made him a warg—merely lit his cigarette, the flame flaring in the near dark as he cupped his hands around it. "Don't have to touch her." He shook the flame out, drawing in a sweet lungful of smoke as he sneered at Adam. "That's the beauty of this."

Adam hadn't understood.

"Throw him in there with her," Cane told Colton, who was struggling to shove Eden through the door. "I told you what I wanted, McClain. You refused. This is punishment."

Eden gripped the edges of the door like an octopus, kicking at Colton's shins.

Adam stared in horror at Cane as he began to understand what the devil wanted with him.

"No, I don't have to touch her," Cane said with the faintest of smiles. "You get to do the honors yourself. Consider it your first meal, unless...."

Unless he did what Cane wanted, and delivered his friend, Luc Wade, up to the same curse he himself had been inflicted with.

"I warned you," Colton muttered as he slammed the door shut and came back for Adam. "Cane always finds a way to get what he wants...."

Adam blinked, and Colton's face swam out of memory. All these months of hunting the bastard and here he was, right here. Adam's fist curled. He'd never gotten to repay Cane for the misery of this curse—Luc beat him to it a year ago—but if he wanted a target, then Colton was right here. He could finally take his fury out, finally get some blood in return for the hand he'd been dealt.

All he had to do was kiss good-bye any chance of rescuing Mia's sister....

That thought brought him up short. Adam hadn't realized he'd stepped forward until he was an inch from the bars. Colton didn't move. Merely watched him with those black, emotionless eyes. Slowly he tipped his chin up, as if daring Adam to do it.

They stared at each other. Rage burned through him, like a wildfire through his veins. He was shaking. *Jesus.*

Rykker laughed. "Doesn't look like you were old friends." He kicked the cage, but Colton never flinched, and so Rykker resorted to spitting through the bars at him. "Fucking wargs. Caught him a month ago. Then he broke out three weeks ago, trying to get into the slave pens. Let's just say, he won't be trying that again."

"Oh, we weren't ever friends," Colton muttered, his voice raw as if with disuse. "No, never that, were we, McClain?"

That froze the blood in Adam's veins. He met Colton's gaze again. All it would take would be a single sentence from Colton's lips and his cover was blown.

A faint smile curled up Colton's mouth. *Do it?* asked the arch of his brow, as if the exact same thought was running through his mind.

Adam stared at Colton, swallowing hard. Everything depended on this moment. Everything.

"No," Colton rasped, moving away toward the stone bench that served as a bed. "McClain was hunting me. Haven't seen you in a couple of months."

"Lost the scent," he snarled. And that was when he'd lost his motivation, ending up in Mia's bar.

Colton shrugged. "I don't think your heart was truly in it. If you'd wanted my head that badly, you could have caught me twice. I watched you ride by from a couple of gulches, you and that kid at your side."

"Oh, I wanted your head." He stopped himself from grabbing on to the bars of the cage just in time, and stood there quivering. One touch would reveal him, as surely as the sun rose in the east. "After what you did to my sister...."

"I didn't touch her." Colton slid a sidelong look at Rykker, and picked his words more carefully. "If I recall, once you did as Cane asked, I was the one who returned your sweet sister back to her home. If I'd wanted to hurt her, I had my chances. You were the one who tried to burn me alive. You and that bastard you rode with."

Luc. That was the last time they'd ever worked together, when he and Luc trapped Cane and Colton inside the hut, and flicked a match. Too late to save themselves perhaps. Then Luc vanished into the wilderness, and Adam headed out to find a spot to kill himself.

Colton's reticence made him catch hold of his temper. Colton could have given him up then. Only, he'd chosen not to. Why? Adam paced. "Can't say I regret that moment."

"Well, isn't this just fascinating," Rykker said, and Adam recalled they had an audience.

There were a thousand things he wanted to say to Colton, but now was not the time. He stabbed a finger toward the cell. "This bastard's dead. Tell Vex he's bad odds."

"Funny thing," Rykker replied, "'cause it turns out he's our current champion."

"Rykker," someone called. A reiver poked his head through the door. "Zarina sent a message. Wants you to meet her outside, right now."

Rykker paused. "What? Right now?"

"Now," the reiver replied.

Rykker scowled. "You two"—he pointed to the reivers who'd guarded Adam's back—"you're on the door.

Gnat, with me." Jerking War Dog's leash he was through the door, taking all of his men with him.

Rykker slammed the door behind him, and Adam realized he was too late when the lock clicked into place. He slammed against the door.

"Let me out, you bastard," he said as his world plunged into darkness, and Rykker laughed through the door.

"Have fun in there, McClain. Maybe I'll come and fetch you after I pay my respects to your woman."

No! The warg howled within him.

Time to make their move. Mia's heart pounded in her throat as Jake picked the lock into the cells below the arena. She gestured across the street to where Ellie waited with Sara and Bethany. All three of them darted across the street, into the shadows where Mia waited.

"Got it," Jake whispered, easing the door open.

"Go," Mia said, shoving Bethany ahead of her.

The second they were inside the storage rooms under the arena, Jake shut the door. Ellie flicked on the flashlight she'd brought, looking around. Metal gleamed. An underground garage, filled with enormous war machines and rally cars. At least there was no one here.

"The cells must be on the other side," Jake murmured. "You ready for this, Mia?"

"Yeah."

As ready as she could be. Ever since Jake returned without McClain, her heart had been in her throat. Why the hell had McClain gone off with Rykker? She understood the need to not piss off Vex, but surely Rykker was up to no good. Everything seemed to be moving too fast. She wanted desperately to rescue her sister, but without McClain their odds were poor.

And a part of her was purely terrified on his behalf. What had happened to him? If he could have returned, then he would have, surely.

Swinging her shotgun into her hands, she started out across the garage. She wore as much ammo as she could without drawing attention in the streets, and both knives were at her belt, but she still felt woefully unprepared.

"We get McClain," Jake said, "then we head for Sage and the others. If this general arrives tonight, we're up shit creek without a paddle."

"Got it." Mia moved between cars, following the flashlight's path to the opposite door.

"What are you doing here?" demanded a firm voice, just before she reached it.

Zarina Cypher stepped out of the shadows, dressed in head-to-toe black, her hand sliding to the butt of the gun at her waist as she eyed them suspiciously. She ignored Ellie and the girls, focusing all of her attention on Mia and Jake. "You guys shouldn't be in here."

Ellie was the one who saved the day, withdrawing her pistol from beneath her robes and pointing it at the back of Zarina's head. She clicked the safety off. "Don't move, bitch."

"Tell me," Colton muttered, pacing inside his cell. "What are you really doing in Rust City?"

"None of your business."

Colton stretched his neck from side to side. "It's not as though you've got anywhere to go. And the second that bastard gets back, you're a dead man."

"You wish." Adam paced the hallway. There was only one way out of this room. All of his nerves stretched on edge. He'd beaten his fists bloody against the door in the first couple of minutes, but, as Colton mockingly pointed out, it was built to withstand wargs.

Which meant Mia was out there on her own, and he could barely tolerate it.

Other wargs shuffled in cages nearby, watching with beady eyes. Some looked beaten down, resigned to their fates. Others simply looked hungry.

"I don't really," Colton said quietly.

"What?"

"Wish you dead."

Adam looked at him for the first time. "All of this happened to me *because of you*."

"Partly. I know. But Cane's dead now. I'm free, and all I ever really wanted was to vanish. You just couldn't let that happen." Colton sighed. "What are you really doing here? You seemed just as surprised to see me as I was to see you."

"Ran across a town the reivers just hit," he snapped. "I was trying to rescue some of their people. They brought them here."

Colton's dark lashes shuttered his eyes. "You smell like a woman. Intimately."

He lost it, stopping just in front of the cage, his hands shaking as if he wanted to reach through and slam Colton up against the bars. "She's got nothing to do with you, so keep your filthy mouth shut."

Colton cocked his head. "I would. But there's someone coming."

What? He heard it then. Footsteps in the hallway outside.

The cell door unlocked, and Adam pointed his pistol directly at the door. Rykker had been gone for ten minutes, and Adam had no idea when—or if—he was coming back. Sweat dripped down his spine. He just hoped Jake got Mia out of there before Rykker found her.

The door opened, and Jake burst through.

Adam pointed the pistol at the ceiling, letting out a relieved breath. His eyes sought Mia and found her, shoving Zarina Cypher through the door with her shotgun digging into Zarina's back.

"What are you doing?" he demanded. "Are you guys crazy?" Vex would obliterate them if she realized they'd kidnapped her daughter.

"It's complicated," Mia said, handing her shotgun to Ellie and then throwing herself into his arms. "Aren't you glad to see us?"

He allowed himself the briefest moment to hug her back. *More than you could ever know.* "Rykker locked me in here, then went to pay you a visit," he said gruffly. "I didn't know what was happening to you. It's been killing me."

"When he gets there and finds we're gone, he's going to be suspicious," Jake said.

Right. They needed to move, and now.

"Everyone's gearing up for the war games out in the streets," Jake said. "There's a big crowd out there, starting to drink. Which means this is the worst place to get caught, because there'll be reiver attendants in here shortly, getting the wargs ready for the games."

"Let's do this—"

Zarina took that moment to smash an elbow into Ellie's face, knocking the shotgun from her hands. It all happened so quickly, and Adam shoved Bethany out of the way as Zarina smashed a roundhouse kick into Jake's head.

Jake went down, then Zarina spun on Adam, darting under his outstretched arm and aiming a punch to his ribs.

Adam blocked the blow, and used her own force to spin her under his arm, and slam her face-first into the wall. Twisting her arm up under her shoulder blade, he applied just enough pressure to keep her there.

"McClain!" Mia gasped.

"Got her."

There was a split second where he thought it was done, and then Zarina pushed away from the wall just enough to twist back under her own arm, driving a roundhouse kick straight toward his face. His ears rang as her heel connected with his jaw.

Maybe he hadn't applied enough pressure? He hadn't wanted to hurt her.

Metal clicked, as someone removed the safety on their gun. "Don't move," Mia said, in a cold hard voice, and as he blinked and looked up, he realized she was pointing her pistol straight at Zarina's face.

"Pull the trigger," the other woman sneered, though her hands were half in the air. "You'll have every reiver within hearing distance down upon you."

"I don't think so," Mia countered, cocking her head. "Can't you hear that?" Something in the distance echoed, like a drumbeat. Or maybe boots stamping on the wooden stands of the arena. "They're all heading into the arena. And even if they did hear it, all I'd have to do is fire off a couple more in the air and shout a bit, and they'd think I was celebrating." She smiled, and it wasn't very nice.

"What do we do with her?" Mia asked.

Zarina glared bloody murder up at them from where they'd gagged her and thrown her in one of the cells.

McClain scrubbed at his mouth. "Fuck. This is not good. Vex will notice she's missing. And we can't keep her quiet."

"Then we have to move now." Mia rested her hand on his arm. "Rykker will be back soon. We don't have time to wait until we've sounded this place out. We can use Vex's games as a distraction. Free the girls, create some noise to cover our tracks, and then get the hell out of here."

Zarina cocked her head, as if listening intently to them.

McClain gestured her aside, his voice dropping. "We don't know enough about what to expect at the stronghold," he whispered fiercely. "If we rush this, we might have to make a choice between Tom and Sonya, and Sage and Thea."

"We split up," she countered. "Jake and Ellie can hit the slave markets. You and I take Vex's stronghold and get the girls. Everyone will be at the games. You saw what it was like last night."

He hesitated.

"If Vex realizes Zarina is missing, then she'll turn this place inside out. You know that. And Zarina will spill what we're up to. We don't have a hope in hell then. Then there's this general who hasn't arrived yet."

Slowly McClain tilted his head toward Zarina. He and Jake connected for a moment, and Mia shivered.

"I can't just kill her in cold blood," Jake argued. "No way."

A sigh escaped McClain. "Me either."

They all looked at one another. Bethany and Sara held each other subconsciously.

"Okay," McClain continued. "We're going to have to do this fast and hard. Ellie, you and Jake return to the rooms and get the rest of the weapons. Then you need to take the slave markets and get everyone out."

"Everyone?" Ellie faltered.

"I'm not leaving any of these people here as slaves." Confidence seemed to fill McClain now the decision had been made. "That gives us more hands to carry guns, and more people to fight with us."

"Where do we get that many guns from?" Mia asked.

"The armory," Jake murmured. "Vex has an armory nearby. She's a trusting soul."

Behind them Zarina started kicking in the straw in the cell. McClain's hand shifted to the gun at his hip. "As soon as you get the slaves, hit the armory then head for the vehicle lot. Take what you can and slash the tires on everything else. After that we need a distraction."

"I hope you're not talking about lighting a match again," Mia muttered.

"People out first," he countered. "Then we watch this shit hole burn."

"Deal. I'll even light the match." She took a deep breath. It was finally happening.

Boots echoed on stone. McClain moved between her and the stairs.

"Zarina?" Rykker bellowed, leading three of his men down into the cells. He froze when he saw all of them there. "What the fuck are you doing?" His eyes narrowed in suspicion and he reached for his gun. "I knew you were up to something."

Everything happened so fast.

Mia slammed into the wall as McClain shoved her out of the way. "Get down girls!" He and Jake hauled their weapons clear.

"Easy now!" One of the reivers called, looking nervous. "Jesus, Rykker. What the fuck?"

Stalemate. There were four weapons drawn, and the uneasy-looking reiver seemed to be thinking about adding his own. Mia froze.

"Draw that gun and you're dead first," McClain warned him.

"I knew you were trouble," Rykker said, with a sneer. "Should have trusted my instincts."

"Easy," McClain warned, "or no one's walking out of here alive."

Where the fuck was her shotgun? Mia's mind blanked. All she had were her two knives, and the pistol at her belt. She'd given the shotgun to Ellie. Blood rushed through her veins, drumming in her ears.

Noise rustled as Zarina thrashed on the floor of the cell they'd shoved her inside. Rykker saw her, his eyebrows lifting. Then he smiled. "Got the drop on the Warlord's brat. That'd be a first." His smile turned oily. "Guess we'll take care of you, then we can deal with her. Guess what, honey? It looks like I'll be taking what I was promised from you, after all." This was aimed at Zarina. "Afterwards we can just pretend these fuckers put a bullet in your skull."

Mia's heart thumped in her chest. She hovered on the balls of her feet, her hand curled around Sara's upper arm in case they needed to leg it, but she didn't dare move.

Footsteps thundered on the stairs behind the reivers.

"Rykker?" someone called.

"Down here!" Rykker half turned his head, and that was when disaster struck.

"And you call us the monsters," Colton said, lashing out through the bars of his cell.

He grabbed the unarmed reiver, hauling him back against the bars so hard that his neck snapped.

Rykker and his remaining reiver turned on Colton, shots firing. Some of them hit the metal bars and ricocheted off. The reiver's broken body jerked as Colton used it to shield himself, but then McClain drove both Mia and Ellie into the wall, using his body to protect them.

Jake was firing. Noise thundered through the cells. Shouts. Gunshots. Mia jerked every time a gun went off. McClain shot over his shoulder, still protecting them.

"Jake?" he bellowed, when everything fell silent.

"I'm good," Jake rasped.

"Kill them!" Rykker yelled, and more gunshots shattered the silence.

More reivers flooded the cells. Three... four of them?

"Take cover!" McClain hauled Mia to her feet, sending her and Ellie darting ahead of him.

Mia slid to her knees behind a barrel in the corner, and dragged Ellie in with her. Sara and Bethany were already tucked in the corner, curled around each other.

Everything fell silent again.

Jake? Her head spun in shock. It all happened so fast. What was going on? Where was Jake?

"Looks like your friends can't shoot for shit," Jake called. "Now you're on your own."

Jake. Mia's heart slammed against her ribs in relief. She drew her knife, though hell if she knew what she was going to do with it.

"Just drop the gun, Rykker," McClain warned. "You might still walk out of this alive."

"Two against one," Jake pointed out.

Mia peered around the barrel. Dead reivers littered the floor. One of them moaned a little. And Rykker stood surrounded, both Jake and McClain taking careful steps toward him, with their pistols trained on him.

"You know what?" Rykker's mouth curled up, all on one side. Blood dripped from his arm and thigh, but he held a pistol trained on Jake, and the shotgun on McClain.

"Fuck the pair of you. How 'bout we even the odds?" he asked, then aimed the shotgun at McClain's chest and pulled the trigger.

Everything in Mia's world froze, her vision narrowing.

"Adam!" she screamed, as he began to fall.

twenty-one

RECEIVING A CHEST full of hot lead felt like razor blades slicing straight through him. McClain slammed back into the wall, his knees giving out, and his hands clapping over the bloody wounds. A chill ran through him as he slid slowly to the ground, hot blood pumping through his fingers.

"Adam!" Mia screamed, sliding to her knees at his side.

Couldn't... breathe. Fuck. He clapped a hand to the worst of the wounds, his lungs whistling sharply as fluid bubbled inside them. Everything hurt. But it felt distant, as though shock insulated him from the worst of it.

Rykker had shot him in the chest.

And just like that, everything collapsed in upon him. Adam's head swam as pain lit his chest on fire. All he could see was Mia's worried face. Beautiful. She was beautiful, even now. He tried to touch her, but his arm wasn't working properly. Pressure popped in his ears as his head began to swim.

"Don't you dare!" Mia yelled, easing him onto his back. "Ellie! Someone help me!"

Adam coughed as his chest heaved. Couldn't breathe. Damn it. He tried to suck in air.

"Hold your hand down firmly," someone yelled. "It's pierced his lung. Jesus, let me out of here."

Mia's hands were on him, and Adam tried to shove her away. "Don't!" he tried to say, and coughed. *Don't get... my blood on you.*

It would take a bite, or a scratch from his warg claws to curse her, but he didn't want to risk it. Who knew what poison was running through his blood?

Jake slammed into Rykker, wrestling for control of the shotgun. Adam coughed again, and blood spattered Mia's shirt. Jesus. What was going on? He could hear the two men fighting. But he world was starting to close in around him. He couldn't quite see. Something tangled in his numb fingers. Mia's hand?

"Don't you dare, don't you dare," she called, her face following him into the dark.

"*Mia*," he whispered, and wondered if she even heard the faint sound on his lips.

"Jake!"

A rough grunt greeted her yell. Mia caught a glimpse of Jake's black shirt, and then both he and Rykker slammed into the cell wall. Clearly he wasn't going to be much help. Something wet her cheek. Tears. She was crying. *No. No. No.* This wasn't happening.

"Here," Ellie said, resting her knees under McClain's head. "I've got him."

Mia stripped out of her loose shirt, scrunching it into a fistful and slamming it over the bloodied wound in McClain's chest. He gasped, clapping a hand over hers. Their eyes met, and she shivered as the cool air met her bare skin. The only thing covering her was her white tank. Correction: previously white tank.

"It's okay," she told him, her voice weirdly distant and calm. "I'm *not* going to let you die."

"Mia…." A rasp.

"Don't waste your breath." There was a horrible whistling sound, and it was coming from his chest.

Lungs are punctured….

Don't think that.

"You are *not* leaving me like this," she breathed, assessing the damage. Ten wounds, possibly more. He'd been standing at least twenty feet from Rykker when he was shot. "Damn you, why?"

McClain's pained eyes met hers. "I'm—"

"Not supposed to speak." This time it was a growl.

Most of the damage had been to his abdomen and side, which made her feel sick. *Punctured stomach. Sepsis.* Her mind kept going down dark alleyways, even as she worked to stanch the worst of the bleeding. Even though he'd taken at least seven shots in the side of his abdomen, it was the two or three in his chest that bothered her.

Grunts sounded nearby. Jake swore, then a shotgun discharged.

Mia screamed a little, ducking down, even though the gun hadn't been pointed anywhere near them. Jake punched Rykker, and then the shotgun hit the ground with a clatter. He slammed Rykker back against the cell door.

Surely someone would hear the noise. She didn't know what to do. There was so much blood, and if Jake didn't take Rykker down now, then there might be more of it.

"Let me out!" the warg in the cage bellowed, rattling the door on his cell until he could no longer bear the burn of the silver on the bars.

The two men staggered toward them, shirts tearing as they wrestled. Rykker was bigger, but Jake knew every trick in the book.

"Jake!" she screamed, curling over McClain protectively as they staggered back into her.

Both men went down, and she took a boot to the thigh. McClain's hand curled around her wrist as though he was trying to protect her.

"Son of a bitch," Jake swore, landing flat on his back.

Rykker pressed a knee to his chest, his hands curling around Jake's throat.

"Jake!" Ellie screamed.

"G-get the gun," Jake choked out.

Mia didn't know what to do. She couldn't leave McClain. Beneath her hands his chest began to shake. He was still bleeding, still trying to breathe, a horrible rattling sound that made her feel sick.

But if Rykker took Jake down, then she and McClain were sitting ducks.

"On it!" Ellie scrambled for the spent shotgun. Gripping the hot barrel with her blood-slick hands, she slammed the heavy butt down across Rykker's shoulders. It was just enough to break his grip on Jake's throat. Jake slammed his palm up under Rykker's chin, and went after him when Rykker rolled.

Ellie stood there with the gun raised again, as if she didn't know what to do. The two men grappled again. Jake drove Rykker into the silver-coated bars of the warg cell, and head-butted him.

There was movement within the cell. A shadow loomed behind Rykker's shoulder and he made a shocked noise, his eyes shooting open wide as he gasped.

Jake slammed his forearm across the reiver's throat, but the bastard slumped against him one fist curling Jake's collar, as if to plead for help.

"What the...?" Jake stepped back, and Rykker hit the floor face-first, his back a bloody ruin.

In the cell, the warg withdrew bloody claws through the bars. "I'm McClain's friend, Johnny Colton."

Ellie turned the shotgun on him even though she had no shells. Jake's shoulders heaved, and he took a limping step sideways, clutching at his ribs. Bethany and Sara cowered in the corner.

"Are you all right?" Mia gasped.

"Peachy." Jake leaned against the opposite wall, as though, now that the fight was over, he could barely keep himself on his feet. "He never mentioned you."

"He wouldn't," Colton replied dryly. "When I say 'friend,' I use that word loosely. But we... know each other."

McClain's chest gave a racking heave beneath her hands. She touched his face, leaving bloodied fingerprints there. "Is there a medical kit somewhere around here? Something? Anything?"

Ellie shoved Rykker with her boot, and his body rolled over like a slab of heavy beef.

Down. Glassy-eyed and dead.

Ellie looked up at Colton. "I don't know whether to say thanks, or not."

The warg's dark eyes met her own. "Don't thank me just yet." His gaze slid sideways, to where McClain gasped beneath Mia's hands. McClain's face was rapidly turning gray. "He's dying. Let me out and I might be able to help."

"Yeah, right." Jake crawled toward her, his face paling when he saw the damage. "Mia—"

"I know you've tended wounds before," she broke in, ignoring what he was about to say. McClain's skin felt clammy to the touch, and his eyes rolled back in his head. She pressed her fingers to his throat. The second she found his thready pulse, a wave of relief burst over her.

"Please, Jake," Mia whispered in desperation. "I can't lose him. I can't!"

Not when she'd just found him. Not when she'd only just begun to open her heart to him.

She shot a look at Bethany. "Your mother's a healer...."

"I know a little, but not enough for this," Bethany cried, tears sliding down her cheek. "I don't know what to do."

And she'd been through too much in the past couple of days to pull herself together.

Jake shot Mia a look from where he had peeled back the shirt she'd used to staunch the blood. He swallowed visibly. "Mia...."

It was the kind of tone she didn't want to hear. Words she knew she wouldn't like. "No! Don't you dare say it." Even though her hands were covered with blood, she wouldn't believe it. McClain still breathed. There was still a chance.

Her eyes pricked with tears.

"He's got a punctured lung," Jake said hesitantly.

"I can help him," Colton's voice insisted.

"I thought I told you to shut up?" Jake snarled.

But Mia looked up at the warg. "How? Are you a surgeon?"

"No."

"Then how can you help?" Her eyes were hot. She didn't think she could afford to give herself any false hope right now. "Don't bullshit me. Not now. Can you save him?"

Colton tilted his head toward the wall and the ring of keys that hung there. In the distance someone screamed as the war games kicked into gear in the arena above them. "I can save his life. But you need to act now, or you'll lose the chance."

"Why should I trust you? McClain clearly didn't," she replied.

There was a long thoughtful silence, as he considered the prone man at her feet. "I have a lot of amends to make. Starting with McClain." He met her gaze again. "I can save his life, Mia. But you won't like it."

"Jesus Christ, Mia!" Ellie snatched at the keys, trying to find the right one.

A chill sprang down Mia's spine as she eyed Colton's hands, still covered in Rykker's blood. Her mind caught up to what he was trying to say. Nobody deserved that fate. She'd rather see McClain die peacefully than turn his life into a nightmare. "I won't let you make him a monster like you are. He wouldn't want that."

Jake caught her hand. He swallowed. "He won't have to."

Colton's lips merely twisted. "True. But the clock's running out, Mia. Time to choose."

twenty-two

IN THE END it wasn't a choice. McClain's breath started to rattle in his lungs, and Mia met Ellie's eyes. "Do it," she whispered, feeling like an inmate taking that last long walk. "Open Colton's cage."

"Mia," Jake warned, but she was no longer listening to him.

"You got a better idea, Jake?" Ellie put the key in the lock, listening to the metallic click. "You'd better not be lying to us, Colton. You'd better not make him a warg, or hurt him."

"What about me?" Zarina called from the cell next to Colton's. She'd spat her gag out and lay on the floor, still hogtied.

"We'll deal with you later," Ellie told her.

And then she unlocked the cell.

Colton moved fast, but Jake had the shotgun now and had reloaded with shells from Rykker's belt. He pumped the shotgun, and Colton held his hands up in the air.

"I'm not going to hurt her. Or him." Colton knelt by McClain's side and rested a hand on his forehead.

"Is he...?"

"Still alive," Colton murmured. "Though not for long." Grabbing McClain's shirt by the collar, he started dragging her man toward the cell.

"What are you doing?" Mia demanded.

Colton laid McClain on the floor in the middle of the cell. "You... Jake?" When Jake nodded, he gestured to the cell door. "Make sure you're ready to lock it if need be." He looked between the bars of his cell toward Zarina. "I'd roll a little further away if I were you."

Mia didn't understand. But Jake nodded and handed her the shotgun before slipping the keys in the lock. He held the cell door slightly ajar.

Colton looked up at her, and she saw some sort of message in his eyes that she didn't want to understand. Then he started unbuttoning McClain's shirt. "Be prepared," Colton said softly.

There was something hanging around McClain's throat. The wolf's head medallion he wore.

With a sharp jerk, Colton tore it from around McClain's throat, then danced back out of reach.

McClain screamed, his spine arching off the floor. She'd never heard anything like that in her life.

Zarina's eyes bugged out of her head, and she swore and rolled across the floor away from him.

"What did you do to him?" Mia demanded, but Jake shoved her out of the way, and Colton slid back through the cell door, slamming it shut behind him.

Ellie locked it.

Inside the cell McClain spasmed violently.

Mia couldn't just stand there. She grabbed the bars of the door, but Jake wouldn't let her open it. "What did you do to him?" She turned on Colton. "You promised! What did you do? Did you scratch—"

"No! He didn't scratch him." Jake dragged her back, hauling her into his arms. "Mia, he's... he's changing. I told you about the medallion on that warg up north, didn't I? This is who McClain's always been. Or what. I—I should have told you the moment I realized what he was."

And that was when she saw the horrible truth.

Muscle bulged in McClain's thighs as if something moved under the skin. Fur sprouted along the backs of his hands, and his jeans tore as his body began to change. McClain screamed again, his mouth elongating and razor-sharp teeth erupting through pale gums.

A warg. McClain was a warg.

"The transformation can heal him," Colton murmured, watching sadly. "They tried to create something pre-Darkening that could win any war. A soldier with faster reflexes and greater strength than any other, one that could heal from almost any wound. Of course, it all went horribly wrong, and then the Darkening hit. Man shouldn't mess with nature."

Mia stumbled back as Jake dragged her away from the cell, her entire body numb with shock. The change continued violently, an enormous hulking monster tearing itself free of McClain's clothes. The screams of pain faded, leaving behind the angry huffing of something... not human.

"Adam," she whispered, letting Jake wrap his strong arms around her.

McClain rolled to his elbows and knees, still jointed like a wolf-man, albeit one with teeth and claws. Light glinted off his tawny fur. For a second she almost thought she saw something human in his eyes. Then his gaze locked on Jake, and he threw himself at the bars, the impact making them shudder.

Mia squealed as Jake hauled her out of the way.

"Let her go!" Colton snapped. "He's reacting to you."

Jake surrendered her with a hard swallow. "What do you mean he's reacting to me?"

Colton shot her a look, one hand held out in a placating manner. "She's his woman, no?"

No. Not like this. Mia's jaw dropped open. "He's a monster," she said, shock stealing her words.

And McClain lifted his muzzle to the sky and howled, a long, sad, echoing sound.

Jake and Ellie took the girls to see if anyone heard the ruckus in the cells, taking the shotgun with them. Colton showed the others another way out that nobody had seen, barred the main door, then knelt beside her to wait. McClain—or what had once been McClain—paced the cell.

"How?" Mia asked hollowly.

"Usual way," Colton muttered, raking a hand through his silky black hair. "He got clawed up. Turned."

She shook her head. "No. How does this... this amulet stop him from changing?"

She could remember Jake sitting in her bar, telling her about the warg up North who'd lived among a town unnoticed for years. Had that been McClain? She couldn't quite wrap her mind around this. Wargs were monsters. That was an inescapable Badlands truth, one that little children learned at their parents' knees.

But McClain....

She kept getting flashbacks to moments when he'd smiled at her. The night she'd fallen asleep in his arms, feeling not just safe, but... something else. As though nothing bad in the world could ever touch her again. The way he'd been drinking in her bar for that entire month, as though fleeing from something. That time he'd saved them all from the revenants at the tor, heedless of his own safety, volunteering to help virtual strangers save their people, when their friends in town wouldn't even lift a finger.

How could she put the two together? Hero and monster. How did that mesh?

If you knew my truth, Mia, then you wouldn't smile at me like that....

She felt sick in the stomach. With her history, she'd kept herself at arm's length, especially when he'd admitted that he had secrets. But now she knew them... she couldn't hate him for keeping them. He'd known she wouldn't look at him the same way.

Ugh.

"I don't know." Colton shrugged. "I never needed one to keep me from shifting."

She eyed him sideways.

There was a stillness to the man that made him seem like he was always watching the world around him. "You control it?" she asked.

Colton scratched at the stubble on his jaw. "I'm different to him. I was born this way. It's never been a problem for me." Dark lashes shuttered over his eyes. "The first change happened during puberty. I was under Bartholomew Cane's thumb then, so maybe that's it. He was the warg who changed McClain, and another man named Luc Wade. He... he was—"

"A monster?" she suggested.

"Yes, but you think a warg is a monster." Colton looked at her. "A warg is a beast. It's hungry, it's thirsty, vicious, and violent, but... that is the nature of the beast within. It thinks of survival—of food, and water, and fucking—and it has no concept of human things, like revenge or sadism. That's the human inside it, not the beast. Cane was pure, cold evil. He did what he did because he liked to. Seeing people suffering... he got off on it."

"Why can none of the others control the shift?"

In the cell next to McClain, Zarina sat up, her arms still bound behind her. Somehow she'd slipped the ropes around her feet, but she seemed more interested in what Colton was saying than in escaping.

Colton shrugged. "Maybe they could if they taught themselves to? It's not easy, but if you have the right motivation.... Well. Last year Bartholomew Cane meant to bring McClain and Luc Wade to heel, so he captured Luc's kid, Lily. Used Lily to draw Luc and his woman, Riley, into a trap. When Luc got there, Cane forced him and Riley into a room together for the night. Took Luc's medallion off him. Cane wanted Luc to tear her apart with his own claws. Luc turned, but he didn't hurt her, and in the morning, during the middle of the fight, I shot Cane."

Mia drew back in horror. She couldn't even imagine wishing such pain on another person, warg or not—to force them to kill someone they loved. Colton was right. That was pure evil.

"I can force a partial shift," Colton said, and lifted his hand. It began to shift, hair crawling up the back of his hand, and claws erupting through his nail beds. "The only other man I've met who could do this was Luc, but he couldn't seem to stop himself from transforming when night falls. I can." He tipped his head toward McClain, then shook his hand and watched as it began to revert. "And he doesn't seem to be able to control it at all."

Zarina cursed under her breath. "That's impossible."

Colton wiggled his human fingers at her. "Sorry, sweetheart, but it's not."

The color bleached from Zarina's face.

It was too much to take in. Mia wrapped her arms around her legs and drew them in to her chest. "What do I do?"

She'd been trying to tell herself that there was no future between her and McClain, but the second he'd been shot in the chest, she'd felt the weight of that loss threaten to crush her. She'd begged—prayed—that he wouldn't be taken from her, and now her prayers had been answered.

In a way.

Mia buried her face in her hands. McClain still paced the cell, watching her and growling every now and then if Colton got too close to her. She was so grateful that he was still alive, but she couldn't bring herself to look at him. Everything she'd thought about him had been blown to ashes.

"What were you planning to do," Colton asked carefully, "if you hadn't found out?"

Nothing. Walk away. Maybe. She didn't know. She knew what she'd been telling him, and herself. Loudly. Vocally. One night and all that bullshit. But something inside her had known that there was something different about McClain. He was not the sort of man she'd have ever forgotten. And maybe there'd been the occasional thought of "what if" that lingered in her heart.

What if he didn't walk away at the end of this?
What if they rescued Sage and the other girls, and survived?
What if there could be more than just one night?

He was it for her. She might not have accepted it just yet, but she knew what she felt for McClain was like nothing she'd ever felt before. Mia's shoulders slumped. "My people will never accept this."

"I don't think it matters if your people accept it or not." Colton watched her with wise eyes. "You've clearly spent some time together, and all this time you never realized what he was hiding."

That's because she'd thought it was impossible. Wargs haunted the desert nights. They tore people apart and killed indiscriminately. Or at least that was what she'd always believed, even though Jake hinted that they could pass as human. It just seemed *inconceivable*.

But here sat Colton, and he seemed human enough.

"I thought the two of you were enemies," she said. "You almost sound like you hope I stay with him."

Colton shrugged. "It'd be nice... to know that the dream could come true, you know?"

And she realized that it wasn't McClain he was speaking about at all.

Her heart gave a sideways shift in her chest. She hadn't been thinking about this from McClain's perspective at all.

I lost everything, he'd once admitted, sitting in her bar. Every action he'd taken toward her since then had been gun-shy, because he fucking *knew* that he could never have what most men dreamed of.

Unless she could come to terms with all of this.

As if he understood what was in her heart, McClain suddenly rattled the bars and howled.

And Mia didn't know what her answer would be.

"We've got a problem," Jake whispered, sidling out of the gloom. He shot a glance at McClain, who prowled his cell, and swallowed hard. Both Bethany and Sara followed him closely, as if afraid to leave him.

Ellie followed on his heels, gripping the shotgun with white knuckles. "We've found a way out, but—"

"What?" Mia almost didn't think that she cared.

"They just finished the third match," Jake announced. "There are reivers crawling through the other wings, dragging wargs out of their cages. We've been lucky so far but... I heard the announcer say they're taking a brief break and then going to bring out the champion."

Colton shoved to his feet, rolling his shoulders loosely. "Which means me."

"The second they get in here, they'll realize someone died," Jake said.

Too much blood on the floor to hide.

"And we can't hide him." A thumb jerked toward McClain.

"Unless...." Ellie's gaze shifted to Colton. "They might think it's him, if we get Colton out of here."

"No way," Mia snapped. "They'll put McClain in their death match instead, and he's not in any condition to fight."

"Then what do we do?" Ellie asked.

Mia's gaze shot to McClain. He prowled the cage on two legs, hideously hunched over, his tawny fur rippling over obscene muscles.

"I don't know," Mia blurted. She'd never been helpless, but her brain felt like it was wrapped in fog right now. Like it couldn't make decisions. *Shock*, an analytical part of her mind said.

She needed to pull herself out of this. There was no time to work her way through the minefield she'd suddenly found herself in.

The truth was, they were in dire straits. They'd done their best to hide the reiver bodies, but there was too much blood on the floors. Someone would notice that Rykker and his crew were missing.

And they couldn't just leave McClain here for the reivers.

That didn't even account for the fact that Sage and the others were still trapped and her, Jake, and Ellie's covers had been blown. Fuck. How were they supposed to get out of this alive?

"Two hundred reivers," Jake murmured, looking at her with the same horror on his face. The last few days were taking their toll on him too. "We can't handle those odds. Not with only three of us, and everything up shit creek at the moment."

"Four," Colton pointed out.

"McClain's our fourth, not you," Mia snapped. "And we can't let him out of the cage right now. We need to regroup."

Colton suddenly cocked his head. "I can hear voices."

Funny how she'd never really questioned McClain's superhearing before.

Maybe you didn't want to?

"I'm not leaving without Thea," Ellie declared, but she looked so young in that moment. More determined than hopeful.

"Or Sonya," Sara declared, seeming to find her voice for the first time. She shrank as they all looked at her. "We can't leave them. Sonya stayed behind so we could get out. She thinks we're coming back. I can't leave her like that."

Mia's heart raced. "We need ammunition, a means of escape, and a distraction." Those plans still applied. Her gaze slid to Zarina thoughtfully. "*And* we need a hostage."

"Sage can work a shotgun," Jake replied, snagging the keys from Ellie and hauling open Zarina's cell. "We have to get the girls out. Fast. That gives us better numbers. We still have surprise on our side."

But that meant leaving McClain behind. There was no way they could handle a warg right now.

"You promise to behave?" Jake demanded, hauling Zarina to her feet. "Or should we just shoot you now?"

She surveyed them all, but her expression remained thoughtful. "I'll come. But no ropes."

"The ropes stay. You make one wrong move and I'll put a bullet in your back. Let's go," Jake told her, shoving her toward the cell door.

"No! I'm not leaving him." Not like this.

Jake grabbed Mia by the upper arm. "If we don't leave, then we'll be outmanned and outgunned. How do we get Sage out then?" His face contorted. "I need you, Mia. I can't rescue my wife alone. They're going to sell her tomorrow, if she's still here. To some Confederacy general. We'll never get her back then."

"I'll stay," Colton said. "I can maybe put the amulet back on McClain, and try and talk him through the shift back. I'm probably the only one who can survive him in this state."

She stared at him helplessly.

"Incoming," Colton muttered.

The handle turned as someone tried to open the main door to the cells. "Hey!" It twisted again, as the newcomer realized this way in was locked. "What the fuck?" He hammered on the door. "Who's in there? Open the door!"

"Go," Colton said, gesturing them toward the small tunnel he'd showed them. "If you're free, then you can come back once you get your sister. You come back for him, and you get me out too."

"But what if...." What if they killed McClain when they found him like this?

"He's valuable to them," Colton said, interpreting her fears. "They'll save him for the ring."

"Why would you sacrifice yourself?" Jake demanded.

Colton looked up. "There are some debts that must be repaid. I had a hand in making McClain what he is. Maybe you don't understand that, but there are some things you can't walk away from, not if you want to live with yourself." He shrugged. "Plus, if they see me running around free they'll shoot me on sight. It won't be something I can just recover from either. They use silver bullets for wargs, and all the handlers down here are equipped with them. And if he's here"—he tipped his head toward Mia—"then she'll come back for him if she gets a chance."

Mia didn't want to go. Didn't want to leave McClain here alone. But as Jake dragged her slowly, she let her feet fall into line. Sage first. McClain would understand.

"I'll come back for you," she promised, her gaze meeting McClain's silvery-green eyes for a moment, before she could no longer hold it.

Then Jake dragged her down the passage, just as the door broke down behind them.

twenty-three

ADAM GRIPPED THE bars, his biceps flexing as he tried to tear the steel apart. Jaw ground together, he winced as the newly-knit wounds in his chest pulled, and his hands burned from the silver coating the bars. The second Colton put the medallion back on him—almost ten minutes ago now—he'd made the slow, torturous change back to human, his skin rejecting the shotgun pellets. He'd spent every second since then trying to escape.

Especially after several reivers burst in and found him halfway between man and warg. They'd run out to tell Vex, which didn't leave him a lot of time.

"You ain't getting out."

"Fuck off, Colton." Adam finally tore his hands from the bars in defeat. His chest ached like a son of a bitch, and it wasn't just from being shot.

Mia. He could see her horrified expression as plainly as if she stood before him still, the look in her eyes.... That damning look. A lump in his throat made swallowing difficult. He'd lived this truth before. Seen his townsfolk, his friends, look at him the same way when his true nature had been revealed almost a year ago. Time didn't make this moment hurt any less. He'd spent the past year using Colton as his goal to keep moving forward, even as he refused to look to the past, or accept what had happened. In that time he'd grieved, but he'd also refused to let anyone else get close to him.

Until now.

"Just saying." Colton picked at a thread on his combat pants, before looking up, those dark eyes locking on Adam. "You don't think we haven't all tried?"

Of all the hells.... Rearing back, he smashed his palm against the bars. It hurt and did nothing to calm his rage, but at least it felt like he wasn't giving up. "Shut up."

Fabric shifted as Colton clearly slid to his feet. He hadn't put up much resistance when the reivers came in and found all of the blood on the floor. Simply held his hands in the air and entered his cell again, while they tried to figure out what to do. "I can't help thinking that this is fate—"

"I said... shut up," Adam growled, tilting his head toward his enemy. "Or I'll make you."

A line of bars separated them. Colton looked unimpressed at his threat, and rested one arm on the single horizontal bar that ran at chest height. He rapped his other knuckles against the bars, withdrawing with a flinch when the silver coating burned him. "Yeah. You seem pretty tough behind those bars."

Ignoring his nakedness, Adam took a step closer and Colton tensed. "Why are you even here?" he demanded.

"Someone had to stay with you, and I figured you'd prefer not to tear one of your friends apart if you lost control. Besides, your woman looked a little shell-shocked. Keeping secrets, were we?"

"I should have killed you the first time I met you."

A shrug. "Probably." Their eyes met. "Would have done us both a favor."

And with that, they were both back in the past, seeing Bartholomew Cane's face again—the psychopath who'd created them all, keeping Colton on both a physical and mental leash.

He didn't want to sympathize with the bastard. But it was hard not to. Adam's experience with the man had begun and ended in little more than two nights. Colton spent years under Cane's heel.

"How'd you get caught?" Adam finally asked, sinking onto the frigid stone bench. "You're not stupid." After all, he'd managed to avoid Adam for at least a few months.

"Found a small town in an uproar. Reivers had taken three of their women. Thought I might as well do something about it. Only problem was, I walked right into a trap. Townsfolk sold me out to keep the reivers off their own asses."

Typical strategy in some parts of the Badlands. It made it impossible for towns to band together when they couldn't trust outsiders, and therefore made creating a militia against the reivers damned near impossible. Adam grunted.

"The reivers took me out of my cage one night to have a little fun with brands and hot iron,"—this time Colton's smile was vicious—"and let's just say all hell broke loose that night. I cut free, Cypher's raiding party found the remains, figured out what had done the job, and War Dog tracked me down." He rapped on the bars with his knuckles. "Home, sweet home ever since."

"So you fight in the arena?"

"I kill in the arena." When they locked eyes, he saw the chill disregard in Colton's eyes, as if he used it to distance himself from the nightmare. "You're looking at Cypher's most valuable property."

"Guess that makes two of us." Adam clasped his fist in his palm, rubbing at his knuckles.

"You know they'll probably pit us against each other if your woman doesn't make it back? Cypher will want revenge on you for sneaking in beneath her nose."

Made sense. Adam looked away. The chance he'd been waiting for all year, yet now he'd almost lost all enthusiasm.

Or maybe tracking Colton down had become a crutch. Something to give his life focus, until Mia strolled into his vision, with those hands on her hips and that eyebrow arched.

Don't think about her. His ribs felt empty again— hollow all the way through. She was better off getting the hell out of here.

"I've been here for over a month," Colton said quietly. "It's taken all the rusty edges off me. You won't stand a chance."

Adam looked up. "And I've got nothing left to lose."

"How's the chest? Looks like a hot mess still."

"Feels like déjà vu." Colton had been the one who shot him over a year ago, when he'd been trying to escape

Adam's town. "For some reason you're always involved in my downfall."

Another shrug. "Are you talking about the cells here? Or that pretty girl following you around?"

"It's unlikely I'll see her again." He looked away. He just hoped she did the smart thing and rescued her sister, then got as far away from here as she could.

"Doubtful." Colton straightened, stretching out the kinks in his shoulders. "From the way she was following you around, she looked like she'd staked some kind of claim."

"Yeah," he snapped, cracking his knuckles. "Well that was before I pulled my incredible transformation act, thank you very fucking much."

"You're breathing," Colton returned, "which is more than I can say for your chances if I hadn't. So my fucking pleasure."

Adam pushed to his feet, feeling too small for his own skin. He paced in small circles. Dying felt like an easy way out, one he'd thought about before, if he were honest with himself. What always stopped him was the fact that he truly wanted to live. He just wanted to shed himself of this forsaken curse, even though he knew there was no cure. No hope.

And now he was trapped in this hellhole, what was left? Dying looked like something he might be acquainted with in his near future, and that made his gut clench with denial. No. He didn't want to die.

He wanted... well, he wasn't getting what he wanted, but a man could still hope.

"I need to get out of here," he said, looking around.

"Good luck with that," Colton muttered. Apparently he'd given up toying with Adam and had slumped onto the cold stone bench. "They'll be back as soon as they've reported in to Cypher."

"So we can't get out of the cells," he muttered.

"Only time any of us gets out of here is when they've got us scheduled for a match." Colton lay down, dragging his shirt over his head. No help there. "If you're lucky they'll blood you first with whoever they've got in the arena at the moment, and it won't be with me."

Lucky. He frowned. From what he'd seen that night at the arena, there was only one gate in and out of the sandy cage, which clearly led back here to the warg cages. The wire dome around the arena was at least twenty feet high, and reinforced with electricity. By the time he tried to climb it, his hands would either be raw, or he'd be dead from a stray bullet.

"Anyone ever tried to escape the arena before?" he asked.

"Yeah." Colton's shirt lifted with his breath, but apart from that he stayed still. "Two weeks ago one of the wargs tried. They crucified him. Took turns at him. Wasn't pleasant."

"Then he shouldn't have gotten caught," Adam muttered under his breath, and Colton lifted his shirt off his face just enough to peer sideways at him.

But it didn't matter.

Now he had something else to focus on, apart from losing Mia or dying.

The door slammed open, and Vex strutted into the cells. She had a lit cigarette in one hand, and she'd drawn her eyebrows on in red pencil that matched the bright gleam of her Mohawk.

"Jesus. H. Christ," she said, looking Adam up and down. "What happened? You get clawed up?"

"Let me out," he growled.

Vex laughed. "Put your hands on the bars," she said, "and I will. After I make sure you're human."

He wouldn't pass that test. Adam shook his head.

"Thought so." Her gaze cut to Colton, then to the blood on the floor. Vex stepped over a puddle of it, suspicion racing through her eyes. "Looks like someone died in here."

A reiver hurried through the door. "It was Rykker. Found him and his men stuffed in a cell that was meant to be empty." He swallowed. "Someone shoved a hand through his back and tore his heart out, but he'd also been shot."

That made her eyes narrow. She turned her attention back to Adam, as though he suddenly had a use again. "*What* happened in here?"

Cold sweat slid down his back. He had to protect Mia and the others. "Rykker said you wanted me to see the wargs who would be fighting tonight. When we got here he changed his mind. Didn't like my plans to encroach on his turf. Things got messy." He shot a dark look at Colton. "I shot him and his men, and then this bastard killed him. I got... I got clawed and tried to hide the bodies. Thought I could get away with it, but that's when the itch started. I locked myself in here before I could go warg." He closed his eyes briefly. "Didn't want to risk going back to find Mia."

"That what happened?" she asked Colton.

He eyed Adam sideways. Then nodded.

Relief flowed through him, but Adam didn't dare show it.

"You shot Rykker *and* his men?" Vex asked. "That sounds like you got the jump on them."

Adam pressed his lips together.

"Where's your woman?" Vex demanded.

"Don't know," he lied. "Last I saw her she was back at the rooms." He forced himself to hesitate. "You won't... tell her, will you?"

Vex snorted, stubbing out her cigarette on the bars of his cage. "Won't need to." She graced him with an evil smile. "Guess she'll just have to see for herself when you enter the arena. That's what you get for killing my favorite. Maybe I can find someone to console her?" Turning around, she gestured to her men. "Make sure he's ready. He can go in with Slash. He seemed to like him so much last night."

"Vex!" Adam caught the bars of the cell and flinched.

She looked back, just before she exited the room. "You don't make demands on me anymore, warg. No matter how pretty you look."

"I locked myself in here to save your people," he shot back. "And mine."

Vex shrugged. "Your mistake. You shouldn't have gotten close to *him*." She jerked her head toward Colton.

"No! If I fight," he told her, "then I fight him." He stabbed a thumb toward Colton.

"*What the fuck*?" Colton muttered.

Vex's eyes narrowed. "You don't get to pick and choose. I'm the master of your fate now. Not you."

"I know. I know. But you want to impress your general? Give him a good fight?"

She paused.

"I can give you a good fight," he promised. He needed to sell this. "Colton and I have bad blood between us. I was hunting him before I came here, and the bastard did this to me. I want one last shot at him. One last shot and I'll make it good, I promise."

Vex put a fresh cigarette between her painted lips, and lit it. She shook out the match, and then drew deeply on the cigarette. Adam swallowed. *Come on*. He knew he needed to play to either her vanity, or her future plans. Preferably both.

"Done," she said finally, blowing out a cloud of smoke as she turned to the handlers. "Make them the last fight, just in case the general arrives. He's already late. And oil them up or something. I want to see those muscles *gleam*." She shot one last look at Adam. "The general might not even make it tonight. But I've got a sudden hankering to see your blood on my sands tonight."

Adam sighed with relief as she strode back through the door.

"You stupid son of a bitch," Colton spat, as the reivers swarmed the pair of them with long poles with collars on the end.

Adam ignored him as they collared him through the cell bars.

He had a plan.

Vex's stronghold first.

Mia's heart thundered in her chest as she put her back to the gate that led to the courtyard. Jake ducked against the other side of the gate, meeting her eyes. Both of them held shotguns. Bethany and Sara hid in the nearest doorway, holding each other's hands. Neither of them would be much good here.

All of their group were running on pure adrenaline, and the choice had been hard. The slave pens were easier to hit, and they'd have numbers on their side if they freed the people held there, but Vex wouldn't be away from her stronghold for long. Even now, the moon shifted in the sky overhead. The war games kept Vex and her coterie of reivers away, with only a light guard on rotation at her stronghold. It was the best chance they'd get.

And both Sage and Thea were held here.

"Where's Ellie?" Mia whispered.

"Here." A shadow ducked out of the night. "Let's do this."

Ellie went first, unarmed and wearing the slave collar. Inside the gates, a man's voice coughed appreciation. "Hey now, darlin', what are you doing out here all on your lonesome?"

"There's someone out there, across the street," Ellie cried, milking terrified young maid for all she was worth. "They were stealing something from Vex's jeep out front."

"What?" The guard strode through the gate, his shotgun in his hand. Instantly, Jake stepped up behind him and clapped a hand over his mouth and chest. He dragged the reiver back into the shadows of the arch, where he cut his throat.

"It's clear," Ellie hissed.

One heartbeat. Two. Mia's gaze roved the street. Nothing moved. She took a sideways step back through the gates, aiming the shotgun into the corners before nodding. "We're good, Jake."

Jake hauled Zarina in through the gates. He'd gagged her again, and Zarina glared bloody murder at them. "Where's the other guard?"

Vex's handful of reivers weren't like the others. Reivers were lazy, vicious, and cared only for themselves as a rule, but Vex's men looked more like vicious guard dogs, than street curs.

"There should be two on the gate," Jake muttered. He passed Zarina off to Ellie, who grabbed her by her bound wrists. "Watch her."

Stepping forward, he trained his pistol around the courtyard. In the distance feet hammered in approval and hooting hollers filled the night. Someone was either dying in the arena, or bleeding.

Mia swallowed. Not McClain. She had to keep telling herself that. Right now she needed every ounce of focus she could muster, or she'd end up with a bullet between her eyes.

A shadow pushed out of the bushes, struggling to zip up his fly. "Yaris? Is that you?"

Jake flipped a knife through the air, and the reiver died with a gurgle.

"Nice throw," Ellie muttered, fetching the blade from the reiver's throat and wiping it clean on his clothes.

"Thanks." Jake took it back. "Courtyard's clear."

Upstairs. Mia's pulse began to tick a little faster. They were so close now. Her hands began to shake as adrenaline pumped through her.

Another guard appeared out of nowhere upstairs. Mia pumped the shotgun, and blew a massive hole in his chest.

Jake shot her a look. "There goes our element of surprise."

Her hands shook. "Sorry." *Instinct.*

Jake swore under his breath, then started running as boots pounded on the concrete floors. "Get Sage and Thea out! I've got this."

Two more reivers spilled out of the stronghold. Jake shot one, and the other slammed into him, taking him to the ground.

"Jake!" Mia pumped the spent cartridges out of the shotgun, then paused.

"Come on!" Ellie cried, dragging Zarina down the corridor. "Jake knows what he's doing. You two stay here with Jake!" she told Bethany and Sara.

Cursing, Mia charged after her. McClain had sat them all down that afternoon, and drawn a detailed map of the stronghold out of sand. She knew where her sister was being kept.

There was one more guard in the dark interior. He looked up as they burst into the hallway, and Ellie shot him before he could blink. "Jesus," she whispered, as the body hit the floor. "I just killed him."

"Better him than us." She knew exactly how the other girl felt. She'd been there a couple of nights ago. Mia hauled her and Zarina along. "This way!"

They found the entrance to the women's cells. It was locked, a small electronic device winking at them from the door. A glass device rested on the pad, with green light leering through it.

"What the hell is it?" Ellie asked, poking the box. "Is there a code or something?"

"If Sage were here, she could probably work it out." Sage knew electrics, and ran a thriving electronic salvage business. Mia slid her hands over the steel door. No handle. Nothing to grip. She shoved the door.

Nothing.

"No wonder Vex wasn't worried about anyone escaping," Ellie said softly. "She knew no one could get through this door. What do we do now?"

"Stand back?" Mia aimed the shotgun at the door, near where the hinges ought to be.

Zarina made a gurgling sound behind the gag.

Mia pointed the gun at her face. "Shut up."

Zarina bared her teeth around the gag, then tilted her head

"I think she's trying to tell us something," Ellie said hesitantly.

Mia jerked the gag from the other woman's mouth. "What?"

"If you untie me, I can get you through that door," Zarina panted. "All you'll do with that shotgun is invite ricochet. It's bulletproof. I'd rather not die from your stupidity."

"Mia," Ellie murmured, grabbing her by the wrist.

She didn't take her eyes off Zarina, but she nodded. The other woman's motives were unclear, and she certainly wasn't acting as Mia had expected. Zarina wanted something. She just had to find out what.

"You make any sudden moves," she warned, drawing the knife at her belt, "and Ellie will shoot you."

The ropes cut off the circulation in the other woman's hands. As soon as Mia sliced through them, Zarina stifled a groan, trying to rub her hands together. Color flooded into the pale skin. "I had my doubts when you first called on my mother, but now I know you're not here to buy slaves. You're here to rescue them."

"That's my sister in there," Mia told her. "And Ellie's girlfriend. The two girls are from our town."

"And the others with you?" Zarina asked, "They're not wannabe reivers either."

"Bounty hunters," Mia muttered. "Jake's my brother-in-law. Why do you care?"

Zarina looked at them thoughtfully. "You're going to get yourselves killed. The general's two hours away, and he's got fifty men riding with him."

"Then we'd better get out of here quickly," Mia countered.

There was a tense moment.

"I can open the doors," Zarina said. "And help you get out."

"Why would you do that?"

Zarina rubbed her hands, loose strands of hair framing her face. "There is a condition."

That made more sense. Mia lowered the shotgun. "What?"

"You take me with you," Zarina replied, quite seriously.

Silence. Both she and Ellie looked at each other.

Mia didn't understand. "You want to come with *us*? Why? Is this a game?"

"Do you think you're the only one who wants free of this toxic dump?" Zarina snarled. "I want out and I am willing to do whatever it takes to escape. And if you take me with you, I can show you how to get out of here without getting killed. Vex's got warning systems in place. The second she finds something is out of place she's going to turn the sirens on. That pack of rabid dogs out there isn't smart enough to find their way out of a wet paper bag, but they'll hunt at her call, and there's enough of them to make sure you don't get three miles away from here. They'll be tripping all over themselves to bring you back. Though you might not survive. Or you'll wish you didn't."

Warning alarms. It made sense. Mia froze. She'd thought Vex seemed complacent about leaving this place virtually unguarded. "How do we know that we can trust you?"

"That warg skin my mother wears? It belonged to the man I once loved," Zarina replied, and a flash of anger lit over her features. "She made sure he was infected, and then she skinned him alive in front of me. For daring to disobey her."

Jesus. Bile burned in her throat. She couldn't even imagine....

"I want to see her fall," Zarina continued in a dangerously soft voice. "I want to see this hellhole burn. And I want out. Vex controls everything that comes within her radar, especially me. She's decided she wants her legacy to continue, which means she wants to offer me up to her favorite reiver until I fall pregnant. That was Rykker until a few hours ago, provided he brought her a new haul. I can't live like this anymore. And as far as I can see, you're my best chance at getting out of here. I knew you were up to something the other night, when I saw you and that tall one, McClain, hovering around Vex's stronghold."

"You saw us?"

Zarina rolled her eyes. "I wanted to know more about why you were here. You didn't look like reivers, and Vex was suspicious."

"Enough talk. I trust her," Ellie said, "and we don't have the time to question her motives further. Open the door, and you've got my vote."

Zarina strode toward the door with predatory grace, and pressed her thumb down on the glass pane. The green light blinked, and then the door opened up.

Both Mia and Ellie gaped.

"It's keyed to Vex and me," Zarina explained. "Biometric tech the General's men use to pay for black market slaves. They throw something fancy at Vex every now and again to get her salivating."

"You don't seem impressed."

"There's one thing I hate more than my mother. And that's men who pretend they're morally upright citizens, while they're keeping slaves in dark holes."

"Didn't hear you protesting before," Mia pointed out. "When she was talking slave trades in your parlor."

Zarina shot her a dark-eyed look. "You *have* met my mother? The last time I tried to run she whipped me bloody. I'm her only surviving offspring. That means she won't kill me. It doesn't mean she won't hurt me, and if I push her too far she'll have me bred, and then she'll take the child and I'll become collateral damage. I'm as powerless here as anyone else."

"Let's do this," Ellie said, stepping through the doorway first.

"You in front of me where I can see you at all times," Mia said, and pushed Zarina in the back with the shotgun.

There were five doors with the same fingerprint scanner inside the narrow hallway within.

"This one is your sister." Zarina pressed her finger on the panel. The door blipped again, and then opened.

Mia's heart suddenly pounded in her ears. She stepped closer.

Sage faced the door, her hands curled into fists, and her whole body quivering. Her mouth fell open when she saw who was standing there. "Mia!"

Sage slammed into her, and Mia curled her arms around her sister. She couldn't squeeze her tight enough. All this time, she'd been focused on marching toward this moment, but a part of her had doubted if she'd ever see Sage again.

McClain had done this. Without him, they'd have never gotten this close. Tears leaked from her eyes. "You're safe," she said, over and over again.

"I can't believe you guys came," Sage whispered, drawing back. She rubbed her face dry. "Are you stupid, or what?"

"Definitely stupid."

Sage hugged her again.

"We've got to go," Mia said reluctantly. She held Sage's hand, leading her back into the hallway. "Jake's fighting off the guards."

"Is he okay?" Sudden concern turned Sage's voice dark.

"Don't know." She wouldn't lie to her sister ever again. "He might need backup."

Ellie and Zarina reappeared, with Thea behind them. Thea sobbed quietly, as if she couldn't quite believe it either.

"We've got to move fast," Mia told them. "I know you've both been through one hell of an ordeal, but this isn't over yet. We need to hit the slave markets and get the others out, and then we still have to escape. Questions will have to wait until later, got it?"

Both women nodded. Sage held out her hand, and Mia realized her sister wanted the spare pistol tucked in her belt.

"I'm not being defenseless ever again," Sage said, when Mia hesitated. "And I won't let them take me if this goes to shit. Not alive."

She could understand that.

"Let's go rescue Jake," Mia said, nudging Zarina ahead of them.

twenty-four

THIS TIME ADAM knew what to expect when the reiver guards dragged him toward the arena.

The crowd pounded their boots on the timber stands above him in an almost tribal rhythm, dust whispering between the cracks in the floorboards. BOOM. BOOM. CLAP. BOOM. BOOM. CLAP.

Light flashed as certain reivers hauled the domed lights in slow circles, taking in the leering faces, the pumping fists. Every sound was interspersed with the occasional shouted scream for blood, for flesh.

Adam shivered, the nerves in his body trembling. The moon hovered in the east. He could feel it in his veins now; the monster whispering in his ear. It could smell the blood, taste the bitter sweaty scent of the reivers' hunger for violence on his tongue. Adam swallowed, his fingernails digging into his palms as he forced it back down. With his medallion back he was in charge of the monster again. But he could never forget how easily it had taken him in the cell, or the look on Mia's face when it did.

"You stupid son of a bitch," Colton muttered, on the other side of the silver mesh that kept them apart in the tunnel until they entered the ring. "They were going to play you against one of the weaker wargs. I can't believe you volunteered, you dick."

Adam merely focused on the ring. The mesh fence surrounding it was still at least twenty feet high. There was no way he was getting over that.

Not without help.

His lips pressed together. He didn't want to involve Colton. Adam sure as hell didn't trust him, and there was an ugly part of him that simply didn't want to extend any kind of olive branch at all.

But he wasn't ready to die yet.

And maybe Mia wouldn't come back for him—a part of him hoped she wouldn't—but there was enough doubt there that he wasn't sure. She knew what he was now. There was no future between them. But he'd seen her stand up to her townsfolk and push herself into dangerous situations in order to rescue others.

Mia was the type of woman who wouldn't walk out of here without coming back for him, if she thought she owed him.

And he couldn't let that happen.

"Only one of us walks out of this alive," Colton muttered. "I'm not going out of here on a stretcher so they can throw my body to the pigs. I paid my debt to you in that cell. I saved your life. So I don't owe you anything anymore. Fuck you, McClain. You had an option out."

"Maybe I didn't like Vex's option."

Colton flexed his fists, jumping up and down lightly on his feet as he watched the spectators howling. "You got a better one?"

The metal gate in front of him sprang open, and someone behind him prodded him with one of the poles—wrapped in barbed wire—that they tended to carry around here. "As a matter of fact I do," Adam shot over his shoulder as he staggered forward into the arena.

There was blood spattered on the sand at his feet. As he and Colton waited, he'd seen some of the reivers dragging a body out by its heels. The crowd had barely been glutted by the warm-up act.

Nerves chased themselves in circles in his stomach. The monster shivered through him. *Blood. Flesh. So close to warm human flesh....* After years of wearing the medallion, he'd become complacent. But had the medallion ever controlled the monster within him, or merely found a way to suppress it as it lurked hungrily inside his body? He thought of Luc Wade, who'd once told him that fear wasn't control.

You have to face that bastard head-on, Luc told him once.

"And here we have our challenger!" boomed the voice of the violet-haired announcer. Scars bisected her cheeks. "Captured only tonight, in the bowels of Rust City itself! I present to you, Scythe."

The crowd roared. Maybe they liked the look of him, or maybe it was just the fact that he had at least two inches on Colton, which might give him an edge, or predict a longer fight. His oiled-up muscles gleamed under the hot lights, and someone had at least found him a pair of jeans, though they'd paired that with a leather collar that offended him on all levels.

He knew now what it meant to lose everything: his name, his freedom, his humanity. Adam's lip curled up in a silent growl that was barely human as he glared back at the crowd defiantly.

"And facing him in the ring for the first—and most likely—last time is the mighty Rattlesnake!"

The crowd lost control as Colton appeared with a shove. Some of the female reivers grabbed at their crotches and hooted, shouting down offers at Colton. Some of the men did too.

Across the arena, their eyes met, and he knew that Colton felt the same sickened feeling as he did. For the first time, he truly understood what it felt like to be considered nothing. To not even have his name.

Vex Cypher held up her hands as the crowd chanted and stamped their feet. "And what do we say to the monsters, my pets?"

"Die!" someone screamed.

"Fight!"

"Are we not mighty?" Vex bellowed. "Who rules the night? The monsters? Or the people of Rust City?"

"Rust! Rust! Rust!" came the chant.

Jesus. He'd felt hatred from humans before, and knew what disgust and fear felt like. This was something else. This was joy at the thought of his inherent suffering. A lust for his misery, his defeat.

A condemnation of his own worth.

You are nothing, said the screaming voices. *Just a moment of amusement for us before we bury you.*

301

The chanting grew louder. Both he and Colton were turning in slow circles. He couldn't see the general anywhere. Maybe he hadn't arrived yet.

But Vex didn't throw him back in the cells. She probably liked the idea of watching him die too much.

Instead she let the crescendo build, watching the crowd with glittering eyes. She knew how to own her reivers. Maybe one of them might overthrow her one day, but Adam doubted it. He knew fanaticism when he saw it. She was giving them what they wanted, and so they'd love her for it, even when she tightened the leash and played them off against each other, one by one.

"Fight!" she finally screamed, bringing her arms down sharply at her sides.

Something silver arced high in the air, and a single knife flashed into being as someone threw it into the ring. Colton was already sprinting for where it landed, point first in the sand.

Adam shoved himself into gear, darting forward to meet him. If Colton got his hands on that knife, then he might as well kiss the game good-bye.

Colton slid to his knees, and Adam drove into him a second before his hand curled around the hilt of the knife. The impact rolled them both across the sand. Both of them were covered in oil and he couldn't quite get a strong enough grip. A knee drove into his thigh, so he hammered his elbow into Colton's jaw.

Colton blinked, his fingers digging for Adam's eyes. Adam used his heavier weight to drive him into the ground, and locked Colton's elbow into place.

"If you help me, I can get over the fence," he whispered in Colton's ear.

Then he rolled away as Colton flung a flimsy blow at him, offering Colton time to get on his feet.

The crowd booed and hissed.

"Kill him!" they screamed. "Give us blood! No mercy!"

Colton's dark eyes flashed in curiosity as he climbed to his feet. Rolling his shoulders he looked around, as if surveying the crowd, but Adam could see him taking stock of their surroundings.

"Blood! Blood! Blood!" Someone in the crowd started up a cheer, one hastily taken up by the rest.

And they thought he and Colton were the monsters. Adam wiped the sweat from his brow, feeling sick.

Colton danced toward him, fists held up defensively. "What have you got in mind?"

Thank fuck.

They hammered together, both of them seemingly wrestling for control. "Throw me over. There." He grunted as Colton drove a fist into his side. "I'll take down the fence's electrics. Then you can follow."

"You're fucking crazy." Colton slammed his cupped fist into the muscle above his collarbone. "They've got gun turrets at both ends."

Adam grunted and locked his cupped palms behind the other man's head, bringing their faces close enough to share breath. "You draw their attention at one end, I take out the other one. Or would you rather die for their amusement?"

Another flash of dark eyes. They went down and rolled, Colton hooking a leg around his as both wrestled for supremacy, but his heart clearly wasn't in it. He was thinking now. That lock should have broken Adam's ankle, but he shoved free with a hard knee to the muscle in Colton's upper thigh.

Both of them broke apart, panting. Colton's eyes darted. His back was close to the huge electrical generator at the southern end of the arena. With a faint nod, he held his hand up and twitched two fingers. *Come at me.*

Adam started sprinting toward him. Hell if he knew if he trusted Colton or not, but this might be their only chance.

The crowd roared their approval. At the last second, Colton slid to one knee, cupping his hands together in a stirrup.

Adam's foot hit Colton's clasped palms, and then he was sailing up, up, arms and legs windmilling as if he were running through the air as the fence rushed toward him.

The crowd's roar turned into a scream of thwarted rage—and fear.

And then Adam cleared the fence.

twenty-five

THE SLAVE MARKETS were closer to the arena than Mia would have liked, and just as lightly guarded.

Vex's reputation kept most of the reivers from attempting to steal from her, Zarina explained, as they slipped from shadow to shadow. There'd been enough demonstrations in the past that nobody in their right mind would seek to thwart the warlord.

"They'll have two guards on rotation there," Zarina muttered, her dark eyes focused on the markets. She pointed toward the pair of stone gates that led into the market from each end. "Another two in the back. They're not the problem. The alarms are. Right now the war games will be keeping Vex's attention, but she's going to start wondering where I am soon. And if one of the guards here makes it to the nearest alarm, then we're done."

"You're saying we need to separate," Mia murmured.

"Hit them all at once." Zarina nodded. "The bad news is that we're close enough to the arena now that we can't risk using guns. Maybe Vex will ignore the odd shot. Hell knows that reivers like to waste bullets. But if she hears enough in a concentrated burst, she'll send someone to investigate. She's not stupid."

"I can take them down without a sound," Jake replied.

"But you're just one man," Zarina countered. "There are four guards, in four different areas. I've got the advantage of surprise. They won't be expecting it from me."

"That's two of us. Mia?" Jake looked at her.

Shooting that reiver the first night in Vegas had been harder than she'd expected. It grew easier every time, but Mia didn't think she'd ever get used to killing someone. And whilst Jake had taught her to punch and fight as a young girl, she didn't have the same instinct the other two did.

Mia focused on the gates. Sage and the others were out of the question. With the pale robes that barely covered their skins, they couldn't pretend to be anything other than what they were dressed as: slaves.

"I can do it," she said, slipping Jenny's knife into her hand.

Jake squeezed her shoulder. "Take the girls with you. If there's anyone here who needs backup, it's probably you. I'll hit the ones at the back, if you and Zarina want to take the guards at each gate."

"Let's do this." Before she lost her nerve.

Jake moved to go, but Sage caught his wrist. They'd had a brief reunion in the courtyard at the stronghold, tears flooding Sage's eyes as she threw her arms around Jake's neck and simply held him. Not long enough, clearly, for Sage grabbed his collar and hauled him close for a swift kiss. "Watch your back."

Mia looked away.

"Always do," Jake muttered. "You watch your sister's."

They pulled apart.

"Keep an eye out for Rondo," Zarina called in a low voice. "He's dangerous. He'll be the bigger one with the gut on him, and if he gets you in his hands, you're dead."

"Got it." Jake slipped into the night.

"Go right," Zarina told Mia. "It's either Zeke or Millar on the gate there, and they're the easiest to take."

Trusting her went against every grain in Mia's soul. Zarina could be double-crossing them. All she had to do was slip away and sound the alarm herself.

"Ellie, go with her," Mia said, tossing her the shotgun.

Startled eyes met hers, then Ellie nodded. The young woman had hardened in the past few days. No longer the local cattle baron's daughter, now she had blood on her hands just as much as the rest of them.

"You two walk behind me, as though I'm wearing your leashes," Mia said, eyeing the gate right in front of her. She could see a shadow under the arch, the faint flare of a cigarette gleaming at the bastard's mouth. There was no cover between here and the gate. She couldn't sneak up on him, which meant subterfuge. "Eyes downcast, nice and meek. At least until I put a knife through his throat."

"Give me the knife and I'll do it." This from Sage.

Maybe Ellie wasn't the only one who'd hardened. Mia handed her the spare she carried. "Don't use it until you get a free shot. Let's do this."

Mia strode across the dirt road as though she belonged there. She mimicked the low, hip-swinging strut she'd seen on Zarina.

Instantly the reiver on the gates stepped forward, plucking his cigarette from his lips. "What d'you want?"

Mia smiled. "What do *you* want, handsome?"

That made him take a second look at her. He put the cigarette to his lips again, eyeing the pair of breasts that threatened to spill out of the black tank she wore. "What I want isn't the sort of thing you say out loud to a lady."

"Who's the lady around here?"

His smiled grew wider. "In that case, I'd be interested in getting you out of those leather pants. And getting into them."

Mia slid a hand up his chest, her nose wrinkling at the stench that came off him. She maintained her smile, the hilt of her knife sliding into her palm. "Maybe that can be arranged."

"That sounds...." The smile on his lips faltered as he caught a better look at Sage. "Hey, where's her leash?"

Whoops.

Mia swung a punch at him.

Her left was her weaker hand, but she needed to keep hold of her knife. Knuckles crunched as she connected with his nose. *Jesus.* This wasn't like hitting the wheat bag Jake had strung up for her at fifteen.

The reiver staggered back and Thea drove into his midriff, taking him down like a professional. Mia suffered a moment of surprise, and then she leapt in too. Grabbing a handful of his hair, she tried to stab him but he threw her off.

"Bitches."

A sharp knee sent Thea flying. Both she and Mia scrambled to their feet, but Sage stepped in, hammering a rock down on his head. The reiver's eyes rolled back in his head, and he slumped to the concrete.

Sage stood there panting, holding the rock high.

"I think you got him," Mia said.

Sage lowered the rock with shaky hands. Then she drove her boot into his side. "Scum."

"Scum or not, we need to get him out of here." Mia checked under his eyelid. Out cold. She grabbed him by the vest and hauled him into the shrubby bushes near the gate, blisteringly aware of how loud that had been.

"Hey," someone called. "What's going on there?"

Shit. Her pulse jacked through her veins. Mia stepped forward, but three reivers paused in the street just outside the gates.

"What are you two doing out?" demanded the one in the front, eyeing both Bethany and Sara.

Mia took a menacing step forward, and something in her expression must have triggered the reivers. Their smiles faded and the leader's hand lowered to his hip and the gun there.

"That gun better not clear your holster, Eduardo." Zarina Cypher strode into view, scowling at the three reivers.

Eduardo yanked his hand away with a respectful nod. "Cypher. Found these four slaves down here, and this woman. They're not—"

"They're here to meet me," Zarina told him, and faced him with just enough aggression in her tone that he actually backed away. "Are you impeding my guest and her slaves?"

Guest? Mia's gaze shot to Zarina.

"Aren't you supposed to be guarding the armory?" Zarina pushed him firmly in the chest, so that he staggered back a step. "You want my mother to know you're in here trying to get your hands on one of the slaves before they go up for auction? You know soiled goods don't fetch a quality price, Eduardo."

"We weren't—"

She grabbed a fistful of his shirt and leaned close, her voice dropping to a menacing whisper. "You fucking lie to me and I will cut your tongue out myself. I know what you're doing here. I know what you planned. I can smell it all over you. And if I ever catch you anywhere near this place again, I'll cut your fucking balls off and feed them to the pigs." She shoved him back into the arms of his two companions. "But I'm feeling lenient today. All three of you get out of here, before I change my mind. Return to your post."

Eduardo shot them a panicked look, then turned on his heel and fled, with the other two reivers at his side.

"You going to use that pig-sticker?" Zarina asked, arching a brow in Mia's direction. "I'll just warn you that if you try, I'll do more than take it off you."

Mia tucked the knife back up her sleeve. "You're letting them go?" What if they said something to someone?

"Eduardo had his hand on his gun," Zarina replied, glancing at Ellie as she checked Thea over. "You want to try and take it off him, sure, be my guest. But Eduardo's not someone you mess with. He won't say anything. Not after I just threatened him. He'll be sweating buckets, hoping I don't mention this to Vex."

"Any trouble?" Jake called, appearing out of the shadows like a cat.

"Nothing we couldn't handle," Mia told him, staring flatly at Zarina.

"Let's go get our people then."

It seemed to be going smoothly. Too smoothly.

Jake found the keys to the first row of slave pens, and broke in. The pens were covered in tin, and the narrow hallway stunk of unwashed bodies. It was stiflingly hot in here. Sweat dripped down Mia's spine.

Straw rustled as Jake flipped on the flashlight he'd worn clipped to his belt, and whispers broke out as the people in the cages saw him.

"Easy now," he whispered. "I'm not here to hurt you."

"What's going on?" someone called inside the pens.

There were people in cages in here. Her people. And others. Some of them crouched in the straw, peering up at them with sleepy eyes.

Tom Hannaway saw them, his mouth forming an O. "Jake?"

"Get ready, kid," Jake said, unlocking his cell. "We're here to bust you all out."

An excited babble filled the chambers.

"Quiet," Ellie rasped, helping drag a dirty Tom out of his cramped cage.

Mia guarded the door with Zarina, as the others worked their way inside, greeting those trapped in cages. Lights created a halo over the arena in the distance, and sound buzzed. The outcry was so loud Mia didn't think that any of the reivers would even hear it right now if she fired her gun.

McClain.

Her heart twisted in her chest, and nervous energy buzzed beneath her skin. So far the plan seemed to be falling into place.

Next step was escape.

But if she ventured down that path with the rest of her people, then there was no coming back.

"*Blood, blood, blood!*" came the distant chant.

And Mia made her decision. She'd done what she came here to do. Sage was free, and the others were out of their chains. Time to fulfill her promise to McClain.

"How long 'til the war games are over?"

Zarina tilted her head. "Sounds like this is the last match. They save the best for last, and that"—she pointed her finger toward the arena as a horn called—"is the final siren. They just started."

"We'd better get moving then," Sage muttered, helping a young woman out of one of the cages she'd been cramped in. "Get these people out, and head for the cars."

"Armory first," Zarina said, "unless you want to face reivers with your bare teeth. Only problem is: they have electric locks installed. You'll need the code, and I don't know it. It changes on a weekly basis."

"I can get through an electric lock," Sage promised. "All I need to do is short-circuit a few wires."

Mia paced a little. This was the first section of the market. She couldn't see Sonya anywhere, which meant she must be in the other section.

"How long until Vex leaves the games?" she demanded.

"Could be over in fifteen minutes," Zarina replied, watching her closely. "Could be an hour. Why?"

"I've got to go back." She'd promised him, after all. There was no way she could walk out of here without McClain, and the others were nearly out of their cages now. Just one more row of slave pens, and then they'd head for the vehicles. Which meant she was running out of time.

"Mia." Jake looked up at her, the torchlight searing his eyes a weird blue. "We don't have time."

"I am *not* leaving without him," she snapped at him. "Warg or not, he helped us when he didn't have to, Jake. I won't repay that with treachery, so you can either leave me behind or help me rescue him."

"You've got a death wish," Zarina said.

"I know *you* wouldn't understand the concept of loyalty," Mia shot back, "but this is what good people do when they give their word. McClain is coming with me, or

I'm staying with him. That's my choice, and none of you will change it. I'll help you guys get the others out of the pens," she said, loading two shells into the shotgun. "Then I'm going back for McClain."

"Mia—"

"No, Jake." She looked up. "You were right. We had to get Sage out first, and all of the other women. But I've had time to think through the shock of finding out what he is. McClain didn't have to come on this rescue mission. He chose to. And I don't know why—I think I *need* to know why—but that doesn't sound like a man who meant to hurt any of us." *Me*, was what she really meant. Mia swallowed. "Whatever the future holds, I owe him this. If I don't get him out, then I won't ever be able to look myself in the eyes again."

"I can't leave you here," he began to argue, gesturing toward Sage. "What about your sister? She needs you."

Sage caught Jake's hand and squeezed it. "If he came here to help save me, then I'm not going anywhere without him either."

Jake swore under his breath.

"Thank you," Mia whispered.

Sage smiled a little sadly. "You'd do nothing less for me."

"Which do you want more?" Zarina asked. "The other slaves? Or McClain? Because you're not going to have time to do both."

Mia and Sage exchanged a look. She was so grateful she had her sister back—Sage was the only other person who could understand what she was thinking without her even saying it.

"We separate," Sage said firmly. "We'll head for the armory—Mia, how are you going on ammunition?"

"Low."

"If you do this, then you need all the help you can get," Sage warned. "Give us another five minutes, then hit the armory with us. That will give you everything you need to free him."

"Done. And then I'll go get McClain." Mia exchanged a grim smile with Zarina. Trust or not, Zarina was the best person to get her what she wanted—access to the warg cages. "You want out? Then you're with me. That's the deal."

"I didn't agree to that."

"No," Sage said, backing Mia up. "But you're not a very popular person with a lot of the people we're about to free, so I don't think you have much of a choice. Earn your redemption. If you can't bring Mia and McClain back, then we're not taking you with us."

Zarina's jaw dropped.

twenty-six

ADAM LANDED IN the center of the stands, among a couple dozen startled reivers. He'd cleared the fence, which meant he was halfway there. Now to take out those generators.

One of the reivers gaped at him, then drew a knife. Adam lashed out blindly. He was lost in a fog of rage and fury, lost in the claws of the warg within him. It wanted blood, and he wanted out. Both purposes meshed for the moment.

"Kill him!" someone screamed.

And they came at him like a flood. A flood of reiver scum that he actually welcomed.

By the time he came back to himself, he was standing in a pool of torn bodies, with a knife in his hand. He couldn't remember how he'd gotten it, but his arms were drenched in blood, and there were various cuts and grazes up his arms and along his ribs. As he looked down, they healed almost miraculously.

The warg was too close to the surface right now. The pewter medallion around his throat flared cold, as if in warning.

The rest of the reivers hung back from him. Sanity wasn't usually a prerequisite for reiver membership, but he'd just cut down at least twenty of them and now they were wary. Whipped curs, the lot of them.

"Come on," he spat, curling his lip a little as he darted toward a pack of them.

Bullets ripped through the air as the reiver on the gun turrets swung the massive repeating rifle toward him. Reivers went down beneath its hail, and Adam threw his arms over his head as he ran.

"Stop!" Vex screamed, as reivers bolted from him.

The cover fire fell silent. Clearly she wanted him alive.

The reivers in front of him scattered, and then his path was clear to the enormous generator tower that ran the fence and the lights. The giant generator was solid steel welded together, but the cables that lit the fences ran through the air above him. If he could take one of them out, then Colton could clear the fence.

The only problem was that they were live wires.

Adam leapt from stand to stand. He'd made a promise to Mia, and he intended to keep it. But to do that he needed Colton.

"Shoot him in the legs!" a woman bellowed, and Adam glanced at Vex's box. Half a dozen shotguns were trained on him.

The reivers around him scrambled to grab him. He lashed out with claws that had sprung from the tips of his fingers, seemingly out of nowhere. A partial shift. He'd seen Luc Wade use claws like these in the past, but he'd never been able to control it himself. Never wanted to. This time he took advantage of them.

Raking through flesh and bone, he lurched forward, diving low as shotgun fire echoed. Reivers screamed as they were hit. Adam kept going, using their bodies to cover his own passage.

A reiver leapt at him from above, an axe in his hand. Adam sidestepped, grabbing the man by the belt and arm and hauling him in a low circle around him. He let go just as they hit maximum velocity, and the reiver flew through the air.

The reiver hit the wires, his weight snapping them from the top of the tower. He hit the ground, jerking and screaming, froth forming on his ragged lips. Instantly the static buzz of the arena's fence went silent.

Problem solved.

Adam turned, but the ring was empty. His heart skipped a beat.

Colton hadn't waited around to see how he escaped. Instead he'd vanished back into the tunnels, the treacherous cur.

Now what?

"You cowardly bastards!" Vex had a whip out and was using it to slash and cut at her reivers as they tried to flee. She cast it aside in frustration, then locked gazes with him. "Five hundred gold pieces to the reiver who brings me that filthy warg's head!"

That slowed the pack of reivers. Some of them kept running, but others turned, greed lighting their eyes. Five hundred gold pieces was more than most of them had ever heard of. Hell, it was more than *he'd* ever dreamed of.

"Dead or alive?" asked a vicious-looking woman wearing a fur vest, and painted stripes of white across her pale skin.

"Do I look like I give a shit?" Vex snarled. She paced the platform, then her face smoothed. "Actually. I want him alive. I want to do the honors. There'd be nothing better than a matching warg fur for my bedroom floor."

Jesus. Adam looked around. He needed a weapon. Snatching up the electrocuted reiver's axe, he hefted it just as twenty or so of them turned on him.

Adrenaline had kicked him along this far. He wanted out. And he wanted to find Mia, to make sure that she and the others were safe. That stiffened his trembling arm as exhaustion began to make itself known. He'd have to cut them down quickly, or else he'd start to lag. Having the warg right beneath his skin was both exhilarating and draining.

Adam stalked across the timber stand. Vex and her reivers were between him and the exit. He could go back over the fence, but there was no way out at the end of that tunnel.

Shit. He'd backed himself into an unintentional corner. Of course, he'd also expected to have Colton at his back right now.

"What are you waiting for?" he asked, as the female reiver crouched low and stalked him.

She grinned, revealing rotting teeth. "She said she wants you alive. That doesn't mean you have to be in one piece. I'm going to cut off your balls and wear them in a pouch around my neck, wolf-man."

She attacked, coming in low with her own axe. Adam jumped her swing, and buried the sharp end of his own axe in between her shoulder blades. She went down with a scream, and then the rest were upon him.

Weapons flashed as they swung at him. Adam cut and hacked, kicking reivers in the face when they got too close, and then slamming his heel on vulnerable ribs when they went down.

There were too many of them though. His arm started to shake, his ribs burning with the pulse of his lungs. One of the reivers he'd downed grabbed his heel, and Adam took the full brunt of a baseball bat right in the ribs. Then there was a giant trying to rip his head from his shoulders.

Move, he screamed at himself. *Or die.*

Grabbing hold of the bastard, he drew his fist back for a punch, but the reiver's eyes widened at something over Adam's shoulder, and he started scrambling to get away.

What the hell?

Wargs scrambled up the fence like monkeys, launching themselves into the crowd from the top of the wire. Reivers screamed as some of the wargs went full shift, rending with claws and teeth.

Colton hadn't fled. Instead he'd gone back into the warg cells and set them all free.

They tore through the crowd, a wave of monstrous fury that cut the reivers down with impunity. Vengeance, hot and bloody, and suddenly the sounds of reivers reveling in the spill of blood—warg blood—turned to shrieks of pure fear as the reivers found their own blood wasn't quite as entertaining.

He'd never been a bitter man, but there was a small part of him that enjoyed the sudden turnaround.

Adam punched the reiver in his grip, and turned to survey the chaos. This changed everything. Suddenly he wasn't one man battling against dozens, he was on the winning side.

Colton landed beside him.

"What took you so long?" he demanded.

"Slight fucking problem with the guards." There was blood splashed across Colton's cheek. "And I thought you could handle a few reivers."

"Are you insane?" Adam breathed, looking around at the wargs. Nothing would stop them now. Wargs were monstrous at the best of times, but after being tortured and forced to fight? They'd be insatiable. "There are still slaves here. Innocent people...."

Colton's dark eyes narrowed. "None of these wargs asked to be a monster. They were innocent too, once upon a time. And I'm not going to leave them to rot here so the reivers can get their fun. Some of them might be monsters, but they deserve a clean death, not to be a fucking spectacle."

Adam grabbed him. "Mia's out there."

Colton's fist curled in his collar. "Then you better get to her before they do."

His heart kicked in his chest. The crowd was running, screaming, being mowed down by a flurry of vengeance. And a part of him liked it. A part of him reared its ugly head and smelled the blood in the air. *Yes. Hunt,* it whispered.

Adam reined it in. *Mia*, he told himself, forcing his lungs to work steadily.

Mia, the warg echoed, as if it wasn't quite certain what to think about her.

Adam shoved his way through the crowd of reivers. They were all trying to get through the narrow exits, and that was where they died, packed in like schools of fish. Vex and her party vanished through her personal exit, and she'd left her guard behind to hold the wargs at bay.

By himself he wouldn't have been able to escape, but with the wargs set free.... He couldn't help admiring Colton's sheer ingenuity.

"This way," he said, and started leaping up the stands toward Vex's exit.

"You want me with you?" Colton called incredulously.

Adam turned. "Help me get Mia and the others out, and the debt you owe me is cleared."

It ached to say it. Nine years of betrayal stretched between them. Colton had been Cane's little bitch-boy, a warg who hadn't voiced too much protest when Cane took him and Eden. A part of him struggled to forgive that moment when Colton had thrown Eden inside the hut with him, sentencing her to die unless Adam gave them what they wanted.

But this needed to end, one way or the other.

Colton's expression wavered, an inner fight that Adam could barely guess at. "Okay."

It felt like the air changed around them. Never friends. Not even true allies. But no longer enemies.

Hell if he knew what to call it.

By the time Colton joined Adam, the reivers had found some composure. Shots rang out, a hail of bullet fire that ripped through both reivers and wargs alike. Adam shoved Colton closer to the back of the stands. They were going to have to jump. Far below them, the rooftop of the tin shanty gleamed in the hot afternoon sun.

"This is your brilliant idea?" Colton demanded.

"We'll both survive the fall."

"If I break a leg, I'll haunt you until the day you die," Colton shot back, and looked down again, his temples darkening with sweat. "I hate heights."

Vertigo crawled in Adam's gut. He didn't really want to do this either. But the choice was taken from the pair of them when a shot clipped the makeshift timber stand he stood upon.

"Now!"

Launching himself off the top of the stand, he felt gravity kick in a second later, with a gut-plummeting whoosh.

Arms windmilling, he tried to prepare for the landing. His boots hit the tin roof with a jarring impact, and he went straight through.

A table shattered beneath his weight. Adam flipped off it and tumbled into a ragged heap on the floor just as Colton plummeted through with a scream.

The shanty collapsed around them. Metal screeched as the tin sheets on the walls tumbled against each other, and dust sprang up. The roof caved in, and Adam shoved an arm over his face as one of the timber roof beams fell toward him. It clipped his arm, then slammed into the floor next to his head.

Silence.

Dust.

Everything hurt.

"You still alive?" Colton groaned. Tin shifted in the corner.

"I'm still... trying to decide." Adam focused on breathing. The fall had taken the wind out of him.

Colton lost it, and laughed. "You son of a bitch. That was the stupidest fucking thing I've ever done."

Wincing, Adam pushed the beam aside, trying to drag his legs out from under the section of roof that had fallen. His lungs shuddered. Something in his side ached like someone had stuck a hot poker in it. Cracked rib?

"We're not out of here yet," he warned. "We need to get moving."

"I'd much rather lie here for a few more minutes."

There was no time for that. Shots ricocheted outside, and the sounds of dying screams echoed through the streets.

Mia was somewhere in the midst of it all.

Adam hauled himself grimly to his feet. "No rest for the wicked. Come on."

twenty-seven

"ARE YOU SURE you're up for this?" Mia whispered loudly as Sage broke open the fuse box that kept the armory door shut.

"More than sure," Sage growled. "I am going to burn these motherfuckers to the ground."

Okay. Her pacifist sister with her sunny disposition and constant smiles had vanished. Maybe Sage needed to work through her anger. Maybe destroying Rust City would be the perfect thing for her. Mia contemplated her sister's face, her gaze lifting to Jake's. He frowned at his wife's back, but then nodded to Mia. He'd watch over her.

Zarina shook her head. "I think she's caught some of your stupid, or something."

Sage tugged wires out here and there. "Nearly there."

"This will get us into the main warehouse," Zarina said, "but the ammunition is kept in a separate locker within. Guns are easier to get your hands on round here, but the ammo's the real deal. Bullet trade dried up after the border dispute down south three months ago."

"How many guards inside?"

"One on active duty," Zarina replied curtly, looking around. "A few more in the back on stand-down. But we're going to have to be quick now. We're in a fairly suburban area here, and if anyone leaves the games early...."

Sparks fizzed, and Sage stepped back from the fuse box as the lock clicked open. "Electricity down. We're in," she said, setting her fingers into the handle on the door.

Jake helped her, and slowly the enormous steel door began to slide open.

Mia and Zarina went through first, covering the main warehouse with their shotguns. Crates were stacked neatly in rows. A faint light gleamed overhead, but most of the warehouse was cast in inky blue shadows.

"Hey!" Shouts echoed ahead as a reiver shook out the match he'd been lighting his cigarette with. He frowned as he saw the size of the group, then recognition dawned, and he turned and reached for something.

"Stop him!" Zarina yelled.

The alarm. Mia saw the red button now. The reiver's fingers almost brushed it, but a gun retorted and his body gave a jerk before it hit the floor. There was a small red hole in his temple.

"Got it," Jake said tersely, lowering his smoking pistol. "Get moving, guys. Someone might have heard that."

Too late. A couple of reivers burst through the doors at the back. Jake shot one of them, but the other dodged.

Zarina took the time to smash the control panel on the alarm system. "That'll slow them. It's the only alarm in this side of the building."

Mia shot the other reiver. Shotgun pellets ripped his chest open and he went down.

"Nice shot," Zarina said, dragging her along with the rest of the group.

She'd been aiming for his head. Mia looked at her treacherous hands. Still shaking. She felt so disembodied.

"This way," Zarina called, pointing them toward a smaller door. "The ammo's kept in here. Sage?"

"Got it." Sage used some sort of metal tool she'd picked up somewhere to jack open the fuse box. She cursed as one of the wires sparked and shook her fingers.

Reivers poured through the main doors behind them. They must have heard the shots. One of the younger girls tripped and went to her knees. Jake hauled her to her feet and shoved her behind a crate. He flinched as bullets slammed through the air around him, and Mia thought she might have been the only one who saw him get hit.

"Jake!" She jerked through the fleeing crowd to grab his arm.

"Just a... graze," he panted, shooting back over his shoulder. His eyes were wild, however. "Get them hidden, Mia. I'll cover our back."

"Sage!" she bellowed. "Can you open the next door?"

She thought she saw her sister's red head bob up through the crowd. "Trying my best."

"Can we shut it behind us? Wait until we're through though!"

"Do you think I'm stupid?" Sage yelled back.

"Let's cover their tracks," Mia said, and started shooting toward the reivers with her pistol. She'd run out of ammunition pretty quickly, so she took shots every few seconds, trying to keep the reivers pinned down behind the crates they hid behind.

Jake caught on and every time she paused, he filled the void with his own bullet, until he clicked empty. He'd lost accuracy, however. Blood soaked his sleeve.

She had to be getting close to running out herself. No time to reload the shotgun. "Sage!"

"Get in here," Sage yelled.

Then Zarina was there. "Reload," she commanded and lifted two pistols, just as the reivers started to creep around the crates in the center of the room.

Bang. Bang. Bang.

Two went down. Mia dragged Jake through the open doorway as Zarina followed them, steadily walking backwards. All of the reivers hit the floor. Mia sighed a breath of relief.

Jake panted, leaning against the wall with his hand clapped to his shoulder. Sage tried to peer at his wound, but he shook his head.

"Get what you need," Mia told everyone. Most of them were staring at her, as if a little shell-shocked. "We have to make a run for the vehicle lot, which means taking out the gun turrets on the main gate. Can anyone shoot?"

"Aye," a big man she'd never seen before said. "I know what I'm doing. Name's Trick."

"Think you can get everyone organized?"

"Will do," he rumbled, and turned to those they'd rescued from the slave pens. Ellie smiled at her and gave her a thumbs up. She'd help.

Screams echoed through the distant air. Mia, Zarina, Sage, and Jake all looked up. Light streamed through the open windows above. They were covered with wire and too narrow to squeeze through, but she could hear everything outside near the arena. Sounded like a bloody riot out there.

"Is that normal?" Mia whispered as everyone started ransacking the ammunition.

"No." Zarina stared at the windows, her body taut with tension. "Something's going on."

"McClain," Mia whispered. She just knew he had something to do with the riot.

As if in answer, the huge flare lights overlooking the arena flickered... and went dark. The room plunged into blackness.

"The generator's down," Zarina whispered, "which means the fence won't hold whatever's in that arena."

Shots hammered through the air outside. It sounded like a repeating rifle. Mia couldn't stop her feet from moving. What was going on in that arena? She had to go and see. Even if the glimmer of hope in her heart was but a spark.

Zarina hauled her back.

"Get your hands off me!" Mia hissed.

"You've got no weapons and barely any ammunition. What are you going to do? Head-butt reivers? You're a liability to him right now."

Good point. Mia dragged a couple of belt loops full of shotgun shells over her shoulders, and reloaded the shotgun.

"Ammo up," she told Zarina. "You're with me. That was the deal."

"If Vex sees me, then I'm a dead woman. This is my ticket out, Mia. You're asking me to throw that away."

Mia opened the clip on her pistol. She paused. "I need you. I can't navigate these streets without you. Please."

Zarina looked away, her shoulders tense. "This is a bad idea."

"You said your mother killed the man you loved. If you had a chance to go back to that moment and stop her, you'd do anything to save him, wouldn't you?"

Zarina cursed under her breath. "He's probably already dead."

"Then why are they still shooting?"

Both of them listened.

"Don't you want to spit in her eye?" Mia breathed. "Take back everything she's ever taken for you? Repay her for what she did to your man? Do you think you can just run away and put all of this behind you? You can't escape her, or what you've done. But maybe you can make amends."

Zarina shuddered. "Yeah. But if we fail...."

"We're not going to fail." Mia's eyes lit on a rocket launcher.

And suddenly a plan formed. Plan B.

She dragged it out of its case, along with a couple of the grenades. She'd been lost ever since that moment

330

when she realized that McClain wasn't human. Her feet kept moving and somehow she'd managed to run and fire weapons but her mind had been in shock ever since, as if it could only focus on one thing at a time, and barely that.

This cleared the fog.

Once upon a time, she and Jake had been playing around with an old gas canister, a plastic tube sealed at one end, and a crate of oranges. They'd both gotten the hidings of their life from that moment too. But she knew a little about trajectory, and could imagine firing something like this.

She was going to get to McClain, or she was going to die trying. And if she did die... well, she was going to take every reiver in Rust City with her.

"How do you work this?"

Zarina shot her a careful look, then picked up the rocket launcher and hefted the end of it on top of a crate. "Like this," she said, and demonstrated how to load it quickly, her hands moving over the grenades as if she'd handled them before. She cocked one eye shut and lifted it onto her shoulder, then pretended to pull the trigger. "Bang.... Wait a couple of seconds and then...." She made an exploding sound through her cheeks, her clenched fist springing wide. "You shoot this, and you make sure you aim high and not at anyone."

Mia took the launcher, juggling its weight. "How big is the explosion?"

Zarina paused, glancing around for Jake and Sage. They hadn't noticed Mia's preoccupation. They were too busy trying to bandage Jake's arm. "You sure you should be holding that?"

"You going to try and take it off me?"

"Hell, no." For a second Zarina's eyes lit up. "I would love to see the look on Vex's face when she sees you coming."

"You will see it," Mia pointed out. "Let's go."

Adam couldn't find her.

Street after street, all he saw was violence and death. Reivers lay scattered and torn in the dirt, along with the odd warg. In the distance, some of the reivers near the main compound manned the gun turrets and bullets chewed the dirt there.

A warg bolted past on all fours, its matted fur wet with blood.

"You drew claws in that arena." Colton swung his arms out to the sides, and claws gleamed at the ends of his fingers. "Think you can do so again?"

Luc had been able to do the same. Adam grit his teeth. He'd never bothered to learn. Suppressing his warg nature had been all that mattered, and now that he was out of the ring he'd lost the claws he'd sprouted. "The axe is good enough for me."

"Suit yourself," Colton replied with a loose shrug. "But you're the one who fears the beast. I'm the one who controls it."

Colton headed down another dusty street, and Adam frowned. What did he mean by that? Could Colton control the actual shift? Or control the warg when it wanted out?

What would that mean if you were a warg? Was there a way to shift forms with his human mind still in control, so that he'd never have to fear letting it out again?

No time to find out. But definitely later.

Focus on Mia. He hurried after Colton. Once Mia and Jake freed her sister, they'd have headed for the armory and the vehicle lot, if they moved according to the plan.

He didn't know what he'd say to her when he found her. The expression on her face when he went warg kept flashing through his mind. Horror. Shock. Her feet taking one explicit step back away from him.

A reiver staggered out of a narrow alley between shanties, and Adam cut him down with the axe.

He wrenched the axe out of the reiver's chest blankly. Whether or not Mia wanted him anywhere near her, he wasn't about to leave her to this. As soon as he got her and the others safely away from here, they could talk. Until she was safe, nothing else mattered.

"Which way?" Colton asked, standing in the middle of the next intersection. Bedraggled washing hung from lines between houses, and there was water—hopefully water—running in a dribble through the middle of road.

Adam caught the edge of Mia's scent. He spun around, staring along the road. She'd been here. And not long ago, not if he could still smell her.

"This way."

He started running, his heart pounding. If he could still smell her, then she was still alive.

And that was when he smelled the rank odor of the warg.

They weren't the only ones tracking her.

Colton smelled it too. "McClain...."

"Shut up." He leapt a pile of rubbish, and skidded to a halt in the next intersection. A scream jerked his head to the left.

And then he was sprinting again. *Mia!* He could hear her now, hear her gasping.

"Help! Help!" she cried.

Another corner. Something growled and there was a scuffle of dirt, along with a pained yelp.

"Incoming," said a low-voiced woman.

A net or something dropped over him. Adam's feet tangled in the bottom of it, and he narrowly avoided impaling himself on the axe head as he hit the dirt hard. In front of him, he saw the warg he'd been tracking wrapped in what looked like a clothesline. A woman stepped over it and blew its brains out, and then a pair of boots stepped in front of him.

He looked up.

Right into the double barrel of a shotgun.

"McClain?" Mia jerked the shotgun up and gasped.

It was her alright. He'd recognize those long legs anywhere. And far from being the damsel in distress, it looked like she and her companion—was that Zarina Cypher?—had things well and truly in hand.

Colton skidded to a halt behind him. "What the...?" He began laughing, and continued even when Mia turned the shotgun on him.

"Easy," Adam told her, trying to escape the net she'd dropped on him. "He's with me."

"Good thing we rushed down here to save them," Colton drawled.

Adam closed his eyes. One of these days....

Mia yanked the net off him, and he rolled to his knees and dragged himself to his feet.

Then a warm, soft body slammed into his, her arms curling around his neck.

Mia. Oh, God, Mia.

He didn't know what to say. He'd been expecting her to spit on his boot, or turn her back again. Adam swallowed the hard lump in his throat, and slowly, gently closed his arms around her.

It felt like heaven. A part of him had wondered whether he'd ever again get to hold her in his arms. Everything that could have gone wrong had been plaguing him, but to see her here... to hold her... to know that she was safe, and that she'd walked into his arms as if she felt she still belonged there... he hadn't realized how much he'd needed her to do that.

"We were coming to get you," Mia told him, her entire body shaking. "But then all of these reivers started fleeing the arena, and we had to take cover. The next thing we knew there were wargs everywhere."

"Are you crying?" he asked in surprise as he drew back to look at her.

"No." She brushed her eyes dry with a stubborn look on her face.

His heart dropped through his boots. Somehow his hands were on her face, and her cheeks were wet beneath his fingertips. It floored him. Those tears were for him.

But not for long.

Mia shook him off, touching the bare skin across his abdomen. For a second he didn't know what she was doing. Her movements slowed as her warm fingers traced the oiled skin there. Where he'd been shot.

He swallowed again, his voice coming out rougher than he'd intended. "I'm whole."

And he was back in that cell again, seeing the look on her face when Colton took the medallion off him.

"Sorry to interrupt," Zarina drawled, "but we've got to get out of here before my mother rouses the rest of the reivers."

Adam looked up.

"She's with us," Mia explained. "She wants to escape, and she's been helping us."

"Sorry to disappoint you, but your mother's getting the hell out of here," Colton said. "The last I saw, she was heading for the helipad."

"*What?*" Zarina stiffened.

"Let her go," Mia murmured, still looking at him with dazed eyes. "She can't hurt us now."

"No. You don't understand. That helicopter was a gift from one of her contacts in the Confederacy. She supplies them with women—or men—so they can keep them in hidden facilities to use as sex slaves whenever they want. There's an entire consortium of rich Confederacy citizens who owe Vex a lot. She can't make it over the wall the Confederacy are building, but she can head straight for one of their military outposts. She'll spin it so that you guys attacked the town, and tried to take all of her slave trade. They've got weapons and tech we can't even dream of, and if she gets her way, she'll come after us, and she'll bring the militia with her. General's already on his way."

"They don't have any sway in the Wastelands," Colton argued.

"Who needs sway when you've got tanks and enough guns to blow your little towns to pieces?" Zarina replied bluntly.

It wasn't the words, so much as the fact that Zarina Cypher—stone-cold killer—had paled, that got his attention.

"Then we stop her," Colton said.

"Which way is the helipad?" Adam asked.

Mia reluctantly let go of his shirt. Adam wanted to grab her hand, anything to keep her in close proximity, but Zarina was right.

This wasn't over yet.

twenty-eight

THEY FOUND THE helipad after a hellish slog through streets cluttered with bodies and hungry wargs.

A huge engine kicked into gear even as they neared the chain-link gates. Wind whipped out from behind the tin fence as something began rotating, slowly at first, then kicking into gear. The tin fence shuddered.

"She's getting out of here!" Zarina screamed.

"How do we stop it?" Adam roared back, trying to be heard over the massive engine. His shirt blew back in the wind the contraption created. He'd heard of helicopters, but he'd never seen one himself and the sight of it was a thing to behold.

The blades whipped faster and faster, and the helicopter began to rise. Zarina screamed in impotent fury, firing her pistols directly at the helicopter.

"Drag her out of the way!" Mia insisted.

"*What?*" He turned around and saw her lift a fucking rocket launcher onto her shoulder. Jesus. "Mia!"

"Get Zarina out of the way," she replied, focusing on the helicopter.

Adam dove forward and grappled Zarina into submission. She screamed and kicked and tried to head-butt him, but he maneuvered her out of the way, getting a mouthful of her brown plait for his efforts.

"I want her dead!" she screamed. "She can't escape. Not like this. No!"

"Mia's on it," he bellowed.

Zarina stopped fighting him with a sob. She looked up as the helicopter began to find purpose in the sky. Mia calmly tracked it with the launcher and then pulled the trigger.

There was an explosion of fire out the back end of the launcher, and Mia staggered as the grenade launched with a whizzing hiss. Its flight path steadied in the air as it flew determinedly toward the helicopter.

"Take cover!" Colton bellowed, and drove Mia into the ground.

Adam caught a glimpse of Vex's face as the startled warlord caught sight of the rocket heading directly for her, and then the world turned molten.

The back blast of the explosion flung both he and Zarina off their feet; a heated wind that stole breath from lungs and dried his eyes in their sockets. Adam landed flat on his back, then rolled, dragging Zarina beneath him. He clenched his eyes shut as flames swept over him, heat blistering his bare skin. The helicopter hit the ground with another explosive boom that echoed in his bones. The very dirt beneath him seemed to shake, and one of the helicopter blades whined past him and impaled a nearby hut. Adam flinched. *Mia*! Sound screamed in his ears; the shriek of dying metal. Bits of debris bit into the exposed skin on his back. *Christ*. His ears rang, and Adam grit his teeth. How much more could he take?

And then it was over.

Adam gasped as he collapsed atop Zarina. He couldn't get the smell of burnt... everything... out of his nostrils. Slowly he lifted his head. Zarina's breath came in ragged sobs. But the only thing that mattered was Mia, and when he saw her wobble to her knees across the street, the lump in his throat almost choked him.

He'd been closer to the blast than she had been. Mia's shirt looked like it had lost a fight with an angry badger, but apart from that she seemed untouched and as much as he hated to admit it, he probably had Colton to thank for that.

Bastard. It was growing hard to keep finding the energy to hate him.

"She's dead," Zarina whispered, hauling herself to her feet and staring at the wreckage. Nearby, a doorway that had been hovering in mid-air finally collapsed.

Fire bloomed in places. His skin still felt hot and tight, like it had shrunk two sizes. The helicopter had taken out a handful of shanties and the flames spread from shit hole to shit hole. Adam caught the faint tang of burning flesh in his nostrils, and deliberately started breathing through his mouth as he hauled himself to his feet with a wince. His back would heal.

"I never... I—" Zarina looked lost.

The words faded into the background.

He stared at Mia. She stared back.

"Plan B," she told him, as if that all made sense.

And it suddenly became very clear to him. He'd been trying to keep her at arm's length for days. The excuse had always been *don't hurt her, don't break her heart when you walk away.* But the truth gave a little twist in *his* heart. It had also been about protecting himself.

He no longer cared what had happened in that cell. All he'd been thinking until this moment was that the right thing to do would be to walk away. Again.

But how long could he keep running?

And he realized what she'd been saying to him in that alley, when they first met. That hadn't been rejection. She'd been trying to find him, just as much as he'd been trying to find her.

Taking trembling steps, Mia reached for him. Adam slung an arm around her shoulders and dragged her against his body. He was insanely tired, all of a sudden, and his entire body ached.

And they needed to talk.

Just as soon as they got out of this hellhole.

"Well," Colton said, shattering the moment. "Looks like you got yourself a real warrior there. Good luck with that, McClain. Now, we'd better get out of here before those fires spread."

"Amen," Mia whispered.

twenty-nine

BY THE TIME Mia woke up, the sun had risen and she was in a car bumping along the desert floor.

The pillow beneath her was warm. Like, really warm. She lifted her head a little, using her hand to push herself up. Everything hurt, and her eyes felt grainy from exhaustion. Something hard flexed beneath her and Mia looked up into green eyes. The morning sunlight was that soft hazy color that sometimes turned the desert to gold, and it was doing the same now with McClain's blond eyelashes.

She'd fallen asleep on him. She was also pretty sure she'd been drooling.

"Sorry," she said, pushing herself upright and bumping into Zarina, who was crammed in the seat on her right.

"It's okay," McClain muttered, sliding his arm back from where it had been resting around her.

Her stomach fluttered. There were a thousand things she wanted to say to him, but she didn't exactly want an audience for it.

And she wasn't quite sure what he was thinking either.

The events of the night before flooded through her memories. Running through the night after she'd *blown up* the helicopter; finding Sage and the others either hotwiring jeeps or slashing the tires on the ones they didn't need; and the awkward tension between her and McClain as they both pretended nothing had happened in the cell before it all turned to shit.

Too much to do at the time, she'd told herself. She'd deal with McClain once they got free of the entire mess.

Only... now they *were* free. And she still couldn't find the words.

They'd escaped Rust City with most of the slaves who'd been there. Vex was dead, most of the reivers either fleeing the wargs or bleeding in the streets. There'd be no more slave raids from Rust City. No more warlords or reiver bands. She still couldn't quite believe it.

Mia craned her neck to look behind them. Dust billowed out the back of the car. In the distance smoke billowed in the sky. "No sign of pursuit?"

Sage met her eyes in the rearview mirror. Somehow her sister was the one driving. Jake snored in the front seat next to her, his arm strapped across his chest with a bloodied bandage. "Nothing worth mentioning. I think those reivers that got out were more concerned with avoiding the wargs."

"Great." She sank down in the seat. "How long have I been out of it?"

"Five or so hours," Zarina said, with a snort.

Not nearly long enough. Mia's head lolled back onto McClain's shoulder as darkness sucked her under.

They stopped driving around four in the afternoon. Zarina wanted to push on—she was clearly fleeing her own demons—but the rest of them were exhausted.

Mia made herself busy by setting up camp and seeing to the other slaves they'd freed. There were around thirty of them. Men, women, even older children who hadn't yet been shipped south. A huge win by any standards, but maybe it was exhaustion that kept some eyes hollow. She smiled weakly as she rubbed her hand through one boy's matted hair. How anyone could do something like this to another person was beyond her.

"Thank you," one woman murmured, sipping the water that Mia had brought up from the stream.

"What's your name?"

"Risa."

"You're safe now," Mia said softly. "Make sure you get some sleep tonight. I'm sure we'll start early in the morning."

Risa looked up. "Where are we going?"

"We're heading north to Salvation Creek, the town I'm from. There'll be warm blankets and food there for you as you recover. As for the rest? That's up to you. I'm sure you'd be welcome to stay."

Tears wet the other woman's eyes. "I didn't think I'd ever be free again. It doesn't feel real just yet." She swallowed. "Thank you so much for all you've done for us."

Mia smiled, then left Risa staring into her cup of water. She still didn't feel like celebrating, but hearing Risa's words gave her a good head start on it.

Where are we going? kept whispering through her head. *Home, we're going home,* she argued with herself, but it didn't feel right. That restless itch she'd felt when she was eighteen was back again, and this time she thought she might know more about what it indicated.

Jake had taken Sage off to the creek to talk. She knew what he was going to tell her sister, and nervous butterflies lit up inside her stomach, no matter how much she tried to distract herself. Sage needed to know and they'd both promised to tell her, but she still felt weird about it.

So much had changed in the space of a week. Mia looked down. She'd washed herself in the creek and wore clean clothes—her last set—but she still felt dirty somehow. Rust City wasn't going to leave her alone just yet. She wore its ghost inside her skin. Best to keep her hands busy. Keep checking on the former captives. It gave her something to do.

As for the other cause of her distress, McClain was off hunting with Johnny Colton, and returned with two wild deer about ten minutes later. She didn't ask how they'd tracked it. *Supersenses, remember?*

How could she forget?

She'd thought she was hiding her dilemma well, but after a few minutes of awkwardly trying to find something to do, Zarina stepped into her path. "What's going on?"

Mia shook out the dusty blanket she'd found in the back of one of the jeeps and examined how clean it was. "What do you mean?" The blanket was riddled with holes, but there were no signs of blood or filth like she'd expected. Probably lice though. Reivers weren't the cleanest people. "I'm waiting for dinner to cook."

"Yeah, right." Zarina squatted by the campfire. "You're very carefully avoiding a certain warg three fires over."

Mia's gaze flickered up. McClain stripped the deer with efficient strokes, his back to her as he knelt by another fire. The firelight gilded his close-cropped hair, turning it molten and almost touchable. Mia tore her gaze away. She couldn't help feeling that little twist in her chest every time she saw him, even though they'd barely said a word since she woke up in the jeep that afternoon.

He could probably hear every word they said.

"That's really none of your business."

The words soured the expression on the other woman's face. "Yeah. Okay. I probably deserve that. I get it. We're not friends."

"Zarina," Mia said with a sigh. "It's got nothing to do with who you are, or what you've done. And... I wouldn't say we're not friends. You came with me when I needed you. That earns you some rights." She glanced across the distance again. McClain had gone. Mia's voice dropped. "I just don't want to talk about it until I've got it clear in my own head."

"Talk or not," Zarina pointed out, "if you don't make your move, one of these others will. That's a fine-looking man, and he just helped rescue some of those women from slavery."

"You're not helping."

"I'm not trying to." Zarina's dark eyes gleamed in the firelight. She stabbed a stick into the fire, toying with the hot coals. "We did it. We actually escaped Rust City. And my mother's dead, and...."

And Zarina needed to talk to someone. Anyone. Mia put the blanket down. "You'd be welcome in Salvation Creek."

"I don't think so." Zarina cast a haunted glance around the clearing at the people her mother had taken as slaves. "I'm the warlord's daughter and these people know me. They're never going to forgive me."

"Are you going to forgive yourself?"

Zarina looked away. "It doesn't matter."

Yeah, right. Mia recognized guilt when she saw it. "You're no longer a warlord's daughter," she pointed out. "Some things are going to have to change. Maybe it starts here?"

"Maybe. I'm going to move on I think, Mia." She shrugged, and graced Mia with a careless smile that rang false. "See a bit of the world."

Mia sighed. If Zarina put a bit of distance between herself and the ghost of Rust City, then maybe she could start to work past it all. Mia knew *she* needed the distance. "Here's to new beginnings... for the both of us."

That roused a genuine smile. "To new beginnings."

"And regardless of what you decide to do, you'll always be welcome in my home," Mia said, but her vision caught on something that stole nearly all of her attention.

Sage had returned to camp, and from the look of her eyes, she'd been crying. *Hell.*

"Go on," Zarina muttered. "I don't know the full story, but I can see that something's going on with her and her husband. She needs her sister right now."

That was if Sage still considered her a sister. Mia swallowed.

"How could you not tell me?"

Mia kicked the toe of her boot through the creek's water. "I didn't want to hurt you."

"And do you think this doesn't hurt me now?" Sage demanded in a hoarse whisper. "My entire marriage has been a lie—"

"I *know.*" There were no excuses she could offer. Just a complicated mess she'd never known how to work her way out of.

Sage pressed her fingers to her temples. "All this time I've been on tenterhooks, trying to manage the pair of you in my life. I knew something was wrong. You hated him. Do you know what that felt like? Managing the both of you? Trying to see you when I could, and then spend time with my husband when he was home. Keeping the pair of you apart as much as often. That hurt, Mia.

"And I've spent years trying to work out what happened between you both. Did he have another woman out there? Another family? Was it Mom and Dad's deaths? Did he say something? Was it me? What? I kept thinking that if I could just hold on to him, just love him enough, then he might stay with me. Do you know what that feels like, to spend so much of your life wondering?"

"I'm sorry. I didn't want to hurt you. And you seemed okay with it all. You never said anything."

"That makes two of us. There's a lot you can hide behind a smile," Sage cried. Tears ran down her cheeks, turning her pale skin blotchy. "When I was pregnant... it was the only thing that made him happy for a while. I pinned so many of my hopes on that child, even though I knew the pains weren't normal. I thought it could save our marriage, but then I lost the baby... And I never told anyone how bad it was inside my head, because I never dared upset the applecart."

Mia dragged Sage into a hug. She was crying now too.

"And he hurt you," Sage blurted. "How do I forgive that? All these years you locked yourself away, and I kept hoping you'd find someone for yourself, but he cost you that."

The pair of them cried on each other's shoulders. Mia couldn't help clutching at Sage a little, as if she could still lose her.

"I won't pretend I'm not angry," Sage finally whispered. "But I know you only meant to protect me. You always do. But this time you fucked up, Mia. No more secrets, okay. I can't handle that shit anymore."

"Promise," she whispered.

Sage wiped her eyes.

"What are you going to do about Jake?"

"I honestly don't know," Sage admitted. "He's been the only thing I could think of for the past few days. I was so desperate to see him again, even when I hoped he wouldn't come. I love him, Mia. But I'm so angry with him. He ruined our family."

"Look," Mia said. "Jake and I have had our differences in the past few years, but I have to admit that this week.... You're all he's thought about. He would have done anything to get you out of there safely. And I'm not making excuses for him, but... I guess I've forgiven him. I saw how much he loves you, Sage. He would have died for you."

"You're the last person I thought would ever forgive him."

"I know." Mia let out a relived breath. "But I don't think I'm the same person as I was before. I'm tired of feeling bitter and tired of... I don't know. Just existing, I guess. I want more."

"Good," Sage said bluntly.

"I thought you'd hate me more. I don't know what I'd do without you. You're my everything, you're my—"

Sage held up her hand, looking weary. "I know I am. That's the one truth I will never doubt." Fire suddenly flared in her eyes. "But have you ever thought about what kind of a burden that places on me? I love you, Mia. And I know that I'm the center of your world. And while that's the most comforting thought in the world sometimes, it makes me uncomfortable too. Mia, I know I'm your everything, but the sad thing is that you *have* nothing else. You can't keep living for *me*. And I know why it happened, I know you needed to protect me when Mom and Dad died, and that it gave you a lifeline to hang on to. But that was over ten years ago. I'm an adult with my own... my own life. Even if things don't work out with Jake, I'll find something. But you.... Jake hurt you and you locked yourself away from the world, and I didn't know why. And you kept living in this bubble-like world. Making your whiskey, running the bar, keeping men at arm's length, with me as your focal point in life. And you can't keep doing that. Not for my sake, but yours. I want to see you move on. I want to see you with your own life, your own man, your own... family. I want so much more for you because I love you, and it hurts me to see you stagnating the way you did."

It shocked her. She'd never thought about it in such a way. Had she really done that? Latched on to her sister and used Sage as the pillar of her life, not just for Sage's sake, but for her own?

Sage let out a faint laugh. "And here you have a man, a good man, one who looks at you like you're the moon and all the stars in his world, and I'm so frightened that you're going to push him away."

Mia opened her mouth but the words didn't come out. "He's—"

"Do you love McClain?" Sage demanded. "Before you say anything else, do you love him?"

She didn't know how to answer that. Everything had happened so quickly, and she hadn't had time to sort through her feelings, let alone deal with the emotional fallout of discovering McClain's secret. "It's not that simple."

"Yes, it is," Sage replied. "Do you love him, Mia?"

"Yes! But it also scares the hell out of me."

"What's holding you back? Are you still scared that you can't trust him?"

"He has a secret," Mia blurted.

"Is it the kind of secret that keeps you from letting him into your heart? I want to believe that one of us can be happy. No, I think I *need* to believe it."

Adam had *known*. He'd known how she'd react and all day he'd been keeping his distance, even as there'd been an ancient sense of sadness in his eyes. It stymied her now. The monsters shouldn't be afraid of the humans, but he was. He was afraid she'd reject him again, afraid to get too close to her.

Or maybe he was waiting for her to make the first move.

"I don't know if he's the type of man I thought he was," she admitted slowly, then held up her hand when Sage went to open her mouth. "He's a warg, Sage."

"*What?*"

She told her sister the story about the medallion. "He wears one around his neck. I've seen it a couple of times, but I have to admit I was... focusing on other things whenever he took his shirt off. I didn't even put the two stories together until he was shot. All the signs were there, but why would I? He's a damned hero, and wargs were always the nasty critters in the night as far as I knew. McClain even told me himself—*you won't look at me the way you do now, if you knew my secret.* He's right. I don't know what to think." Her voice dropped. "I... I had sex with him." *Wild, dirty, crazy sex. And it was incredible....*

"Jesus." Sage scraped her hand over her mouth. "But it's nearly night. I don't understand...."

"The medallion keeps the monster trapped within him," Mia admitted. "What do I believe? He helped destroy a slave town, Sage, because he said that every man or woman there deserved to be free. This entire trip he's been looking after me, taking care of me, of my people. My heart tells me he's a good man, but I'm so scared. What do I do?" She gave a breathless laugh that sounded somewhat ragged. "He got to me. I finally let a man in, and now I'm scared that he's not really a man."

Warm arms slid around her, and Sage dragged Mia's head against her shoulder. "Shush. You'll work it out. I won't pretend it doesn't scare me, or that this is an easy decision for you to make, but... I've seen monsters this past week, those in the shape of men and women. Whatever he is, McClain's not that type of monster and I think you know it. I guess... you just have to decide if it's worth the risk."

Was it? Mia breathed in the fresh scent of the wind blowing off the creek and rested her head against her sister's shoulder. She was tired of not taking risks. And every time she thought herself round in circles, she kept running smack-bang into Sage's declaration. *You have nothing for yourself, Mia....*

Maybe it was time to stop overthinking everything?

Maybe it was time to let her guard down, just a little?

Mia kissed her sister's hand and then slowly drew away. "Whatever he is or isn't, I think this is a discussion I need to be having with McClain," she told her sister.

"Finally."

thirty

"HEY."

Mia paused at the edge of the tor where McClain was standing, staring up with absolute absorption at the full moon only just edging into the sky.

It wasn't as though she'd thought she could surprise him, but when he turned to look at her, the silver light of the moon staining his tanned face, there was no surprise in his expression. "Mia," he said gruffly. "What are you doing? I said I'd take the first watch tonight."

"I asked Ellie to keep an eye out," she replied. He'd laid his sleeping kit out up here, as far away from the camp as possible. "I can't remember the last time I saw you sleep."

A shrug. "It's what I do."

He turned away from her as if to hide his face, but she caught his wrist. "No," she said. "It's more than that. What are you hiding from?"

"Mia—"

Stepping closer, she lifted a hand to touch his face but he was turning away, a movement that might have come across as rejection if only she wasn't so certain what he was trying to hide from her.

"Not a good time," McClain muttered, catching her wrists and leaning forward to rest his forehead against her temple. His chest rose and fell as if his blood rushed through his veins, and his skin felt like a fever raged inside him.

How could she ever have mistaken him for human?

"Isn't it?" she whispered. "Why?"

Please. Please tell me about it. She wanted him to speak to her, to share his burden. And maybe she knew why he wouldn't, but by keeping her at arm's length he was sacrificing any chance the pair of them had.

He just shuddered and looked away, which wasn't good enough.

"It's the moon, isn't it? It calls to you." Mia slid her hands inside his shirt, feeling the bristle of hair down his abdomen. McClain's lashes shuttered his eyes, but the tension within him ratcheted tighter. He looked up then, meeting her gaze with eyes of pure silver. A hungry, hunted look filled them, not entirely human.

But suddenly, she wasn't afraid.

She was angry and furious, but no longer bitter. Her heart felt like a butterfly emerging from a long sleep in its protective cocoon. Its wings were light and the world was beautiful, but there was danger there too. And her butterfly-heart could either accept the risk and take flight, or bury itself back into that stony cocoon and die a short, bitter death of nothingness.

Mia took a deep, shuddering breath. Time for some truth. Time to risk it all, to live again. "That moment when you got shot was one of the worst moments in my life. My mind keeps replaying it over and over in my head... that look on your face, and the feeling that I'd lost you before we even had a chance to begin. I won't pretend all of this hasn't been a shock, but there's a part of me that's glad you're a warg and you survived that."

With those words, she pushed his shirt open, revealing the heavy pewter amulet around his throat.

Suddenly, she was the fearless one.

It was the most wonderful feeling in the world. She knew the dangers here, and she realized that what she was holding in her hands was more precious than she'd ever expected. He might not dare give it to her, but all the same, his heart was in *her* hands and she was in the position of power.

McClain stood still, her palms pressed against his chest, holding his shirt open. The heat of his skin was delicious—the temperature dangerously spiked from where it had been the other day, when she'd lain with him. A full moon fever dancing through his veins and gleaming within his eyes.

Warg eyes. The silver cat-shine of them flashed through his irises, then was gone again, as if he locked the beast tight within him.

"You shouldn't be here," he said in a broken voice. The grip on her wrists slackened, and for the first time since she'd met him, Adam McClain looked like a single blow might fell him. Her heart ached at the sight, for he was the strongest, steadiest man she'd ever met.

That was the moment Mia knew she was not wrong. She hadn't misjudged him. The risk was acceptable.

McClain was both monster *and* man, and the man hated its other half. What would it be like to know what you were? To know that no God-fearing person would ever look at you like you were just a man ever again, if they knew the truth? To believe that you could never get close to another person—to never trust a lover with the truth—for fear of watching them walk away.

It would be the loneliest life of all, and her heart broke for him.

McClain's people had turned him away. It was written all over him, and the effect that such a betrayal had had. She might have been furious about the secret he'd kept from her—especially after her experience with Jake, and the damage that secrets did—but for the first time she was able to look at all of it through unjaded eyes. McClain never wanted to hurt her. All he'd ever dared risk was a single night in her bed, but she had the suspicion that he wasn't just trying to protect her in such a thing, but also himself.

Never get close. Never lose your heart. Never take that risk again. God, she knew exactly how he felt deep down in his bones. And it was lonely and heartbreaking, and became a slow burial of oneself. She couldn't do that to him.

And as Sage said, she needed to stop doing it to herself.

"I'm not going anywhere, Adam McClain. You're such an idiot." Closing her eyes, Mia stretched up on her toes and brushed her mouth against his. "But I know why you didn't tell me. And I can't blame you. Perhaps it was for the best?" She breathed the words against his lips. "Because I don't know if I could have accepted the truth before now. But I do. You're a warg," she whispered. "A warg. But you're not a monster."

McClain gasped, breaking away from her. "Mia—"

"Kiss me."

Their mouths found each other in the dark. Just a taste, once, twice. His body went rigid, as if thoughts were still ticking away at the back of his mind, telling him all the reasons they shouldn't be doing this. She slid her tongue between his lips. *Yes*, her mouth said. McClain's lips chased hers as she retreated, and she felt the tremor in his body as he gave in.

Their lips fused together as Mia's hand slid down that rock-hard chest of his. *So firm.* She flexed her fingers against the muscle in his abs. How long had she wanted to do this? The man was a fucking god carved from stone, all smooth lines and hard planes, like a river had slowly, lovingly carved out curves in its cavern walls. And she was drowning in the taste of him, the feel of him beneath her hands.

Mia saw her future opening up in front of her.

This man. This man was all she wanted for herself. She curled her arms around his neck in a fervent *yes*. It was so much simpler like this. Just feeling, instead of thinking so bloody much.

McClain's hand slid down her back, pushing her hard against him. The kiss deepened, consumed. It felt like she'd thrown oil on the fire, for McClain's hesitance gave way to true hunger. His body was a solid wall against her, engorged cock pressing insistently into her hip. Hands firm. All over her. Teeth sinking into her lower lip—

McClain broke the kiss, gasping as he drew away from her.

"Wait!" Mia caught his hand, trying to catch her own breath. "What are you doing?"

"It's difficult right now." His voice was harsher, lower, not quite human. His eyes *gleamed*, before darting away from her as if to hide himself. "I want you."

"Then have me."

The breath punched out of him. "Mia." He raked his fingers through his short hair, almost sharp enough to cut his scalp with his fingernails. "You don't know what it's like, burning beneath your skin. I can keep it at bay most of the time, but it's harder now with the moon, and with you...."

"Promise you're not going to unleash your wild side on me?"

"*What?*"

Mia dragged her fingernails over his denim-clad thigh. Their eyes met, a serious question in hers. Her humor slipped, but then it had only ever been a façade. "This won't change you, will it?"

He shook his head. "No, Mia. I've never lost control... not with... this." Touching the pewter medallion, he brushed his fingers there. A confession loomed in the sudden tightening of his shoulders. "The hunger gets worse at this time of the month. The need.... I'm not entirely human in my desires."

"A bit of PLS?"

He didn't get the joke. Or maybe he wasn't in the mood to do so.

"Pre-lunar syndrome," she said

When she brushed the back of her fingers against his jaw, McClain grew agitated. "I want to take you. Right here, right now. I want to push you onto the ground and fuck you." His eyes blazed as he nipped at her fingers. "Is that what you want? For I won't be gentle. It won't be like last time. I'll fuck you, and then I'll do it again. I'll rut over you 'til morning and it will be teeth and nails in skin, with you screaming into my shoulder. It will be... a claiming."

He looked ashamed as he sank down onto a boulder.

Mia considered him, only for a moment. Then she slid into his lap and began to unbutton her shirt.

"Mia." His voice was raw. "This is truly your last chance to say no." The vein in his temple was throbbing, and she could see the truth in his eyes. "If this happens tonight, I don't think I could let you go come morning. This is the point of no return for me. For you."

"I'm not saying no," she told him firmly, then leaned closer to lick his jaw and breathe the words in his ear. "Fuck me, Adam. Show me who you are. Trust me. Trust me to guard your heart. Trust me to take what you can give. Claim me. The second I kissed you was the point of no return for me."

A growl in her ear. Nervousness bit through her, but she arched her throat back, granting him access. Granting him surrender.

Constrained, in-control-of-himself Adam McClain lost it. Hands skimmed up her body, his teeth sinking into her throat as he suckled hard.

Mia cried out, her entire body jerking. *God. Yes.*

Grabbing her by the hips, he stood and wrapped her thighs around him, taking her mouth in a furious kiss. Then her back hit his blankets and he was looming over her, pressing her down onto his sleeping gear. Another furious kiss. Hands caught in her shirt and he tugged like he was trying to get it over her head, then simply tore it clean up the center.

Maybe she should have been frightened. His eyes were pure silver now, but as his hard body came over her again, blotting out the moon, she knew she didn't have anything to fear. Hands unclasped her bra, and then his mouth was on her breasts, the rasp of his stubble making her cry out. Heat enveloped her nipple as his mouth closed over her, and Mia rocked beneath him, arching up into the hard thrust of the erection trapped behind his jeans.

Felt so good. She couldn't stop touching him. All these long days of denying herself... gone now. And now she wanted more.

Mia found the buttons on his jeans and tugged them open. McClain's cock spilled into her eager hands. As she licked his neck she could taste the soap on his skin from the quick bath they'd all had down at the river earlier.

"I love you," Mia whispered in his ear. It was easy to do when he wasn't looking at her. Maybe she'd be able to say it under the light of day, one day soon.

McClain growled, and those clever fingers worked their way inside her jeans and then her panties.

It wasn't enough. She wanted them off. Pushing his greedy hands aside, she dragged her jeans down her legs, and McClain helped her with her panties. Then he was over her again, that firm erection brushing between her legs.

"Yes!" Mia whispered.

She was already wet with anticipation when he spread her thighs and drove his cock inside her. No chance to catch her breath from the fierce pleasure of the invasion, for McClain was all over her, biting at her throat, thrusting his hips against hers, pinning her wrists to the ground.

It was nothing like their previous night together.

Here was Adam McClain unleashed, and her one last thought as she came with a shocking scream of pleasure was that she wouldn't have it any other way.

Sunlight warmed his skin, chasing away the desert night chill.

Adam blinked sleepily, feeling utterly worn out. His muscles ached, and there was a rapid burning in his back that told him something was healing, but for the first time in years he felt fucking awesome.

And then memory came flooding back in, half-cast vignettes of the night before assaulting him like rapid-fire bullets. Mia. Kissing him. Beneath him. Her body, soft and warm. Crying out, gasping in his ear... her nails digging into his back.

Mia. He'd had sex with Mia.

No, not just had sex. Rough, dirty, animal sex. He'd fucked her, downright claimed her, and all night too.

And she knew what he was.

Panic danced along his nerves and he stiffened, realizing that there was a warm, soft weight in his arms. His arm hung negligently over her waist, and their hands were still clasped, as if they'd finally fallen asleep like that.

You're a warg, she'd whispered. His entire world tore itself apart at hearing those words from her pretty mouth, and then... her palm cupping his jaw as she touched him. It had been like a knife to the heart. She'd owned him in that instant, but his first instinct had been denial. How could she touch him like that? How could she look at him as if she still saw him? Him, Adam. Not something else, something monstrous. How could he trust it? Had it been a mirage? A dream? A conjuring of his desperate mind?

You're a warg. But you're not a monster.

God, how many times had he prayed for a woman to look at him like that and say those words? Hope wove through him like a treacherous snake.

Adam lifted his head off the blanket that was rolled around them, his gut muscles clenching as he took stock of the situation. Hell. Mia was pressed up tight against him, her lush bottom pressing into his groin. And his cock was *definitely* aware of that fact.

"Morning," came her whisper and she stretched, pressing back into him, before stiffening. A sleepy eye glanced back over her shoulder. Then she smiled.

It was like the sun suddenly appearing over the horizon, in his chest. That smile. It owned him.

"Please tell me you're not pointing that thing at me."

Adam eased back against her, swallowing hard. Easier to pretend that nothing momentous had happened. He needed time to process this. "That thing? I'd be affronted, but you sound entirely too pleased with yourself this morning."

Mia almost purred. "I am pleased. I am also thoroughly, unashamedly debauched. Do you know the worst thing?"

His heart launched into his throat. "What?"

"Colton's giving your bike back today, and I think Sage and Jake need some alone time in the jeep. I have to get onto the back of a motorbike." A wince furrowed her brow. "And sit there for hours. I don't think I can even walk, let alone ride."

Jesus. "Are you sore?"

Mia turned and snuggled into his arms, her head resting on his shoulder. "A little. But in the smuggest way." Dark lashes tipped up, revealing a pretty brown eye. "I like your dark side, McClain. He's very intense. Very demanding."

Adam had no idea how to answer that. So he simply lay with one hand cupping his head and Mia snuggled in against his side. "I feel like the luckiest man alive today."

"You should get laid more often. It turns you into a teddy bear."

He smiled. For years he hadn't felt like he deserved to feel happy, but there was an incredible lightness in his chest. In his heart. Then reality returned.

This wasn't over. It would never be over for him.

"Mia, I don't know if I can control this... this thing inside me." He shuddered. "That night in the cell was only the third time I've turned. All these years the medallion kept it at bay." Rubbing at his chest, he continued. "I feel it inside me now, all the time. The more I turn, the more it wants out."

"I don't think you'll lose control," she replied. "If it were going to happen it would have been the other night, with all of the blood and violence around you."

"I was distracted the other night."

"With what?"

His voice lowered. "Finding you. That's the one thing the warg and I tend to agree on." He rolled over, sliding his arm around her waist. "Mia.... You.... I—"

"Yeah?"

His heart skipped a beat. "You're everything I ever dreamed about," he blurted. "It scares the fuck out of me that I could lose you."

"You're not going to lose me." Her hand slid up his chest, and that determined look came into her eyes. "You couldn't get rid of me if you tried."

"Will you marry me?" The second he said it, he wished he could take it back. Not because he didn't mean it, but because her eyes nearly leapt out of her head. "I know it's sudden. I know I'm not...."

Not human.

Those fingers curled around his own. Mia shushed him with a kiss, her lips sweet and undemanding. A gentler kiss, one that spoke of something so much more. "Yes," she whispered, drawing back. "I think it's time I finally took something for myself, and I'm claiming you, Adam McClain. All for my own. I love you. I've said that twice now, and I mean it. But it also means that I want a future with you. No matter how bad things get, I know I can face them with you at my side."

He'd faced burning buildings, wargs, and an entire town full of reivers and barely batted an eyelid. Surely he could say this one thing. "You're what I've been looking for all these years, yet never dared hope I'd find." *I love you.* He'd never dared say that before to her. He'd never really understood the concept, for how could he ask for love when there was so much loathing inside him? But seeing himself through her eyes made it a little easier to accept it. A little easier to allow himself to feel it. "I want you at my side for the rest of my life, and I know I can fight this thing inside me if I have you."

They shared another long kiss before he drew back, content to simply hold her. Simply running his hands through her hair felt amazing. His cock stirred, but it was about more than sex in this moment. And they'd have to get moving soon.

Even if he wanted to stay right here in this moment all day.

"How did it happen?" Mia asked, resting her head on his chest. "Colton said a little bit in the cells, but I wanted to hear it from you."

This was the last thing he ever wanted to talk about, but after all of the secrets between them he didn't dare refuse her. Yet... strangely enough, this was also the first time he'd ever been able to be truly open about his curse. Eden never wanted to hear about it after her ordeal, and he'd always wanted to protect her from the harsh reality of his life.

Adam stroked a hand through Mia's black curls. They were softer than he'd imagined, and he couldn't resist the urge to twist one around his finger. "I was in my early twenties, working as a bounty hunter out on the Rim with a friend of mine, Luc Wade. He had a wife and daughter, with another little one on the way, and one time he stayed behind when I went out hunting.

"There'd been rumors of a warg haunting settlements out to the east, in the no-mans-land near the Great Divide. I met these two men out there who claimed they were looking for the same warg. The older man was Bartholomew Cane. The younger was Johnny Colton."

Mia looked up sharply.

"They wanted to join up with me, to track this warg down. In hindsight there were little signs, but then the moon and the night didn't seem to affect them, so I grew complacent." He tensed a little. "We found a warg—the one we thought was doing the killing—and we put him down. That night we rode back toward my town to celebrate. We were nearly home when Cane pulled out a bottle of gin he'd been saving, for a 'special occasion' he said. I woke up screaming with claws buried in my gut. Cane near ripped me apart...." His voice softened to a whisper as he remembered it. That moment when he'd lost nearly everything in life, but most importantly, he'd lost a future.

Mia stroked his arm. "That bastard."

"He said I was his then. That I belonged to him, and that he'd sired me. Thought we made one hell of a team, and that he wanted one more to ride with us. All I remember is a full day sweating in the dirt, convinced I was going to die. Kind of determined to, actually. But then later in the day I realized that the claw marks were itching like crazy, and that every time I glanced at it, they looked like they were a little less red, a little less inflamed. Healing maybe. That was when I knew.

"Cane said he liked my kind and that he wanted another to ride with him. He offered me the medallion. Colton's grandfather made them or knew something about them, and Cane said that they controlled the beast. I could be a man forever with it, a man with special talents. That was how he described it. But if I accepted the medallion, then I had to get him another man to make into a warg. That was the deal—the price for having something so precious."

The words shriveled up inside him. This was the moment of his deepest shame.

"I'd been talking all trip about my friend, Luc, and Cane wanted him. I couldn't do it. Jesus. I thought about it though. I actually thought about it." He curled his arm around her, his heart beating faster. "In the end I refused. Luc had a wife, and soon-to-be two kids. What kind of monster would I have been if I did that to him?"

Soft fingertips stroked along his arm. "You've never been that kind of man."

"You don't understand how tempting it was," he admitted. "I knew I was doomed, but what if there was a chance to live as a man still...."

"Those of us from the Burned Lands have been trained to survive since birth," Mia pointed out. "If you didn't at least think about it, I'd have been worried you were a robot. You didn't do it though, did you?"

Adam sat up, letting her hand fall from his arm. "In the end... yeah, I did."

Mia sat up too, tugging his blanket up to her breasts. "What?"

He looked at her. Nobody wanted to admit his or her guiltiest secret, but he couldn't keep this inside him anymore. It had been eating away at him for years. "Cane had ways to make a man do what he wanted." He hesitated. "I'd never met that type of man before, and I haven't come across one since. Colton actually warned me. Said I should just do it, but I wouldn't listen. I'd drawn my line in the sand. I wanted to spit in Cane's face and this was the way I'd do it.

"Cane beat me unconscious, and when I came to Colton was gone, and I was chained up. He didn't return until the sun was starting to set. And he had my sister, Eden, with him."

There was a flash of vision, of Eden looking at him in confusion. "*Adam, what's going on?*"

And of losing himself, of coming back out of the shadows slumped on the ground with his hand still knotted in the chain that refused to give, with Cane laughing at him. Not Eden. Of all the weaknesses he owned, his baby sister was his most vulnerable.

"He wrestled Eden inside this old hut that we were camping next to," he rasped. "And then they shoved me inside it with her. Her or Wade, Cane kept telling me. And they shut the door and locked me inside with her just as the moon was rising and the night started whispering through my veins."

"Oh, my God," Mia whispered.

Adam reached out, blundering for her fingers. He needed the touch to ground him. "I lasted half an hour, then I could feel the shift starting to win out. So I gave them what they wanted. I lured Luc out of bed with some story about a warg near town, and I led him right into Cane's grasp. He was my closest friend, and I betrayed him to the monsters in order to save my sister. He lost everything. He left his wife, Abbie, so he wouldn't hurt her. I tried to keep an eye on her for him, but... reivers hit her settlement and killed her. That was how I came to take in Lily, his daughter."

"Hey." Mia knelt closer, forcing him to look at her. "I know you wouldn't have made that deal if it was just your life on the line. Just as I know that any threat to someone else, especially your sister, would have just about broken you.

"You're one of the good guys, Adam. Never doubt that." She slid into his lap, sliding her arms loosely around his shoulders. "I couldn't have done this without you. I would never have gotten Sage back, and I know it. It sounds like this Cane gave you an impossible choice, and you took the best way out of it you could. All of this lies on his shoulders. Not yours. I hope you shot the bastard."

Adam buried his face in her shoulder. Mia cradled him closer. It had been a long time since anyone held him like this.

He breathed in her intoxicating scent. Mia was desert air and gunpowder, with faint notes of sage and whiskey. He couldn't believe she was in his arms. "Colton beat me to it."

"You've talked about Luc Wade before," she said. "Back in town at the bar. He married this woman you loved."

"It wasn't love.... I don't know what it was," he admitted, meeting her eyes. "Riley's one hell of a woman and I thought she fit into my life like the missing puzzle piece I'd been looking for. I never understood her though. Not truly." And it was true. What he'd felt for Riley was ambitious and driven; she was the crown on all he'd achieved, the wife that would rule at his side. He'd created a life for himself in Absolution that fitted what he thought a human would want. He'd brought people together, become their master and protector. A house of his own, a role in society where everyone looked up to him—him, the monster in their midst. It had never truly been about what he needed, but more a façade. A shield.

He'd been playing a role he'd thought he had to. Acting the part of a human man.

And Riley, who was strong, tough, and competent, was exactly who he'd thought should stand at his side.

Hell. He'd never thought of it like that before. All of it had been pretense. The town, the future he had planned.

He'd even named the fucking town *Absolution*.

"What was that?" Mia asked, reading his face.

Adam looked up. There she was, backlit by the sun. She'd washed herself last night in the stream, and her black hair was a riot of untamed curls. The sun lit them on fire, turning the ends a coppery brown.

And he had his second major epiphany for the morning.

Her. It was her.

He'd liked Mia from the moment he met her. He'd wanted her in his bed even more. She'd been refreshingly candid, sarcastic, and biting. And she saw straight through him all of the time. But she'd been holding up walls just as much as he had, the pair of them dancing around each other.

You'd be bad for me, she'd once said, *and I for you*. And it had been true. Back then, they would have been. Two wounded souls who would never be able to meet in the middle.

Everything had changed. He was no longer looking for his map and compass in life. He'd found it. The last week had been brutal, but he'd needed to strip himself bare, to confront his inner demons and accept them before he could even come close to accepting what he wanted in life.

He wasn't human. He never could be. There wasn't a cure for his condition.

But he could live with it and learn to stop fearing himself so much. Colton seemed to be able to control his inner beast. Even Luc managed to find peace with himself last year, when Cane performed his favorite trick again and threw Luc in a locked cell with Riley. He'd thought Luc had been dreaming, to admit that he'd gone warg and hadn't hurt Riley, but it was true.

Mia hadn't run screaming for the hills. Last night proved that she had the mettle to stand at his side, and not only that, but she actually cared for him, despite his curse.

I love you, she'd whispered in the dark of night, as if that made revealing her secrets safer. He knew she was scared of opening herself up, but so was he.

"You're starting to freak me out." Mia tapped his shoulder playfully. "You're staring at me like I have two heads."

Adam swallowed slowly. "I'm staring at you because I just realized that I love you."

Her lips parted in surprise, then she smiled.

"I want you," he admitted. "I want a future with you, and everything that comes with it. I've always wanted a wife and children, but I don't think I wanted them for the right reasons—I wanted a smokescreen, not a family of my own. Or maybe that was tied up in it, hell if I know.... But you. I want you for myself. For the real me, both man and monster."

"Stop calling yourself a monster."

He shook his head. "We can't pretend it doesn't exist, Mia. I'm done pretending."

Those gorgeous brown eyes narrowed. "This Cane sounds like a monster. You're just a man with a beast riding beneath his skin. Words matter, McClain. Call it your beast, or the warg within, but stop calling yourself a monster."

"Adam," he argued. "I want you to call me Adam."

"That's not the point. You're...." Mia looked flustered again, her eyelashes fluttering as she peered down at him shyly. "*Adam.*"

A word full of intimate meaning. Of longing.

He'd never heard his name sound like that on anyone's lips before. It was something a man could get used to.

Catching her up under the hips, Adam twisted until he could lay her flat upon her back on the blankets beneath him. Cradling himself between her thighs, he looked down at her, drinking her in as if to imprint the sight of her on his memory.

"Still sore?" he whispered.

"Maybe a little," Mia replied, then dragged his head down for a heated kiss. "But there was something you said about my lips... and your cock?"

Mmm. Sounded like heaven.

"Hello!"

The voice jerked him out of the pleasure of the aftermath of Mia's tender destruction of him. Adam started, then realized it was Sage, standing courteously behind the rock overhang that hid them from view.

"Are the pair of you decent?" Sage called.

Mia erupted into a sudden laugh, her eyes warm with scandalous need. She'd just come up from under the blankets. "No! Don't you dare come around that corner."

"Okay." There was a hint of laughter in Sage's voice. "I guess you worked out that argument brewing between you and McClain. Just letting you know I'm cooking breakfast if you want some. Then we need to hit the road. There's still no sign of pursuit, but some of the others don't want to tempt fate. That general might still be out there somewhere."

Mia looked down at him, sliding a pair of fingers over his mouth. Adam bit them, then smiled up at her. He flipped her over onto her back, then started working his way down her body.

"Tell her I won't be needing breakfast. I'll have already eaten," he whispered, and licked his way south of her navel.

Mia's eyes widened, and she dragged the blanket over his shoulders as he vanished lower. "Be right down, Sage!" She curled up on her elbows. *"Don't you dare!"* she whispered at him, shooting a shocked look toward the rock wall her sister stood behind.

"Yeah, right," Sage called, but he could hear her footsteps vanishing into the distance. "Just don't be too long."

Smooth, silky brown skin.... She was beautiful. And he could scent her wetness, smell how eager she was for him to touch her. Eager for *him*.

"McClain," Mia scolded. "We need to... *oh*."

Adam took his time worshipping her. Every last lick of her sweet pussy notched her a little tighter.

"McClain!" Mia gasped, her fingers curling into his hair.

"I thought you said you were tender?" He spread her thighs wide. "Let me kiss it better...."

And then she stopped pushing him away and started moaning.

By the time they returned to camp, most everyone had packed up. Mia walked slowly, her fingers firmly laced between Adam's. She'd never felt like this in her life. Relaxed, sated, happy. Happy was definitely a new emotion for her.

And one she wanted to share with him.

"So are you thinking of staying in Salvation Creek awhile?" she murmured.

Adam looked down at her. "Trying to get rid of me already?"

"No." She squeezed his hand. "But once we get Sage settled and make sure everyone's alright, I think it's time you headed north. From what you've told me, your sister must be wondering where you are. She'll be worried about you, and I'd like to meet her."

A long pause greeted this statement.

"I know there will be some folks you don't want to run into," she said quickly. "But I also know that you'd give anything to see your sister again. And Lily."

Adam swallowed, the lump in his throat moving. "Yeah. Yeah, I would." He paused, and turned her to face him. "Thank you. For giving me the courage to consider that."

Mia smiled shyly. "You've done so much for me. I feel like I'll never be able to repay you."

Warm hands cupped her face and Adam leaned down to brush his mouth against hers. "You have no idea how wrong that statement is. You give me strength, Mia. And you give me hope. I haven't felt that in a long time."

It was the sweetest kiss they'd shared. One to warm her from within. Mia let her hands slide to his waist, as his tongue eased her lips apart. A lazy, heated kiss that turned her insides to mush, because she knew it wasn't just lust anymore. This. This was what it felt like when she no longer had the words to tell him how much she loved him.

But all too soon a branch cracked under someone's foot, and Mia drew back.

"Sorry to interrupt." Zarina breathed hard, as if she'd been running. "Colton's gone."

"Gone?" Adam repeated, and the silver in his gray-green eyes flared intensely.

Mia watched his expression, feeling a little tense herself. Then Adam visibly relaxed, his shoulders lowering. "Let him go," he said with a shrug. "He earned his freedom."

Giving Mia's waist a squeeze, he headed for his motorbike, his hand in hers.

"He stole your bag," Zarina called after them.

Adam simply slid an arm around Mia's shoulders. "He can keep it," he threw back, giving Mia a squeeze. "I've got all I need, right here."

epilogue

JOHNNY COLTON PAUSED in the shadow of the canyon, rifling in McClain's bag for the water canteen. Remaining alert—just in case the bastard followed him—he lifted the canteen to his lips.

God, it felt good to taste fresh, clean water. Sweet enough to wash away a multitude of sins. Just not enough to wash away his. Colton swallowed, then wiped his mouth and screwed the lid back on. There wasn't enough water on what was left of the planet to remove his sins.

Keep moving. Keep out of sight. He stowed the canteen, and then slung the bag over his shoulder as he leapt from boulder to boulder, climbing high into the edges of the rocky tors that lined the basin of the Badlands. The only advantage working in his favor right now was the fact McClain had a handful of injured men and women to worry about.

He trekked for hours, sweat pouring down his body as he hauled himself upwards, sometimes by his fingertips alone. It didn't matter how far he managed to retreat—the ghost of Rust City haunted him. Not just the deeds he'd done there, the kills he'd made in the arena to survive, but the reminder of what he truly was in the eyes of the world.

He knew the warg within him didn't make him evil. No matter how much his estranged uncle, Bartholomew Cane, tried to make him into something else, after he rode into the small outpost where Colton lived with his parents and smiled pure vengeance at his father.

No. That had never been in any doubt. But Rust City stripped away the remaining illusion that there was any kind of place in the world where he could fit in. Or even hide. He'd spent years under that psychopath's sway, finally earning his own freedom a year ago with a lucky bullet. Since then he'd spent his time alone, keeping an eye over his shoulder for McClain's shadow, and sometimes creeping close enough to hear children singing in the settlements or men and women laughing, when he grew lonely enough.

He'd begun to think there was a place in one of those settlements for him. Hell, McClain managed it for years, until his secret came out. Luc Wade had found a woman who loved him enough to overlook the fact that he turned hairy if he lost his medallion. Maybe, just maybe, Colton thought he might have been able to find a place of his own, one where he could pretend to be something else—someone else—for a while. That same yearning had been his undoing in the end, when the townsfolk of Bitter River sold him out to the reivers to keep the bastards off their own backs.

Never again.

Colton made camp in a small cave up high in the mountains, high enough to give him a good vantage point where he could see anything coming. No sign of McClain, heck, any pursuit, but he couldn't be too careful. Too many people wanted to kill him.

Too many people had good reason to.

What now? Colton seduced the fire to a generous glow, then worked his way through the methodical task of cooking dinner. It all tasted like ash in his mouth, and afterwards he merely curled up in his stolen blanket, watching the coals slowly flare to red-hot embers and then die back down with the shifts in the breeze.

Christ, he was tired. So fucking tired.

Propping his back against a rock, he stared into the glow of the embers as the sunlight slowly died on the horizon, darkness creeping closer until it was a warm cocoon. Something in the bag at his hip kept digging into him, until he finally shoved it aside.

The bag fell over, and the edge of something poked out of it. An envelope? He frowned and reached down for it, revealing three of them.

Paper rustled. Letters. Well-handled, the edges of the paper stained and worn. McClain wasn't the type to leave a diary, but it might be useful for tinder if he ran out of scrub bush. He was about to crumple them back up when a few of the words caught his eye.

...I know you feel the darkness within you, that you think it is all that remains of your life, but you're wrong. There is still so much light in you, and the others are beginning to see that.

Come back to me, Adam. Come back home. You belong here with me, with all the others. Your life doesn't have to be one long vicious fight. There's more to it than that. You deserve more.

Love always,
Eden

Colton slowly lowered the paper. It felt somewhat sacrilegious to read a letter so personal when it belonged to someone else, but at the same time, it also felt like the letter was addressed to him too. It spoke to something deep inside him, something he thought long buried.

Hope.

He flipped to the next one, written three months ago, losing himself in the warmth of a home that this Eden conjured. He couldn't help but wonder if she truly believed in the dreams of hope she was spinning—could she be that naïve?—and yet, it stirred something within him that he'd long though hidden.

Eden.... Colton frowned.

If he closed his eyes, he could almost summon memories of her. A young girl, not quite twenty perhaps, when he'd first encountered her—when Cane first set his sights on her. Tall, coltish figure, wavy brown hair burnished with just enough gilt to show that she spent her time outdoors.

She'd been McClain's Achilles' heel. The bargaining chip that pushed McClain over the edge when Cane demanded his soul—and Luc Wade's betrayal.

She was almost a shadow of a memory. Not fully formed. Not entirely whole in Colton's mind. Just one of hundreds that he'd left behind in his wake when Cane forced him to heel.

He ought to burn the letters. Should even track McClain down and give them back....

But instead he breathed in the soft scent of woman that still clung faintly to the paper, and conjured up whispers of a woman who was no longer that girl he remembered.

A woman who knew the part he played in her brother's downfall.

Colton slowly lowered them. No point in chasing stardust. He needed to keep moving, maybe take on some bounty work somewhere.

And stay far away from Eden McClain and all that she conjured.

Taking the letters, he held them over the fire. Something held him there. *You're a man, not a monster,* her voice whispered in his mind, and even though Colton knew she'd been speaking to her brother and not him, he couldn't bring himself to do it.

He slowly tucked the letters back in the bag.

And cursed himself for a fool.

coming 2017...

If you enjoyed *The Last True Hero*, then get ready for *The Hero Within*! Book three in the *Burned Lands* series, it will be available late 2017, so make sure you sign up for my newsletter at www.becmcmaster.com to receive news and excerpts about this release!

Can't wait for more *Burned Lands* action and romance? Check out my *Blue Blood Conspiracy* series. I recommend starting with the first book, *Mission: Improper,* featuring Caleb Byrnes and Ingrid Miller, who are drawn into a spy conspiracy in steampunk London.

When Byrnes receives an invitation to join the Company of Rogues as an undercover agent pledged to protect the crown, he jumps at the chance to find out who, or what, is behind disappearances in the East End. Hunting criminals is what the darkly driven blue blood does best, and though he prefers to work alone, the opportunity is too good to resist.

The problem? He's partnered with Ingrid Miller, who won a private bet against him a year ago. Byrnes has a score to settle, but one stolen kiss and suddenly the killer is not the only thing Byrnes is interested in hunting. It's James Bond meets Dracula...

Thank you for reading *The Last True Hero*! I hope you enjoyed it. Please consider leaving a review online, to help others find my books.

Not ready to leave the Burned Lands? Read on for a preview of what's next for Johnny Colton and Eden McClain...

The Hero Within

BOOK THREE: THE BURNED LANDS SERIES

As the only healer in a war-stained town, Eden McClain is devastated when the Salt Plague sweeps through the wastelands she calls home. Suddenly she's racing against time to save her people–and her niece–before it's too late. When she hears whispers of a cure, she knows she can't cross the dangerous Wastelands by herself to get it. She needs a guide. And she's just desperate enough to turn to a man who once betrayed her.

Redemption comes at a price...

After years of living on the leash of a dangerous psychopath, Johnny Colton is finally free, but that doesn't mean he can wash the blood off his hands. The easiest way to deal with the past? Just stop caring. Which is working perfectly for the rugged outlaw, until a beautiful ghost from the past rigs a trap for him. The last person he wants to see is the woman who haunts his dreams, but as Eden points out, he owes her one.

Each step leads them further down a dangerous path of seduction that neither can quite accept—but are they also walking into a deadly trap? The only way to survive is for two past enemies to learn to trust each other.

ABOUT THE AUTHOR

Bec McMaster is the award-winning author of the London Steampunk series. A member of RWA, she writes sexy, dark paranormals, and adventurous steampunk romances, and grew up with her nose in a book. Following a life-long love affair with fantasy, she discovered romance novels as a 16 year-old, and hasn't looked back.

In 2012, Sourcebooks released her debut award-winning novel, *Kiss of Steel*, the first in the London Steampunk series, followed by: *Heart of Iron*, *My Lady Quicksilver*, *Forged By Desire*, and *Of Silk And Steam*. Two novellas—*Tarnished Knight* and *The Curious Case Of The Clockwork Menace*—fleshed out the series. She has been nominated for RT Reviews Best Steampunk Romance for *Heart of Iron (2013)*, won RT Reviews Best Steampunk Romance with *Of Silk And Steam (2015)*, and *Forged By Desire* was nominated for a RITA award in 2015. The series has received starred reviews from Booklist, Publishers Weekly, and Library Journal, with *Heart of Iron* named one of their Best Romances of 2013.

In 2016, she debuted the Dark Arts series with *Shadowbound*, the Burned Lands series with *Nobody's Hero*, as well as the second London Steampunk: The Blueblood Conspiracy series, with *Mission: Improper*.

Bec lives in a small country town in Victoria, Australia, with her very own Beta Hero; a dog named Kobe, who has perfected her own Puss-in-boots sad eyes—especially when bacon is involved; and demanding chickens, Siggy and Lagertha. When not poring over travel brochures, playing netball, or cooking things that are very likely bad for her, Bec spends most of her time in front of the computer.

For news on new releases, cover reveals, contests, and special promotions, join her mailing list at www.becmcmaster.com

ACKNOWLEDGMENTS

Writing fast-paced, sexy, paranormal romance is the best fun imaginable, but as with every project I take on, I couldn't have done it without a lot of help from these amazing people:

I owe huge thanks to my editor Olivia from Hot Tree Editing for her work on this manuscript; to Mandy from Hot Tree Edits for the proofread; my wonderful cover artists from Damonza.com for kicking this one out of the park with McClain and those sexy abs; and Marisa Shor from Cover Me Darling and Allyson Gottlieb for the print formatting. To the CVW and the ELE, thanks for keeping me sane, and being my support groups! Thanks for helping me pick which cover to go with, and for all of the advice, tea and chocolates. Special thanks go to my beta readers, Kylie Griffin and Jennie Kew–who ask me all of the hard questions and crack me up with cat references (more than a few in this manuscript!). And to my family, especially my mum, who helped keep me sane in the last few days before Christmas before this book was due. Decorating my Christmas tree was probably not on your list for Christmas Eve, but you don't know how much I appreciate it. But the most thanks go to Byron, who is always there for me, and who helped me out so much during the crazy deadline rush of this book. I couldn't do what I do without his help.

Last, not certainly not least, to all of my readers who support me on this journey, and have been crazy vocal about their love for the London Steampunk series, and anything else I write! I love sharing my books news with you guys, and hearing how much you're enjoying these new dark worlds I've chosen to write!